The Critics on Peter James

'Peter James has found his own literary niche, some-where between Stephen King and Michael Crichton'
Mail on Sunday

'Gripping . . . plotting is ingenious . . . in its evocation of how a glossy cocoon of worldly success can be unravelled by one bad decision it reminds me of Tom Wolfe's *Bonfire of the Vanities*'   *The Times*

'Probably James's finest novel to date. I have not read a work so focused and intense in its depiction of the classic Orwellian nightmare'   *Shivers*

'A thought-provoking menacer that's completely techno-logical and genuinely frightening about the power of future communications'   *Time Out*

'James has been compared with Stephen King, but in many ways he's better'   *Daily Express*

'An awesome talent . . . one of the few writers working in the genre today whose work is always a pleasure to read and a disappointment to finish'   *Starburst*

'A well-paced thriller that delivers maximum emotional torture'   *Chicago Tribune*

'This compulsive story is a tale of the search for immortality . . . I cannot remember when I last read a novel I enjoyed so much'   *Sunday Telegraph*

Peter James was educated at Charterhouse and then at film school. He lived in North America for a number of years, working as a film-maker (his projects included the award-winning *Dead of the Night*), before returning to England. His previous novels have been translated into twenty-two languages. *Prophecy* has been made into a highly acclaimed television film, starring Nigel Havers and Sophie Ward. *Host* has been made into a television film starring Peter Gallagher and Mimi Rogers, directed by Mick Garris, and *Alchemist* has been made into a four-hour television mini-series, starring Grant Shaw, Ruth Gemmell and Edward Hardwick. All his novels reflect his deep interest in medicine, science, technology and the paranormal. Peter James lives in Sussex.

Peter James

PROPHECY

ORION

An Orion Paperback
First published in Great Britain by
Victor Gollancz in 1992
This paperback edition published in 1999 by
Orion Books Ltd,
Orion House, 5 Upper St Martin's Lane,
London WC2H 9EA

A CIP catalogue record for this book
is available from the British Library

ISBN: 0 75281 737 X

Printed and bound in Great Britain by
Clays Ltd, St Ives plc

To Jesse

ACKNOWLEDGEMENTS

As ever, I am indebted to many people and organizations whose help, knowledge and input has been invaluable. In particular, a very special thank you to the following:

The Viscount Hampden for allowing me to use Glynde Place as the model for Meston Hall (although I should add that Glynde Place is in very considerably better condition than Meston and I have made changes both to the house and grounds). I should also add that the Halkin/Sherfield family are entirely fictitious and bear no relationship to any of the Viscount Hampden's family nor previous occupants of Glynde Place.

Brian Inglis. Roderick Main of Scarab Research for his invaluable help also on coincidence (and for the coincidences!). Robert Knox, Deputy Keeper of Oriental Antiquities at the British Museum. Frances Wollen. Canon Dominic Walker OGS. Dr Robert Morris of Edinburgh University. Miss Eleanor O'Keefe of the Society for Psychical Research. Jane Henry. Ruth West. Brian Dickinson. Tim Mair. Pippa Hooley, Bovine Consultant. Councillor Pam Stiles. Kathryn Bailey. Sophie Allen, Game Boy Consultant. Dr Nigel Kirkham. Dr Tim Carter. Dr Duncan Stewart. Dr Brian Kirkland. Mick Harris. David Garbutt. Nina Mackay (for lightning calculations on the backs of envelopes!). Ray Hazan and Peter Marshall of St Dunstan's. Adrian Elliott. Mark Towse. Peter Orpen of AVT. Dr Robert Wilkins. Roy Gambier of the Shuttleworth Collection.

I am indebted also to the hard work of Sue Ansell;

to my agent, Jon Thurley; to my editors, Joanna Goldsworthy and Richard Evans and my copy-editor Elizabeth Reeves. And to Bertie, for not eating all of the manuscript. And to my wife, Georgina, who through all the bludgeonings of chance kept me bloody but unbowed . . .

PROLOGUE

The man and boy walked along the London street trying to keep clear of the gutter, the man hurrying, clutching the boy with sharp, bony fingers, turning down one dark alley then another, like a rat that has learned its way through a maze.

The boy was confused and uncertain; he did not know who the man was and did not like him. His mother and the man had talked in low voices and his mother had not kissed him or looked him in the eye when the man had taken him away. They had walked for a long time through the failing light and the rain, and he was tired and hungry. And becoming afraid.

After a while they stopped in the rear yard of a large house and the man knocked loudly. The door opened a few inches and dark, suspicious eyes peered out. 'Come in,' a woman said and the door opened wider. The man pushed the boy ahead of him into the kitchen.

The woman frightened the boy. She was tall, dressed in a black gown, and had a skeletal face with eyes that seemed to scold him.

'How many years has he?'

'Eight,' the man said.

'He stinks.'

'He needs a wash, that's all.'

The woman studied the boy carefully. He had fair curls that were unkempt and matted, large blue eyes and a snub nose; his lips were drawn sullenly down, and his clothes were little more than grimy rags; his feet were bare. 'Wait here,' she said.

The boy stood gazing at the stone floor, aware of the flames in the hearth and the pot above it from which came an acrid, unpleasant smell.

After a few moments the door opened and the woman came back in, followed by a tall man with a limp. He was wearing a gold, full-length robe, and had a cruel, vain face framed with a carefully trimmed beard. He stood in the doorway and smiled approvingly at the boy. 'Yes,' he said. 'You have done well.'

He came closer to the boy, dragging his club-foot across the floor with a scrape, and stood still again, admiring him. 'Very good.'

The boy was impressed by the man's robe and by his noble appearance. The man moved closer, then in one fast movement tore the clothes off the boy, letting them drop around his ankles.

The boy looked at him in shock. The nobleman took a step towards him and laid a hand on his shoulder. The boy whipped his head around, bit the man's wrist hard and bolted for the door on the far side of the kitchen.

The man who had brought him grabbed him by his hair and held him tightly. The nobleman roared with laughter.

'He is fine and spirited. You have done *very* well, for a change.'

'Thank you, my Lord.'

'Yes,' he said. He eyed the boy's body with mounting satisfaction. 'I will reward –' He broke off as a commotion beyond the kitchen disturbed him. He frowned; they were early. Much too early. They were not due for at least two hours yet, surely? He turned, staring through the open door and down the passageway.

A man in a tall black hat, a high white collar and a

black coat over tight, ribboned breeches strode through the doorway. He was followed by a group of soldiers wearing the red coats, grey breeches and waist sashes of the Parliamentarian Army.

His grey eyes scanned the room then fixed on the nobleman. He spoke with a humourless smile. 'Good evening, Francis,' he said. 'Have I interrupted some sport?'

'What do you mean by this intrusion, Thomas?' The nobleman stared with a vexed expression at the soldiers who were clustered inside the door; their faces beneath their buff leather hats carried an air of intent that disturbed him.

The man in the black hat looked at the woman and the rat-faced man beside her. 'Who brought this child?' When they remained silent, his voice became hard and stern. 'Who brought him?'

''Twas I,' the rat-faced man said.

'Clothe him and take him back.' And then, to the woman, 'How many servants are here in the house now?'

The woman glanced at her master as if for approval to speak.

The nobleman's vexation was tempered by uncertainty. 'Thomas, I'll not have this. Take your men and leave forthwith.'

The man in the black hat ignored him and continued to stare at the woman. 'I want all the servants to be gone immediately and not return until curfew time. Understand?' He turned and nodded at the soldiers.

They moved forwards and seized the nobleman's arms. His expression turned to fury. 'Thomas – my brother, man! For God's sake! What do you think you are doing?'

'For God? For *God's* sake?' his brother echoed

mockingly. 'What dost thou know of God whom thou hast abandoned these five and twenty years?' He led the way out of the door and down a passageway into a fine hall with a black-and-white tiled floor, candles in ornate sconces on the walls and gilt furniture. The soldiers, headed by their sergeant, frogmarched the robed nobleman, ignoring, as his brother did, his protestations.

They went downstairs into a dark, evil-smelling cellar and halted at a door outside which a candle burned. Thomas jangled a key tauntingly at his brother, unlocked the door and led the way into a huge cellar chamber.

A massive fire blazed in a hearth beneath a brick flue on the far wall, the echoes of its cracking and spitting resounding like gunshots around the brick walls and flagstone floor. There were stone tablets fixed to the walls, some containing five-pointed stars, others squares of numbers. Skulls and bones, human and animal, were laid out on shelves between lit black candles.

On a raised dais like an altar at the far end was a bed covered with tasselled cloth. There were massive black candles at each corner and, beyond, a leather-bound book lay on a lectern.

The man in the black hat nodded at his brother, whilst the soldiers stared round in awe and horror. 'The fires of Hell already lit, my Lord?'

'I'll have no more of these games, Thomas. What do you want?'

''Tis no game, Francis, I assure you. None but that of your own making. I must depart, for I've a long way to go before dark. I'll take my leave of you, if you'll forgive me. Sergeant Proudlove will attend your needs; a good man by all accounts and a father of three young boys.'

He nodded to the sergeant who had a blunt face with a broad, flat nose and dull eyes, and walked out. Ignoring the shouts of his brother, he closed the door of the chamber behind him.

'Like to sport with young boys, your Lordship?' the sergeant said.

As the nobleman looked at him, and at each of the deadpan faces of the other six soldiers, the heat of his anger began to turn into the cold uncertainty of fear. 'Your intrusion is intolerable,' he said stiffly.

'We has but only one more intrusion to make and we'lst be gone, my Lord.' The sergeant grinned and several of the other soldiers let out coarse sniggers. Then he nodded and they gripped their prey tighter.

'Unhand me at once, I say! What do you mean by all this?'

The sergeant pointed to the bed. The soldiers pulled the nobleman over and thrust him face down on to it. The sergeant removed his waist sash and tied it across Francis' mouth as a gag, yanking it so tightly that there was a grunt of pain. Then he carefully eased up the gold robe, exposing the nobleman's naked, bony backside. Francis began to struggle harder, grunting louder. The soldiers moved as if they had done this before, four of them each using his own body weight to pin down an arm or a leg, the other two sitting on the small of his back. 'Careful not to bruise him,' the sergeant said.

He walked slowly across to the fire, knelt and picked up the poker then ambled back to the front of the bed and held the poker up so that Francis could see it. 'Thou enjoyest sporting with backsides, let's see how thou enjoyest this, my Lord.'

The nobleman's eyes widened; the cruelness of them was gone now, replaced with a look of pleading. He mumbled desperately and incoherently through the gag.

The sergeant removed from inside his jacket a slim hollow ox-horn and checked that the poker would slide freely through it. Then he placed his hands on his captive's buttocks, which were slippery with the perspiration of fear, and pushed them apart, locating with his eyes the circular orifice of the anus. Using some of his own spittle he lubricated the end of the ox-horn, then again located the orifice and slowly but firmly inserted the horn, easing it in further and further.

'Gently does it, my Lord,' he said. 'Wouldn't want to hurt you.'

There was a guffaw from the soldiers. The nobleman struggled, his buttocks twitching fiercely, but the sergeant continued pushing the tube in for several inches until only the tip was still showing.

A low whine of fear escaped through the gag. Rivulets of sweat ran down the small of the victim's back. Sergeant Proudlove carried the poker across to the fire and prodded the tip deep into the burning coals. The nobleman grunted, trying to speak, to call out to him, but the sergeant stood in steadfast silence, watching the poker, carefully pulling on a thick gauntlet.

After a few minutes he removed the poker. The last twelve inches of the tip were glowing red and white hot. He walked around and held it up in front of the nobleman's face. 'Ready, my Lord?'

The nobleman's eyes skittered as if they had broken loose in their mountings. Another, longer, whine of fear came through the gag, then another. He tried to speak, choked on his own saliva and coughed, then tried frantically to speak again. He writhed and thrashed, throwing one soldier off his back on to the

6

floor, and pulling an arm free. A soldier grabbed it again, pinned it down and the other climbed back on to him, holding him down grimly. The sergeant thrust the poker back into the coals, holding it for some seconds with his gloved hand. The nobleman whined again, then again.

The sergeant removed the poker, walked up to him, gripped the hollow horn, which had slid out a couple of inches, carefully inserted the red-hot poker into the end of it as if he was locating his sword into his scabbard, then slid it in, pushing firmly and grimly.

There was a sharp hiss and bubbling sound as it burned through the soft rectal flesh, and the sudden sweet smell of roasting meat.

A convulsion of agony bulged every muscle of the nobleman's body and a scream tore free of the gag and bounced around the room like an unleashed demon; it came back at the soldiers from the ceiling, from the walls, from the floor: a screeching banshee that became louder every second as the sergeant pushed the poker relentlessly, holding it with both hands, twisting it, working it further and further in, forcing it up through the rectum, the colon, tearing through the peritoneum, melting and cauterizing a passage through the liver, gall-bladder and pancreas; through muscles, tendons, gristle, piercing the stomach wall, stirring the nobleman's bowels and organs like a giant pudding until the poker was in up to the handle.

The victim arched backwards, scattering all six of the soldiers. His neck twisted like a serpent, his head almost turning completely backwards as if his neck was broken. He stared the sergeant full in the eye and for a moment the sergeant thought he was going to clamber off the bed. Then the nobleman's mouth contorted as if it were melting, and let out a low, barely audible moan of agony; slowly this began to rise into a howl, becoming louder and louder until, in its crescendo, it seemed to detach itself from the writhing, almost inhuman, object on the bed and explode in an independent ball of energy.

The soldiers stood back, covering their ears now, unable to bear the sound that threatened to shatter the insides of their own heads. Even the sergeant released his grip and covered his ears.

Long after the poker had cooled and the nobleman lay motionless in his own slime and vomit, his fingernails embedded into the palms of his hands, the scream remained, echoing back at them as if it would never fade.

CHAPTER ONE

The father and son walked along the London pavement in the warmth of the spring mid-morning sunshine. The father ambled at a leisurely stride; a tall man in his late thirties, in an unbuttoned Harris Tweed coat, whose thoughts seemed to be elsewhere, as if he was pondering the cosmos above him rather than concentrating on his immediate environs.

He had a strong, open face, with handsome features and an amiable, if rather absent-minded, expression. His brown hair was parted high and was a little long, covering the tips of his ears and the top of his collar. His bearing was distinctly aristocratic, but in spite of his City suit he looked more like an academic than someone who fitted into a business community.

The five-year-old boy had his mother's looks: short ginger curls, a serious, freckled face, wide, innocent green eyes. He was wearing a tiny corduroy jacket, grey flannel shorts, grey knee-length socks and polished black shoes. He wished his father would walk faster; this part of London did not interest him – except for the Dungeon and the Tower, and the Docklands train, and they had already done those. The thought of the shop in Regent Street filled him with an excitement he could barely contain, and the prospect of the tube train they were going to take to it was something he looked forward to also, but now that they had left the boring office where he had had to wait for an hour with nothing much to read, his father seemed in no hurry and he panicked for a moment.

'Daddy, we are going to Hamleys, aren't we? You promised.'

'Hamleys?' The father stared at his son as if he had momentarily forgotten him.

'You promised!'

'Righty ho, suppose we'd better head there, then.'

The boy looked at his father, never sure when he was joking and when he was serious. 'Is this the right way?'

'We've got to wait for Mummy.'

The boy's face fell. 'Where is she?'

'At the hairdresser's. She's coming to my office at half past twelve. That's in twenty minutes.'

'That's not for ages! Where are we going now?'

'I have to pick up Mummy's wedding bracelet from the mender.'

The boy's face fell further. 'You said we were going to Hamleys.'

'We're going to have lunch with Mummy, *then* we're going to Hamleys.'

'I want to go now! You promised!' The boy was sobbing.

They were blocking a busy pavement, being jostled by passers-by. There was an alley-way beside them, with a café a short distance down on the right. The father pulled his fractious son past an employment bureau, a travel agent, a heel bar and a few other shops, then stopped outside a dingy, unprepossessing sandwich bar with words above it, in twelve-inch-high dayglo letters, two of which were missing: SANDW CH S LUIGI CAFE. Four small suction cups held a white plastic menu against the inside of the window. EAT IN OR TAKE AWAY was printed along the bottom.

'Look, they have milkshakes,' the father said. 'Let's have one.'

A small queue stood at the counter and all but one of the tiny handful of tables were taken. There was a strong smell of coffee and of frying food; a dying fly fizzed and crackled in the mesh of an ultraviolet trap. Two posters, discoloured with age, one of Amalfi and one of Naples, were stuck to the back wall.

His father propelled his charge to the empty table and sat him down. The boy placed his fists on the table. 'You promised! You promised – you –' The boy was silent suddenly and a strange look came into his eyes, a mixture of both fear and recognition as he stared past his father at the counter.

His father turned his head, surprised, failing to see what he was looking at. Behind the counter a thin, unshaven man in his fifties greeted a customer with a cheery: 'Hi, how y'doin? What y'gonna 'ave today?' Next to him, a short, plump woman with lifeless black hair and a haggard, drained face, was buttering bread. There was a sharp ping and a girl in a white apron removed a dish from the microwave.

'Chocolate milkshake?' the father suggested, pulling out a handkerchief and wiping the tears from his son's face. He went to the counter and bought a milkshake and an espresso.

The boy concentrated on his drink, his tantrum forgotten. Soon he was spooning the dregs from the bottom of the glass, and then he became absorbed in scooping up the last of the froth with a straw.

When they left the café and were walking back down the alley into the street, he asked, 'Are we meeting Mummy, now?'

'Yes, for lunch. Then we're going to Hamleys, and then the Planetarium. You want to see the stars, don't you?'

The boy nodded dubiously.

In the distance, they both heard a siren; it sounded like a bag of stones being swirled through the air.

'Daddy, why does Mummy always go to the hairdresser every time we come to London?'

'Because she likes to look nice,' he was told.

They walked on for a moment in silence. The shops here contained nothing to distract the boy. Stationery. Men's clothes. Masonic regalia. A bank. A silversmith.

The swishing of the siren was coming closer and the boy heard the roar of an engine. They stopped, waiting for the lights to change to cross the road. A cyclist pedalled across, wearing a crash-helmet, his face covered in a smog mask which the boy thought made him look frightening. Then he saw a woman with short red hair on the other side of the road, and for a moment he thought it was his mother and tugged excitedly on his father's hand, wanting to pull him across the road to greet her. Until he realized she was a stranger. His mother had long hair.

The siren was still coming closer. The boy looked up at his father and tugged his sleeve. 'Daddy, do you think I should have my hair done in London?'

The father tousled his son's curls fondly. 'Like to come to Trumper's with me next time I go?'

The boy nodded, waited until his father was looking away, slid a hand up and flattened his hair down again. Then he looked across the road at the woman with red hair. She looked like his mother again now. It was his mother! It was. His heart leapt, then her hair blew in a gust, and it wasn't; it was someone quite different.

The lights changed to green, and the boy ran forward. Something jerked him back, holding his collar, a sharp yank. There was the roar of an engine, a shadow bearing down, the siren deafening now. The red-haired woman was halfway out in the road. His mother? Not his mother? She was staring at him, her mouth open. She was trying to run backwards now.

Tyres screamed. A shadow crossed, blocked his view for an instant. A van with two young men in it braking furiously, slewing across the road. Going to hit the woman.

'Mummy!' he screamed.

The woman was splayed out on the van's bonnet. It was careering across the road, mounting the pavement. A man in a business suit dived out of its path. A traffic-light post snapped and the coloured lights shattered on to the road. Then came an explosion like a bomb as the van, with the woman still on the bonnet, smashed through the plate-glass window of a bookshop.

The woman seemed to elongate then disappear. For an instant the entire surroundings seemed paralysed. In the silence there was nothing but the sound of breaking glass. The boy saw a chunk of window fall. He heard a scream, followed by another. Doors slamming. A siren winding down. Policemen leaping out of a car. Doors of the van opening: one easily, one with difficulty, the man inside forcing it. The van's engine was still running.

'*Mummy!*'

The boy broke free of his father's grip and ran in terror across the road, through the crowd that was forming, pushing his way, sidestepping the opening door of the van. Another pane of glass crashed down. Blood. Books scattered everywhere. A poster lay on the ground, covered in blood. An assistant was standing in the shop, hand over her mouth, screaming. The boy stared in the direction she was looking. His mouth opened but no sound came out. The woman's body lay on the floor, blood jetting intermittently from her neck. Red bubbles lay on the grey carpet tiles. A rubber mask with hair attached lay nearby, leaking blood into a fallen dumpbin of paperbacks.

Then he realized it wasn't a rubber mask. It was his mother's head.

CHAPTER TWO

August 1991

Summer had finally come to London a week ago after two months of almost continuous rain, and already the grass in the parks was parched. Seven days of heat seemed to have drawn every last drop of moisture from the soil – from the pavements, from the cement in the eternal building works – and dust that was loose and weightless hung like a permanent haze in the air. Frannie Monsanto had breathed it in, washed it out of her hair at night. She felt it now, clinging like pollen to her skin, which was already sticky with perspiration.

Normally Frannie's Mediterranean genes reacted automatically to sunshine, flooding her with a deep sense of well-being. But at work today she had been glad of the coolness of the basement vault of the Museum, and she was thankful to be heading away from the claustrophobic oven of the city and *en route* to catch a train up to the Yorkshire countryside.

The rush-hour tube was crowded and she felt faintly ridiculous holding the double bass, her overnight suitcase wedged between her legs. Air blasted her face through the open windows: hot, rank draughts that smelled of soot and something more unpleasant, reminiscent of unwashed feet, as the carriage rocked and screamed through a long stretch of darkness.

Frannie was twenty-five, with attractive Latin looks and a slender figure that she kept well toned by twice-weekly aerobics, and by swimming fifty lengths on Sunday mornings at her local pool. Like many Latins, her family had a tendency towards fatness in middle age, and Frannie was determined never to let that happen to her, the way she was determined about many things in life.

Capriciousness sometimes broke through her barrier of reserve and, on rarer occasions, a fiery temper; but mostly Frannie applied herself with single-minded quietness and dedication to her work. She did not consider herself academic, or intellectual, and had to compensate by sheer slog. That was how she had got into university in the first place, and how she had got her degree in Archaeology and Anthropology. Frannie would have been pleased just to have scraped a third and had surprised herself by getting an upper second. She had scarcely been able to believe her good fortune when she had been offered a post as a research assistant at the British Museum within weeks of leaving university, where she had remained since.

She had wispy chestnut-brown hair that was clipped to each side of her head and rested on her shoulders, a straight nose, intelligent olive eyes and an expressive, sensual mouth prone to smiling, although at heart she was a serious girl. At five feet four inches, she wished she was a little taller, but by and large she was happy about her appearance.

She was wearing Nike trainers, blue jeans, an orange T-shirt and a black cotton jacket. Slung over her arm was a large untreated leather handbag she had bought in Naples four years previously on a family visit, and which was now comfortably hammered from its daily use. Frannie was not particularly interested in clothes and loathed shopping for them. In any event, archaeology did not pay well and she was saving as hard as she could to buy a small flat of her own and get out of the crummy place she rented. Jeans were fine for her work and she lived in them most of the time, except when she had a smart date.

She had had no such date for a while. It had been over six months since her relationship with her last boyfriend had ended and, to her surprise, she was really enjoying her freedom. She was reading a lot, catching up on movies, going to exhibitions.

It would not last, she knew. Something intrinsically excited her about men, and sex was something she enjoyed deeply.

'Dreaming of nothing in particular?' said an advertisement on a panel in front of her.

A lanky youth with goofy front teeth stood opposite her. He looked at her face, down at the double bass, then back at her again. She caught his eye, stared back, and he looked away hastily. The train swayed and she nearly lost her balance, bumped into a large man in a singlet, with tattoos on his arms, and the double bass rocked precariously. She was already regretting having so readily agreed to bring it.

It belonged to Meredith Minns, a fellow Archaeology student at the University of London, with whom she had shared a room for their last year there. Meredith had wavered all that year between becoming a professional archaeologist or musician, then had fallen in love with a farmer and was now living in North Yorkshire, had produced two children, one of whom Frannie was a godmother to, and seemed content being a farmer's wife.

When she had invited Frannie up to stay, she had asked if she would mind collecting the instrument from a man who was repairing it in Covent Garden. Meredith had told her to take a taxi and she would pay, but Frannie did not like squandering money, neither her own nor anyone else's, and she had decided when she collected it that although it was bulky it was not heavy, and she could manage it on the tube. Now she was beginning to realize she had been a bit optimistic.

The train was slowing and she gripped the grab-handle harder, lurching towards the goofy-toothed youth. Bright lights slid past the window as they came into a station. She saw the sign KING'S CROSS, and the train halted. She lugged her case and the double bass out, along the platform and on to the escalator.

On the station concourse, long lines stretched back from the ticket offices and the platform gates. Commuters hurried, some trying impossibly to sprint through the crowds.

People clambered over suitcases; a toothless old lady halted her luggage trolley, lips chomping impatiently, waiting for Frannie to move out of her path. But Frannie had not noticed her; she was standing, trying to fathom out the departures board. YORK, she saw, 17.34. PLATFORM 3. She looked around for a luggage trolley but could not see one, and hefted her double bass and suitcase over to a queue at the ticket offices. An announcement rang out. Beads of perspiration trickled down her neck. She bought her ticket, then queued again at the platform gate. The train was coming in now, and the Tannoy announced: 'Arrival of the 14.52 from York. British Rail apologizes for the late arrival of this train.'

She saw carriage doors opening in line before the train had stopped moving, and the empty platform erupted in seconds into a surging wall of people. Frannie heard a shout and a small boy ran past the ticket inspector and headlong into the mêlée, followed by a harassed-looking man. Frannie gripped her ticket in her teeth, picked up her case and slid the double bass forward, stopped, repeated the procedure until she had reached the gate, then handed the ticket to the inspector.

He clipped it without looking at it, distracted by a colleague, and handed it back. She struggled forwards, the double bass getting heavier by the moment, got a few yards down the platform then stopped for a rest. Somewhere in front of her she heard a child shouting.

'No! I don't want to! I don't want to!'

The sound rang out above the clattering of feet. Several people glanced around.

'I hate you!'

The crowd was thinning and she could now see a boy of about eight – the boy who had run through the barrier a few minutes before – fighting to free himself from the grip of the man who had been chasing him and who was pulling him down the platform towards the gate.

'Let me go, let me –' As they reached Frannie, the boy suddenly stopped shouting and stared at her intently. Frannie felt a strange sense of recognition, as if she had seen him before somewhere. The man looked familiar also. In his mid-thirties, she estimated. Tall, a handsome, distinctive face; brown hair parted high up; he reminded her a little of the movie actor Harrison Ford and she wondered fleetingly where she had seen him before; perhaps he was an actor, or maybe a politician.

He stopped, sensing the boy's change of mood and interest, and smiled apologetically at Frannie; he seemed a little embarrassed by the child's behaviour. The boy was looking curiously at her double bass.

'Can I – er – give you a hand?' the man said in a quiet, assertive voice that carried both a hint of humour and the plummy confidence of the English upper classes. He was wearing an old-fashioned but rather stylish linen suit, a faded denim shirt and a pink-and-green tie, and he had an endearing air that made Frannie instantly attracted to him.

'It's OK,' she said. 'Thanks – I can –'

'It's – er – no problem. Which carriage do you want? Have you got a reservation?'

'Any carriage – I didn't reserve.'

'Where are you going?'

'To York.'

'Oh right – we'll – umm – take you down to the front – it'll be easier for you the other end.' He picked up the double bass and the suitcase.

'Really, it's –'

'What's in there?' the boy asked, touching the case. He was serious-looking, with an open, freckled face and curly ginger hair.

'It's a double bass,' she said as she walked behind the man, the boy walking beside her.

'Why's it in the box?'

'Because it's easier to carry.' She smiled, feeling a curious affinity for him.

'We've just been to an air museum and the zoo,' the boy said.

'Have you?' Frannie said politely.

'Whipsnade Zoo, in Bedfordshire. I had a ride on an elephant and on a camel. The camel sat down first so I could get on. They always do that. Did you know?'

'I didn't realize they were so polite. Which did you like best – the camel or the elephant?'

The boy thought for a moment. 'I think the camel – because if you have one you don't have to remember to give it water every day. But they can kill you.'

'Can they?' she said, amused by the boy's reasoning.

'Oh yes,' he said solemnly.

'How about here?' said the man.

'Perfect. That's very kind – just leave them here.'

The man lugged the double bass on to the train and wedged it into the luggage space at the end of the compartment. Frannie picked up her bag, but he took it insistently from her, carried that on to the train too and put it beside the double bass. 'Beautiful city, York,' he said.

'Eboracum,' Frannie replied, then immediately wondered why she had said that.

He gave her an intense look, as if he was examining an exhibit in a glass case. His eyes were a brilliant, cornflower blue, beneath thick eyebrows that were well apart. 'Ah,' he said with a warm grin. 'A Latin scholar.'

Frannie smiled back. 'No, I'm not a scholar, I'm afraid.'

'I'm having piano lessons,' the boy said.

'Are you?'

'Yes. My teacher's not very nice, though. I'd like to learn the guitar when I'm older.'

Frannie caught his father's eye. Caught the *frisson* of interest that flickered in it. He hesitated, as if about to say something, then he blushed and glanced at the boy.

'Well – er –' the man patted his pockets. His jacket was crumpled and his shoes were old brown brogues, well polished but battered. The boy was by far the neater of the two, in a white open-necked, button-down shirt, grey shorts with turn-ups, white socks and laced rubber-soled shoes. 'Better not – er – get stranded on the train,' he smiled at Frannie, hesitating again, as if trying to summon the courage to say something else.

'Thank you,' Frannie said as they parted. 'Thank

you very much.' She wished she could have kept the conversation going, but found herself watching him walk towards the exit, the boy at his side.

She went into the compartment, which was beginning to fill, and managed to claim a seat by the window. The image of the man's face stayed in her mind. Excitement burned inside her. The fleeting look of recognition of something in his eyes; of the mutual attraction. She wanted suddenly to get up and run down the platform after him. To prevent the parting that had just taken place.

Except, she might just have been imagining his interest. And at least she hadn't made a fool of herself. She smiled, feeling good suddenly. Good to have found herself attracted again to a man after so many months. She sat back, opened her bag and took out two magazines, *Antiquity* and the *Antiquaries Journal*. And she also took out the novel she was reading, *Take No Farewell* by Robert Goddard, which seemed oddly appropriate, she thought.

As the train jolted, then jolted again and began, silently, to roll forward, she flipped open one of the magazines at the last page, where she always started. But it was an hour before she was able to settle down and concentrate on her reading.

CHAPTER THREE

The traffic was snarled. Engines blattered and rattled and horns blared. The air above the bonnets of cars was corrugated by the heat and the gold spikes of the railings across the road bent and shimmered like reflections in a disturbed pond. Beyond them the British Museum sat, serious and graceful in the block it occupied in Bloomsbury, bounded by four roads like an island to which time was anchored.

In the rooms and galleries beyond the graceful portals, fragments of the past were laid out and neatly labelled, tens of thousands of years of chaos put into semblances of order: *Ancient Iran*; *Coptic Art*; Italy *Before the Roman Empire*. Visitors could stare through polished glass at the corpse of a man preserved in a peatbog; at jewelled crowns from the heads of dead emperors; at clay tablets and carved gods and Ming vases and fragments of neolithic artisan soup mugs; at pages of manuscripts left open as though waiting for their long-dead authors to return for final amendments.

Few people left the building unimpressed, untouched by something, by a memory or a thought, by a sense both of man's insignificance and of his resources, by an awe of being in a place the sum of whose parts was greater than any single human being could ever be.

Behind the quiet order of the galleries lay a labyrinth of corridors, book-lined offices and basements where many of the thousand-strong staff worked, and where some of the priceless exhibits had been stored during the war. Frannie's office was cramped and one of the few without a window, but she did not mind. She loved this museum and still, some mornings, after nearly three years, got a kick just out of walking in through its majestic front, unable to believe that this was really where she worked. And sometimes, when the monotony of her current assignment got her down, she reminded herself that it was early days in her career and there were more exciting landmarks ahead.

She had been working for twelve months on checking and recataloguing the countless basement treasures not on view to the public because of lack of space. It was tedious work, but she was learning all the time, broadening her knowledge both in her own subject, oriental antiquities, and beyond. After Christmas she was going for the first time to the Himalayas, for six weeks, on a dig. She was looking forward to that, and her mercurial boss, Declan O'Hare, the head of her department, had been hinting about a new and more exciting project at the Museum to follow.

In truth, the hope and excitement she had felt after leaving university had been dulled just a little by the tantalizing enormity of reality. By the knowledge that one human being with a trowel could unearth at the most a few square feet a day. Maybe a dozen square yards in a fortnight. That he or she could dig on the same small site for a lifetime and still examine only one tiny part of it, and find only fragments within that. There was far more still buried than had ever been discovered. Earth did not yield its secrets easily. It seemed at times as if there was some superior force at work, toying with them all, letting them build up theories then fragmenting those theories. As if the rules did not permit that you could ever piece together the whole.

Part of the excitement of archaeology for Frannie was to look at artefacts, to hold them and try to let the past come back to life in her imagination. It was something she had found herself doing ever since she had first read a book on Roman history at school. Caesar's world had come vividly alive through those pages, and the hundreds of historical books she had devoured since then. It had come alive through tiny fragments – the spoon handles, brooches, beads, rims of pots, pieces of tessera – that she had unearthed on the digs she had done.

On fine days Frannie spent her lunch-breaks outside, usually taking a sandwich to a bench in a nearby square. Sometimes one of her friends working in the West End managed to bus over and join her, or else she might be accompanied by some of the younger crowd from the Museum, but today was an exception. She felt a sense of dread as she left the massive front hall, negotiating the stream of visitors, and went out through the gateway between the black-and-gold railings into the solid, fumy jam of Great Russell Street.

She had been scared of dentists all her life. Her stomach felt like a hollow metal bowl as she walked down Charing Cross Road and turned into the narrow alley where she stopped beneath the small plastic DENT-IST sign that needed a wipe. Once inside and upstairs, she announced herself to the blonde receptionist.

'Francesca Monsanto. I have an appointment with Mr Gebbie,' she said.

The girl checked her name off a list. 'Go through – first door on the right.'

Frannie went into a tiny waiting-room with half a dozen plastic chairs. A messy-looking woman with a bag of groceries spilling on to the floor beside her chair eyed Frannie hopefully, as if willing her to jump the queue.

She sat down, opened her handbag and took out her diary, determined to distract herself while she waited. Ignoring the National Health booklets scattered on a small coffee-table, she opened the diary by pulling the ribbon marker and checked the weekend and the week ahead. Clive Bracewell's party on Saturday night. It would be a crush in his tiny flat just behind the Portobello Road, but he knew a lot of people and there was always a chance of a decent spare man being there.

Clive was a research assistant at the Museum like herself. Life at the Museum wasn't that different from college, she reflected. Similar social functions, similar cliques. The same air of studiousness. It was more serious, and there was an underlying good feeling of purpose and shared aims. She had a good circle of friends there, but tried not to make it the whole focus of her life, and she particularly treasured get-away-from-it-all occasions, like the recent weekend in York with Meredith Minns, that were completely away from this community.

A breezy voice broke her train of thought, 'Mrs Lowe?'

The grocery bag rustled as its owner walked heavily through the door. Frannie put the diary back into her handbag and noticed that there were some magazines among the booklets on the coffee-table. She spotted *New Woman* lying beneath a copy of *Private Eye*, and tugged it out. As she did so, *Private Eye* fell on to the floor and lay up-ended, its covers spread open. Frannie leaned over and picked it up. It was open at the personal ads page. 'Eye Love' was the headline of one column. She glanced at it out of curiosity.

'BALDING 50-SOMETHING not fat if stomach held

in. Own London house plus inadequate income. Separated. Chain-smoker not interested in star signs. Any offers?'

'NICE BOTTOM washes quite regularly, clever 28 and tailormade for the beautiful young London career woman. One only remaining. A giveaway at 24p . . .'

'FEMALE SEEKS eccentric to delight in. Midlands. Box . . .'

She wondered what sort of people put these ads in. Whether they were like herself. Or whether they were desperate. Maybe it was all in code. She glanced across the page and read down the 'Eye Need' column.

'DESPAIRING STUDENT urgently needs funds to continue education. Genuine. Thanks. Box . . .'

Then a headline in another column caught her attention: 'GIRL WITH DOUBLE BASS! Are you the girl who was struggling down the platform of King's Cross Station carrying a double bass, on Friday, 10th August, catching a train to Eboracum? I am the man who helped you. I'd like to see you again.'

Frannie looked at the advertisement in disbelief, thinking for a moment she must have imagined it. *Eboracum.* The Roman name for York. She had mentioned it to the man and he had understood it.

She read through the ad again, feeling strangely disconcerted. Yet a tiny pulse of excitement beat deep inside her. There might have been other girls struggling with other double basses down that platform. But not going to *Eboracum.*

'Jesus!' she blurted out in excitement, and then felt slightly foolish. A brake of caution suddenly applied itself in her mind and she wondered for a moment if she was the butt of some elaborate joke. She bit her lip and looked up at the ceiling, and then around her.

Then she read the ad once more. It had to be her!

Had to be. A grin spread across her face as if she was sharing the joke with the man she had met. Of all the tens of thousands of people reading this ad, it was for her, her alone. And she had seen it.

She tried to recall the man's face, but it was hazy. The intense stare of his blue eyes, the resemblance to Harrison Ford. The warmth in his face, in his voice. The strange way the boy had looked at her. The ginger curls, the freckles; the serious, tear-stained face.

She remembered the humour in the man's face as he had spoken to her. The pulse of excitement beat again, more strongly. Crazy; she could remember that sudden thrill of attraction, could feel it now. It was like that sometimes; you met a total stranger and you immediately clicked, as if you were soul mates.

Frannie dug her pen out of her bag, took her diary out again and wrote down the box number of the advertisement, then the address of the magazine.

It was only as she closed her diary that the doubts began. As if there was something not quite right, that she had not yet spotted. The big snag. She shrugged them off, read the ad again, and grinned again. She was still smiling ten minutes later as she walked through into the dentist's surgery.

When she got back to the Museum, complete with two new fillings, Penrose Spode was seated at his desk with the quiet demeanour of a statue of Buddha. And the same aura of benign domination. He was her colleague and they shared an office.

Like most of the offices in the building, it was taller than it was wide, the walls on all four sides lined floor to ceiling with books and catalogues. The word-processor terminals and digital telephones on each of their ancient wooden desks looked incongruous, as if they were stage props that had been put on the wrong set.

Their desks faced each other: Spode's, like himself, immaculate; the stacks of paper laid out in careful geometric asymmetry in contrast to the post-nuclear-holocaust appearance of her own desk. Spode sat very erect, his chest indented, the knot of his lichen-coloured tie protruding the same distance as his Adam's apple; his black hair drawn smooth and flat like sealskin; his eyes small and myopic behind lenses like magnifying glasses and frames the size of protective goggles; his closed mouth, small and tight, formed a perfect circle like a rubber bung.

He was a man of twenty-eight with a dry, anarchic humour and an obsession with routine, punctuality and consistency, which he maintained were essential for a harmonious life. He did everything at the same steady pace, as if aware that energy was a commodity not to be squandered, and went about his work and his life with an air of constipated inertness. Archaeology was his world; he had no outside interests and he exercised by cycling to work on an old-fashioned upright bicycle. His clips hung on a hook on the back of the door, along with his crash-helmet, smog mask and fluorescent sash.

Frannie's hurried late arrival from lunch seemed to throw the rhythm of his concentration and, between entering the room and settling at her desk, she noticed him type and erase the same line three times on his word processor.

He stopped, clearly irritated. 'I didn't know you would be up here this afternoon,' he said. 'Thought you were down in the basement.'

'Dentist,' she mumbled through her frozen mouth.

He sighed as Frannie noisily opened and shut a drawer in her desk, looking for plain paper.

'Oh – there was a call I took for you,' he said. 'A Mr Jupp from the Bodleian. He says he's found the reference you wanted.'

'Thanks,' she said, distractedly.

'He said he thought you'd be extremely pleased.' There was a slightly pained note in Spode's voice as she continued to rummage, cleared a space on her desk, laid down a sheet of paper and started to write.

'He asked if you could call back before three,' Spode said, looking at his watch pointedly.

Frannie did not notice. She was concentrating on her handwriting, trying to make it legible for once. She wondered whether it was sensible to give her home address and phone number just in case, then realized how embarrassed she might be if he rang her at the office. Penrose Spode always listened to her calls with one ear. She decided to include her home number but not her address. Even so, her surname was not common and he could get the address by matching her name and number but she felt it at least afforded her some protection if he turned out to be a nutter.

She tore up five attempts before she was satisfied that she had got the tone right:

'I am the girl who was carrying a double bass down the platform of King's Cross Station on Friday, 10th August. Were you the very kind man with the young boy who had just been to the zoo? I would be delighted to see you again. Francesca Monsanto.'

She called at a post office on the way home, stuck a first-class stamp carefully on the envelope, then held the letter for a long time before letting it drop, with a strange feeling of finality, through the slit of the post box into the darkness.

As she walked on towards the tube station, there was a light spring in her step.

CHAPTER FOUR

Frannie's misgivings began a couple of hours after she had posted the letter. It was nothing she could put her finger on, more the feeling that what she had done was rash and she needed to be careful. There was something about the chance of having seen the advertisement that nagged her.

She wondered where else he had advertised, and whether he had done it of his own volition, or had been goaded into it for a bet by friends. And she wondered, more darkly, whether he did this as a regular way of picking up women.

She had posted the letter on Friday and it would have reached *Private Eye* on Monday. Depending how quickly they forwarded it, she knew that the earliest he could receive it would be Tuesday. Even so, every time the phone had rung over the weekend she had stiffened and answered it with a mixture of trepidation and excitement.

At the party on Saturday night she had confided in Carol Bolton, who was her closest friend at the Museum. Carol had surprised and worried her by being alarmist. She told Frannie that if he contacted her she should make sure they met in a public place, and offered to go along and lurk in the background as her minder. Frannie promised she would meet him in a public place, but said she would not be able to relax if she knew Carol was lurking, watching her.

On Monday she had lunch in a café round the corner from the Museum with Debbie Johnson, an old friend, with whom she had been at school from the age of thirteen. Debbie had a rough-and-tumble impishness about her; she was short, but prettier than she normally allowed herself to look, with large doe-like eyes and fair hair that sprouted like wild grass around a badly tied bandanna.

'Hm,' said Debbie, 'he sounds *very* dishy. Nothing like that ever happens to me.'

Debbie worked as public relations officer for a chain of fashion shops and was always enthusiastic about everything, which was one of the many things Frannie liked about her. She told Frannie she thought it sounded incredibly romantic but, like Carol Bolton, warned her to meet in a public place. Even if he was a maniac, she said, he could hardly murder her in a crowded bar.

They discussed whether the fact that he had been on his own with his son meant that he was divorced or a widower, or even that he was happily married and seeking an affair. Debbie ruled out the happily married option; she did not think he would have dared risk an advert. Frannie agreed with that.

There was no call on Tuesday. Frannie did not go to her aerobics on Wednesday in order to be at home in case he rang. But the phone remained obstinately silent.

He called the following night when she was in the bath. It was half past nine. She had for the moment forgotten about the ad and the letter, and was thinking about the argument she had had with her parents when she had gone to their Bethnal Green flat for Sunday lunch, as she usually did. Her mother had loosed off one of her regular salvoes at her for being nearly twenty-six and not married, not even going out with anyone; for not having started to make babies.

Her father had been in one of his despairing moods

in which he shook his head at her and questioned her wisdom in choosing archaeology. He could not understand how his daughter could get into university then not go into industry or law, how she could be content to make do on a meagre salary and spend her time looking at what he called old stones and bones. Frannie had heard the same argument with weary monotony two or three times a year ever since she had first made the decision to study archaeology. During her university years her father had not been so forceful, wondering perhaps at the back of his mind whether she had a smart commercial motive he had not spotted. Now, when he was in a bad mood, he vented his anger at his own failure to prosper at Frannie's betrayal, as he saw it, of all he had worked for. She had no ambition to be rich. He could not understand her. He and her mother had sacrificed everything to come to England to try to make money.

She had replied angrily that she could not understand how they had run a café for thirty years in London's Square Mile and made no money. Lunch had ended in a shouting match, with her kid sister Maria-Angela taking her side and her brother Paolo taking her parents' side. The row had eventually petered out, but the acrimony had not, and she had returned to Clapham on Sunday evening angry at herself for having erupted, angry at her parents, and with a sense of desolation about her life.

Her parents had worked hard, they had tried, they had given her the opportunities. Maybe they were right and she was letting them down. It was much easier for animals who left their families for ever the moment they could feed themselves, she thought. Then she remembered the numerous times she had gone back to her parents after she'd split up with boyfriends or was just down in the dumps, and they'd sat with their arms around her and talked wisely, made jokes, made her feel strong again, and she felt lousy for having shouted at them.

She lay back in the bath in her rented flat, her knees drawn up. The bathroom was crummy: a tiny, cramped, windowless room with a mean, narrow bath-tub that was too short to stretch out in and taps that had been loose ever since she had moved in three years ago. Despite her frequent calls to her landlord's office, the wash-basin was still coming away from the wall and was so small it was almost impossible to get both hands in together.

The hallway by contrast was vast, larger than both her bedroom and the small sitting/dining-room. It was dark and dingy, with massive pipes that gurgled and vibrated alarmingly in winter when the central heating was on, serving as an echo chamber for the boiler that switched noisily on and off at irregular intervals. One day, she was convinced, it would explode and blow the entire terraced house above her down.

She sat up and began to soap her breasts. The first ring of the telephone startled her, and water slopped over the end of the bath as she stood up, the soap submarining down between her legs.

She knew instinctively that it was him, and as she scrambled out she tried to recall his face, tried to picture him, but all she could see was a little boy with ginger hair and freckles pointing at the double bass. She managed to conjure up a crumpled linen suit but the face above it eluded her.

Water streamed down her face and her neck. Her fingers slid without purchase on the door-handle and she wrapped an end of the towel around it to open it, then hurried out, straggles of wet hair draped down the side of her face and the back of her neck, across the hall and the pea-green carpet of the sitting-room to the brown telephone which sat on a cheap, spindly table of its own.

'Hello?' she said, trying to sound nonchalant, but it came out as a strangled squawk.

'Is that – er – Francesca Monsanto?'

She recognized the voice immediately. The hesitation, then the quiet authority.

'Yes, speaking,' she said. His voice clarified his image and a clear picture of him flashed in her mind.

'It's your railway porter here.'

The remark threw her for a moment, then she laughed. 'Oh – right – hi – you got my letter?' she said, aware too late of the dumbness of her reply.

'This morning.'

Water ran down her cheek. There was an awkward silence. 'I – er – posted it on Friday.'

'How – ah – how was the concert?' he said.

'Concert?' she said blankly.

'In York?'

'Concert? Oh –' She gave a nervous laugh that sounded like she had swallowed a fish bone. 'It wasn't my double bass. I was taking it to York for a friend; it was being repaired in London.'

'Ah – I see – I – I thought you were a musician.'

'No – I'm – not terribly musical at all.'

There was another awkward silence. 'I'm sorry – I didn't introduce myself – I'm Oliver Halkin.'

'Hello,' she said, the formality of her tone striking her as absurd.

'Are you any connection with the company?'

'Company?'

'Monsanto – it's rather famous in textiles.'

'No – I don't think so.' Without meaning to, she

35

found herself noting the people who were walking down the street. Above the parapet she saw trousers, then a woman's legs. Water trickled down the small of her back into the towel.

'I'm really pleased you saw the ad,' he said.

'It was pretty amazing seeing it!' She relaxed a little. 'I never thought – I – I don't read *Private Eye*. I saw it by accident.'

'You were awfully decent to write.'

'I – I didn't really believe it was for me, you know? I thought it must be for someone else. Except for the Eboracum bit, that was clever.'

'Could we – er – meet up? Perhaps I could – er – could buy you some lunch?'

Lunch. She liked the idea of lunch. Daytime. There was an almost disappointing innocence about it. Lunch wasn't easy for her, it was meant to be an hour; not that anyone kept a stopwatch on it, but she felt guilty about abusing it. She remembered Carol Bolton's caution, and Debbie's. Lunch would be safer, although she did not believe he could be a threat to her. And she could compensate by working late. 'Great! Thank you.'

'Do you work in London?'

'Yes.'

'Are you anywhere near the City?'

'In Bloomsbury.'

'Right. Is next Tuesday any good for you?'

'Next Tuesday? I'll just check.' She clamped the receiver against her towelled thigh, her brain racing. Tuesday. Nothing. Her diary was through in her bedroom, but she knew she was free. 'Tuesday would be fine.'

'I'm trying to think of somewhere that's easy for you. Do you know Greville Street?'

'Off Gray's Inn Road?'

'Yes. There's a wine bar in a little alley called Bleeding Heart Yard. We can sit outside if it's nice.'

'Great. I'll find it.'

'One o'clock OK for you?'

'Yes, fine,' she said. 'See you then.'

Frannie found the Bleeding Heart wine bar more quickly than she had expected and was ten minutes early. She had dressed in the only really smart summer outfit she had, a navy two-piece, a white open-neck blouse and her one pair of decent navy shoes, and she had felt good when she had left the Museum twenty minutes ago. Now she was a bag of nerves.

She walked on past the courtyard and crossed over to the cool of the shaded side of the street, out of the cloying lunch-time heat, wondering if there was some subtle humour in his choice of venue that was eluding her.

She checked her reflection in a shop window, making sure her face and nose had not gone shiny, then ambled on edgily, unable to stand still, glancing at other windows but barely registering what was in them. Instead she was thinking about him. Oliver Halkin. All worked up, she thought, for someone I met at a railway station and will probably never see again after today. Someone whose face I can't even remember clearly without his voice to prompt me. She even wondered whether she would recognize him instantly or not.

At five to one she made her way back up the street and into the pretty, cobbled courtyard with tables outside laid for lunch, several of which were already occupied. A waitress asked if she had a reservation and she told her there might be one in the name of Oliver Halkin.

The girl disappeared inside, then came back out a moment later. 'He's not here yet.' She led Frannie to a table in the sun, saying 'Would you like a drink?'

'I'll wait for a few minutes,' Frannie said.

She sat, glancing around. There were three women at the next table, smartly dressed and chattering. Two men sat at the table in front of her, one having soup, the other pulling an artichoke apart. A blond man in a brightly checked jacket walked arm in arm with a smartly dressed woman across the cobbles, and into the interior. She heard the faint clatter of cutlery, the clink of glasses around her, and smelled the aroma of grilled fish.

A tall brown-haired man hurried in from the street; he was the right age and build and she wondered, just for an instant, whether it could possibly be Oliver Halkin. He caught her glance and hesitated, looking at her expectantly but equally without recognition, then walked past her and inside.

A striking-looking woman in her early thirties, in a white trouser suit and jangling gold chains, strutted past, heels clicking on the cobbles. Her wake of perfume drifted over Frannie. A siren wailed a few blocks away. Then Oliver Halkin came in.

She stood up as he ambled towards her with a shy smile on his face, everything else in the courtyard dissolving into the background. He stopped in front of her, seemed to pluck up courage and held out his arm, stiffly, giving her hand a firm, curiously formal shake. 'Francesca. Sorry I'm late – the traffic –' He raised his arms then let them drop to his side by way of apology. 'You haven't been waiting long?'

'Just a couple of minutes. I was a little early.'

He was taller and more powerfully built than she remembered, and in the bright sunlight she could see he was closer to forty than thirty-five. He was dressed similarly to before, although he looked smarter and fresher in a well-pressed linen suit, a blue-and-white striped shirt and a tie which had what looked like hippopotamuses on it. He was as good-looking as she had remembered. Even more so.

They studied each other for a moment, as if each was uncertain of their memory and was seeking reassurance, then he leaned forward and lowered his voice conspiratorially. 'You know, you look much better without your double bass.'

'You don't get to meet such nice strangers without it.' She smiled, surprised by the flirtatiousness of her reply. Now that he was here, her nervousness had gone almost completely, and she was feeling the same immediate attraction to him that she had before.

He sat down opposite her and the waitress came over with two menus. 'Can I get you something to drink?' she said.

Frannie opted for a spritzer and Oliver joined her. He glanced down towards his lap, then up, touched the edge of the table as if he was going to adjust it, then seemed to have difficulty in deciding what to do with his arms. He folded them, unfolded them, then rested his hands on the edge of the table. They were large, strong-looking hands with slender, elegant fingers and rather bluntly clipped nails, which he examined for a moment before looking directly back at her. She noticed the signet ring on his wedding finger.

'So, tell me about Francesca Monsanto.'

She interlocked her fingers in her lap, amazed how relaxed she still felt. 'You tell me about Oliver Halkin first.'

'There's nothing very exciting to tell.' Oliver tapped his menu as she grinned at him disbelievingly. 'I'm a widower with a son of eight, Edward, whom you've met. I have a farm which my brother runs – I help him out at weekends. And I'm a mathematician at a bank in the week.'

'Oh?' She tilted her head inquiringly.

'Yes; mathematics and flying have always been my two big loves. But I can't afford to fly much these days.'

'Do you have a plane?'

'I have an ancient Tiger Moth I've been restoring. But she's not airworthy yet.' When her eyes widened, he said, 'Your turn! Tell me about Francesca now.'

'Right, well . . .' She pursed her lips and smiled, infected by his own expectant air. 'She's an archaeologist.' She paused to take in his reaction, which seemed to be of approval. 'She has graduated in Archaeology and Anthropology at the University of London. She's a Libra.' She thought for a moment, swinging her tongue inside her mouth. 'Her lucky number is four and her favourite colour is blue. She's quite superstitious. She has two brothers and one sister.'

The waitress arrived with their drinks and as Oliver leaned back a little Frannie noticed his broad shoulders. She brought to mind an expression about the boy being father of the man. In Oliver Halkin she could see both. There was a boyishness about his features, his hair, about the faint trace of sadness in his eyes, and yet a manliness in his physique, in the lines of his face, the crow's-feet, in the confidence with which he carried himself, the assurance with which he sat here like a lion in its own habitat.

'What do they do?' he asked. 'Your brothers and sister?'

'My little sister Maria-Angela's at catering college.

My eldest brother, Vittorio, is a doctor – he's a house-man in Durham, and my younger brother, Paolo, is a lorry driver.'

'Quite a mixture, your family.' He held his glass forward. 'Cheers.'

'Cheers,' Frannie said.

He clinked his glass against hers and there was a rich chime. Their eyes met and Frannie felt a beat of excitement as she drank. He lifted his menu. 'Shall we order? Get these out the way.'

They studied the menus in silence for a few moments. Frannie ordered melon followed by turbot, and Oliver Halkin ordered pâté and the turbot.

She wondered how his wife had died but did not like to ask. 'Which bank are you with?' she said.

'It's a small merchant bank, called the Halkin-Northrop.' He raised his eyebrows. 'I shouldn't think you've heard of it.'

'Halkin? Is that a family connection?'

'More by name than much else, these days. We don't own many shares any more. They give me something to do out of kindness.'

'I don't believe that! What do you actually do there? Chairman?'

'No, gosh, I'm just a sort of consultant. I dabble away with my mathematics and every now and then if I get something right they give me a pat on the head and a biscuit.'

'You do their accounts?'

'No. I'm a statistics analyst. I study trends, patterns, assess the odds of risks. We do quite a bit of reinsurance financing – I have to try to work out things like how many people are going to be killed in road accidents over the next decade, how many in plane crashes and how many are going to get bitten by dogs.' He smiled wryly. 'Or how many cavalry officers are going to get kicked to death by horses.'

'Do many?'

'It's a very consistent figure.'

'I've never been much good at maths.'

'Have you ever been interested in it?'

'No, I've never really thought about it very much – probably because I'm so hopeless at it.'

He looked reprovingly. 'That's a shame.'

'Why?'

He patted the table with the palm of his hand, lightly but with a sudden look of zeal on his face, and leaned forward. 'Because so many bright people do ignore it. So few teachers make it exciting at school – they teach it as just another boring thing you have to learn.' His eyes brightened, coming alive like a dormant fire blasted by bellows. 'Archaeology – beauty – symmetry. Think about the proportions of buildings, of vases, furniture. Mathematics and design are inseparable. The design of objects,' he raised his side plate then put it down; 'the design of the world.'

'Of the world?' she said.

He picked up his glass and swirled the liquid inside it. His eyes were alight and Frannie was captivated by his enthusiasm. 'Mathematics is the most exciting thing of all. It holds the key to the universe.'

She looked at him and asked dubiously. 'In what way?'

'You said you're a Libra. Do you read your horoscope?'

'Sometimes.'

'Do you believe in fortune-tellers?'

'I'm not sure. I suppose I do, a little.'

'I'm a fortune-teller.'

Her eyes widened. 'Do you have a crystal ball?'

'No. Just a calculator.' He smiled. 'At a simple level, mathematics can predict the most extraordinary things.'

'Like what?' She leaned towards him.

'I can tell you how many people are going to die next year, in every country of the world, in any kind of accident you can name. And from any kind of disease. What's more, I'll be more accurate than any seaside clairvoyant.'

Frannie savoured her spritzer then cupped her glass in both hands. 'Except you can't predict who the victims will be, can you?'

He smiled. 'No, that's right. Not yet.'

'Not *yet*? You think you'll be able to one day?'

'There are patterns to everything. By understanding patterns you can make order out of chaos.' He raised his glass. 'I'm getting far too serious.'

'No, I'm interested.'

He drank and then set the glass down with exaggerated care. 'Tell me about your parents. What do they do?'

The time slipped by easily, almost unnoticed, as they chatted. Their table had become a private island where they sat alone, absorbed in each other and undisturbed except for the arrival of food and more drinks and the removal of plates, and at some point, even when Frannie already thought she was feeling far too drunk, a bottle of Sancerre was presented and poured. She became increasingly surprised at the things they had in common. Attitudes and interests. She told him how she had first become interested in archaeology as a child, from a book on the Romans at school, and had persuaded her parents to take her to stately homes and museums at weekends.

Oliver elaborated on his love of mathematics and how he believed that it was both an art and a science, one which could ultimately solve all the mysteries of the universe. She talked about her love of archaeology and how she believed that it was through uncovering the secrets of the past that the mysteries of the universe would be solved.

Finally, Frannie noticed there was no one left in the courtyard except themselves. She looked at her watch, and saw with shock that it was four o'clock.

Oliver took her back to the Museum in a taxi, and asked her if she would have a meal with him on Friday. She told him she would like that very much.

She hurried back up the steps into the shadow of the colonnaded portals, stepping on air, her guilt at being so late back cushioned by the haze of alcohol.

An hour later, as she began to sober up, she had a slight sense of unease about Oliver and she was not sure why. He seemed almost too good to be true. It was as if there was something about him that did not totally fit together; a piece missing from the equation. Something about himself that he wasn't telling her, perhaps; that he was either hiding or holding back. And she was still bothered, also, by the feeling that she had seen him before.

Normally Frannie was confident and looked on the bright side and she found it unsettling to feel this way. All the more so as she realized quite how deeply she fancied him.

CHAPTER FIVE

Debbie Johnson rang her late on Wednesday evening, curious to know how her date had turned out. Just back from her aerobics, Frannie tried not to say too much, afraid it might be bad luck to talk about it too soon. She promised to call her friend back on Saturday and report on Friday's date.

As she hung up, the phone rang again. It was Oliver. He apologized for having made her so late in getting back to work on Tuesday afternoon and she told him it had not mattered, although actually she'd been carpeted by the unpredictable Declan O'Hare. They chatted easily. He asked her what she had been doing at work and she told him she had spent the day cataloguing Indian daggers and had then been to her aerobics class; and he said he had just got back from playing tennis. There had been a pause in which she had been tempted to say, 'Why don't you come over?' but she did not want to seem pushy or too keen. It was enough that he had called. And she was secretly pleased that at nine o'clock he was at home and not out on a date.

On Thursday evening she washed her hair but could not settle down and relax. She was unable to concentrate on reading, or on the television and instead spring-cleaned the flat. She knew she was behaving like a besotted teenager and was angry with herself. But she could not help it.

On Friday she left work punctually at half past five and hurried home, having a sudden, uncustomary panic about what to wear. She unhooked the black dress, a high-street version of Chanel, which she had decided on. She liked it because it was short and neat, but she was worried in case it didn't make her look attractive enough for Oliver Halkin. She tugged several more outfits out, but nothing else looked right, so it was going to have to do.

A narrow rectangle of sunlight lay across the bed-room floor, touching the edge of the white rug she had bought in Petticoat Lane a few months ago to try to brighten up the room. Sometimes it could feel dark and oppressive even though the walls were white and the ceiling was high, and at times it had an atmosphere that made her feel distinctly uncomfortable. A window opened on to a basement well which only accentuated the subterranean feel of the room.

Frannie had hung a couple of Egyptian prints on the walls, and on the mantelpiece were her family photo-graphs, as well as two small fragments of tessera that she had pocketed from one of the first digs she had ever been on, and which still gave her a thrill. In spite of all the objects she handled daily at the Museum, nothing quite measured the feelings she got from the few treasures of her own.

She had finished getting ready by twenty past seven and had forty minutes to kill. She looked around the sitting-room. Her efforts of last night had improved it a little. It was the first flat she had ever had of her own and she did not mind the cheap furniture and the drabness because it had given her freedom and inde-pendence. She always enjoyed playing hostess when her friends came round. But most of them were as used to the flat's less-than-impressive air as she was. It was only now, with Oliver coming, that Frannie suddenly found herself gazing uncomfortably at the ugly vinyl sofa and armchairs, the dining-table with its peeling mahogany laminate, and the shabby net curtains.

The only stamp of her own personality on the room lay in the framed posters of past exhibitions at the Museum, her books and her pride and joy – a small, plain earthenware Roman vase that sat on the coffee table. It was pear-shaped and rather dumpy, with the handle and part of the rim missing, and had been carefully glued back together by the amateur archaeologist who had dug up the pieces in 1925.

Often Frannie wondered about the life of the Roman artisan who had made it, imagined what he or she had looked like. The clay indicated it had been made in Italy and brought over maybe by an immigrant like her own parents. She had paid five hundred pounds for the vase three years ago in the Portobello Road, on the day she had received the letter from the Museum telling her she had got the job. It had been a spur-of-the-moment bit of madness that had blown her savings, but she had never regretted it.

She switched off the overhead light, leaving just a table light and the wonky lamp standard and that made a further improvement, made the room seem almost cosy. Another year and she would buy somewhere of her own. It would be tiny but it would be tasteful, she resolved.

She picked the Jilly Cooper novel she had just started off the sofa, made a mental note of the page number and closed it, tucking it into her bookshelves, and pulled out instead a paperback of Guy de Maupassant short stories, which she opened and placed casually, face down, in the same position on the sofa.

As eight o'clock approached, Frannie began to feel nervous. She went into the bedroom, and felt a bit reassured by the girl who stared back at her from the mirror. The short dress showed off her legs and her figure well. She had frown lines from anxiety so she deliberately relaxed and smiled. A sultry girl with dark, shiny hair that framed her face and touched her shoulders smiled back. The girl looked OK.

She looked great.

She went back into the sitting-room, sat down and picked up the Maupassant, glancing through, unable to concentrate. She could hear muffled gunshots ringing out from the television in the flat above. Her watch said eight-fifteen. Then eight-thirty. He wasn't coming. Chickened out. Stood her up. Going to end up spending the evening watching the box.

Then she heard footsteps. A shadow crossed the curtains. The doorbell rang.

She jumped up, went into the hall and opened the front door. Oliver Halkin peered over the huge bunch of flowers in his hands, looking relieved that he had found the right place. 'Sorry I'm so late,' he said. He pushed the flowers forward as if he was slightly embarrassed by them. 'I hope you – sort of like these –'

'Wow!' she said. Their scents blotted out for a brief moment the rank, humid smells of London at night, of unemptied dustbins, exhaust fumes and dust, reminding her that there was another world of parkland and countryside. 'They're gorgeous!' She took the flowers, brought the heads close to her nose and inhaled deeply. 'Thank you.' She kissed him spontaneously on his cheek, but he made no response and the gesture left a moment of awkward silence between them.

He was wearing a navy double-breasted suit that looked good on him, a soft-collared blue shirt and a yellow tie. His hair seemed more carefully groomed than before and he was wearing black Oxfords that looked fairly new. The neatness of his appearance belied her original image of him. When she offered him a drink, he looked at his watch, then back at her, expressionlessly.

'I think perhaps we ought to make tracks – I booked for eight-thirty.'

'I'll just put these in some water.' The flat suddenly seemed dingier than ever. She ushered him through into the living-room, then walked with a heavy heart into the kitchen, and ran the cold tap into the sink; a feeling of unease was establishing itself inside her. He seemed a bit distant.

As she went into the sitting-room she was pleased to see him staring with interest at the Roman vase.

'Is this one of your finds?' he said.

'Yes – well – sort of – I found it in a shop.' Her confidence had gone and she realized she was sounding stiff and nervous.

'How old is it?'

'About 50 BC.'

'Good Lord.' He squatted and stared at it more closely. 'I've got one very similar at home. I'd no idea it was as old as that. What would it have been used for?'

'Probably for water or wine. I could have a look at it for you if you like.'

'Yes, I would.'

'I sometimes feel guilty about owning it.'

'Why?' He stood up again.

She shrugged. 'I suppose it's the same as I feel about the treasures locked away in the vaults in the Museum. That things from the past like this ought to be accessible to everyone – that maybe it shouldn't be tucked away down here – a secret little treasure hoard.'

'You could always open your flat to the public.' He grinned, fleetingly.

'Great idea. England's first stately basement!'

He laughed, and although it was a little forced, the atmosphere seemed to improve between them.

It was now dark outside. She followed him to a small Renault that was either grey or blue beneath a London patina of grime and dust; it was badly dented down the passenger side, and there was a row of holes where a chromium or plastic strip had been torn away.

He held the door for her, scooped a clutch of papers off the passenger seat, and she climbed in. The interior of the car was full of clutter. She carefully placed her feet between several library books that lay on the floor. A residents' parking sticker, Borough of Chelsea, was stuck on the windscreen beside the licence roundel, plus another permit that she could not read. Several parking-tickets in cellophane bags lay in the indent above the glove compartment, along with a packet of Fisherman's Friends, a couple of ball-point pens, several loose pieces of paper and a tennis ball.

She pulled the seat-belt over her chest and found the buckle. He climbed in and sat slightly hunched, his head touching the roof lining, as if the car were a suit that was a size too small. He twisted the ignition key and the engine clattered into life, then he turned towards her. 'I apologize if I'm not quite with it at the moment. I had a bit of grim news just before I came to pick you up.'

'I'm sorry,' she said.

'No – it's –' he shrugged. 'My son's on holiday in the South of France, staying with some friends who've a boy his age – they have a villa down there.' His voice tailed and he pulled the car out, accelerating harshly. 'I just had a phone call this evening – they had a ghastly accident on a speedboat yesterday.' He braked at the junction and peered sternly out into the main road, as if he expected the traffic to stop under his withering gaze. 'Apparently they all went out in the boat to find a bay for a picnic and water-skiing. On the way back they ran over a swimmer – a girl.'

'God!' Frannie said. 'Awful. Is she –' she hesitated. 'Badly hurt?'

'She was killed.'

'That's terrible.'

He accelerated decisively out into a gap, alarmingly close to an oncoming car.

'Is your son all right?'

He drove on without replying for some moments. 'Fine. Edward's fine.' He said it rather oddly, she thought; quite defensively.

'Shock sometimes hits people later,' she said, remembering the time she had been a passenger in a motorway pile-up four years ago, and one of the cars behind had caught fire. Just a few flames under the bonnet at first. Everyone had tried to get the trapped driver out, but the flames had soon engulfed the car and beaten them back. She'd watched him banging the windscreen and yelling until she could bear it no longer and had had to turn away. It had been a week later that she'd had the first nightmare about it. She still dreamed of it now, occasionally.

'Yes,' he said.

'Who was driving the boat?'

'I'm not sure. It wasn't Edward.' He was about to say something else, then was silent.

'What a horrible thing for a child to see,' Frannie said.

'I had a word with him over the phone. He seemed fine – far more concerned about whether I'd got his Scalextric working again – there was a problem with the transformer.'

She smiled. But there was no humour in Oliver's

expression and he lapsed into silence. She watched him, the glare of each passing street light flaring on his face then fading. Something about his taut profile reminded her of a rabbit when it is caught in the glare of the headlights and doesn't know which way to turn. Just for a moment. Then the impression was gone.

The restaurant was a cheap and cheery trattoria, with red-and-white tablecloths, strips of fish netting and wickered Chianti bottles strung from the walls. The air was heavy with cigarette smoke, and stronger, sumptuous smells of hot olive oil and garlic, of searing meats and grilling fish. All the tables were occupied and the place had a crammed, lively atmosphere which made Frannie immediately feel comfortable.

A waiter with an accent Frannie recognized as Neapolitan led them down a staircase into an equally packed basement. There was a burst of raucous laughter from a large party of people in their twenties at the far end. Only two tables were unoccupied and he led them to one tucked in a corner alcove near the party. 'You like an aperitif, perhaps?' he said as he pushed Frannie's chair in.

'Yes, I – er –' Oliver raised his eyes quizzically at Frannie.

'Love one.' She felt in need of a drink.

'A couple of your cocktails.'

'*Due Vito Fizzo*,' he proclaimed, presented each of them with a large, handwritten menu and wheeled away. A packet of *pannini* lay beside each of their places. Oliver picked his up and tore open the top.

There was a deafening eruption of laughter from the party behind them, and Frannie instinctively turned her head. As she did so, a chuckling face looked familiar. The luxuriant hair was shorter than when she had last seen it, but there was no mistaking the thick lips, the burly frame, the booming voice. She watched as Seb Holland banged the table and called out: 'Hey, Luigi, bring me an alligator sandwich and make it snappy!' He turned, roaring with laughter at his joke, to his companions.

She hadn't seen Seb since university, over three years ago. He was going into his family business, she remembered. They were in insurance, something large in the City, and he looked like a prosperous City businessman now, in his chalk-striped suit and loud tie. Their eyes met and he beamed in recognition, stood up, stumbled slightly drunkenly out of his chair, came over, and leaned across the table. 'Frannie! Hi! How are you? You look gorgeous.' He gave Oliver Halkin a cursory glance. 'Sorry, 'scuse me,' he said. 'I've always been in love with this girl – might try and pinch her from you later on if I get pissed enough.' Seb Holland's voice was slurred with booze and he spoke too loudly.

Frannie blushed and introduced the two men.

'Hello,' Oliver said. There was a brief silence as Oliver and Seb frowned at each other in vague recognition.

'Met you before,' Seb said. He was having difficulty in standing upright without swaying, and held on to Frannie's chair-back.

'Yes,' Oliver said good-humouredly, 'I – seem to think we – have –' He frowned which made him look rather fierce, Frannie thought.

'Halkin? Halkin-Northrop bank?'

'Yes,' Oliver said. 'Seb Holland? Any connection with Holland Delarue?'

'Yah.'

'Ah!' Oliver's face relaxed into a beam as recognition dawned. 'I know Victor Holland.'

''S'my brother.'

'Good Lord! Your brother! I play tennis with him occasionally at Queen's.'

'Didn't you come to our Christmas party last year? That's where we met.'

'At your rather super building?' Oliver's eyes narrowed as if he was trying to remember its name. 'That's right. We talked about cricket! How is Vic? Haven't seen him for a while.'

'He's fine.'

'Good – well –' Oliver looked awkward suddenly, as if unsure how to end the conversation. 'Give him my regards.'

'Yes, I will.' Seb turned to Frannie. 'So, how are you? What are you up to?'

'Fine. Working at the British Museum. How about you?'

'Great.' He sniffed. 'Getting married next month. That's my fiancée.' He pointed at the table, but Frannie could not work out which of the girls he meant. 'Lucy – d'yever meet her?' He screwed up his eyes as if finding it hard to focus. 'No – that was after university. Getting married next month,' he repeated. 'Hey, you must come! Send you an invite. I've still got your family address. We must have a drink sometime before that, anyway.'

'Love to. Congratulations.'

'Yah, thanks.'

Frannie was secretly pleased at being recognized; it helped her stand on her own two feet with Oliver. Seb showed no signs of moving away and she felt a bit embarrassed about prolonging the conversation. 'Still in your family business?'

'Yah, it's OK. Spend half the time in the States.' He sniffed. 'Still see any of the people I'd remember?'

'Meredith. I stayed with her a couple of weekends ago up in York.'

'Meredith! Great girl! Really liked her. How is she?'

'Fine. Very married.'

He grinned, then looked solemn. 'Hey – remember Jonathan Mountjoy?'

'Yes.' She remembered him clearly, a tall, quiet boy, always intensely serious, who never said very much.

'Poor bugger got shot dead in Washington a few weeks ago.'

Frannie stared at him in shocked silence. Her stomach felt as if a drum of cold water had been emptied into it. 'What – what happened?'

'Mugger. Gave him his wallet apparently and the bastard still shot him.'

'God, poor Jonathan!' she said. 'That's awful. Horrible.' She shivered, feeling oddly disoriented suddenly.

Seb dug his finger into his breast pocket and pulled out a card. 'Give me a buzz – come and have lunch or something sometime.' He gave Oliver a smile. 'I'll tell Vic I met you,' he said, then moved away from the table, hesitated for a moment and turned towards Frannie. 'Great seeing you.'

'You too.'

Jonathan Mountjoy. Shot. Dead. Gone.

'Were you at school together?'

Oliver's voice startled her. She collected her thoughts and smiled at him apologetically. 'University.'

A waiter presented them with their cocktails.

Oliver raised his glass. 'Cheers,' he said, quietly. 'It's good to see you again.'

'You too,' Frannie said and sipped the pink-tinged fizzing concoction. It had a pleasant taste of apricots but she barely registered it.

'I'm sorry about the news – about your friend being killed.'

'Thanks,' she said heavily. 'I didn't really know him that well – hadn't seen him since university. But he was nice.' She hunched her shoulders and smiled more brightly. 'Doesn't seem as if either of us are having much good news tonight.'

'No,' he said. 'Well – except that you're here, and that's pretty good news.'

Their eyes met. 'Thank you,' she said.

Someone at Seb's table was telling a story and a girl was squealing in protest. Frannie felt a chilly draught from the air-conditioning against her neck, then a sudden rash of goose-pimples down between her shoulder-blades. She drank some more of the cocktail, but could not feel any effects from it yet. Oliver Halkin and Jonathan Mountjoy's death were now inter-twined in her mind, as if somehow connected. She tried to control the crazy notion that the news was an omen about her and Oliver. That she should pull out now, while she still could.

A waiter hovered; they looked at their menus and ordered, then there was an awkward silence. Oliver shook a stick out of his packet of *pannini*, then laid both the stick and the packet down, aligning them carefully so they lay parallel to his cutlery. 'Penny for your thoughts,' he said.

'I was thinking about the coincidence – of bumping into Seb – and that we should both know him.'

Oliver broke a piece off the end of his *pannini* stick and ate it in silence. 'Coincidences make me uneasy,' he said.

'Why's that?'

He shrugged, then lowered his eyes to the tablecloth, as if embarrassed by what he was about to say. 'I've had rather too many in the past few years; not very happy ones. I find them bad news. They bother me. Probably sounds daft.'

Frannie smiled back at him, surprised that he was superstitious. 'They happen to everybody, surely? Don't you ever have harmless coincidences – like when you're thinking about someone and they phone you?'

'I'm not sure there is such a thing as a meaningless coincidence.'

As she watched his serious face, she began to feel excluded, and her sceptical grin faded. 'What's happened to make you feel that way?'

He fiddled around for some moments with the *pannini* packet, then responded in a way that did nothing to make her feel better. 'I suppose the worst was my wife's death.' He moved his hands in a gesture of helplessness.

'I'm sorry,' Frannie said. 'What happened?' She felt that she needed to know.

He leaned forward, pressed his fingernail hard into the tablecloth, and with intense concentration began to make a straight line across. 'Almost any sort of coincidence,' he said distantly, as if he had not heard her question. 'Bumping into someone like Seb Holland. The same number coming up a couple of times. Anything.'

His expression suddenly changed into a distant smile that seemed to be directed at the universe in general rather than at her. 'The French mathematician Laplace said that chance is the expression of man's ignorance.'

'Is that what you believe?'

He picked his glass up by the stem, cupped the base in the palm of his hand and twisted it round slowly, studying the contents with an air of suspicion. 'Chaos. All these bubbles firing off in here at random. But the effect works; it tastes good and it's intoxicating. Order from chaos! See?' He continued to hold the glass in the air as if in a mood of childish contentment.

'Perhaps the next coincidence is going to change your luck,' she said and drank some more.

'Maybe,' he said, unconvinced.

An image slipped silently through her mind. Jonathan Mountjoy wearing a battered old greatcoat, standing with his hands in his pockets, staring into space. That was how she remembered him, always slightly out of it, in his own world. Dozy, silent Jonathan, handing over his wallet, then the gun coming up, firing.

Over.

She swallowed, placed her hands on the tablecloth, reached out awkwardly for her glass, then stopped as she realized there was nothing left in it.

I'm not sure there is such a thing as a meaningless coincidence.

'Mozzarella for the signorina!' A waiter placed their plates in front of them, then brandished a pepper grinder above Oliver's minestrone. He gave the handle several sharp, crunching twists.

Another waiter appeared with a bottle of wine, which he ceremoniously opened. Frannie looked at her plate, but her appetite had gone. She wanted someone to tell her that it was quite safe to fall in love with Oliver Halkin. She looked across the table at him. He was tasting the wine, holding the glass with one hand, the other lying on the table, large and solid, the winder of his watch nestling in the hairs of his wrist. The sadness had returned to his eyes and she felt an urge to put her own hand out and touch his, to reassure him, to reassure herself.

Her attraction towards him was growing, but her

unease grew with it. Almost as if he were reading her thoughts, he smiled at her.

They talked deeply throughout the meal, which Frannie managed to pick at, mostly discussing their views on the meaning of life, and carrying on their arguments from where they had left off at lunch on Tuesday. She found him challenging to talk to, and he opened her mind further to the world of mathematics and physics. Starting to relax, she told him she had tried to read *A Brief History of Time* but had abandoned it halfway through, and he laughed and told her he'd abandoned it a quarter of the way through, and talked her through the theories in a way that made more, if not total, sense to her.

Frannie had two Sambucas with her coffee, and was pleasantly drunk as they left the restaurant shortly after one; she felt on safer ground with him now. As she fumbled with the seat-belt she was vaguely aware that it was she who had done most of the drinking tonight. She had not even noticed whether Seb Holland was still there or had left.

Oliver dropped her home and escorted her down the steps to her front door. She hoped he would not make an advance because she would find it hard to resist him if he did, and she wanted it to be special when they made love, and she was too drunk for it to be like that now. 'Would you like to come in for a coffee?' she said.

'I – ought to get back – it's pretty late.' He looked awkward suddenly. 'I was wondering – Edward's coming back tomorrow – this is his last weekend at home before he goes back to school.' In the haze of the street-lighting Frannie could see that he was blushing, and wasn't sure what was coming next. 'If – if you're not doing anything, would you – like to come down to the country for the weekend? He took a bit of a shine to you at King's Cross.'

She tried to think of the implications, but her heart overruled everything. There was a party tomorrow that she was not particularly looking forward to, and she was meant to be going to her parents for Sunday lunch, but had already been thinking of ducking out of that. After the fracas of last Sunday, she could do without seeing her parents for a few weeks. 'I'd love to,' she said.

He looked really pleased. 'How about if I pick you up at about ten?'

'Do I need to bring anything?'

'Some wellies. I don't know what the forecast is. We're very informal. And swimming gear.'

'I'll be ready at ten.'

He held her gaze for a moment, gave her a light peck on the cheek, walked back up the steps, and stood waiting until she was safely inside.

As she closed the front door and pressed the latch, she felt as if she had been scooped up and put on a pedestal. Her emotions came to the surface so that her earlier fears were buried by a glow of pleasure and a sense of anticipation. The very word *country* conjured an image in her mind of a ramshackle farmhouse, with a flagstone floor and log fire, acres of fields and woods. She could see them taking long walks, maybe having lunch in a pub garden. Lazing around a swimming-pool, with sheep on the far side of the fence. The boy had taken 'a shine' to her. Edward. She was pleased about that, rather flattered.

She went through into the kitchen, switched on the light and stared at Oliver's flowers in the sink, then hunted for something suitable to put them in. She remembered a plain white vase with a green ceramic bow which she had been given a couple of birthdays ago by Meredith Minns, and retrieved it from behind a stack of bowls.

She carefully arranged the flowers in the vase, feeling wide awake and almost deliriously happy, then carried it through into her bedroom and placed it in the centre of the mantelpiece, spreading out the white and peach carnations, the yellow and orange lilies, smelling their scents in turn, then standing back to admire them.

It was after two when Frannie went to bed, and she set her alarm for eight. After she switched the light out she lay awake for a long time, her brain buzzing.

When she eventually slept, she sank into a sinister dream in which she was running through dark empty streets in a city. Ahead of her she could see Jonathan Mountjoy, silhouetted against a high-rise building. But although he was not moving and she was sprinting, she was not getting any nearer. Footsteps were clacking down an alley. Someone was running towards him holding a gun. She tried to scream at him, to warn him, but her voice would not work. She could see the gun pointing at him, the wild, shaky hand holding it. 'Jonathannnnnnnnn!'

The shot woke her with a start.

People were screaming. The sirens of the police and the ambulance were wailing. Then she realized it was a real siren, somewhere in the distance. But the shot had been here, in this room. A bang, or a slap.

Someone in here.

A deep chill of fear spread through her. For a moment she was too scared to move. Then slowly she put out her hand, groping for the light switch. Snapped it on.

The darkness leapt back into the walls. She stared around with frightened eyes. Only an eerie silence filled the room. Nothing moved, nothing breathed, but something was wrong. Shadows from the lamp lay across the ceiling; a fly sat directly above her. She stared at her prints on the walls; at the wardrobe. Her throat was parched, her mouth dry. She stared at the mantelpiece. The mantelpiece where she had carefully put the vase with the flowers.

The vase was still there but there were no flowers in it.

She sat bolt upright. The flowers lay strewn across the floor, as if they had been hurled there by someone or something in a rage.

CHAPTER SIX

Oliver turned up shortly after ten, wearing a rugger shirt, baggy red trousers and ancient laced yachting shoes; he carried Frannie's bag to an elderly mud-caked Range Rover.

'What happened? Did you put the Renault in a grow-bag?' she asked.

He laughed. 'I just use the Renault for hacking around London; it's so clapped out I don't think it would survive a long journey.'

The interior of the Range Rover was as cluttered and untidy as his Renault, with the addition of crumpled rugs and an assortment of chewed rings and rubber bones on the rear seat. 'Captain Kirk's,' he said by the way of explanation.

'Captain Kirk?'

'Edward's dog; he treats this bus as his kennel.'

They drove south out of London, through traffic that was heavy and slow at first, but which thinned out on the motorway. The sun beat down ahead of them out of a cloudless sky. Frannie had on a checked shirt, with a thin jumper slung around her shoulders, white cotton trousers and trainers, and she felt cool and comfortable in her clothes. Her thoughts were less comfortable and she felt tired, her eyes sandpapery from the fitful sleep she had had.

The flowers churned in her mind. She had checked the flat, but the windows were shut, the front door was locked and no one could have been in. She had put them back in the vase and in the morning they were still there, and she had begun to wonder seriously whether it had simply been a dream. Or just a household accident to which she'd overreacted.

She asked Oliver more about his farm, trying to build up a picture of it. He told her his manager and younger brother, Charles, was a very committed Green, and the farm was now almost completely organic. They were building up large herds of organically reared cattle and sheep, although both were fraught with problems, and he explained some of them. She learned also that Charles was divorced and had custody at the weekends of his son, Tristram, who was the same age as Edward.

Oliver was not a driver she would have liked to have been following, she thought. He drove well if a bit fast most of the time, but occasionally, when he talked about something that particularly excited him, he would go for several miles oblivious of an indicator he'd left flashing, or forgetting to change up into top gear so that the engine raced, maddeningly. Several times she had been quite convinced he was not going to stop for a red light, and had found herself jabbing her foot down.

Now, cruising on the motorway, everything had settled down. The windows were open and air billowed through the car, batting strands of Frannie's hair across her face, and she lounged back in her seat, beginning to relax, surveying the scenery through her sunglasses.

As London receded, the disconcerting memory of her sleepless night receded with it. The weekend ahead was full of promise and she was determined to enjoy herself. Her return journey seemed a hundred years away, and she wondered whether she and Oliver would have become lovers by then.

The friends with whom Edward had been staying in France were catching a ferry to Dover this morning and would be dropping him home around midday. The accident on the powerboat had clearly distressed Oliver; he had not talked about the boy very much, yet she had the feeling that Edward had a strong influence on him. She realized how very little she really knew about Oliver. Their conversations had all been about their subjects, their views on life, and they had talked only very sketchily about their families. She had not been able to draw him back on to the topic of his wife's death and she was curious to know both how she had died, and what the coincidences were that had distressed him so much. But she did not want to be morbid.

The silhouette of the South Downs, like a huge barrier wedged across the horizon, drew closer, and a few miles on they turned eastwards off the motorway, on to a busy country road. They drove into a heavy stench of manure, but even that she found refreshing after the cloying, greasy air of London.

'Where does Edward go to school?' she asked.

'A place called Stowell Park. A prep school about ten miles away. It's easy for picking him up at week-ends.'

'Does he board?'

'Yes.'

'He doesn't mind?'

'No. That's what he wants to do.'

Through an opening in a hedgerow she glimpsed a flurry of activity at a car-boot sale. 'Did you board?' she asked.

'Yes, from the time I was seven.'

'How did you find it?'

'I hated it. I loathed school altogether.'

'Why?'

He shrugged. 'I couldn't do what I wanted, I

suppose. And I didn't care about team games.' He smiled and scratched his ear. 'I was only interested in mathematics and aeroplanes as a child. We could only do one afternoon a week of gliding, and that was in summer, and I used to think the maths teachers were a load of bozos.' He smiled again. 'I don't think I was very well adjusted to school. Did you like it?'

'Yes, most of the time, I loved it. Particularly history, and the classics. I used to long in the holidays for term to start. People probably thought I was an awful swot.'

'And they all thought I was a lazy bugger who didn't like being prodded. They were probably right.'

'And Edward really enjoys it?'

'Yes,' he said, then he went silent for a while.

They drove along a bypass, past an old town built over a hill; at the top she could see the ramparts of a castle.

'Lewes,' he said. 'County town of Sussex.'

'Where Simon de Montfort defeated and captured Henry the Third in 1264.'

He glanced at her quizzically.

'Once the home town of Gideon Mantell, who discovered the dinosaur,' she added. 'Originally a Saxon stronghold then a Cluniac priory.'

'Smart alec!'

She grinned.

They drove through a deep cut in the Downs and along a wide, flat valley for a couple of miles, then slowed and turned into a lane that wound up a steady gradient, bounded on both sides by overgrown verges. As they drove down a dip, she saw a tarpaulin of mist suspended over a boggy field. They passed a 30mph speed-limit sign, then another sign that was partly obscured by a cluster of tall nettles: MESTON. PLEASE DRIVE SLOWLY.

66

The lane levelled out. There was an elegant Sussex flint farmhouse ahead on the left, and she wondered if he was going to turn in there, but he drove on, without glancing at it, into a small, unspoilt-looking village of flint houses. They passed an old-fashioned village store, a pub called the Sherfield Arms and a Norman church that Frannie thought looked interesting.

The lane climbed steeply out of the village, bounded on the right by a continuous brick wall, beyond which she could see thick, mature trees in a rather grand, sweeping park, and on the left by a railed field. Oliver changed down a gear, and as they rounded a bend, Frannie noticed something odd rising above the brow of the hill ahead. It looked like a giant bird suspended in mid flight. As they got closer she could see that it was one of a pair of massive carved stone wyverns on top of brick gate pillars.

Oliver slowed and indicated. A white sign with black lettering, on a weighted pedestal, said: MESTON HALL. OPEN TODAY. 10a.m. – 5p.m.

Frannie looked at Oliver but his expression told her nothing. The wyverns towered above them, menacing creatures with snarling faces and scaly tails. He turned in through the gates and drove down a formal drive, walled on either side by tall yew hedges, towards a handsome flint stable-block. There was an archway through the centre of it, above which a gold clock face was housed in a domed Venetian cupola. The hands said 11.40.

They drove through the arch, and came out into a junction flanked by more yew hedges and with signs pointing in various directions: CHAPEL. TEA ROOM. CAR PARK. HOUSE. GARDENS. FARM. Another, on a free-standing plinth, said: THE MARQUESS OF SHERFIELD REGRETS ANY INCONVENIENCE TO VISITORS DURING NECESSARY BUILDING REPAIRS.

Uncertainty welled inside her; she wondered if Oliver was playing a game on her. He followed the drive in the direction labelled HOUSE and CAR PARK, and as they rounded the end of a hedge, the house suddenly appeared in front of them.

It was a red brick Elizabethan stately home, as large as many of the great houses she had visited with her parents when she was a child, built in a fold on the hilltop and dominating the entire valley.

The architecture was romantic and imperious: brick chimneys that rose majestically into the sky, banks of tall, mullioned windows with Gothic drip-stones, the baronial front door in its own crenellated tower. A gravel drive ran in front of the façade, separating it from a formal, stone-balustraded lawn below which the park swept away down into the valley.

'Is that it?'

He nodded with a guilty schoolboy smile.

The road ahead was marked NO VEHICLES BEYOND THIS POINT. To the right was a ticket hut, with a wooden bridge beyond that spanned a ditch into a sloping field containing a massive gnarled oak and half a dozen cars parked haphazardly. In spite of its grandeur, the house had a forlorn air of neglect about it. The grounds also, as if it was a struggle to keep them up, and probably a losing battle.

Oliver braked to a halt as a solidly built woman in her sixties hurried towards them, her hand raised in a greeting. A springer spaniel raced past her and stood outside Oliver's door, barking furiously. He opened the door and the dog scrambled in and on to his lap, licking his face.

'Captain Kirk! Hello, chap! Hello! Hello! Say hello to Frannie!'

The dog jumped on to Frannie's lap, its tail thumping as she stroked it, then scrambled frantically over Oliver's lap, jumped back down and barked expectantly at them.

The woman reached the car and paused for breath, wheezing heavily, and gave Frannie a quick but absorbing glance. She had a kind, rather handsome face, and was wearing an ill-fitting cobalt-blue T-shirt printed with the words MESTON HALL, EAST SUSSEX in gold letters. Her voice was doughty, with a faint rural burr. 'Good morning, Lord Sherfield.'

'Morning, Mrs B. How are we doing?'

Frannie looked at him, her surprise increasing. She began to feel slightly out of her depth. The woman ran her eyes over her again, making Frannie feel like an object in a display case, and she felt a flash of irritation that Oliver made no immediate effort to introduce her.

'Not a bad week,' the woman said. 'And a good start so far today. About a dozen already.'

Oliver nodded approvingly. The dog was still barking. 'Quiet!' he yelled.

The woman wheezed again, and dabbed her brow with the back of her hand by way of signalling her dislike of the heat. 'Good day yesterday in the tearooms. Party of ramblers. Twenty-four of them. All had high teas.'

'Excellent. Jolly good. Well done.'

The engine rumbled busily and Frannie sat with a polite smile on her face, aware of the woman's scrutiny. There was obviously a lot that she had not been told and she hoped she could get through the next twenty-four hours without showing herself up in any way. She listened carefully as the woman addressed Oliver again. Despite a feeling of nervous excitement verging on panic, she was determined not to miss a trick.

'We can do a lot more with that catering side. We

ought to consider keeping it open during the winter. I think we could do a good trade with the ramblers.'

'Yes – ah – yes, I'm sure you're right – I'll – er –' he nodded thoughtfully, glancing at Frannie. 'This is – ah – Miss Monsanto,' Oliver said. 'Mrs Beakbane.'

Mrs Beakbane arched her back and tilted her head sideways in order to present herself with a better view of Frannie. 'How do you do?' she said in a pleasant but rather servile tone that Frannie found slightly embarrassing.

'Hello,' she replied, feeling her way.

Oliver pushed the gear lever forwards. 'Right, I'll – ah – see you a bit later on.'

'Oh, one more thing – young Cliff Webber in the village is anxious to have a word.'

He disengaged the gear. 'Cliff Webber?' He looked distant.

'Charley Webber's boy.'

'Ah.' Oliver still looked a little blank.

Mrs Beakbane glanced around as if to make sure no one was in earshot. 'Getting married. Wants to talk to you about a house.'

'I was planning to go down to the estate office this afternoon.'

'I'll let him know to pop in, shall I?'

'Yes, right, about three o'clock.'

He drove on slowly, with Captain Kirk chasing along beside, down on to the gravel and along the front of the house. 'Mrs B,' he said, 'can be a bit of a dragon but she runs the place with an iron rod.' He stopped and waited patiently for a Japanese youth to take a photograph of his girl by the front door.

Frannie turned to Oliver with a quizzical air. 'Lord Sherfield?'

He had the grace to look slightly embarrassed. 'I – I

don't use it very much. My wife used to –' He fell silent.

'So you're a peer?'

'Not a very active one, I'm afraid. When I'm not at the bank I spend most of my time trying to keep this place going.'

Frannie stared out of the window. Close up, the neglected condition of the house was much worse. The stone casements had been painted at some stage, and now the paint was flaking off. Chunks of the masonry had fallen away. The brickwork badly needed repointing, and the bricks themselves had been rubbed raw by centuries of wind and rain. Green slime coated the walls behind the downpipes of the guttering. Shrubbery climbed unchecked, blocking the light from some of the windows, and had even found a way inside some of them.

She focused on the coat of arms carved in a stone tablet above the front door, noticing a wyvern among the symbols, and a Latin inscription that was too worn to read. The Japanese smiled cheerily and Oliver drove on again. Frannie felt an air of unreality as she attempted to take it all in, trying to accept that this was not a dream, that this really was Oliver's home and she was going to be staying here. She pictured her father's approval.

The drive ended at a low wall, beyond which was an ornamental circular pond, with a stone fountain that was not working. A large sign said: PRIVATE. NO VISITORS BEYOND THIS POINT.

Oliver pulled on the brake and switched off the engine. Outside the car, Captain Kirk's barking penetrated the silence. Frannie jumped down, and the dog suddenly went mad, chasing its tail around in several wide loops, skidding on the gravel, then it jumped the wall, skirted the pond and hurtled off towards some beech trees beyond. She shut her door; the clang hung in the air for a moment, then there was complete silence again. It was broken after a few seconds by the distant bleat of a sheep.

Oliver opened the tailgate and hauled their bags out. She walked across the lawn to the balustrading and surveyed the acres of parkland into the valley, savouring the smell of the grass. Rolling meadows, one of which contained a couple of horses, and another a large flock of sheep, dropped down towards the dense, mature woodland that covered the floor of the valley, and through which she could see pearly glimmers of a lake. The woods rose up the far side and gave way near the top to downland pasture sprinkled with sheep. The entire vista was peppered with stone obelisks, classical columns, statues and follies, adding further to the unreality for Frannie.

She turned to Oliver, who was standing quietly beside her, holding their bags. 'It's really stunning,' she said, her excitement tempered by unease, then a sudden feeling of anger. 'I could kill you,' she added.

'Why? What's the matter?'

'Why didn't you tell me about all this? Did you think it would frighten me off?'

'How was I supposed to tell you?'

She walked on a few steps, pushing her feet through the swaying fronds of grass. 'I don't know.'

'Why are you upset?'

'You've made it embarrassing for me. I haven't even brought a decent dress.'

'God! We're not formal – it's only you and me.'

'And all your staff?'

He put an arm around her and squeezed gently. 'You look wonderful as you are, you don't need a ball gown. We live in jeans down here.' He gave her a light kiss on her cheek. 'Come on, let's go and dump our bags.'

She gave him a glare that was part anger, part smile. 'How long have you lived here?'

'Since 1580.'

'I didn't realize you were that old.'

The corners of his eyes creased in a smile and the breeze lifted his hair and rearranged it across his forehead. 'Halkins have lived here ever since it was built. It hasn't always passed from father to son – the lineage has become a bit diluted over the centuries.' He turned and carried the bags through the gap in the walls, and as she followed she saw to her surprise that the house continued with another wing. It was in the same style as the façade, but set well back behind a group of rectangular parterres that badly needed tidying. Beyond it she could see a row of greenhouses and the wall of a kitchen garden. A plume of thick blue bonfire smoke reminded her that summer was nearly over.

'This is the bit I – ah – we – inhabit,' Oliver said.

She followed him along a narrow gravel path bounded by a rampant herbaceous border, down the side of the house, past a bumble bee clinging like a circus acrobat on to the swaying stem of a climbing rose, and a hydrangea that was out of control, then stopped at the front door. It was oak, in the same style as the main front door of the house, but not extended forwards. Above it, Frannie noticed there was again a carved heraldic crest with a wyvern on one of the lozenges.

As Oliver slid the key into the lock and turned it with a sharp clunk, her brain registered something familiar about the Latin motto that was written in the scroll beneath the crest. In the distance she heard the single, mournful toll of a bell, and glanced at her watch. It was 11.45.

She looked up at the crest and read the motto again. *Non Omnis Moriar*. Automatically, she translated it to herself. *I shall not altogether die.*

Oliver held the door for her and she frowned as she stepped into the large, dark hall. Although she had come across that motto in her Latin studies at school, she had come across it somewhere else, also, and the thought disturbed her. She was not sure why.

CHAPTER SEVEN

Oliver waited for Captain Kirk, then closed the front door. It was pleasantly cool inside and very dim. Frannie realized she still had her sunglasses on, and removed them, but even when her eyes had adjusted it was not much brighter. Sunlight shone through the narrow windows, creating a dramatic chiaroscuro effect and trapping motes of dust in its rays.

They were in a large panelled hall with a flagstone floor partially covered with fine rugs. In the centre was a round inlaid table with a vase of fresh flowers. A wide oak staircase rose up to a half-landing on which stood a suit of armour.

Frannie's gaze fell on a squat bronze container in the shape of two back-to-back rams, standing on the floor. She went over to it, examining it more closely. It was cold and felt smooth in spite of the intricate carving representing the coat. She turned to Oliver, feelings of inadequacy forgotten, excitement brimming inside her. 'How long have you had this?'

Oliver looked at it with a faintly bemused air. 'Never quite worked out what it is,' he said.

'It's Chinese,' she said. 'Called a *zun*.'

'*Zun*?' He mocked her with his eyes.

'They would have put wine in it. Know how old it is?'

'About two hundred years, I should think. It was brought back from the Orient by one of my ancestors – the family used to have business interests out there.'

Frannie studied the carving of the horns and squinted carefully at the pattern in the poor light. She raised one end up with some difficulty, and looked beneath one of the legs. 'I think it's Shang dynasty; somewhere between 1700–1050 BC.'

Oliver appeared startled. 'My father used it as an umbrella stand,' he said.

She wondered if he was joking, then realized from his expression that he wasn't. 'It's priceless.'

'We've got all sorts of bits and pieces here. Nothing's ever been properly catalogued. Maybe I should hire you to do that.'

'So long as everything's Oriental or Roman I'll be OK; I'm not much good on anything else.'

'There was a Roman villa here originally, before the house.'

'Has anyone ever done any excavations?'

'In about 1820. They found a tessellated pavement and baths, then they filled it all in and planted beech trees on top.'

'God, why?'

'I think they got fed up with people coming and poking around.' He picked the bags up. 'Right – let's dump these.'

They climbed the stairs, which were lined with painted panels of hunting scenes, went through a pedimented door, past a fire bucket and extinguisher which added a rather institutional feel, she thought, and down a wide, dark landing. Their shoes squeaked on the polished wooden floorboards.

Oliver stopped by a door and pointed to the end of the corridor. 'That takes you through into the main part of the house – the section that's open to the public – if you want to have a wander any time. You'd have to buy a ticket, of course.'

'A ticket?' Then she saw his expression and realized he was teasing.

He opened the door for her. Frannie went into a large, sparsely furnished bedroom that smelled of musty fabric. In spite of the sunlight streaming in, the room had a cold, damp feel, as if it were rarely used, and it had not been redecorated for decades.

Oliver pressed the light switch by the door and seemed surprised that the bulb came on, regarding it for some moments with an expression of almost primitive wonder, then he switched it off and carried Frannie's bag over to a *chaise-longue* at the end of a funereal-looking two-poster bed. 'There's a loo just down the corridor, second door on the left, and a bathroom next to it. I'm afraid the Elizabethans didn't go in for *en-suite* bathrooms.'

Frannie gazed out of the window across the valley. 'Incredible view. How much of it's your land?'

'To the north as far as the main road we turned off, and to the south down to the river, which you can't see from here.'

'Your land goes as far as the village we came through?'

'I – um – own the village.'

'Own it?'

'Yes.' He scratched the top of his nose, and had the grace to smile. 'There are about seventy houses – all peppercorn rents. A lot of the farmland's tenanted out, so most of the houses are let to the farmworkers.'

'How feudal!'

'Very. Look, you'll want to freshen up or something. I'll go and make some coffee and meet you downstairs.'

In the bathroom there was a chipped and stained cast-iron bathtub and wash-basin. When she turned the brass tap it rattled with a sharp knocking sound for some moments, then rust-coloured water hurtled out with the ferocity of a fire hose.

She checked her face in the large mirror and tidied her hair. An air of unreality surrounded her, almost as if she had entered a new dimension where she didn't really know the rules.

A strong smell of coffee filled the hall as she went downstairs and along a short passageway into a large kitchen that had a homely, lived-in feel. Copper pots sat on a rack above the Aga oven; strings of onions and another of garlic cloves hung from hooks; toy cars were strewn across a Welsh dresser; a chewed plimsole lay on a decrepit sofa. An open door led through to a scullery.

Oliver was seated at an old pine table, phone to his ear, tilting back precariously in a chair and tapping his knee with a pencil. Behind him, a red light glowed on a gurgling percolator.

'Yup, well, I'll be in the estate office for an hour or so this afternoon but that's all. I'm not going to have too much time free this weekend.' He winked at Frannie as she came in.

In a corner, Captain Kirk was busily digging toys out of his basket and rearranging the blanket inside it, snorting and panting, his tail wagging furiously. The windows looked out on to an internal courtyard that was in the shade. She could see a rusty barbecue and some garden furniture.

'OK, three o'clock. See you then,' Oliver said with some reluctance and hung up. 'No peace for the wicked.'

Frannie looked at him.

'Tenants. Always problems. I'm like a marriage-guidance counsellor half the time.' He sifted uninterestedly through a stack of post. 'The really frightening thing is that they actually take my advice.'

'Perhaps you give good advice,' she said.

'No, I just sound convincing.' He went over to the dresser and unhooked two mugs.

'How many staff live here?' she said.

He shook his head. 'None.'

'None?' she said, surprised. 'Doesn't the woman who met us – Mrs Deakdene?'

He put the mugs on the table. 'Beakbane. No, she lives with her husband in the village. She stays here and looks after Edward if I have to be away, and there are four ladies who come in every day to clean.' He frowned at an envelope and ripped it open with his finger, glanced at the letter then dropped it in the waste-bin.

'What about cooking?'

'Either Mrs B or me.' He tapped his chest with his thumb, then switched the percolator off and filled the mugs. 'I'm afraid it's a bit frugal and rather primitive here. All the money gets gobbled up on maintenance. The house went through a long spell when almost nothing was done and it's now in a pretty desperate condition. Sugar or milk?'

'Black, thanks. Do you get any grants?'

'A bit – English Heritage and the local council – but you only get a portion of the total cost or a small contribution.' He took a bottle of milk out of the fridge and eased off the top. 'There's subsidence on the north wing, where the scaffolding is. It's costing three quarters of a million to underpin and make good the damage.' He smiled grimly.

'Is that why you're open to the public?'

'We don't make much from the public. There are about six thousand visitors a year at three quid a head, and we pick up a bit from brochures and teas and things, but it all goes on wages for the staff. We have to employ a sitter for each room, for instance. But we have to be open to the public to qualify for grants for the repairs – we're getting about £400,000 towards the costs.'

'And you have to find the rest?'

'Yes.' He brought her mug over to her and put it on the table. He stood beside her and gave her a long, fond look. 'Thanks for coming.'

She smiled, touched. 'Thanks for inviting me.'

There was an easy, warm silence and Frannie wished suddenly that Edward was not about to turn up, and that they could be on their own together. 'Did you inherit this from your parents?'

He sat on the edge of the table and blew into his mug. 'My father made it over to me to avoid death duties. They moved into a smaller house on the farm.' He stared into the rising steam. 'To avoid inheritance tax you have to survive for seven years after handing the property over. He died twenty-four hours before the seven years was up.'

'God! So you had to pay?'

'Yes.' He shrugged. 'They were pretty crippling. I'm still paying them off.'

'Did you have to sell anything?'

'Our two finest paintings – a Canaletto and a Vermeer.' He hunched his shoulders and pulled the mug closer to his chest, as if he were drawing warmth from it. 'I don't believe in flogging things off. I feel that each person who lives here has an obligation to pass on what he inherits intact, and in better condition. I have to do what I can, and one day, I hope, Edward will do what he can.'

'The *zun* would be worth a lot, if –'

The doorbell rang and there was a sharp rapping of the knocker at the same time. Captain Kirk raced across the kitchen and down the passageway, barking furiously. Oliver put his mug on the table and jumped down. 'Might be them!' he said and hurried out.

Frannie hesitated, uncertain whether to follow. She heard the sound of the door opening and then a commotion of voices.

'Edward! Hey, hey, hey! How are you?'

'Captain Kirk! Hello, Captain Kirk! Good boy! Daddy, guess what? We nearly had an accident! We nearly had a crash!' Although Frannie had only heard Edward's voice once before, she recognized it instantly.

'No we didn't, stupid!' said another boy's voice, very insistent.

'We did, Daddy! This car pulled out right in front of us. We had to brake really hard.'

'The car was miles away, stupid. We hardly had to brake at all!'

'Clive, hi!' Oliver said. 'Caroline! You all look wonderful!'

A collage of photographs on the wall caught Frannie's eye, and she walked across to it. There were several of a pretty red-haired woman of about her own age, one of Oliver, a boy she recognized as Edward, and the woman – whom she presumed must be Oliver's late wife – standing by the wing of a small aeroplane. The resemblance between the woman and the boy was striking. Unable to restrain her curiosity, Frannie looked more closely at Lady Sherfield and noted the classical English rose features. The designer countrywear. She felt she could imagine the voice: cut glass, precious, confident. And hard?

There was a happy innocence in the photograph. A family together, going off somewhere or just posing. She looked at the woman again, wondering, absurdly, whether it was possible to tell from a photograph that someone was going to die. Then she stepped back, disturbed by the darkness of her own thought. She felt awkward doing nothing, she wanted to look interesting in case Oliver brought his visitors in to meet her.

'We're bloody tired,' said a woman's voice in the hall. 'The hotel we stayed in last night had lorries thundering past non-stop.'

'Hey, Daddy, I had snails for dinner,' she heard Edward say. She was beginning to feel like an eavesdropper.

'No you didn't,' said the other boy. 'They weren't real snails, anyhow.'

'Yes they were. You can't have pretend snails.'

'They weren't, were they, Mummy?'

'Like some coffee, or a drink?'

'We ought to get going,' a man's voice said. 'Caroline's mother's expecting us for lunch.'

'I've got a surprise for you, Edward!' Oliver said.

'What? Tell me!'

There was a sudden silence as if Oliver was whispering. And Frannie felt her remaining confidence evaporate. She heard footsteps and turned round, prepared to be intimidated. Edward was standing in the doorway, in a white T-shirt, jeans and espadrilles. His face was tanned, bringing out more freckles than when she had seen him before, and the tip of his nose was peeling.

His intelligent, brown eyes widened and his mouth broke into a grin that was an exact replica of Oliver's. 'Hey! You're the lady from the railway station!'

She relaxed and grinned back, warming to him instantly as she had before. 'That's right.'

He looked more serious suddenly. 'We nearly had an accident.'

'Did you?'

'A woman pulled right out in front of our car. Uncle

Clive had to brake very hard indeed.' He paused. 'He's not my real uncle, but I call him that.'

'How was your holiday?'

He stood, studying her without replying, as if he had not heard her.

'Ghastly business,' said the woman out in the hall.

'Who was driving the boat?' Oliver's voice asked.

'Jean-Luc's boy, Albert. He's normally quite a careful lad. You know what it's like. The kids love driving boats – Edward drove it quite a bit too, and Dominic. Problem was that the adults were a bit pissed – had a boozy day – left the kids to it really.'

'And no one saw the swimmer?'

'She was quite a long way out but it was fairly calm. He should have been able to see her, and he wasn't fooling around or anything. He can't explain it. Poor Jean-Luc's in a terrible state.'

'Can you water-ski?' Edward asked Frannie.

'No.'

'I can mono-ski now. It's really great. I can get out of the water with one ski. Dominic couldn't do that; he could only start on both skis then kick one off.'

Another boy came into the room. He had a fat, aggressive face, untidy tufts of fair hair, and was wearing a gaudy shirt and Bermuda shorts. He stopped a safe distance from Edward, his face screwed up into a knot of anger and shouted at him. 'You know something? You're weird! Really weird! And you're really stupid and I never want to see you again. You're a stupid, stupid bumhole!' He ran straight at Edward and pummelled him on his right arm and chest, then ran out of the room.

Edward stood his ground without flinching, barely even acknowledging the assault, and Frannie admired his restraint. 'Dominic got scared to go into the water because he saw a jellyfish,' he said as if nothing had happened.

A tall, fine-boned woman appeared in the doorway, looking tired and hot from travelling; her dry blond hair was scraped back beneath a floral printed headband and she was wearing a creased, lightweight shift-dress. Her face had a haughty, rather disdainful expression, and she had a matching accent, elongating each of her words as she spoke, with virtually no movement of her lips.

'Oh, hello,' she said.

'Hello,' Frannie replied, feeling slightly undermined by her.

The woman gave her a thin, patronizing smile and went back down the corridor.

In the hallway, Frannie heard her say: 'Is she the new nanny, Oliver?'

Bitch, Frannie thought.

Oliver sounded embarrassed. 'No – that's Frannie – let me introduce you, I'm not thinking –'

'No, we really must be on our way,' the woman insisted. She and the man called their goodbyes to Edward in turn.

'Box jellyfish can kill you within seconds,' Edward said, ignoring the farewells.

Oliver called out: 'Edward, they're off, come and say goodbye and thank you.'

Edward screwed up his face, then marched reluctantly out of the door.

'I'm going to give you a ring, Oliver,' the woman's voice said. 'There's someone I absolutely want you to meet. Great friend of mine, stunning looking. Just been through a horrendous divorce. I think you'd like her. And this is the best bit: she has a degree from Cambridge in mathematics! I'll fix something up in the next couple of weeks.'

Frannie strained hard, unsuccessfully, to hear Oliver's reply, feeling a strong twinge of jealousy, and a desire to go out into the hall and throttle the woman. She seemed to be the odd one out. She suddenly wondered if she should have stayed in London and gone partying after all.

The voices faded. With relief, Frannie glanced back at the photographs, thinking about the boy's attack on Edward and his oddly mature response. There was a shot of Edward fishing in a small rowing-boat on a lake. Behind him was a boat-house and overhanging trees. The water was flat and he was holding his rod with deadly serious intent.

'Can you ride?'

Edward's voice startled her. 'No,' she said, turning round.

'I could teach you, if you like. My horse Sheba's very docile.'

She smiled. 'I'll have a go.'

His face lit up. 'Would you? She's quite old – she's fourteen; she's a hunter.'

'Do you hunt?'

Outside there was the slam of a car door. Then another. Then a scream that started low and slowly and built up to a high-pitched howl like a siren. It took her a moment to realize that it was a human scream.

'I think I'd quite like to hunt, really, but I'm worried because it's cruel,' Edward said as if he could not hear the scream at all.

'I think we'd better see what's happening,' Frannie said as the scream worsened. She went to the door. Edward stayed where he was. She ran across the hall, out of the front door and down the gravel path.

There was a commotion around a silver Volvo estate car parked beside the Range Rover. The blond woman was shouting hysterically. A balding, rather plump man was trying desperately to open the rear door of the Volvo. He had one foot pressed against the wheel fairing for leverage while he heaved with both hands on the door handle.

The scream was coming from inside the car.

The boy's face was visible through the open rear window. It was he who was screaming, his face stretched and twisted in agony.

Frannie saw to her horror that his hand had been shut in the hinged end of the door; his fingers were trapped between the edge of the window frame and the door pillar.

A man was running towards the car. So were Mrs Beakbane and another woman in their Meston Hall T-shirts. The woman in the bandanna, the boy's mother Frannie presumed, clambered frantically in through the opposite door, leaned across, and pushed the door from the inside.

The boy's screaming continued, getting even louder, whooping with pain and shock. Droplets of blood slid down the paintwork, deep crimson against dusty metallic silver. Oliver ran across, found a grip on the door's top edge and pulled too. Both the balding man's legs left the ground for a moment as he used every ounce of leverage he could. The door finally came open with a splitting sound like a safe that had been jemmied.

For a brief instant the screaming stopped. And the footsteps.

Three fingers detached themselves from the door pillar, one after the other. At first Frannie thought the boy was relaxing his grip. Then his fingers fell limply on to the gravel. In the silence she could hear each one land.

*

Oliver took charge. He sent Mrs Beakbane to phone for an ambulance, and told Frannie to come with him. They sprinted into the house and through to the kitchen. Edward had disappeared but in her panic she hardly noticed. Captain Kirk bounded in after them, barking.

'Towels, that drawer!' Oliver said, turning on a tap, hunting around the room with his eyes. 'Soak them!' He yanked open a drawer, then another, rummaged through it and pulled out a long knife steel. Frannie bundled tea towels into her arms and dunked them in the sink. He helped her wring them out, then they raced back to the car.

The boy's stunned mother held a bloodstained handkerchief over his hand. Oliver took his arm and removed the handkerchief. The forefinger was hanging from a thread of skin. Blood spurted unevenly from the stumps of the other fingers; some pattered like rain onto Frannie's trousers as she knelt with wet towels at the ready, and she swallowed the bile that rose in her throat. The boy screamed relentlessly, emptying one lungful of air after another and pausing only for choking gulps. A slick of warm blood struck Frannie's cheek, then another her forehead and she felt it sliding down towards her eye. She turned away, swallowing hard again, fighting not to be sick, unable to look at the hand or the boy's twisted, boiling face.

Oliver swathed the hand in a tea towel, and she helped him wind it around the wrist, then repeated the process with a second one. He put a third over the top, and with Frannie and the boy's mother's help, using the knife steel as the lever, wound the towel tightly into a tourniquet. The boy's father leaned over, agitatedly crowding them, a feeble twitch animating his expression of utter helplessness.

Oliver scooped up the fingers and parcelled them in another towel, which he gave to Frannie. 'Pack these in ice.'

The commotion had attracted the attention of several visitors, who watched in a group a short distance off. They were talking amongst themselves, trying to work out what had happened. One woman said she thought the dog must have bitten the boy.

'Dom? You OK, Dom?'

Edward was rushing towards them, his face horrified. 'Dom?' He looked at his friend, then at Frannie. 'What's happened?' His eyes shot to the tourniquet. 'Hey, Dom –' He blanched.

As Frannie ran into the house she wondered where he had been during the past few minutes, and why he had not come with her. She unfolded the towel on the draining-board, and stared at the three fingers, each of which was leaking blood. Like joke fingers, she thought. Then a wave of giddiness struck her; her stomach up-ended; she swayed, gripped the edge of the sink and threw up into it. Her eyes streamed and she wiped them with her shirtsleeve, then rinsed the sink out, washed her hands and forced herself into sensible action.

There were several trays of ice cubes in the fridge, and she searched for a suitable receptacle. The screaming was coming closer and Oliver carried the boy in, followed by the parents and Edward. Mrs Beakbane was trying to comfort the boy by assuring him the ambulance would be there any moment. Oliver laid him on the sofa, and Mrs Beakbane went to the sink and peered at the fingers with a surprising nonchalance that made Frannie feel displaced.

'I was a Red Cross nurse in the war,' she said, as if by way of explanation, and helped free the ice cubes, again making Frannie feel inexperienced and in the way.

The screaming abated into an undulating, sobbing moan of pain. Edward hovered, looking very distressed. He put his arm around his friend but the boy shook him away and began screaming again, even more vehemently than before. His mother sat beside him, white-faced.

'Look,' the father said, 'this bloody ambulance could take hours. I'll drive him myself.'

'No,' Oliver said. 'He's got to go somewhere they can do microsurgery – they might be able to sew the fingers back. If you go to the wrong place you could waste valuable time; I think you only have a few hours before the nerve endings die.'

'Six,' Mrs Beakbane said, authoritatively. 'My Harry lost his little finger in a lawnmower but we never found it until the following day.'

The father paced over to the sink, then turned away rapidly at the sight of the fingers. Frannie stood back and let Mrs Beakbane pack them carefully, using all the cubes, then they were placed with a couple of freeze packs inside a picnic cool-box.

Oliver phoned a doctor friend who gave him some names and suggested a hospital less than half an hour away, which seemed to relieve the father.

The ambulance arrived a few minutes later. The boy and his mother went in it, and his father followed in the Volvo. Frannie, Oliver and Edward watched numbly as they left. A couple of short pulses of the siren pricked the air and then there was silence.

They walked back towards the house, Oliver with his head sunk in thought, Frannie uncertain what to say. Edward stopped by the pond. Frannie waited a moment for him, then went inside. Mrs Beakbane excused herself, saying she had to go to a problem she had been dealing with in the tearoom.

Oliver poured the remnants of coffee in the percolator down the sink and turned the tap on. Frannie gathered the two mugs from the table and carried them across.

'It's OK – they can go in the machine.' His words made Frannie feel even more useless. As if she hadn't yet found her role. His eyes skimmed her face and he lowered his voice. 'You have a bit of – er – warpaint on you.'

She touched her cheek with her fingers and saw blood on them. 'Oh, God!'

She hurried upstairs to the bathroom. Her reflection in the mirror startled her. Streaks of blood ran down her forehead and cheeks. Her eye make-up had smudged and run. Her stomach rolled again. Sour bile rose in her throat and she puked it out. Then she stripped off and washed herself, put her trousers and top into the sink to soak, wrapped herself in a towel and went to her bedroom to change.

When she returned, Edward was sitting in the kitchen, glancing in a rather adult way through a newspaper. He looked up at his father.

'Do you think they will be able to sew Dom's fingers back on, Daddy?'

'They can do pretty clever things with microsurgery these days.'

'It's a pity it wasn't his left hand,' Edward said. 'Then at least he could still do sport.'

The comment hung over them and there was a long silence broken only by the sound of Captain Kirk grinding on a bone. Edward closed the *Daily Mail* and began turning the pages of *The Times*. 'You didn't remember to fix my Scalextric, Daddy.'

'I did. The brushes had gone on one of the cars.'

'It's not working.'

Frannie frowned, wondered when Edward would have had time to play with any toys. And what he was searching for in the newspaper.

'It is. Did you switch the transformer on?'

'You're useless, Daddy. You should have taken it to the man in Lewes to fix.'

'Well, it was working last Sunday. I spent an hour on it.'

Edward seemed unconvinced. Oliver looked at his watch. 'Right, let's make some plans for this afternoon.' He shrugged apologetically at Frannie. 'I have to do a few things. Would you like to lounge around the pool? Have a swim? The water's very warm.'

'Can I show Frannie round the grounds?'

Oliver signalled Frannie with his eyes that she did not have to.

She winked, then smiled at Edward. 'Thank you, I'd love that.'

'Can I show Frannie the aeroplane, Daddy?'

'I have to go down and turn the engine over; I might catch up with you.'

'Is your name really Frannie?' Edward said.

'Yes.'

He held out his hand for hers and for a moment she thought he was going to shake it. Instead he held it firmly, pulling her very slightly towards him, as if there was an urgent message he needed to communicate. Then slowly, without slackening his grip, he led her towards the door.

She glanced at Oliver and noticed a strange look of apprehension on his face as he watched his son. The shadow that crossed his eyes was one of fear. She turned to Edward but all she could see was the trusting face of a small boy who has found a new friend.

CHAPTER EIGHT

Frannie and Edward, closely followed by Captain Kirk, ambled past the Range Rover and along the front of the house. A bird chirruped with a ping that sounded like a spoon against china and as Frannie breathed in the scents of the air and felt the afternoon sun on her face, the horror of an hour ago receded a little in her mind; but not the unease. She still wondered why Oliver had kept quiet about his title; quiet about Meston Hall; wondered if it had anything to do with his wife's death, for instance. And was there anything else he was keeping quiet about?

She avoided looking at the gravel in case she saw the stain of blood and stared up at the façade, picking out details of its decaying state: a chunk missing from the coping-stone of the parapet; a cracked window; a bird's nest under the eaves; wasps going in and out of a hole in the roof.

An elderly man with a shiny camera case and a woman in a straw hat were going in through the front door and Frannie caught a glimpse of a marble floor and white columns. Edward pointed across the valley. 'The English Channel's the other side of those hills. Brighton's over there to the right – you can see the glow of the lights on a clear night.'

'Do you like living here?' Frannie asked.

'Yes, quite.'

'Only *quite*?'

'I like some things,' he said, more brightly.

'Have you got many friends here?'

'Yes, I suppose so.' He seemed about to say something else, then changed his mind.

They walked past the end of the house and up the private road towards the junction bounded by hedges.

'Is Frannie short for something?'

'My full name's Francesca.'

'Is that Italian?'

'Yes.'

'Does that mean you're a Catholic?'

'I am a Catholic, yes.' She was surprised by the question. 'What are you?'

Edward was silent for some moments, then he pushed his hands into his pockets and stared down. 'We have our own chapel.'

'Can I see it?'

'There's not much to see.'

'I'd be interested.'

He pointed in front of them. 'It's through there, but it's not worth going in.'

'Couldn't I have a quick peep inside?'

'Why?'

There was something oddly strained about his voice and she almost wished she hadn't pursued the idea. 'I'm very interested in churches,' she said.

'All right.'

They waited for a car full of visitors to pass, then crossed, went through an opening in the hedge and the chapel was in front of them. It was small and narrow, rising out of a riot of weeds and in the same poor state of repair as everything else. A well-trodden cinder path went up to the door, through a tiny graveyard peppered with old tombstones.

The interior felt more cared for. Marble and alabaster tombs were spaced along the sides and there were plaques on the floor. Frannie read one of them. *Lord Thomas Bouverie Henry Halkin. 15th Marquess of Sherfield. 1787–1821.*

While Edward walked on slowly down the centre of the aisle, running his hand nonchalantly from the top of each pew to the next, Frannie scanned the structure of the building, trying to date it. Deep, solid buttresses and well-dressed stones; classic Perpendicular tracery in an elaborate geometric pattern. Geometry, she thought suddenly. Mathematics. Oliver's words at lunch on Tuesday echoed suddenly in her head. *Mathematics and design are inseparable.*

'Every Marquess of Sherfield for four hundred and fifty years is buried in here,' Edward said. 'Except one.' He stood gazing at the floor in front of him. Frannie joined him. He was looking at an onyx rectangle, with a brass plaque in the centre which read: *Lady Sarah Henrietta Louise Halkin, Marchioness of Sherfield. 1963–1988.*

Edward's face reddened, and Frannie sensed a tension in the air between them as if she had intruded into something private. She wondered if that was the reason he had been reluctant to show her in here. She kicked herself for not having realized that his mother would be buried here.

He began to hum softly, and after a few bars she recognized the tune as 'Swing Low Sweet Chariot'. Then he turned and began to saunter as if he was in no hurry – as if he had all the time in the world – towards the exit, humming more loudly now, the way someone might who is alone in the dark and wants to demonstrate that he is not afraid.

Captain Kirk was lying obediently outside. Edward stopped humming and knelt beside him, telling him he had been good. Then they left the graveyard and walked along a cart track that sloped downwards towards a cluster of farm buildings. An invisible barrier separated them. Frannie wondered what to say to repair the situation, realizing how very little she knew about children. She was not used to dealing with the problems of motherless young boys and she simply didn't know what to do. She almost wished that Mrs Beakbane would appear. She had no idea of how Edward felt about seeing his father with another woman.

A vapour trail was unravelling across the sky. Grit crunched beneath their feet. 'You said there was one Marquess who was not buried in your chapel – who was that?'

'Lord Francis Halkin,' he said. 'The second Marquess.'

'Where is he buried?'

'I don't know.' He lowered his voice as if he were letting her in on a secret. 'There were quite a lot of people who didn't like him very much.'

'Why was that?'

'I'd like to be buried somewhere that's completely secret. Where no one knows where I am,' he said, not answering her.

'So you don't have to spend eternity with your ancient relatives? You'd like to meet some new people when you die?'

Edward broke into a fit of giggles. 'I think they'd be *dead* boring, don't you?' He giggled again.

'*Dead* right.'

'*Dead* on!' he said. 'Hold out your hand.'

She held it out and he turned it palm up, then slapped it with his own palm. '*Dead* on!' he said again as he did so. 'You have to do that when you say "dead on"!'

'I'll remember. *Dead* – cert!' She stopped as a stone on the ground caught her eye, knelt, and picked it up. She pulled her handkerchief out of her pocket, spat on it and rubbed one side that was almost flat. She examined it carefully, whilst Edward watched her in silence, then she held it in front of him. 'Look!'

He stared blankly. 'What at?'

Frannie pointed carefully with her finger. 'Can you see? The shape of the shell?'

He peered closer, still uncertain.

'It's a fossil – of a seashell – an oyster or something.'

His eyes brightened. 'Gosh, yes! Is that really old?'

She nodded. 'Ten thousand years; perhaps more.'

'Do you think it's worth a lot of money?'

She shook her head. 'The countryside's covered in them.'

'I've never seen one before.'

'You've probably never looked.' She handed it to him. 'You keep it.'

'You should keep it really, because you found it.'

'It's a present.'

'Hey! That's great, wow! Thank you.'

She walked on, feeling she was getting somewhere with Oliver's son after all. But she was taken aback by his next remark.

'Do you think the dead stay dead, Frannie?'

Mindful of his mother, she deliberately played down her response. 'I don't think that oyster's going to come back to life.'

'Its spirit might.'

A combine harvester chomped through a cornfield on their right. The stubble stretched out into the distance, short and spiky, and Frannie breathed in its dry, prickly smell. Edward was a strange boy, she thought. Old for his years, he slouched as he walked, as if burdened by a thousand worries.

As they approached the rear of a massive corrugated-iron barn, a bang like a muffled gunshot rang out, making Frannie jump. Captain Kirk barked. There was the clatter of what sounded like an enormous ratchet, and another bang. Edward sprinted on ahead.

Oliver's Range Rover was parked on the concrete hard in front of the barn. The barn's doors were open and there was an old-looking single-engined biplane inside, its wingspan taking up almost the entire width.

Oliver had both hands close together in the centre of one blade of the propeller and slowly rotated it anti-clockwise, while Edward stood several feet away, watching him. There was a deep sucking noise from the engine. He rotated the propeller completely a couple of times, then tensed up, gave the blade a sharp downward pull, and stepped quickly back and to the side. There was another much louder bang as the engine fired and died, a splutter as the propeller made a half-turn, then the ratchet sound again as it swung to a halt. A small puff of oily blue smoke drifted over Frannie. Oliver looked engrossed and Frannie began to wonder if he'd simply wanted to be on his own for a bit.

He turned and smiled cheerily at her, pushing his hair back from his forehead with a grimy hand, sweat pouring down his face. 'Got her started last weekend; have to try to run her again for a few minutes to get the oil circulating, but she doesn't seem to want to know.' He gazed at the aeroplane admiringly. 'What do you think of her?'

The plane reminded Frannie of First World War movies. A primitive, open two-seater, with struts and wire rigging between the wings, it sat on a flimsy-looking undercarriage, its nose in the air. Parts of the skin of the fuselage and wings were missing, exposing the skeletal frame beneath and the cylinder block of the engine protruding from the nose. In contrast, the propeller appeared immaculate; it was made of dark, varnished wood and held in place with a polished aluminium spinner.

'It's beautiful,' Frannie said. 'Have you actually flown her?'

'Not this old girl. She hasn't been airborne for about thirty years. I bought her as a complete wreck five years ago. A few more months and she'll be up there.'

'Yeah!' Edward said excitedly. 'Daddy said we can fly to France!'

Oliver looked at his watch. 'I'd better get to the estate office. My three o'clock appointment will be waiting.'

'No peace for the wicked,' Frannie said.

'None. See you in an hour or so.' He began closing the barn doors. Frannie and Edward helped him, then Oliver drove off in the Range Rover.

'Would you like to see the lake now?' Edward said.

'Yes, sure,' she said, feeling slightly out on a limb at being abandoned again by Oliver, and wondering suddenly if Dom's snobby mother hadn't been too far off the mark when she had asked Oliver if she was the nanny. She felt a sudden flash of anger as she wondered whether Oliver had conned her into coming down here in order to look after Edward. Once again, she pictured the party taking place that night in London. Had she made a mistake?

They skirted around the side of a ploughed field, jumped a ditch and came out at the bottom of the visitors' car park. Captain Kirk ran on ahead then bounded back and walked beside them. They climbed over a fence and walked across a broad, sloping meadow. 'Do you like it here, Frannie?' Edward asked.

'It's very beautiful.'

'I had to really twist Daddy's arm to make him see you again.'

She stopped and stared at him. 'Pardon?'

'Daddy wasn't brave enough. He said he'd be too embarrassed and that anyway you might not like him.'

'It was you? You made him put the advertisement in?'

He shook his head. 'I told him that he had to try to find you. He thought you were nice, but he's very shy, really.'

'So how did you persuade him?' Frannie asked.

He looked rather pleased with himself. 'I did keep nagging him a bit. But I don't think he needed that much pushing.'

They walked on through some trees, and Frannie smiled to herself, her anger fading. She was amused by the boy's precociousness. A clock chimed three times in the distance. They passed a collapsed stone folly, and came into a walk of lavender bushes past a cluster of small headstones, most of them overgrown with moss and lichen. On one she could just make out the words: *Sam (Nimo San). Labrador. 1912–1925.*

Edward stopped by a lavender bush, and pointed at it, announcing '*Nana atropurpurea.*'

'What?' she said, unsure if she had heard correctly. She was startled by a growl from Captain Kirk and turned, wondering what was wrong with the spaniel. Then she realized it was growling at Edward.

Edward walked on down some timber steps and stopped by a rhododendron. '*Rhododendron campanulatum,*' he said.

The spaniel growled again more deeply, baring sharp white teeth that rose from gums brimming with saliva; its soft hair seemed to rise and harden like spines and its dark brown eyes boiled inside their whites with a sudden rage that frightened Frannie. The dog was crouching on its rear haunches, as if its rear paws were embedded in the earth, its head craning forward, the growl deepening into a ferocious snarl. It pulled itself forward in sharp jerks as if trying to free its rear legs from the ground and launch itself at the boy, and she dived in panic, grabbing it by the collar to restrain it.

Captain Kirk's head spun round, the jaws showering her with saliva and she just managed to withdraw her hand and jump back before the teeth snapped on air. The dog turned to Edward again, simmering, the snarl deepening. Edward stood his ground in silence, staring back hypnotically. Frannie felt the hairs rising on her own body, the onlooker in a private duel. The dog made a lunge forward towards the boy, then stopped as if restrained by an unseen force. It tried to lunge again, and stopped once more, seemingly made powerless by Edward's concentrated stare.

Frannie watched in horror as the spaniel's hair slackened, then it let out a whine and began to shake, backing away, whimpering, and finally retreating like a banished demon.

There was a strange hush. The sun went behind a cloud and Edward stood in silence, as if nothing had happened. Frannie turned to watch the dog but it was almost out of sight, heading back towards the house. She was shaking, not knowing exactly what she had just witnessed.

'What's the matter with Captain Kirk, Edward?'

He said nothing at first. Then he suddenly pointed to another rhododendron across the track that had white, trumpet-shaped flowers. '*Auriculatum*,' he said.

'Have you been learning Latin at school?' she asked, her voice quavering.

He studied the bush for some moments again, as if he had not heard her, then continued along the track through increasingly dense shrubbery until they came down on to level ground, and Frannie could see water beyond a screen of reeds. The lake was a good quarter of a mile across and longer in length.

She followed him along the bank towards a sorry-looking boat-house, its white paint stained green with moss and peeling away in chunks. Edward pulled open the rotting door with some difficulty and they went into the dank, shadowy interior. A cobweb brushed Frannie's face and she jerked her head to one side, instinctively putting up her hands and feeling the sticky strands on her fingers. Her nostrils were filled with the unpleasant mushroomy stench of rot.

'You get in first and sit down,' Edward commanded, pointing to a narrow wooden pontoon.

Dazed into compliance, she placed a foot carefully in the bottom of the boat, avoiding the oars. It rocked precariously and she grabbed the side with her hand, steadied herself, then brought the other foot in and sat down quickly.

Edward untied the boat, pushed it forward and stepped in, sat down and fitted each of the oars into the rowlocks. They drifted out of the boat-house into the sunlight, now bright again.

As the boy rowed, Frannie felt the pull of the little boat through the water and listened to the splash of the oars. Then Edward let the boat drift forwards on its own momentum, and she let her own thoughts do the same: Jonathan Mountjoy; 'Is she the new nanny?'; Sarah Henrietta Louise Halkin. The onyx slab on the floor. 1963–1988.

'I hope you're not planning to sleep with my daddy.'

Her mouth dropped open in amazement. Edward was leaning over to one side, staring idly at the water the way she had been, with a distant expression on his face. She watched him for a moment, wondering if she had misunderstood. 'Pardon?'

He did not look up or acknowledge her. His face remained blank and unreadable. Was it his mind that was disconnected or hers? she wondered.

A fish rose near them and left behind an eddy of disturbed water that slowly broadened out until the surface was smooth again, as if the water had forgotten it had ever happened. Oliver had told her last night at dinner, when he had been talking about mathematics and gambling, that a coin could not remember which way up it had landed the previous time it was flipped. It was always an even chance whether it would be heads or tails the next time, regardless of how many times one or the other had come up before. Water had no memory either. Humans remembered everything – too much sometimes – Oliver said, so that at times it was difficult to look back clearly to both before and after an event had happened. The brain played tricks constantly, he said.

She watched the small boy with the intelligent brown eyes and sad, freckled face, and tried to work out what trick her own brain might have just played on herself.

Frannie was hot and sticky and her top was damp with perspiration after the climb back up from the lake. They emerged through a ride of giant beech trees at the rear of the walled kitchen garden. The intensity of light had gone from the sun and the caw-caw-kercaw of a pigeon carried through the air like the last post from a lone bugler.

She felt uncomfortable, as if Edward was playing a

game with her for which she had not been given the rules, and she wondered if he was deliberately trying to undermine her confidence. Yet he was only eight; surely he was too young to be that devious? His mood changes left her not knowing whether left was right or right was left. She couldn't find her feet with the boy and she wondered if it was her fault or if there was another reason. She thought about the dog, wondering where it was now and whether its fury had been deliberately provoked by Edward for her benefit. She found that hard to believe because it had seemed so spontaneous.

Edward had become chatty again in the last ten minutes. He asked her more about fossils and she explained to him how you could date the past from them, enjoying seeing the deep interest he took.

As they reached the front door, he said to her: 'Can you play ping-pong?'

'I haven't for ages.'

'Would you like to have a game?'

She smiled, feeling a bit weary. 'All right, but a quick one. I'm tired.'

He gave her such a mischievous look that she felt like putting her hand out and tousling his hair as a gesture of affection, but remembered the faint look of irritation on his face when his father had done that. Something else stopped her too: she daren't.

Before their game, they both went into the kitchen to make themselves a quick sandwich. Frannie finished hers first and she wandered off to look in the library as she waited for Edward. It was a surprisingly small and narrow room that seemed to double as a study. Several large hand-drawn charts were pinned to the walls either side of the desk. One looked like a family tree. Another was a mass of mathematical calculations. All the rest of the walls were lined floor to ceiling with bookshelves, which she would have liked to look at instead of playing ping-pong but she felt that duty called.

Her reverie was broken with the arrival of Edward who, worried in case she changed her mind, led her upstairs and along the dark corridor past her room. As they drew up to the next door, Edward said: 'That's my room. I'll show it to you later if you like.'

'Thank you.'

They passed a couple more doors, then the passage dog-legged left. Edward climbed up a narrow staircase into a huge, gloomy attic-playroom that seemed to span the entire wing of the house and which housed the ping-pong table.

She acquitted herself well at the ping-pong table despite losing. After promising to go with Edward to see the orchard the next day, she made her excuses to him and went to her bedroom. She closed the door, relieved to be on her own for a few minutes.

Through the open window she noted that the visitors' car park was empty and the windows of the ticket hut were closed. A crane-fly flew clumsily around the room, bumping against the window and the walls.

I hope you're not planning to sleep with my daddy.

A bead of perspiration slid down her forehead and Frannie put her hand in her pocket, but could not feel her handkerchief. She dug deeper, but the pocket was empty. She remembered wiping her forehead during the game, and went back up to the attic-playroom. The meagre daylight coming in from the small dormer windows, too high for a child to reach, gave a prison-like feel to the room.

A bird flew past one of the windows and its shadow skated along the wall. The total silence struck her. A floorboard creaked as she stepped on it and she moved forwards, treading more lightly so that Edward wouldn't hear her.

The handkerchief was lying on the floor beneath the ping-pong table and she picked it up and removed a bit of fluff from it. A sad room, she thought, staring around, and tried to imagine Edward playing up there on his own. There was an old rocking-horse, perhaps Victorian; it had probably been here for years, and generations of young Halkins had played on it. Oliver. Oliver's father.

She walked over to the bookshelves and looked at the titles. *William*. *Jennings*. *The Famous Five*. *Biggles*. Old books, some with their covers torn, others with no covers. There were some she used to read herself: *Grimm's Fairy Tales* and *Struwwelpeter* and the *Eagle Annual* and the *Beano Bumper Book*. Then she noticed a photo album and pulled it out.

It was heavy and she laid it down on the ping-pong table to open it. The first picture was a colour photograph of a naked baby lying on its back, gurgling, arms and legs raised in the air.

'Edward. 2 days,' was handwritten in black ink beneath.

She turned the thick page. There were various photographs of Edward's mother cuddling him in a hospital bed. She was fascinated to see this younger version of the Sarah Henrietta Louise she'd already seen in the kitchen collage. She noted the same poise, the same classic features, which made her feel rather plain in comparison. Her suspicions about Oliver's motives in inviting her down began to return. She turned on, through scenes of Edward growing up. She studied them closely, also trying to see his expression, searching for clues about his strange behaviour. Finding none.

As she turned the last page, she saw, folded in the back, a newspaper cutting. Curious, she opened it. It was from the *Mid-Sussex Times*, and dated 10th August 1991. An article in the centre of the page had been ringed with a red pen. Its headline read: SUSSEX MAN SHOT IN US STREET HORROR.

She began reading.

> A Sussex man has been shot dead by a mugger whilst on holiday in America.
>
> Jonathan Mountjoy, 25, a ceramics expert with Sotheby's, had left his home in High Street, Cuckfield, last Friday, for his dream holiday.
>
> Neighbours were shocked by the incident. 'He was a gentle young man who would not have harmed a fly,' said neighbour Ann Wilson.
>
> A spokesman for the Washington DC Police Department said, 'This was a particularly vicious crime perpetrated on an unarmed tourist. We are actively seeking the assailant.'

Frannie stopped and went to the start of the article again to make sure her eyes weren't deceiving her. *Jonathan Mountjoy*. But there was no mistaking his face in the photograph; it must have been taken around the time they were at university, or else he had not changed. The serious looks, almost gaunt with his high cheekbones and short black hair. A kind face. His colleagues were right; he was a brilliant young man, even if he had always seemed to be in a permanent dream.

She remembered Seb Holland in the restaurant last night, telling her about Jonathan's death. A curl of anxiety travelled through her as she remembered

Edward in the kitchen earlier, scanning through the newspapers as if looking for something. Had he cut it out? Or was it Oliver, thinking it would be of interest to her? The print blurred. Confused thoughts whirled through her mind. Oliver cutting it out did not make any sense. He would have shown it to her if he had seen it in the paper, surely, not hidden it in his son's photo album. And the article was a few weeks old.

She folded it up again and replaced the album on the bookshelf. Then she decided to have a bath, hoping Oliver might've returned when she'd finished.

CHAPTER NINE

She had a quick bath, then combed her hair, tugging the tangles free. Dark olive eyes stared back from the mirror. Frightened eyes. They watched the reflection of the closed door behind her. Maybe Jonathan Mountjoy was a relative of the Halkins? A cousin? But if that was the case, why had Oliver not mentioned it at the time?

Maybe it was just coincidence. Things happened that way sometimes. She remembered Oliver's words: *Coincidences make me uneasy ... I'm not sure there is such a thing as a meaningless coincidence.*

She dabbed the shine from her nose. Some people were scared of spiders; some of flying; of darkness; of the number 13; everyone had something they were scared of. Oliver Halkin happened to be scared of coincidences. That did not mean she had to be.

Oliver was waiting for her in the kitchen as she'd hoped. Captain Kirk was asleep on the floor in front of the Aga. 'Edward finally released you?' he asked, winking at her.

'Just.'

'I'm sorry you got lumbered.'

'He's been good company.' She hesitated, wanting to ask Oliver about Edward's strange silences but not able to think of a way of doing so tactfully.

'Would you like some tea – or something stronger?'

'I'd love some tea.' Her eyes fell on the stainless-steel draining-board and she swallowed at the memory of the fingers that had lain there a few hours earlier on the bloodstained tea towel.

'Ordinary or Earl Grey?'

'Earl Grey, please.' She watched his face. 'Does the name Jonathan Mountjoy mean anything to you?'

'Jonathan Mountjoy?' He pulled a tea-bag out of a tin, dropped it into a mug and then poured from the heavy kettle. 'Jonathan Mountjoy,' he said again with a slight frown. 'I think I recognize the name.'

'Last night,' she said.

'Ah! Was it the name of the chap – your friend – who was killed by a mugger?'

'Yes.' There was nothing that she could read in his expression at all.

'Why?'

She blushed. 'I – I got the impression that his name rang a bell with you, that's all.'

He shook his head. 'So where did you go this afternoon?'

'We went first to the chapel.'

'Oh?' Oliver pulled a tin out of a cupboard. 'Like a piece of cake?'

'No, thanks.' She eyed the spaniel. 'How old is Captain Kirk?'

Oliver thought for a moment. 'About three.'

'Is he OK with Edward?'

'Good as gold.' He hesitated. 'Why?'

'I thought he was going to attack him this afternoon.'

Oliver shook his head. 'He has got a bit of a sharp streak – he had a go at some gypsies last weekend, but he wouldn't touch Edward. He –'

'May I watch a video please, Daddy?'

Edward came in holding a Game Boy in his hand, and knelt beside Captain Kirk, who was stretched out on the floor, crooked his arm around the dog's neck and pressed his cheek against him. 'You'd like to watch a video, wouldn't you, Captain Kirk?'

'What do you want to see?' Oliver said.

'*Terminator 2.*'

Frannie watched the dog warily, but it licked Edward's face affectionately with no trace of its previous display. Oliver bent and tousled the boy's hair. 'All right. I'm going to show Frannie round the house. What do you want for supper tonight?'

As he removed his hand, Edward tidied his hair with a faint look of annoyance. 'Fish fingers,' he said. 'Captain Kirk likes them,' he said, looking at the dog fondly. 'Don't you?' He pressed his nose against the dog's.

Frannie looked at Edward curiously, wondering if the boy was being deliberately tasteless or not.

'I think we've had enough of fingers for one day.'

Edward looked crestfallen. 'Why?'

'I don't even know if we have any.'

Edward's face fell further. 'I *want* fish fingers; please, Daddy.'

He stomped his foot and Frannie felt uncomfortable, as if it was her fault he was overtired.

'OK. OK.'

Tears began to trickle down Edward's cheek. Frannie's heart went out to him. Perhaps the loss of his mother was still affecting him. Maybe that explained his behaviour. But not the news cutting. She caught Oliver's eye and he smiled wistfully back at her. A glint of sunshine slipped from an upstairs window across the courtyard, as if a light had been switched out. Edward cradled Captain Kirk tightly to him again, rocking backwards and forwards, tears flowing thickly. Oliver spooned the bag from Frannie's tea and raised the milk bottle as if it were a question mark. She nodded.

Oliver watched Edward for some moments, then

rested a hand on his shoulder and squeezed. Edward spoke without looking up at him.

'I'm scared, Daddy,' he said.

'It's OK,' his father replied. 'It's OK.' He handed Frannie her tea and gave her a weary smile, then he picked Edward up in his arms. 'Who's a tired boy? Sure you want to see a movie and don't want to go to bed?'

'See *Terminator* 2.'

Oliver winked at Frannie and carried the boy out of the room and down the corridor. Captain Kirk followed, excited.

Frannie sat at the table and blew on her tea, thinking of Edward's strange remark to his father. *Scared*. She wondered what of?

Oliver took Frannie round the downstairs first, starting in the basement, showing her the old, disused kitchens with their massive ovens and small high windows that reminded her of the ones in the nursery. She trailed along beside him, feeling slightly awkward, as if she were a sightseer; she was still very uncertain about her role. Upstairs, he showed her a bedroom with a roped-off four-poster where Oliver Cromwell had once spent the night. But it was the objects in the rooms that really captivated her. They seemed to be walking through an endless treasure trove. She recognized an Etruscan bronze mirror just for starters.

On the first floor they went into a long oak-panelled gallery. There were tapestried window-seats, elegant sofas, large tables on which open photograph albums of the family's history lay. The rich pinky-yellow glow of the sun filled the room with an ethereal light that the polished oak floor reflected like the surface of a lake. Massive chandeliers hung above it, each arm ornately wrought into the shape of a wyvern.

'Incredible,' she said, stopping in appreciation. She breathed in the rich warm smell of the wood and was aware of the complete silence.

'I think you're incredible,' Oliver said, putting his arm around her, surprising her.

'Me?'

He pulled her gently towards him. 'Yes.'

She turned to face him and smiled. 'I'm not. I'm very ordinary.' She watched his blue eyes that were staring straight into hers, and felt the strength of his arm around her.

'I say you're incredible,' he said again. 'And you're very lovely.' He squeezed her tighter.

Frannie flushed with elation, and experienced a sudden, intensely erotic pang of desire for him. He released her to walk over to a glass showcase and she followed him. 'Thank you,' she said. 'I think you're very lovely too.' Their shoulders were touching and there was a peacefulness between them; the same easiness again now as there had been when they had left the restaurant last night.

On the wall above them was a portrait of a man in seventeenth-century clothing. His head rose from the ermine collar of a purple velvet robe. The expression on his face was cold, preening arrogance. Thin lips were compressed into an inquisitor's smile. His shoulder-length hair was brushed immaculately in King Charles curls and tiny hands, the size of a child's, clasped a book to his chest. The same book, she realized, that now lay in the showcase on a velvet pad, its faded ink handwritten on what looked like badly preserved vellum. The writing was almost illegible, even without the failing light, and in a language she did not recognize.

Oliver moved and his shadow fell across the glass

and the book beneath. 'That's the one thing I really wish I did not own.'

'This book?'

'Yes.'

'Why? What is it?' There was a typed card in a mounting on the outside of the cabinet. It said: *Maleficarium*. c.1650 AD.

'An instruction manual of satanic rituals. It's supposed to be written on human skin.'

'Seriously?'

'That's what the family has always believed. I've no idea whether it's true.'

She leaned forward with morbid interest. It was as beautifully crafted as it was hideous. She stared at the grain of the pages, tiny criss-cross lines; the colour was a repugnant dark brown. She peered closer, revulsion spreading through her. Frannie had seen preserved human skin on mummies and on tribal artefacts. It always looked leathery, like this. 'Have you ever had anyone test it?'

'No.'

'I could get it done for you.'

There was an expression of wariness on his face. 'I'm not sure I really want to know. It's a bloody evil thing whatever it is. I've never even touched it and I don't think I want to.'

'What's the history behind it?'

'It was written by one of my ancestors – the second Marquess.' He nodded at the portrait.

'That's him?'

'Yes. Lord Francis Halkin.'

'Is he the only Marquess who's not buried in your family chapel?'

He frowned. 'How do you know that?'

'Edward told me when he was showing me the chapel.'

His expression darkened. 'He was a fairly evil man by all accounts.' He eyed the book uncomfortably. 'He was into witchcraft. Black magic. A whole raft of things. He was a sort of follower of Gilles de Rais.'

'I know the name. Who was he?'

'A rather unsavoury Frenchman who liked to have sex with small boys and cut their throats during the act.'

Oliver moved and as his shadow slipped away from the book, the effect made it appear for a moment as if the skin were breathing, and Frannie turned away also, unsettled, not wanting to stand near the cabinet any more. A floorboard creaked as her weight shifted.

He dug his hands in his pockets. The sunlight in the room seemed to be incongruous. She followed him as he walked slowly on. 'Gilles de Rais is reputed to have killed over nine hundred boys – the world's worst ever serial killer. I don't know how many the second Marquess killed. Nor where he got his writing-paper from.' He stopped and turned towards her. 'I can never take the notion of aristocracy too seriously. None of us are descended from terribly nice people.'

'There are plenty of ordinary people who are not very nice either,' Frannie said. 'Plenty of ordinary people commit evil acts and atrocities. You should see some of the weapons I've been sorting through at the Museum. Things like beautifully jewelled Indian knuckledusters with attachments for tearing ears off. Does tearing people's ears off advance mankind?'

'If it stops them being able to wear Walkmans it does.'

She chuckled, then looked back at the display case. 'Why do you keep the book? Why don't you sell it to a museum?'

He shrugged. 'It's part of the house's heritage,

whether I like it or not. There are a lot of other things here that I'm not wild about. I'd love to flog some of the dreary old portraits and buy some modern pieces, help encourage our young artists. But people want to see the family's history hanging on these walls.' He walked on again. 'The book pulls a few visitors – we get some of these odd occult characters travelling hundreds of miles to have a gawp – it's mentioned in quite a lot of reference works. I get two or three letters a year from the born-again brigade telling me to burn it.'

Leaving the gallery, they walked through a doorway at the end and into a dining-room. Places were laid for an elaborate dinner on the round mahogany table.

'This is where my ancestors would have intimate dinners.'

'Intimate dinners for sixteen?' She'd counted the places around the table.

'The table can be extended or contracted.'

A single picture hung on each of the four walls. The one that drew Frannie was a portrait of a man with a strong family likeness to the second Marquess. His face was slightly plumper, but there was the same hard arrogance and a look of fox-like cunning.

'That's the third Marquess,' Oliver said. 'Lord Thomas. He shopped his older brother, the second Marquess, to Cromwell, so he could inherit the title.'

Frannie could see the smugness in the man's face, and could well believe what Oliver had just said.

'It was during the Civil War. The family used to have a house in London – later destroyed in the Great Fire. There was a secret passage beneath it down to the Thames and the second Marquess allowed the Royalists to use it as a safe house in exchange for a supply of boys, the story goes.'

'What happened to him?'

Oliver's eyes roved around the room. 'He was hot-collared.'

'What's that?'

'The same thing that happened to Edward the Second. A red-hot poker pushed up his backside. It used to be a good way to murder someone – didn't leave any visible marks.'

Frannie squirmed. She was glad she could see no family resemblance to the portrait in Oliver's face. She looked at the round table again, cordoned by crimson rope to prevent visitors from helping themselves to the silverware or the cutlery. 'Do you ever use this room?'

'Very occasionally. There was a time when we did period banquets for American tourists.'

'Could we eat here tonight?' she said mischievously.

He looked surprised. 'You'd like to?'

'I think it would be amazing!'

He caught her mood. 'We could, I suppose!'

'Don't you think the house would like it – for it to be used again.'

He knelt down and crawled under the table. 'I'm not sure I can remember how to make it smaller.'

Frannie could see the family crest was embossed on the silver cruets, and on the handles of the cutlery. Much larger, in the centre of each plate, the Halkin motto was clearly legible in gold lettering inside the scroll. *Non omnis moriar.*

The words gave her the same feeling of apprehension she had felt earlier when she had read them above the front door. *I shall not altogether die.* From Horace. She had come across the quotation originally when she had studied Horace at school. But there was somewhere since. She read them again. It was there, on the edge of her mind, like a child taunting her then dodging behind a tree.

Like Edward. She shuddered as she suddenly thought of his strange question when he had been holding the fossil. *Do you think the dead always stay dead, Frannie?*

Non omnis moriar. She repeated the Latin silently to herself, then the translation, staring into the steely eyes of the third Marquess, as if he might help jog her memory. As if he might explain why the words made her feel so deeply and unaccountably afraid.

Spoons of flame hovered unsteadily above the twin silver candelabra; they fluttered in a draught and a hundred reflections shimmied in unison on the polished facets of the crystal goblets.

Frannie had her pullover on over her shirt, but still felt the dewy chill of the night air. Oliver sat opposite her across the mahogany table, which he had reduced right down in size. He was looking relaxed, wearing a denim shirt with the cuffs rolled back, and cradling his glass in his hands. His hair had slid forwards either side of his parting and rested across both temples, but he made no attempt to push it back. There was a mottling around the neck of the bottle on the table and the red of the wine in the glasses was dulled with a faint tinge of brown. The label said: Gevrey-Chambertin, 1971. Steam curled from the thick fillet steaks on their plates.

Frannie helped herself to mushrooms, a large tomato and tiny new potatoes from the foil pack in which they had brought the food. 'Are there any ghosts here?'

His mouth broadened into a warm grin and the blue of his eyes deepened in the candlelight. 'I don't think so.'

'I thought all old houses had ghosts.'

'All old families have skeletons in their closets, but

117

they don't all rattle and wail in the middle of the night.' He cut a piece of his steak. It was beautifully cooked, well done outside, pink inside, the way she liked them.

Frannie cut into hers, watching the band of juice trickle out in the wake of her knife. The sight made her feel queasy, reminding her of the blood from the boy's fingers. Her eyes went warily up to the third Marquess. She heard the sigh of a gust of wind outside, and the hiss of leaves. The window behind the drawn curtain was open slightly, and rattled in the draught.

She looked up at the unlit chandelier for the first time. The candlelight was reflected in its tear-drop crystals. The flames were burning upright again now; tiny ripples of heat warming the air above them. 'How did your wife die?' At last, she'd said it.

Oliver was silent for some moments before replying, then leaned forward as a sudden weariness seemed to sap him, and rested his elbows on the table. He interlinked his fingers beneath his chin. 'I – it was about three and a half years ago.' He gently tapped the base of his throat with his thumbs. 'I was taking Edward to meet Sarah for lunch – it was her birthday and we were having a day in London. She'd gone to have her hair done. We saw her on the other side of the road, and she started to cross towards us. A van being chased by the police jumped the lights and hit her.'

'God!'

'It carried her across the road and pushed her through the plate-glass window of a shop.'

Frannie looked at him in horror. 'You saw it happen? Both of you?'

He grimaced.

'Three and a half years ago?' she said, her voice trembling.

'Yes.'

'Whereabouts did it happen?' she felt her whole body clenching.

'In the City. I had to go to a meeting and took Edward with me into the office. We had a bit of time after it finished, before Sarah arrived, so I thought I'd show Edward the Guildhall. He was in a bit of a grumpy mood because I'd promised to take him to Hamleys and hadn't managed it. We had a drink in a café, then, as we came out into Poultry, we saw Sarah on the other side of the road. I remember not recognizing her at first because she'd had her hair cut short. She started to cross the road and a van being chased by the police jumped the lights and pushed her through a shop window. She was decapitated.'

'God, I'm sorry.'

He studied his wine and said nothing.

Frannie felt a strange and disorienting mixture of shock and surprise. 'Was it a bookshop?' she asked, quietly.

He looked at her oddly. 'Yes.'

'Edward had a chocolate milkshake and you had an espresso?'

'I can't remember exactly –' his face darkened into a deep frown. 'Yes, actually, I think –' He leaned back. 'How on earth do you know that?'

'I was the girl who served you. It was my parents' café.'

There was a long silence. Oliver shook his head in disbelief.

Then a sudden cold draught of air struck Frannie in the face. The flames on the candle heeled over sharply, almost tugging free of the wicks. A shadow moved behind Oliver. It was the door opening. Frannie pressed her nails into the palms of her hands. Oliver turned his head, following her stare.

Edward stood in the doorway in a woollen dressing-gown and corduroy slippers. 'Daddy, I heard a noise in the attic.'

Warm blood spread like central heating through her veins as her fear subsided. She slackened her clenched fingers, breathing out, almost exhilarated in her release, smiling at Edward as he came closer across the room. Oliver stood and put his arm protectively around the boy. 'Did you? Probably squirrels. I'll get someone to set some traps and put down some poison.'

Frannie continued to smile at Edward but there was barely any hint of recognition in his expression. He eyed their plates. 'Can I have some pudding?'

Oliver tousled his son's hair. 'You can have some tomorrow. Come on, I'll take you back to bed. Say goodnight to Frannie.'

The boy mumbled, 'Gnightfrannie,' then turned.

Oliver winked at her. 'Couple of minutes,' he said.

As they walked off, Edward grunted something she did not catch; their voices faded and their silhouettes became part of the darkness that stretched out into the corridor beyond the door. She looked back down at her steak which she had hardly touched and cut another piece, the silence amplifying the sound of her knife on the china. She was thinking back three and a half years, surprised she could remember so clearly what the man had ordered for the boy and himself. Thinking about the coincidence; or coincidences.

She drank some more wine and caught the arrogant gaze of the third Marquess on the wall. She became self-conscious, unable to dismiss the sensation she was being watched by the face in the portrait.

The horror of the death of Oliver's wife played on her mind. She could remember that scene clearly, also. And the stories that came back to her afterwards from other shopkeepers, from her parents. How the woman's head had been severed cleanly by the plate-glass and had rolled to the other end of the shop. How every single book in the shop had had to be thrown away because they had all been sprayed with blood.

She felt a strange mixture of elation and fear. As if there was some curious force of destiny at work and she was part of its master plan. But there was something that Oliver knew and was holding back. Had he known that they had met before? Did he have some reason for contacting her? For bringing her here?

The flames of the candles heeled again as another gust blew outside. There was a sharp crack behind her like a foot on a floorboard but she did not want the Marquess on the wall to see that she was nervous. Houses creaked and cracked all the time. The change of temperature from day to night. Contraction and expansion. The British Museum made the same sounds. She had been on her own many times down in its vaults, surrounded by mummies and unopened coffins; alone in crypts. It wasn't the dead who frightened her, it was the living. She was not afraid of ghosts.

She knew there was no one in the room; the door behind her was closed and she could see through into the darkness beyond the one in front. But when something touched the back of her head, she jumped, her larynx throttling the scream before it escaped. The same something flicked her cheek. Then her ear. A shadow flitted in front of her eyes. A moth, swooping in an uneven parabola in front of her. Its shadow strobed across the table.

Just as her breathing had calmed, the bang right behind her almost shook Frannie off her chair and on to the floor.

She turned in terror. The wall was blank; where there'd been a likeness of a white-faced girl from the past, there was now just a large dark rectangle and a crude hook in its midst. The picture of the girl lay face down on the floor, its frame split by the impact, like broken bones. She heard a deep hiss and the curtains were sucked into the window. Then both candles blew out, and the door slammed shut.

'Frannie?' Oliver's voice.

She opened her mouth and nothing came out. She heard a sharp click. Light filled the room and she blinked. Oliver looked anxiously at her, then beyond at the fallen picture. 'What's happened? You OK?' He walked over to the picture, knelt down and held up two strands of wire. 'Snapped,' he said. 'Bloody flimsy bit of wire whoever did this. Could have injured someone.'

'It nearly gave me a heart attack!'

His eyes moved to each of the remaining pictures in turn, giving each a stern appraisal. 'I apologize for Edward – he normally sleeps OK.'

'Probably still shaken by the accident on the speedboat – or Dominic's fingers – I should think it would give any child nightmares.'

His face relaxed a little. 'You look as white as a sheet.'

'The painting gave me a fright!'

'I'm sorry.' His eyes focused intently on hers and he smiled. 'So. Not such strangers after all!'

Frannie shrugged. 'I had the feeling at King's Cross that I'd seen you before. It's been niggling me.'

'Do you often work in the café?'

'All the time when I was a kid, in the holidays, and when I was at university. My dad used to pay me, which was useful. But I haven't in the new café. The lease ran out and they were forced to move by developers a couple of years ago.' She looked at him quizzically.

He took a step towards her. 'I – I'm really happy that you're here.'

'In spite of our – coincidence?'

He slipped his hands around her waist and she felt the gentle grip of his strong fingers. He tilted his head back a few inches. His hair had slid further down over his temples and the crystals of light from the chandelier danced in his eyes. 'Maybe you're going to change my luck.'

'I hope so.'

They held each other's gaze and slowly their faces moved closer. Their lips dusted each other's lightly, tentatively, then parted. They stared, searchingly, into each other's eyes, then kissed again. She was surprised how soft and tender his lips were, how gently his mouth moved. His fingers pressed harder, held her more firmly, tracing the contours of her back, and she felt safe now, her fears melting, replaced by an intense yearning. She kissed him ferociously, pushing her fingers through his soft hair, breathing in the light fragrance of his skin, feeling the strength of his body.

Their mouths separated again and they eyed each other once more. Oliver cupped her face in his hands and kissed each of her eyelids lightly, then looked into her eyes, with hope and with fondness. 'Let's go to bed,' he said.

CHAPTER TEN

A sharp click woke Frannie with a start from a confusing dream. It sounded like a machine being switched off, or a drawer being shut. She sat up, confused, taking a moment to remember where she was. Then she breathed out and sank back against the pillow, held herself still, trying not to wake Oliver, who was sleeping deeply beside her. The stump of a candle burned unsteadily beyond him. Outside, the hoot of an owl probed the darkness.

She was wide awake, as if something was not right. The owl hooted again, a soft, lonely call, like an unanswered signal through space. The candle fluttered and shadows collided against the walls. Her eyes roamed the room, the dark canopy of the four-poster above them, the thick rugs on the floor, the walls ornately painted with cherubs and Rubenesque women.

Beneath the thin sheet Oliver's arm lay across her stomach. He stirred and his chin, hard with stubble, pressed against her shoulder. Then she smiled at remembered pleasures of the past few hours and her fear subsided. She felt drained, like a spent husk, and yet at the same time deliciously complete, as if the whole principle of equilibrium lay within her. They had made love almost the whole night through, catching brief snatches of exhausted sleep, then waking and starting again. The way they were starting now, the way she could feel Oliver nuzzling her cheek, slowly playing his fingers down her body.

She kissed him back, their lips tacky, their skin

damp with perspiration. He kissed her neck, then her chest, then each of her shoulders. He ran a finger lightly around the base of her neck and kissed that too, then he stared silently, approvingly at her face, and she was wanting him as if it were only the beginning of the night. She drew him to her, caressing him with her hands, kissing him lightly, then deeply, then lightly again; her body taut, resonating with increasing desire at each returned caress, each reciprocated kiss until she had to fight from crying out and clutch him tightly to her, cradling his head in her arms, whimpering with pleasure so intense it was barely distinguishable from pain, repeating his name over and over as if the world would cease to revolve if she stopped.

Afterwards they lay still, gulping air, her nostrils filled with the smells of sex, the salty taste of his skin on her lips. His face lay on the pillow beside her, nestled into her chest, and she stroked his hair, separating the strands, tidying them.

At the back of his parting was a tiny bald patch of white scalp. It made him seem vulnerable. As if she were looking at his skull. She shivered, but continued to stare in fascination. She knew that human beings shed skin constantly, a complete layer each week, shed enough particles of dead white skin to fill a soup bowl every day. She wondered, suddenly, how much skin it took to make a book.

Then she kissed his head, afraid of her thoughts, and buried her face for a moment in his hair.

He turned his face towards her, and looked serious for a moment, searching her eyes with a worried frown.

'What is it?' she said.

At first he said nothing. But then his hand squeezed her shoulder. 'How many languages do you speak?'

A little surprised, she answered him, 'English. A little French. Italian. And I understand Latin,' she added. 'Why?'

'You don't speak any Arabic? Or archaic languages – other than Latin?'

She smiled. 'No. Do you want something translated?'

He said nothing.

'I was quite surprised to hear Edward speaking Latin,' she said.

Oliver seemed to stiffen. 'He spoke in Latin to you?'

She was chilly, suddenly, under just the sheet and snuggled against him for warmth. 'His knowledge of plants is incredible. He seems to know the Latin names of all of them.'

'Plants?' he said quietly.

She lifted some hair from his forehead and pressed it back. 'Bright boy from a bright daddy.'

Oliver was silent again.

They slept.

The room was washed with light when she awoke to the sound of the clock chiming. Her eyes felt raw, the lids rubbing like sandpaper as she blinked. Oliver was sitting on the side of the bed in a paisley dressing-gown, smiling at her. His skin, white with tiredness, accentuated the darkness of his stubble, and with his hair dishevelled, hanging unevenly over his forehead, it gave him a rather savage appearance that she found appealing. His breath smelled minty as if he had just brushed his teeth. 'Morning,' he said.

'What's the time?'

'Six,' he said quietly. 'I don't want you to go, but Edward often comes in – and I –'

She nodded.

He squeezed her hand and looked thoughtfully at her for a moment. 'Have a lie-in in your room – get up when you feel like it and I'll make you some breakfast. Sleep in as long as you want – let's just have a lazy day.'

She heaved herself up and slid her feet out of bed, shaking her hair away from her face. Oliver peeled his dressing-gown off and draped it over her shoulders. 'Wear this.'

She pushed her hands in and they disappeared into the sleeves, then as she stood up she almost tripped over the bottom of it. She bundled up her clothes and shoes and carried them over to the door. Oliver came out into the corridor and they stood like clandestine lovers. He put his arms around her and she said farewell with her eyes. 'See you a bit later,' he whispered and kissed her lightly on the forehead.

She padded barefoot down the corridor, past the door of Edward's room, which was very slightly ajar, and she slowed, tiptoeing along to her own door which she opened, then shut behind her as quietly as she could.

She breathed in the bland smells of her own room, climbed in between the fresh, cold sheets, and fell asleep.

CHAPTER ELEVEN

Frannie had read the story on the front page of her father's newspaper when she was nine. A family on their yacht struck a mine that had been laid by the Germans during the Second World War. It had broken free from its anchorage and could have been drifting in the Channel for days. It was the first mine that had been encountered for a decade, a coastguard said. The whole family was killed.

She counted the chimes of seven o'clock, and wondered why she had suddenly thought of that story now. It had affected her deeply as a child and for years afterwards she had been scared of going anywhere by boat.

She heard seven-fifteen strike, then seven-thirty. She was wide awake, cocooned in a warm glow, too excited to sleep. Listening to the rising cacophony of the birds, she let the brightening light play on her closed eyelids. Finally, she slipped out of bed, pulled on her clothes and went quietly downstairs.

In the hall, she was surprised to hear the sound of a television. It was coming from the snug next to the kitchen, and she stuck her head around the door. Edward was lying on the floor in a Garfield dressing-gown, engrossed in a cartoon.

'Hello,' Frannie said. 'You're up early.'

He stayed glued to the television for some moments without acknowledging her. A large matchbox lay on the carpet beside him. The action reached its climax. Frannie watched the television with mild amusement. A cartoon dog skidded across a polished floor and through an open window. It hung upside down high above a Manhattan street, saved by a man's foot standing on its tail. A circle of darkness enclosed the image and shrank to a small dot. The credits rolled.

Then Edward turned his head. His face was pale and his eyes were red with tears.

Frannie was startled. 'What's the matter?' she said, kneeling down beside him.

'I've had the bad thing again,' he said.

'What do you mean?' she said with deepening disquiet.

He was silent for a moment. 'This is my last weekend before I go back to school.'

She smiled, relaxing, thinking she understood now, and feeling for him. 'We'll try and make the most of today, shall we?'

'Do you like insects, Frannie?' he said glumly.

'No. Why?'

He pressed the mute button on the sound, then picked up the matchbox. 'This is my new friend.'

She stared at the box warily as he slid open the lid. For a moment she could see nothing in it. He tilted it sideways, and tapped it. 'Come on, Mr Bean. I call him Mr Bean because I think he looks like Rowan Atkinson.' She saw twitching antennae. A small, dark brown beetle crawled into view. She felt a twinge of revulsion.

'Did you know Jonathan Mountjoy, Edward?' She lifted her eyes to his face, but all his attention was focused on the beetle.

'Turn round, Mr Bean,' he said and gave the matchbox a light shake. But the beetle plodded on to the end and then began trying to climb out. A new cartoon was beginning. He turned back to the screen. 'I have to see this. Would you like to watch it with me?'

'I'm just going out for a walk – I'll watch some with you when I come back.'

He grabbed the control and turned up the volume, his concentration already absorbed again by the television, and did not seem to hear her reply. The matchbox lay ignored beside him. Like her question.

Frannie had often heard of gifted children who behaved as if they were a little out of sync with everyone else. She wondered if this might be the case with Edward. She resolved to discuss it with Oliver.

She latched the front door, closed it behind her and headed for the lakeside. The morning was beautiful and she stopped to admire it from the graceful stone bridge that crossed the lake at its narrowest point.

As she rested her hands on the stone parapet, she noticed for the first time that they seemed to have aged; although the fingers were still slender the skin had dried and coarsened, probably from all the digs she had been on, she realized. She smelled Oliver rising from her unwashed skin and wished he was here with her now.

For all her recent happiness, a shadow moved through her mind. An undefined doubt chafing. Her feeling that there was something not right had returned. A rusting mine, broken from its anchorage, drifting unseen beneath the surface. Waiting to make contact.

She crossed herself, the habit of childhood.

The feeling deepened as she walked back up towards the house. She took a different path from yesterday and found herself lost for some minutes in the woods. Then she came to a track alongside an unfamiliar cornfield with a pylon in the centre, and worked out that she had gone too far over to the east.

She corrected herself and after a quarter of an hour the scenery looked more familiar again. She recognized the collapsed stone folly she had passed with Edward and some massive beech trees ahead.

As she entered their heavy shade she saw something strange in front of her. At first she wondered if it was a broken strip of foliage hanging down, but as she got nearer she realized it was an animal. It looked like a fox caught in a snare, she thought, her stomach churning. It was hanging by its neck, motionless, from a branch of a tree.

Then she clamped her hand over her mouth, cupping a scream, and stopped in her tracks, horror-struck. She could hear her own panting, and was aware of a dull ache in her stomach.

One dark brown eye watched her, shining like a marble in the ray of sunlight that played on it.

Frannie backed away, stumbled on a rut. The eye followed her every movement but recorded nothing. Unblinking. The open mouth revealed the gums that yesterday had been wet with saliva, but which were now as dry as old rubber tubing. Captain Kirk's limbs were splayed out as if he were asleep on the kitchen floor, instead of hanging from a noose of thin, bare wire.

Threads of fear pulled tight inside her, but she braced herself and walked slowly up to the dog, needing to make sure, just in case she could still do something for it. Just one brief touch was all she needed. Beneath the silky coat, the skin felt like porcelain.

She ran for the house, went straight upstairs and along to Oliver's room. His door was open and the room was empty. Across the landing she heard the sound of a bath draining and pounded on the door.

Oliver opened it, with a towel around his waist, and

gave her a warm smile which froze as he registered her expression.

'I don't know if Edward's seen it,' she said as he threw on some clothes. 'He was crying when I went down, but I'm not sure if that was because of going back to school.'

'Gypsies,' Oliver said grimly, as if he were not really listening, tugging the laces of his plimsoles. 'We had problems with gypsies a couple of weeks ago, camping on our land opposite. Captain Kirk bit one of them.'

They left the house quietly, hoping Edward would not hear them, carrying a bin liner and pliers. They cut the spaniel down. Frannie suggested Oliver should call the police but he seemed reluctant. Instead, he laid the dog in the bin liner in the back of the Range Rover and drove off to his gamekeeper, to have him bury it.

Frannie went back upstairs and ran herself a hot bath. She lay soaking in it for a long while, tired and distressed, trying to piece her thoughts together. Trying to dismiss, but unable to, the incident between Edward and Captain Kirk yesterday afternoon and the possibility that it was not the gypsies who had killed the dog.

Then she remembered the affection with which Edward had curled up on the kitchen floor with his arm around Captain Kirk last night, and she gave up trying to find an answer.

An hour later, the smell of fresh coffee and fried eggs greeted her as she came into the kitchen, and gave her an oddly reassuring feeling of normality. It reminded her, she realized, of one of the most familiar smells of her parents' café.

Oliver was wearing a butcher's apron over a faded denim shirt, and was pushing cloves of garlic under the skin of a chicken on a roasting tray. Edward was kneeling on the floor, his beetle inside a rectangular enclosure of Lego bricks. On the table, among the debris of Sunday papers, cereals and jams, there was an untouched place that she presumed had been set for her.

'Hi.' Oliver exchanged a conspiratorial grimace with her.

Edward did not look up. Inevitably the boy's presence made her feel subdued. Was it because she hadn't worked out whether he was friend or foe? But he was only a child, she reminded herself. And now his dog was dead. 'Feel up to some breakfast? French toast is the chef's speciality today.' Oliver was putting on a good act.

'Yes please,' Edward said, cheerily.

'Hey, you've already had some!'

'Can't I have some more? Please?'

'You really want another piece?'

Edward nodded. 'Daddy, would it be all right if I took Frannie riding this afternoon?'

Frannie looked at the boy in amazement then glanced at Oliver, uncertain whether the boy knew about Captain Kirk or not. He must, she thought, otherwise he'd be looking for him.

The telephone began to ring. 'You're going to a party this afternoon.'

Edward's face screwed up with disappointment. 'What party?'

'Jamie Middleton's ninth birthday.'

'God, Jamie Middleton.' He made a series of mock vomiting sounds. 'Do I have to go?'

'Yes, you've accepted.' Oliver picked up the receiver, covering the mouthpiece with his hand. 'I thought you liked him. You wanted him to come and stay a few weeks ago.'

'He's really silly, Daddy. He hasn't grown up at all.'

Oliver and Frannie exchanged a glance. Oliver removed his hand from the mouthpiece. 'Hello?' he said. 'Clive!' His voice became serious. 'I tried ringing you a couple of times yesterday evening. What's the news?'

Frannie watched him in silence. He said very little, listening mostly, then hung up glumly. Some of the morning brightness seemed to fade from the kitchen with his expression.

'Dominic,' he said. 'They stitched one finger back, but they're not very hopeful. They couldn't save the others – the bones were too badly crushed.'

Edward tapped the floor as the beetle moved towards a wall.

'Poor chap,' Frannie said.

'It would have been better if it was his left hand, wouldn't it, Daddy?' Edward said without looking up.

'You said that yesterday. It would have been better if it hadn't happened at all.' He turned to Frannie. 'Tea or coffee?'

'Coffee, please. Can I get it?'

'Sit and relax, read the papers. Have some cereal?'

Frannie poured herself some cornflakes, which she hadn't eaten for years, feeling hungry in spite of her distress, as if aware that she somehow had to stoke herself up for what was to come. Oliver dropped a knob of butter into a frying-pan.

'Daddy, are you making me another piece? I'm still hungry.'

'I'll make you another piece of French toast if you promise to go straight after breakfast and pick some plums for a crumble.'

'Can Frannie come and help me?'

'Frannie might just want to have a sit down.' He winked at her, rocked the butter around, then broke two eggs into a bowl, beat them, dunked two slices of bread in them, dropped them into the frying-pan.

'Frannie,' Edward said. 'Will you?'

'Yes, sure.'

She found herself smiling at his antics, being cheered by them, as he watched his father and mimed his hunger, hunching his shoulders up mischievously, then smacking his lips greedily.

Oliver served the toast up and poured maple syrup on top. 'Ready.'

'Daddy, look! Frannie!'

As the beetle approached one corner of the Lego enclosure Edward dropped a dried pea in its path. The insect pushed it forwards. 'He's going to score a goal!' Edward said, excitedly.

The beetle changed direction. 'No, stupid!' He blocked its path with his hand. 'That way!'

'Toast's getting cold!' Oliver said, putting the pan in the sink and turning on the tap.

Edward stood up. 'Bye-bye, Mr Bean,' he said and crushed the beetle flat with a single stamp of his foot. Then he sat on his chair and nonchalantly picked up his knife and fork.

Frannie looked at him in disbelief, then down at the beetle's remains. Oliver was rinsing out the frying-pan and had not noticed. Edward cut a piece of his toast, pushed it through the pool of syrup, then raised it to his mouth, a trickle of syrup running down his chin. He chewed enthusiastically, cutting his next piece before he had swallowed.

She looked back at the boy's open, freckled face; at his warm brown eyes and his springy ginger hair. 'Why did you do that?'

He continued eating without replying.

Whatever the reasons for it, his habit of not answering

tended to make her feel a fool. She cut her toast half-heartedly, her appetite gone, and forked a piece into her mouth. The sweet taste perked her a little. She tried not to look at the beetle but her eye was drawn back to it. 'Why did you do that, Edward?' she repeated.

Edward began to leaf busily through the pages of the *Mail on Sunday*, scanning the columns without reading them, as if he was searching for something.

Oliver frowned. Edward continued turning the pages in silence, shovelling his food into his mouth until he had finished, and put his knife and fork down, then he concentrated his full attention on the paper.

Oliver raised his eyebrows questioningly at Frannie and she pointed at the beetle's remains. When he realized what it was his face darkened. 'Edward, did you tread on the beetle?'

Edward ignored him and turned another page.

'Edward?' Oliver sounded angry. 'What did you do that for? Why kill it?'

'Beetles are vermin, Daddy.'

'They're not all vermin. And you shouldn't torture animals.'

Edward simply looked at Oliver as if it were he who was the child.

Frannie saw in the boy's face the same expression, the same power, that had made the dog tremble and back away yesterday, just as it now silenced his father. It chilled her. In Oliver's eyes she read both anger and bewilderment.

'For heaven's sake, Daddy, I wasn't torturing him; I was teaching him to play football. Frannie, have you finished? Shall we go and pick some plums now?'

Edward went to the scullery and brought out two wicker baskets with shoulder-straps. He held one for

Frannie. She swallowed the rest of her coffee, fetched her boots, then followed him outside.

They walked down a recently mown track beside the brick wall of the vegetable garden. The sun was hot, but the breeze was back, stronger, sucking and releasing the bushes and the leaves in the trees with a sound like distant waves. The grass had been left where it had fallen and had turned to hay in the dry weather; the air was tainted with its sharp, peppery smell and the more acrid reek of the cow-parsley that rose untamed either side.

'Captain Kirk's gone away,' Edward said suddenly, rather offhand.

'Gone?' she said, wondering what Oliver had told him.

'He's gone away,' he repeated, then lapsed into silence.

Frannie tried a different tack. 'Edward, in your photo album in the attic there's a newspaper cutting about someone called Jonathan Mountjoy, who was killed in America. Did you know it's there?'

'Yes.'

'Did you cut it out?'

He nodded.

'Why?'

'I don't know,' he said guilelessly.

'Do you cut out other things from newspapers?'

'Sometimes.'

'What sort of things?'

There was no reaction. She looked at him. 'Edward?' Still no reaction. He had sunk into silence, leaving her thrown as usual.

She walked on beside him into a large, hopelessly neglected orchard. There were rows of trees laden with fruit, their branches weighted down, some almost touching the ground. Plums and greengages lay all around in the long, weed-strewn grass – wasps, bluebottles and flies crawling over them, burrowing into them. She trod on a plum, felt it squelch beneath her and looked at the mess of brown, overripe flesh. Through a gap ahead she could see rows of apple trees, similarly laden, the fruit looking less ripe.

Edward jumped up and grabbed a low branch and swung down on it, then released it. The tree shook and plums thudded down all around them. One struck Frannie's head and fell beside her. She picked it up, wiped it on her jeans and bit it. It was soggy and had a faintly rotten taste.

'The Victorias are the best, Frannie,' Edward said, and took her hand. 'Let's pick those!'

'What's the Latin for them?'

Edward did not reply as he walked on, suddenly taking her hand and holding it tightly, hurrying her as if afraid the fruit might disappear. He led her to a cluster of trees laden with large, egg-shaped plums, some green, some yellow with red streaks. 'These!' he said.

Frannie picked one and bit it. It was hard and sour.

'They ripen much later than the others,' Edward said. 'You have to look carefully to find the ripe ones. I'll get one for you!' He released her hand and scampered ahead, his eyes scanning the branches of the next tree. He looked carefully at one large plum that was a deep yellow colour, curling his fingers around it gently as if worried it was fragile, and then pulled it very slowly, his face puckered in concentration. 'Here you are!' He held it out.

'Thanks!' She took it, raised it to her mouth and bit into it. As she did so, something tickled the inside of her lip. There was a strange fluttering sensation in her mouth, then a fierce pain on her inner lower lip. She opened her mouth, spitting frantically. There was a stab like a red-hot needle in the base of her tongue. She tossed her head, spitting again, then again something was flicking backwards and forwards in her mouth; it stabbed her ferociously a second time.

She spat again, then again, tiny fragments of plum flying out. A dark thing came out too, fell, dipping, then rose. A wasp; it flew away unsteadily.

She clamped her hand to her mouth, the pain almost unbearable, pinched her lip between her fingers, then her tongue, to try to ease the excruciating agony. She called out from her throat as another wasp buzzed around her, shaking her head in sudden panic. 'Edward! Help!' She pinched her tongue harder with her fingers, pressed her lips tightly together, stumbled forward, her vision blurred with tears. 'Edward!' A branch struck her face. 'Edward!' Another branch hit her in the eye.

Ammonia for bees, Vinegar for wasps. Her father had said that when she was stung as a child. AB. VW. The thought repeated itself. AB. VW. It became a chant in her head as she stumbled out of the orchard, and back along the path beside the walled kitchen garden, heading as fast as she could towards the house.

AB-VW-AB-VW

Sarson's vinegar. She visualized the bottle. AB. VW.

Sarson's vinegar. There was a bottle on each table at her parents' café. Vinegar and HP Sauce. The pain seared her mouth. She fought back more tears. It was worsening every second.

AB. VW. The words buzzed like a wasp in her brain. Willing herself on, she repeated them over and over in case she got to the house and did not know what to do. Edward was somewhere. She was still carrying the basket for the plums. A keening cry came from deep within her. She pulled her handkerchief out of her pocket and stuffed that into her mouth and stumbled on.

In the orchard, Edward shook another tree, and busily picked the best plums off the ground, checking each one carefully for insects, then laying them gently in the basket, careful not to bruise any, working methodically, remembering he must not fill the basket too much otherwise it would be too heavy to carry.

The house stood ahead beyond the beech grove. The pain would be better after she reached it. The house would stop the pain. Oliver would stop the pain. She ran in front of a young woman posing for her husband's camera as the shutter clicked. 'Sorry,' she said, but no voice came out and the word echoed, trapped inside her brain. Sorry. Sorry. Sorry.

She shook her head from side to side as if this might ease the burning in her mouth. She chewed on her handkerchief. Her lips felt like swollen bladders. Pain ate its way up behind her eyes, down into her gullet.

She opened the front door, charged into the hallway that was pitch dark after the brilliant sunlight, saw Oliver hunched over the kitchen table, phone pressed to his ear, in deep concentration. An egg whisk leaned out of a white china bowl on the table in front of him. The radio was on, the Archers weekly round-up.

'Eleven?' he was saying. 'The eleventh last night?' He gestured a greeting at Frannie with his left arm, barely acknowledging her, tapping the table thoughtfully with his right index finger. 'The same symptoms? Does the vet still reckon it's milk-drop syndrome?'

She turned to Edward for help and was surprised to

see that he was not behind her; she thought he had been following her. She opened a cupboard. It was full of china and glass bowls. She shut it and opened another, which was stacked with plates. Then another and stared through tears of frustration at a wok and an assortment of frying-pans. The pain in her tongue became unbearable. She squeezed it between her finger and thumb.

'Surely the vet must have some idea?' Oliver said calmly.

She yanked open another door, her eyes misting. The shelves contained a food mixer and various attachments. She clenched her mouth even tighter over the balled handkerchief, and managed an inarticulate sound.

'Charles, hang on,' Oliver said. 'Frannie – what was that?'

She was desperate, wondering why on earth he couldn't see her distress. 'Vrrngigr.' The handkerchief blotted up her words.

He looked at her properly and stood up, anxious suddenly.

'Vringar,' she repeated and lurched towards a cupboard. She turned back towards him, pleading with her eyes.

'Christ, Charles. I'll call you right back.'

She was trying all the cupboards, leaving the doors open. China . . . glass bowls . . . frying-pans . . . and then one full of bottles. Pickles, ketchup, Worcester Sauce, soy sauce, olive oil. Vinegar. She reached in. There were three different kinds: light vinegar, cider vinegar, dark brown vinegar. She took the dark one out, pulled the handkerchief from her mouth, unscrewed the top of the bottle and shook vinegar on to it, soaking it, then pushed it back into her mouth.

The acidity shot straight up her nose and her eyes snapped shut. She coughed the handkerchief out into her hand, staggered to the sink, hung over it and gagged. The taps and the stainless steel basin rolled past her as if they were on castors. She felt Oliver's hand on her shoulder.

'What is it, Frannie? What's happened?'

She looked up at him, trying to speak, but her tongue clogged her mouth and her lips wouldn't move properly. 'Wassp,' she hissed, and closed her eyes. When she opened them again he was holding her face in his hands, examining her mouth.

She tapped her lips then peeled the bottom one back. 'Wrsspp. Stnnng. In plum.'

'Wasp? You've been stung?'

She nodded feverishly, pointed to two spots on her lips, then her tongue.

'On your tongue? Oh, God! Did you stumble into a nest?' His face creased with anxiety and his cornflower-blue eyes seemed to lose their colour.

She breathed in sharply, clenching her eyes shut, then exhaling sharply. Oliver stood it for sixty seconds and then announced, 'I'm taking you to Casualty. I've got some sting-relief stuff upstairs but we can't put that in your mouth.' He gently pulled her lips, turning them over, looking inside. He checked the clock on the wall. 'Actually, no, it might be quicker if I try our doctor, see if he's in by any chance.' He picked the phone up.

Frannie opened her eyes. The taste of the vinegar made her gag again and she hung her head over the sink, stared down at potato peelings, the tops of carrots and a teaspoon covered in congealed coffee. The fire in her mouth was getting hotter. She rinsed it out with a glass of cold water and that made it worse.

She caught her reflection in the side of the kettle and tried to examine the marks, but it distorted her face too much to see clearly. She remembered there was a mirror in the hall and went out.

In the dim light, her skin looked pale and lifeless. Mascara ran in black streaks down her left cheek, but she barely registered it. As she leaned closer she was surprised that her lip was hardly swollen at all; just a little puffy. She peeled it back and there were just two tiny red marks that were barely noticeable. She curled up her tongue and could see just a tiny red spot, like an ulcer.

She pressed the handkerchief back in her mouth; the fire cooled just a fraction and the vinegar wrung more tears from her eyes. She wiped them with her sleeve and walked back towards the kitchen, bumping clumsily against the wall, and knocking a couple of pictures.

'Would you?' Oliver said into the phone as she came in. 'She's really in terrible pain.'

She sat down opposite him. A tear fell on to the front page of the *Mail on Sunday* and spread in a small grey stain. 'Bush Gets Tough', said the blurred headline. She wanted to be tough too, was trying to compose herself, to stop crying.

Oliver hung up. 'He'll be here in ten minutes – he only lives at Glynde. He says vinegar *is* the best thing.'

She closed her eyes, nodding gratefully.

He looked carefully inside her mouth again. 'You're not allergic to wasps?'

She shook her head.

'Your tongue doesn't look swollen. You can breathe OK?'

This time she nodded.

He put his arm around her shoulder and squeezed

her firmly; then he kissed the top of her head. 'I'm so sorry. Horrible. It's been a bad year with the wasps, we've been plagued by them.'

As she looked up at him, she caught him staring back at her, searching her face carefully with a troubled expression. Searching not for stings but for something else, trying to read her mind. Then he switched focus and she turned her head, startled.

Edward struggled in through the door, his wicker basket laden with plums, holding it with both hands, his face red from exertion as he carried it proudly to his father.

'See how many I got, Daddy!'

'Frannie's been stung by a wasp,' Oliver said starkly.

Edward looked shocked. He dropped the basket on to the floor, ignoring the plums that spilled from it and ran to her. 'Frannie, no! Wasps! Are you all right?' He looked at her face, his eyes wide open, so distraught she thought for a moment he was going to cry. 'Where?'

She stared back at him warily, and pointed at her mouth. Her expression was accusatory.

'In the plum? In the one I gave you?'

'Ysh.'

His face crumpled as if it had been deflated and his voice rose into a whine. 'There wasn't; there couldn't have been! Frannie, there couldn't, I was really careful – I nearly bit one with a wasp in once and I always look. Frannie, I'm sorry, does it hurt a lot?'

She nodded.

He turned to Oliver. 'I picked it, Daddy, specially for Frannie.' A tear ran down his cheek, and in spite of her pain Frannie suddenly felt a heel for her attitude. 'I did,' he said.

She reached her arm around him and hugged him. Then she buried her face in her free hand as the pain once more became unbearable.

The doctor examined each of the stings diligently and, with profuse sympathy, asked her if she had any allergies, then gave her an injection of hydrocortisone. He told her the pain might continue for a while and to take aspirin.

She spent the rest of the morning in a lounger beside the swimming-pool that was secluded from the prying eyes of visitors by a topiaried yew hedge. Edward stayed close to her as if he had personally taken charge of her recovery, lapsing into long periods of silent concentration on his Game Boy, to Frannie's relief, enabling her to read the papers.

A page of the *Sunday Times* on the ground beside her lifted in the breeze and rolled over with a crackle. She looked up and watched Edward, bent intently over his machine, biting his lower lip in concentration and pushing the buttons. She heard the faint tones of the synthetic music and the muffled explosions, and continued to watch him, as if she could somehow understand him by doing so. She needed to solve the enigma of how he could be so warm and alert at times, then suddenly switch off completely, seeming to be elsewhere. It was disturbing. Despite her earlier resolve, she hadn't liked to raise it with Oliver, because she sensed that she might be treading on forbidden territory.

Maybe there was nothing sinister about it. Maybe it was his mother's death that had caused it. The trauma of seeing his mother decapitated. She wondered how she would have reacted in the same circumstances. Perhaps Oliver was fortunate the child had kept his sanity at all.

She replayed in her mind the moment when Edward had picked and handed her the plum. Saw again the innocence in his face. Tried to compare it to the innocence of his expression on the boat yesterday.

He glanced at her suddenly, and she lowered her eyes to the pool. She watched the pipe that stretched beneath the surface, and the automatic cleaner working its way busily up and down. An unappetizing scum of froth and dead flies had gathered in one corner.

I hope you're not planning to sleep with my daddy.

Her unease was growing.

Edward was regarding her with his warm brown eyes. 'How are you feeling now, Frannie?'

'A little better,' she said.

'Would you like to have a go with my Game Boy?'

'Sure.'

'I'm going to kill every wasp I ever see,' he said.

She smiled. 'You don't have to do that.'

'I'm going to,' he said darkly. 'You're my friend. They're going to be sorry for what they did to you.'

The sun went behind a cloud, and she shivered as a sudden sense of fear swamped her. She remembered the beetle from a few hours ago. And the words Edward had used as he opened the matchbox. *This is my new friend.*

She remembered how he had parted company with it.

CHAPTER TWELVE

They had lunch in the courtyard. The sun shone intermittently between increasing spells of cloud. Oliver had cooked the chicken well, it was moist and lightly flavoured with tarragon, but eating was painful for Frannie and instead she drank too much of the ice-cold *rosé*. Edward waged a relentless war against the wasps, somewhat to Oliver's irritation, trapping them beneath upturned glasses, crushing them with his fork, and drowning one in his glass of Coke. Then he put down his knife and fork, leaving his food almost untouched.

'This chicken tastes funny, Daddy. What have you put in it?'

'A herb called tarragon.'

Edward screwed up his face. 'You always muck things up when you *gourmet* them.' He turned to Frannie.

Frannie smiled and saw that Oliver looked rather crestfallen. She wondered if his wife had been a good cook.

'There's gratitude!' he said. 'Back home for twenty-four hours and he's already criticizing my cooking.' He glared at his son with a mock-fierce expression. 'OK, Paul Bocuse junior, why don't you rustle us up something next time?'

Edward looked back at him seriously. 'Can't we just have things cooked normally? Like Mrs Beakbane does?' He turned to Frannie. 'He reads too many recipe books.'

Before she could speak in Oliver's defence, a man

and a boy of about Edward's age came into the court-yard. The man was tall and sturdy and looked a little younger than Oliver; he had a pleasant face with a healthy outdoors complexion, hair bleached by the sun, and was wearing grubby jeans and an old shirt. The boy had a round, rather watery face, with an impish grin, a high forehead and thin blond hair brushed vaguely flat – apart from one lock which stood defiantly upright. He was wearing a yellow Mickey Mouse T-shirt, clean but creased trousers, and train-ers.

'Charles, hi!' Oliver said, standing to introduce them. 'This is – ah – Frannie Monsanto – my brother Charles, and my nephew Tristram.'

'How do you do,' his brother said rather shyly, shaking Frannie's hand with a strong grip and looking down awkwardly at the ground. Frannie could see the family resemblance in their features.

'Tristram,' Edward said, 'would you like to see my new Game Boy cassette?'

The boy's eyes lit up. 'Yes!'

'Got time for a drink?' Oliver asked his brother.

'No – er – thanks, ought to get going; I've got to pick some stuff up from the vet on the way.'

'When's the homeopathic chap coming?'

'Tomorrow morning.'

Oliver suddenly shouted at the boys, who were scampering off. 'Hey, where are you going?'

'Tristram wants to play with my Game Boy.'

'Another time. Uncle Charles wants to get going.'

Charles scratched his head and looked at Frannie. 'Do you – er – know – er – this part of the world?'

'No, hardly at all.'

'Ah; right.' He looked down at the ground again as if trying to think of something to say.

'You've got problems with your cattle, I gather?' she said. The pain of the stings was being anaesthetized by the wine, but her lip still felt swollen and she wondered if she looked strange.

He dug his hands into the back pockets of his jeans and addressed the ground again. 'Yes, one or two, I'm afraid.' He looked at Oliver, at his watch, then back at her. 'Nice to meet you – excuse us dashing. The children are all being taken off somewhere for a mystery picnic and the mother was very insistent they should arrive on time.'

'Nice to meet you, too.'

'Don't forget the present,' Oliver said to Edward.

'Do I have to give Jamie Middleton a present, Daddy?'

'Yes, of course you do, it's his birthday.'

'I'd much rather give it to Tristram.'

His cousin's eyes lit up. 'Yes, please!'

Frannie felt a sense of freedom as Charles and his mud-caked Land Rover disappeared beyond the far end of the façade; the same way she used to feel as a teenager when her parents had gone out. It was exciting to have Oliver to herself for a few hours. She took his hand and squeezed it hard. Oliver took her other hand and kissed her lightly on the forehead. 'Feeling better?'

'Lots.' She looked into his eyes, seeking reassurance; reassurance that his son had not deliberately given her a plum with a wasp in it.

They lay on loungers by the pool, in the sun. Then, after a while, they went into the wooden changing-hut and made love on the hard, dusty floor. Rays of sunlight played above their heads like the beams of cinema projectors. And the stifling air contained the rubbery smell of some old swimsuits hung up and forgotten.

Afterwards they lay in silence. Frannie held his wrist, pulled his hand to her face and gently nibbled his forefinger. Then she caressed him lightly, feeling the warm, spent air of his breath on her face. Perspiration ran down her forehead and her cheeks, down her neck, and her hair was matted to her head. She watched a spider hover warily above them on its glinting thread. The pain was returning again now, so she sucked in cooling air through clenched teeth and after a few moments the burning subsided a little.

Oliver rolled on to his side, propped himself on his elbow and moved his face closer to hers. 'I'm sorry that you got stung,' he said.

'Do you think Edward could be a little jealous of me?'

Her words seemed to strike him like an electrical current. She detected the sudden change instantly; it was as if he were bristling. 'What do you mean?' He pulled away from her and the warmth left his eyes.

'Nothing,' she said, scared by his reaction.

'You think he did it deliberately?'

'No – not deliberately; not maliciously. I just wonder if there's a part of him that's – you know – that he's not even aware of – that resents me; or anyone you go out with.'

'You really think Edward would deliberately have given you a plum with a wasp in it?' His voice was cold; a stranger's. He sat up, morosely hunched over his knees.

Frannie watched the spider winding itself back up its thread, and was afraid to look at Oliver. 'No. No, I don't mean that.' Then immediately she was angry at herself, because she did mean it. It was exactly what she meant.

★

They swam in the pool separately, like two strangers, Oliver doing bursts of two lengths at a time in a powerful crawl, then lying back against the side, regaining his breath. Frannie meandered up and down in her steady breast-stroke. Each time she stopped, Oliver lunged off again.

They had tea by the pool in the last of the sun, their conversation awkward and banal. Frannie felt choked, trying to retrieve the situation and scared that she had blown it. Oliver did not attempt to touch her and failed to reciprocate with even the faintest squeeze when she took his hand. She cursed herself silently for what she'd said.

Then he left her by the pool, saying he was going to have another attempt at starting the plane, and did not ask if she would like to come with him. She heard the Range Rover roar off, being driven hard by someone in a temper. A few minutes later, the still of the air was broken by a muffled bang that sounded at first like a gunshot. There was another, then a distant but fierce roar that lasted about a second. The same procedure was repeated several times over the next quarter of an hour, until the roar grew into a steady, monotonous drone that went on for some minutes. It seemed to increase Frannie's loneliness.

They were going back to town tonight. Oliver was having a day's holiday to take Edward to London Zoo tomorrow. Frannie thought it strange that when she had first met them they were returning from another zoo; coincidence, she thought; barely worth noting.

In a few hours they would part on her doorstep and she would return to her world. To the flowers in the vase in her bedroom. To an angry phone conversation with her parents about why she had not told them she would not be coming to lunch today. And to an expectant phone call from Debbie Johnson wanting to hear all about the weekend.

All about how she blew it.

The clouds closed like curtains across the dying sun. She shivered as the warmth went out of the day.

The stable clock chimed five times. Each bong rang out, echoing in the still air like a warning. Bong, it pealed. Keep away! Bong. Danger! Bong. *I hope you're not planning to sleep with my daddy*. Bong. *Non omnis moriar*. Bong. *I shall not altogether die*.

The first spot of rain struck her cheek like a tear.

It was raining hard as they came off the end of the motorway into the haze of orange sodium that marked the beginning of the suburbs of London and the end of the weekend. The wipers squeaked and clunked, fresh spats of rain filling the arcs as soon as they were cleared. Tail-lights stretched ahead into the distance. They began brightening in sequence; brakes. A cube of ice-blue light hurtled towards them like a slingshot. It was followed by another. The Range Rover slowed.

'Why are we stopping?' Edward said tiredly from the rear seat.

Oliver changed gear. 'Looks like there's a pile-up,' he replied above the din of the engine and the tape of Michael Jackson's *Thriller* which Edward insisted on being played at an ear-splitting volume.

Edward pressed his face to the window. The traffic filed by a sign: POLICE. ACCIDENT. SLOW. A white car lay upside down across the central pavement, almost cut in half by a street light that was badly buckled. Another car with most of its front missing and its roof sticking in the air, as if someone had had a go at it with a tin-opener, faced the opposite direction. Two people sat inverted and motionless in the first car, their heads slumped forwards. The windscreen had frosted. Frannie looked away, feeling the dread accidents always gave her, but her eyes were drawn back involuntarily.

A siren screamed behind them. A policeman was stopping the traffic, moving everyone over to the side. A fire-engine pulled past them and, moments later, an ambulance. Blue lights slicked across the glossy tarmac.

'How do you think that crash happened, Daddy?'

Several people stood around a lump that lay in the road. Sickened, Frannie saw it was a girl, not moving. A dark pool was flowing from her head.

'Is that lady dead, Daddy?'

'I think she's just unconscious.'

A knot of people were standing around the cars and more were joining them. Two men were pulling hard on a door. As it opened, Frannie heard the shriek of protesting metal above the rumble of the Range Rover's engine and the music. It hit just the right frequency to grate on her nerve endings.

Edward tapped Frannie urgently on the shoulder and lowered his voice. 'I think she might be dead. She's not moving at all.'

A policeman was waving them on, agitatedly. Edward turned and peered at the scene through the rear window. 'Daddy, put the rear wiper on please. Quick. Quickly! I can't see!'

The traffic picked up speed and the accident receded behind them. The image of the girl in the road stayed with her.

Edward said: '*Elephas maximus.*'

She turned.

'*Loxodonta africanus. Giraffidae.*' He spoke clearly but quietly, and at first it was difficult for her to make out exactly what he was saying. '*Diceros bicornis. Diceros simus.*'

Frannie glanced at Oliver. He was looking in the rear-view mirror with a frown. She turned round again. Edward was unsmiling. The inside of the car was cold, suddenly, and she felt her body break out in a chill of goose-pimples. Shock from seeing the accident, she thought.

'*Hippopotamus amphibius. Hippopotamus libieriensis.*' Edward stared ahead, reciting expressionlessly.

'Are these the animals you are going to see tomorrow?' she said.

'*Lama huanacus glama. Panthera pardus. Panthera uncia. Neofelis nebulosa. Panthera leo. Erethizontidae. Hystricidae. Hyaena hyaena. Hyaena brunnea. Hyaena crocuta.*'

There was something compelling about the Latin words and Frannie felt the hairs on the back of her neck rising and something spiralling inside her. Fear. She looked at Oliver who continued looking at his son in the mirror, his face set like a mask. She was unable to read his expression.

'*Crocodylus. Osteolaemus. Crocodylus porosus.*'

'Edward, enough,' Oliver said suddenly.

The traffic had been moving steadily for a while, and familiar landmarks were looming ahead. The grimy, Odeon-style building that was a wine warehouse. The Gulf petrol station. Clapham South tube station. The weak red glow from the mosque-like windows of the Indian restaurant. The chemist. The wine bar and the pizzeria, their outside tables deserted in the rain.

'*Struthio. Gorilla gorilla. Gorilla berengei.*'

'OK, Edward, enough!' Oliver said more loudly and firmly. 'Next right, isn't it?'

She nodded gloomily. There had been no thaw in his frostiness.

'*Anthropopithecus troglodytes. Camelus dromedarius. Camelus bactrianus.*'

'Quiet!' he said, losing his temper. 'Tell us where you learned all that?' He looked in the mirror again.

'Turn right here,' Frannie said.

Edward fell silent.

Oliver turned down the street of terraced houses with cars parked on both sides, drove to the end and left into Frannie's street. He pulled up outside her flat.

Edward peered out. 'Is that your house?'

'I just have a flat there.'

'Can I come in and see it?'

'Not tonight,' Oliver said. 'It's late and you're tired.'

'I'm not, Daddy. Couldn't we just go in for a few minutes?'

'*No.*'

Frannie turned to him, and winced as one of the stings in her mouth suddenly pricked sharply. 'Bye, Edward. Back to school on Tuesday?'

He nodded, then his face crumpled. 'I don't want you to go, Frannie.' He put his arms around her neck and hugged her tightly. 'Am I going to see you again very soon?'

'I hope so,' she said flatly.

Oliver opened the tailgate and lifted out her overnight bag. She slid down on to the wet pavement. Edward looked totally doleful. 'Bye, Frannie.'

'Bye!' She blew him a kiss.

'Hey, Frannie!' Edward said, suddenly. 'Dead on!'

She frowned, then grinned. 'Dead on!' she said, and held out her hand. He slapped it. Then she closed the door, getting wet fast. Oliver carried her bag down into the basement, and held it whilst she fumbled for her key. Then he stepped into the hall with her and put the bag on the floor among a clutch of leaflets. She switched on the light. There was an awkward silence between them. Oliver lowered his head, opened his mouth as if to say something then patted his hands against his thighs. Frannie felt close to tears.

Suddenly he moved towards her and placed his hands on her shoulders and looked her squarely in the face. 'Thanks for coming. I'm sorry about the things that happened.'

She stared back for a while before replying. 'I'm still glad I came. Really.'

His expression thawed and he smiled for the first time since his anger in the changing-hut. 'I – I have an invite to a private view of a painter I rather like, Andrew Kiewzka, on Wednesday. Would you like to come?'

'I'd love to.' She dismissed all thoughts of her aerobics class.

'It starts at seven. I could pick you up from here or the Museum.'

'The Museum might be best as it's early. What time?'

'About ten to seven?'

'The Great Russell Street entrance?'

They put their arms around each other and hugged tightly. 'I enjoyed being with you,' she murmured. 'I'm sorry about what I said. I didn't mean it.' Her eyes were wet; as she clung tightly to him she could smell faint traces of chlorine from the pool on him.

'I'd better go, before Edward decides to come down,' he said. They kissed lightly, then she stood in the front door as he ran back up the steps, his head ducked against the rain, and she waited, listening to the bellow of the Range Rover's engine as it drove off, and the slosh of its tyres.

She closed the front door and scooped the leaflets off the floor. A pizza delivery service, a DIY removals service and a builder called STACKMAN – CHEAPEST IN TOWN! She dropped them on to the hall table. A baby cried upstairs and she heard a man's voice raised in anger. Then silence; just the drumming of the rain.

The gloom of the hall closed around her and she shivered once in reaction. The passage down to her bedroom was dark and a hundred miles long. She walked down it slowly, listening for any sound. As she stood outside the bedroom and gripped the handle, her eyes checked the living-room door; the kitchen door; the bathroom door. She turned the handle and went in and was met immediately by the smell of Oliver's flowers. She switched on the light.

And breathed out.

The flowers were where she had put them, in the white vase with the green ceramic bow, on the mantelpiece. Lilies and carnations. She walked across and smelled them; they were still fresh and their scents were sweet. The phone rang. Probably her parents or Debbie. She let it ring twice, three times, breathed the scents again. Another ring. Then she went over to the bed and lifted the receiver.

It was a man's voice that she knew and yet she could not immediately place it.

'Hello, Frannie?'

Serious; she did know it, but it was different; not the way he usually spoke, whoever he was. It sounded wrong, like a recording played at the wrong speed.

'Hi!' she said, trying not to reveal that she could not place the caller.

'I've been trying to get you all weekend.'

'I've been away.'

Silence.

Paul Bryce. Meredith's husband. That was who it was.

'Oh,' he said. 'Right. You haven't heard?'

The words came out heavily, charged with leaden portent. Her reply was weak, her vocal cords constricted, 'Heard?'

'About Meredith?'

She felt the sudden pull of gravity tugging her jaw, the base of her neck, her stomach, her thighs. The floor pushed up through the balls of her feet and her legs buckled to meet it. She sat down on the bed, her dread rising like water in a lock. 'No? About Meredith?' Whispering now.

'She was killed on Friday morning in a car crash.'

CHAPTER THIRTEEN

The landscape slipped by the window of the train, the colours flat and lifeless as if the sombre grey of the sky had leaked over everything. Chimney-stacks, housing estates, reservoirs, factories, canals, coalfields, lines of traffic at level crossings. Frannie watched a woman unpegging her washing in her back yard. A man stood near a bridge, his dog cocking a leg on a lamppost. A lorry crawled up a hill. Life was going on; the daily business; relentless, remorseless routines, patterns. For all except Meredith and her family.

She used to love this journey so much. Now she was making it probably for the last time. It was a month ago that she had brought the double bass up here and met Oliver and Edward on the platform. Meredith had been alive and Frannie had never imagined she would see Oliver again. She had not even known his name then.

The train shook and some coffee spilled over the rim of the polystyrene cup and scalded her fingers. She took a bite of the soggy breakfast bun; the hot meat and the slimy tomato burned the roof of her mouth. She chewed disconsolately; the food was tinged with the cardboard flavour of its carton. It was half past nine and the train was due in York shortly before eleven. The cremation was at twelve.

On Sunday night she had lain in bed wondering about coincidence and remembering Oliver's comment that there was no such thing as a meaningless coincidence. She thought about the accident involving Oliver's wife and the one they had seen on their way up to London and then getting the news about Meredith. Too many accidents. So many coincidences. Meeting Oliver and Edward at the station after they had come into the café three years before; bumping into Seb Holland in the restaurant and hearing of Jonathan Mountjoy's death; Edward's news cutting; Meredith and Jonathan: two people from the same year at university dead within weeks of each other.

She tried to work out whether there was any significance, any meaning. Oliver had talked at dinner on Friday night about Jung and meaningful coincidence; she had read a little about Jung herself at a time when she had been interested in dreams. Synchronicity. The collective unconscious. Causal connections. The only link she could establish was that they had all happened since she had met Oliver; but there seemed no reason.

She had had a miserable day at work yesterday, in which her mouth had still hurt and she had been too upset about Meredith to concentrate. She had only cheered up in the evening when she'd finally called Debbie Johnson to update her on the Oliver situation and then Oliver himself had rung to say hello. He'd been very sympathetic about Meredith. Edward had come on the line as well and told her about his day at the zoo, his voice sweet and gentle and excited. She had wished him luck at school, wondering again as she hung up about his silences; about his strange Latin vocabulary of plant and animal names. And about the wasp.

She recalled how Oliver's temper had flared when she had hinted that Edward might have deliberately given her a plum with a wasp in it, aware of the very deep nerve she must have touched. Oliver's reaction still bothered her, the way it bothered her that he had been quick to dismiss calling the police when Captain Kirk had been killed. Was he protecting Edward?

Even so it did not diminish the intensity of her feelings for Oliver; if anything, bizarrely, it made them deeper still. She thought back to past relationships and wondered if she had always felt disquieted by the people she had loved the most. But the comparison was hard; she had never before felt as deeply in love with anyone.

The taxi drove in through the gates of the crematorium, and along the smooth drive through the tended lawns to the squat, red brick chapel.

Frannie paid the driver, then stood for a moment rather awkwardly. There were two hearses outside the chapel, a row of black limousines and a large number of people split into small clusters, each a short distance from the next. It was like a cocktail party at which there were no drinks.

She scanned the faces, uncertain which people were gathered for Meredith's funeral and which for an earlier one. She felt chilly in her black cotton two-piece and wished she had on something warmer; she always forgot how much colder Yorkshire was than London.

The men were in dark suits and several of the women wore hats and veils. A smell of mothballs and perfume mingled with the scent of freshly mown grass. She recognized a face from university, but it was not someone she had ever met. Then she saw Meredith's husband, Paul, working his way through the clusters, shaking hands, his normally ruddy face clenched and drained of colour, and she found herself fighting to keep control of her own grief.

The same gutted feeling in response to the news over the phone, which had remained with her since, was now intensifying. The coffin was visible through the rear window of the hearse, rising out of the sprays and wreaths that surrounded it. Two undertakers in black suits were busily unloading and taking the flowers around the side of the crematorium, where they were laying them out. Beyond, Frannie could see an ornamental fountain and a long wall with inscribed stone tablets, and rows of single rose bushes, each bearing a large perspex tag.

The other hearse was empty, its contents currently behind the closed oak doors of the chapel from which she could hear strains of organ music and the muffled singing of 'Jerusalem'. Already, another hearse was nosing its way in through the gates. It hove to at a respectful distance, like a ship waiting for the tide.

Frannie walked into the garden of remembrance and joined several other mourners in looking at the flowers. She found the spray she had sent and read the tag: *Meredith. Love you and miss you always. Fondest love. Spags.*

Spags had been her nickname at university; Meredith had still called her that, and sometimes Paul. A tear rolled down her cheek, and as she pulled her handkerchief out of her bag she saw someone making their way towards her. Her heart sank a little as she recognized Phoebe Hawkins, one of her fellow Archaeology students from university.

Phoebe Hawkins was a strange, rather lonely girl, who kept her own affairs strictly to herself but at the same time was a source of gossip about everyone else, as if she desperately wanted to belong with the crowd, and believed gossip was the currency with which she could buy her way in. She had an angular, somewhat masculine, face that was neither attractive nor ugly, and which was made more severe by her close-cropped hair and wire-framed granny glasses. She was wearing a matt-black smock and leather sandals, and stood badly, her head stooped forwards, the way Frannie remembered. She looked like a tortoise peering from its shell.

Frannie had always felt a little sorry for Phoebe and had tried to include her in things at university, even though she had never really liked her very much. She had never heard Meredith speak of her since leaving and was surprised to see her here. Yet she remembered how Phoebe had always hated to miss out on bad news. The thought had often struck her when they were students that Phoebe appeared to get pleasure from the misfortunes of others.

She shook Frannie's hand with a deadly seriousness that seemed genuine. 'This is terrible, Frannie,' she said.

'Yes, it is.'

'So how are you?'

'OK, thanks,' Frannie said, looking around to see who else she recognized. 'How about you?' she asked, mechanically.

'I'm fine, really well.'

'Spags! You made it.' Paul stood in front of her suddenly and kissed her on both cheeks, mustering a welcome. 'Really good of you to come all this way. I thought you were going to phone and let me know what train you were on – I'd have picked you up.'

'You had enough to worry about.' She smiled. 'I don't know what to say about Meredith. I'm sorry, I'm just – wiped. How are the kids?'

'I don't think they're old enough to really understand.' He glanced inquisitively at Phoebe, but without recognition. 'How do you do?' he said.

'I'm Phoebe Hawkins – I was at UCL with Meredith.'

'Ah, right,' he said politely, but rather formally. 'Very kind of you to come.' He looked back at Frannie. 'Will you come back to the house afterwards?' He glanced at Phoebe. 'You'd be most welcome also. The undertakers have laid on a couple of limousines – just get straight into one when you come out.' He moved on to a man and a woman who were hovering close by. 'Aileen. Richard. Thanks for coming.'

'Heard you are at the British Museum?' Phoebe said to Frannie.

'Yes.'

'Do you know someone there called Penrose Spode?'

'We share an office,' she said, surprised.

'For heaven's sake!' Phoebe's smile showed a warmth and a vulnerability Frannie had never before noticed, and she was beginning to wonder if perhaps she had misjudged her.

'How – how do you know him?'

'We were on a four-month dig together in Iran the summer I graduated. Bit of a strange fellow.'

'A little. He's all right.' Frannie studied her face for any information it might yield about Spode, hoping for something that she could tease him about, and she wondered suddenly whether anything had happened between them. She glanced at Phoebe's hands, but she wasn't wearing a ring. 'How about you – what are you up to?'

'I was working in Bath – at the Roman Baths Museum. But I've just moved up to London about a month ago to the Natural History Museum.'

'How's it going?'

'It's really good, I'm enjoying it.' She hesitated. 'Dreadful way to die for poor Meredith.'

Above the subdued chatter of the crowd, Frannie

heard the clank of a handle, and the chapel doors opened. Mourners filed past a clergyman who stood in the entrance shaking their hands. She looked back at Phoebe. 'Do you know what happened?'

Phoebe Hawkins hesitated, as if reluctant to part with a good secret, then she looked around as if to ensure she was not being overheard and leaned a little closer to Frannie. Frannie could smell her soap, it had a carbolic, institutional smell about it that was unattractive. Phoebe imparted the details proprietorially, as if she alone had been entrusted with them:

'It was on Friday morning, apparently; she had dropped the boy, Charles, at nursery school, and she was driving to some bric-à-brac auction near Harrogate. She was at a traffic-light; when the lights changed, she pulled out and a car crossing on red hit her broadside.' Phoebe stopped, but signalled with a widening of her eyes that there was more she could tell.

'God, poor Meredith!' Frannie said.

'There'll obviously be quite a lawsuit. And the police are going to prosecute him.'

Won't do Meredith much good, Frannie thought but did not say. She noticed another friend she had not seen for a couple of years, but Phoebe did not want to release her.

'At least she didn't suffer for very long,' Phoebe said, 'but it was a pretty horrific scene, I gather.'

'Suffer for long?'

'The car went up in flames. She was conscious but they couldn't get her out.'

Frannie closed her eyes, feeling sick. 'Oh my God!'

'A total fireball; she was burned beyond recognition.'

When Frannie opened her eyes again she saw the

pallbearers were unloading the coffin from the hearse. Meredith was in that. She stared up at the bland, red brick wall. The vapour trail of a jet lay across the sky.

Burned beyond recognition.

She tried to push the image from her mind but she could not. She saw Meredith driving: her hair a tangle, cigarette between her messily painted lips, leaning forward to turn up the volume on the radio, pop music blaring, then looking up and seeing the light go green, pushing the gear lever forward, accelerating. One moment of horror. Stabbing her foot on the brakes. Squeal of tyres. The bang. Then the flames. Trying to open the door that was stoved in, buckled. Other people pulling at the door, the way they had pulled at the door of the Volvo outside Meston, with the boy's trapped fingers. The flames increasing. Burning alive. Meredith screaming, pulling the door handle, pounding on the window. Just like the driver in the motorway inferno she'd witnessed four years ago.

She prayed not.

She swayed on her legs and swallowed the bile that rose in her throat, shivers raking her skin. 'That's awful,' she said, weakly. 'My God.' She closed her eyes again for a moment, immediately opening them, frightened by the image that came into her mind.

'Terrible.' Phoebe nodded at the cluster of Meredith's family filing in through the door behind the pallbearers. 'Imagine having to go and identify her.'

'Do you keep in touch with any of our lot?' Frannie said, trying to change the subject.

'Sarah Hobday's down in Bath doing a six-month project at the museum. And I bumped into Keith Stanley at a seminar at the Middlesex Poly last year. And of course I've been down to see Susie Verbeeten a couple of times.' She hesitated, then added the rider: 'Poor thing.'

Frannie saw a faint trace of the spiked smile of the old Phoebe; it was like the probe of a mosquito drawing something out of everyone she met, exchanging blood for poison. 'Why do you say that?'

'Oh, you didn't hear?'

Shadows rose inside Frannie. 'Hear what?' She remembered Susie Verbeeten clearly: The organizer, always the organizer, but fun too at times, although she tended to know everything.

'She went blind.'

'Went blind?' Frannie echoed in horror. 'Susie?'

'Yes, I thought you knew?'

'I haven't seen her since I left.' Frannie's brain fogged as a new and undefined fear seeped through her. 'How – do – you – I mean tell me – what happened? Permanently blind?'

'Oh yes, there's no chance, her retinas have been destroyed.'

The clusters were thinning around them as the mourners filed into the chapel. 'But how?' Frannie was aware of the desperation in her voice.

'From a virus she picked up in Malaysia. The pollution in the South China Sea – there's some bacteria the locals are immune to but Westerners aren't. It attacks the retinas.'

'But that's – why isn't – I mean – there's nothing they can do?'

'Nothing at all.' Phoebe glanced around. 'We ought to go in.'

Something stirred deep in Frannie's mind. Faint, only faint; like a hibernating monster not quite roused from its slumber. She followed Phoebe lamely into the chapel and sat beside her on the hard, shiny pew, staring silently at the oak veneer coffin on the catafalque. At the single wreath of white lilies.

Death was a lonely place; and a silent place. In a short while Meredith would be wheeled alone into the furnace. Was that necessary when she was already charred beyond recognition? Frannie pondered. And the door would be shut on her for ever.

And maybe God would take her spirit. Maybe she was already with God. Frannie was not sure. Her faith was at a low ebb. She closed her eyes, unhooked her kneeler and slipped down on to her knees, cupping her face in her hands.

She cried softly throughout the service, whilst Phoebe sat stonily beside her. She barely heard the words of the chaplain; Meredith had never been much of a believer and it did not sound, from the way he spoke, as if the chaplain had ever met her.

Odd thoughts came in and out of her mind. Appearance and reality, suddenly remembered from a school essay. Shakespeare wrote about that. About nothing being what it seemed. Susie Verbeeten had seemed strong, indestructible. Leader of the pack.

Blind.

Meredith had been full of life. Charmed. Always cheery, always lucky. Frannie knelt and prayed again, but as she did so she felt a stiffening sensation spreading through her body and a cold sweat broke out on her skin. She was very frightened now. She had to work it out.

Back outside in the drizzle Paul directed them to one of the undertaker's Daimler limousines. Frannie turned to Phoebe. 'Remember Jonathan Mountjoy?'

'Yes. Have you seen him lately?'

'He was murdered in Washington by a mugger, a few weeks ago.'

Phoebe paled slightly. She seemed reluctant to look at Frannie. The driver held the door and they stepped into the rich leathery smell of the interior and sat down. 'Seriously, Frannie?'

'Yes.'

'A few weeks ago?'

'Early August.' Frannie clasped her hands together for warmth and comfort. 'There seem to be a lot of things happening to our year, don't there, Phoebe? Meredith dead. Jonathan dead. Susie blind. Three things. It's a rather horrible coincidence, isn't it?'

Phoebe shook her head. 'No, I don't think it is coincidence.'

'What do you mean?'

She was quiet for a moment, then she asked the driver if he could drop her at the station as she had to get back to London. 'I'll call you, Frannie.'

'What is it?'

'I can get you at the British Museum?'

'Yes.'

Phoebe changed the subject, chatting as they drove through York with false jollity about old acquaintances, watching the passing scenery with bird-like wariness rather than meeting Frannie's eyes.

She climbed out of the limousine at the station. 'I'll call you tomorrow,' she said. Then she went inside without looking back.

CHAPTER FOURTEEN

'Not unless you wish to buy a chariot, madam,' Penrose Spode said into the telephone receiver.

He had a sticking-plaster on his forehead and the tip of his chin was grazed from having fallen off his bicycle on his way into work. His black hair, as usual, was as flat and smooth as sealskin. He sat stiffly at his desk, opposite Frannie, in a shirt that had the same pasty whiteness as his complexion, a green corduroy jacket and a carefully knotted tie the colour of gravy, holding the telephone a short distance from his ear as if it were a bag of dirty laundry belonging to someone else. 'No,' he articulated frostily. 'No,' he repeated.

Frannie was transcribing her notes of tagged but uncatalogued objects stored down in the basements on to the Museum's computers, and she was having difficulty deciphering her own handwriting. She felt cold and tired and her head ached. The morning rain seemed to have followed her into the Museum and was wrapped around her now like a sodden coat. Chilling her body the way Phoebe Hawkins' strange reaction to the news of Jonathan Mountjoy's death was chilling her thoughts.

The rain had fallen all night and the wind had risen. She had lain alone in bed in her flat and shivered, lapsing from time to time into short periods of troubled sleep

'No, most certainly not,' Spode said.

Frannie clenched her throbbing forehead and typed:

Ram-Dao buffalo sword. Jewel-encrusted hide handle.

Gupta Dynasty bone-handled thruster.
Nepalese iron-bladed kukri with copper-banded
   handle.

'Madam,' Spode said. 'As I have told you, I'm
afraid you've been put through to the wrong department. This is Oriental Antiquities. You need to speak
to someone in the Roman department.' He covered up
the mouthpiece. 'Bonkers, complete nutter.'

Frannie was uncertain whether Spode was address-
ing her or the room in general. He had been carrying
on this way all morning, and she had tried to ignore
him, the way she usually did when he was in a tetch.
But she was finding it hard to concentrate on her
work. She had taken some more aspirin an hour ago,
but they seemed to have had little effect. She took
another long pull on the can of Coca-Cola that sat on
her desk; Coke sometimes worked for her as a hangover
cure or when she just felt lousy.

It was ten-thirty. Two and a half hours to lunch.
Her will-power broke and she pulled out of her handbag the Twix chocolate biscuit she had bought for her
dessert. Spode stared disdainfully as she tore open the
wrapping and bit a piece off one bar.

'Yes, madam,' Spode said, 'I *am* well aware of
that.'

The cursor on Frannie's VDU blinked patiently, a
small orange square on the black screen. There was a
moment of quiet, as Spode listened without commenting. Some people walked down the corridor outside.
She heard the jovial Irish accent of Declan O'Hare,
the Deputy Keeper of Oriental Antiquities, and a
guffaw of laughter from whomever he was with. The
door opened and she turned round as O'Hare stuck his
head into the room.

'Ah, Frannie. Looking so smart today. Must have an important date, could it be?'

She smiled faintly, not in the mood for his jocularity. A man in a goatee beard and anorak hovered behind him.

O'Hare went on. 'Frannie is about to be rescued from the eternal drudgery of the basements. The dawn of a new world is nigh. Might even include Penrose if he's very good. Could you come to my office tomorrow at half nine? We're planning a new exhibition and I'd like you to be involved from the ground up. How far have you got with the cataloguing?'

'Nearly finished.'

'Could you get it done today?'

'I could try.'

'Perhaps you could work late?'

'I have to leave at quarter to seven. I'll work through lunch.'

'That's my girl!' He went out and shut the door, and she felt a beat of interest, pleased to have the possibility of a change from the monotony of her current work.

'Madam,' Spode said again into the receiver, 'I think if you check your history books you'll find that the Iceni were not Romans. And that Boadicea was in fact a woman, not a lost Indian princeling.'

Frannie adjusted the brightness of her screen, turning the glare down a little, and stared at her pad. Then her phone rang and she felt irrational panic that it was Oliver calling to cancel. She had an intense yearning to see him again. To hold him. To be reassured by him. She lifted the receiver. 'Hello?'

'Frannie?'

It was another research assistant, Julian Egon. 'Declan O'Hare said I was going to have to take over the cataloguing in the basements. Can you let me have a note of the ones you've covered – save me some time.'

'Sure. When do you need it?'

'No rush. Next couple of days.'

'I'll do it later today.' She replaced the receiver and stared at her unfinished Twix; the chocolate was making her feel queasy.

Penrose Spode hung up. 'Really!' he said.

Frannie raised her eyebrows.

'Bloody female.' He frowned as Frannie drained her Coke. 'You know how much sugar's in that stuff?'

'Probably why it works,' she said, and began to type in the next entry.

The phone rang again. But it was Carol Bolton, asking her if she would like to join a small crowd who were going to be taken around the excavations beneath a construction site after work, and then go on for a Chinese. She thanked her for the invite but said she was already going out. Carol said she could guess who with, giggled and rang off.

Frannie found her fingers and her brain were hopelessly unco-ordinated and she made constant mistakes. Penrose Spode was in a phoning mood and his icy sarcasm to the operators, librarians and archivists made her cringe. She took a break at eleven, asked Spode if he wanted anything, went along to the machine outside the canteen and bought them each a coffee. When she came back he was off the phone and twitching with indignation at some fresh injustice.

'I gather you know someone I was at university with,' she said as she set the plastic cup down on the barren neatness of his desk, and he warily eyed a drop that was trickling down the side.

'Who's that?'

'Phoebe Hawkins.'

He looked at her suspiciously, as if she had made an unwelcome intrusion into his private life, his expression reminding her of a crow guarding its nest. 'Yes,' he said evasively, 'I vaguely remember her. We were on a dig in Iran.'

'Steamy Arabian nights?'

He bristled in silence as if a reply was beyond dignity and made a pretence of returning to his work for some moments. 'As a matter of fact, no,' he said, suddenly, and Frannie realized that Spode's view of the friendship or relationship had been less happy than Phoebe's. She wondered out of pure curiosity what the relationship really had been. From a comment he had once made, she got the impression he lived with his mother, but he always gave ambiguous answers to her questions. None of her other colleagues knew any more, either. In a year of sharing the office, she had found no chink in the armour around his private life.

'Bit of a coincidence!' she said.

He did not reply.

She ate an egg-and-tomato sandwich in the canteen, swallowed it down with an apple juice, bought another Twix, which she dropped into her handbag, and went straight down to the basement. She had two final cupboards to catalogue and she would have finished this storage room. If she worked fast she might just get it done today, as Declan O'Hare had requested. Although the cataloguing on Indian weaponry would not be complete, Julian Egon would have a clear starting-point when he took over from her.

She hurried down the long, gloomy corridor, deep underground, with its overhead fluorescents, rows of fire extinguishers and numbered storage doors packed with treasures. Some were antiquities that had been brought down for safety during the Blitz and never taken up again. Some were objects for which there was simply no room and which awaited a relevant exhibition. Others were items for which the records had been lost.

She opened the door marked 2(f), switched on the light and went into the windowless, airless room. A three-foot-high red marble gargoyle grinned at her, inches from her face. It squatted on top of a stone coffin, guarding it. Its face was hideous and gave her the creeps. Declan O'Hare had told Frannie with an evil gleam that the coffin had never been opened and carried a curse worse than Tutankhamun's.

Artefacts were piled up to the high, vaulted ceiling all around: shelves of statuettes, death-masks, totems, vizors, helmets. A torture chair with upright nails sat in the gloom of the far corner and she eased her way past it to unlock the door of one of the two cedar-wood cupboards she had not yet touched. To her amazement, the cupboard was empty, except for one damaged and jagged brass sculpture of a tiger surrounded by curiously shaped symbols, right at the back. To make sure there was nothing else, she pulled out the steps, and climbed up. Each of the ten slatted shelves was bare.

She climbed down and put her hand around the figure. As she tightened her grip on it she felt a stab of pain in her finger. For a moment she thought she had been stung by another wasp, then she saw dark red blood welling out of the tiny puncture. She sucked it clean, and bound her handkerchief tightly around her finger.

When she turned the figure round, she saw what had cut her: it was the broken-off point of what looked like a sword. Frannie eased the figure to the front of the shelf, surprised how heavy it was, and looked at the old buff tag tied to it. She opened her notepad, and removed the top of her pen, settling down to the usual routine.

The writing on the tag had been done a long time ago, in ink that had discoloured to a watery brown, but it was still clearly legible: *Damaged brass figure of a tiger found at the siege of Seringapatam, Mysore, 1799. Date: early 18th Cent. AD. Donated to British Museum 1865 by William Halkin, 14th Marquess of Sherfield.*

A smile pushed its way falteringly across her lips, like a crack through ice. She tried to convince herself that there was nothing sinister, that it did not mean anything, tried to push away the creeping doubts that had been stalking her since Meredith's funeral. But she had the sudden eerie sensation that someone was in the room with her, watching her. She turned around. Nothing. She looked back at the tiger, read the label again. Then she heard the unmistakable scrape of a footstep. It came from the far side of the cupboard, near the door.

'Hello?' she called.

There was no reply.

'Hello?' she called louder.

Silence. But the ceiling was watching her. The walls seemed to move in a little towards her; her skin felt unseen fingers drawing it in, pleating it. She fought her panic. There was no one down here to hear her if she shouted. She stepped lightly between the shelves, looking for an object to hold, something heavy; the cupboards were full of weapons, hundreds of them. She moved round towards the door, then stopped, astounded. The red marble gargoyle that guarded the unopened coffin was no longer on the lid. It was standing on the floor beside it. Blocking her path.

A low croaking voice beyond the door said: 'I'm just going out for a stroll. You can come out of the coffin whilst I'm gone if you promise to be good.'

Then her boss appeared in the doorway, grinning imbecilically.

'Declan O'Hare! You bastard!' Frannie said.

He rocked his head from side to side and slid his hands into his blazer pockets. 'I always said this room was spooky, didn't I?'

She pressed her hand over her heart. 'God, you frightened me!' Her relief was tinged with anger. 'That really freaked me!'

He grinned again. 'Fear is one of the spices of life, Frannie. How can you respect the past if you don't fear it? You can't love anything in life without being afraid of it. Did you not know that?'

She wondered if he was becoming unhinged. 'No, I didn't know that; there are a lot of things I love without fearing them.'

He stroked the gargoyle's head as if it were a cat. 'Oh yes? Tell me one?'

'My parents.'

He shook his head. 'No, you only love them because the first thing you learned was to fear them. It's the difference between like and love, Frannie. You can *like* all sorts of things – a pretty view, a nice vase – but you can only love something you respect. And if you respect it, you're afraid of it in some way.' He bent down and with some difficulty lifted the gargoyle back on to the coffin. 'Cesare Lombroso said that the ignorant man always adores what he cannot understand. Do you?'

'What is this? Twenty questions?'

'Tell me, do you?'

'Adore what I can't understand? I don't know. What

are you getting at?' She wondered suddenly if there was some connection between Declan O'Hare and Oliver Halkin of which she was unaware. The wording on the tag she'd just read was giving her ideas. Maybe the Halkins were patrons of the Museum or something. Was Declan trying to warn her off? Put her off Oliver? Ridiculous.

He was wandering through the room with his normal, slightly swaggering walk. In his early forties, passionately in love with his work, he had the smooth good looks of a television presenter. He paused to tap a ferocious mask. 'Know why warriors used to wear these in battle?'

'To frighten their enemies.'

He smiled his television presenter's smile. 'No, Frannie. To hide their fear from their enemies.'

'This isn't a very good day to talk to me about fear, Declan.'

'Oh?' he looked at her quizzically. 'Are you OK? What have you done to your finger?'

'Nothing. Just a prick.'

'You look a little peaky. Ah, of course. I'd forgotten. The funeral. Bad?'

'Yes.'

'The Western way of death always is. But that's another story. So, freedom from fear you want today?'

She nodded.

He stared at a death-mask. 'You're a good girl, Frannie. A good researcher – you have a great future ahead of you. Just don't get blasé about the past, that's all.'

'I didn't think I was.'

He gave a brief shake of his head. 'No, no, I don't think you are.' He ran his hand over a crocodile shield. 'Don't you think it would be wonderful if you could access the past? If you could run a machine over something like this and pick up the energy field of the man who once carried it into battle, find out all about him, his thoughts, his emotions, how he lived?'

'Yes, it would be.'

'That's what antiquities do for me, Frannie. Do they do it for you?'

'You mean you can really read the past in them?'

His expressive blue eyes widened. 'Unfortunately not. I wish I was psychic, then maybe I could. There are people who can. Or so they claim. You should talk to Penrose, he knows about these things.'

'Penrose?' she said, surprised.

He rolled his eyes in a rather sceptical affirmation. 'But I'll tell you what I think: we humans can remember everything that's ever happened to us, everything we've ever seen and done. A lot of it we can't access unless we go under hypnosis. It's there, but it's buried. I believe objects and places remember things too; their atoms, their subatomic particles, whatever, are affected by everything that happens close to them. It must be possible to access them somehow.'

'Is that what you want to do? Find a way how? Invent a machine that can read them?'

'No,' he said with a smile, and walked back to the door. 'No, not at all. I'm just a simple archaeologist who digs around in dust for old bones and pots and garden gnomes.' He departed silently on his rubber-soled shoes and she shook her head, bemused by his typical eccentricity.

'Declan!' she called after him.

He stopped by the door at the end. 'Yes?'

'There's a small bronze in one of the cupboards – eighteenth-century Indian, donated in 1865 by William Halkin, fourteenth Marquess of Sherfield. Is there any family connection with the Museum and that family?'

He looked at the ground, clasped his hands behind his back and frowned. 'I seem to think there's some connection between them and the East India Company. And they were quite big patrons of the arts at one time.'

As she reached him he started walking again, through the door and up the staircase. She kept pace with him.

'Strange lot, the Halkins, mad as hatters, half of them. But so are most of the aristocracy,' he said.

'Why are the Halkins strange?'

'Oh – I can't remember which one of them it was – in the eighteenth century, I think – the eleventh or twelfth Marquess's wife died, but he totally ignored it, carried on as usual, had the servants continue to dress her for dinner and bring her down every night. He dined with her for years after her death. Half the servants left because they couldn't bear the charade.' He held the door at the top of the stairs for her. 'And of course there was the old second Marquess in the seventeenth century up to all sorts of occult tricks. Very involved in numerology.'

'You seem to know a lot about them.'

'No, not really. I'm interested in English history, that's all. They were a significant family, in a minor way. A few MPs and soldiers, that sort of thing. I'm not even sure if the line isn't extinct now.'

'It isn't,' Frannie said.

'Ah,' he said without much interest. 'If you want to know more you could try looking them up in the library.'

'Yes, I was planning to.'

'There's a whole section on genealogy. They're bound to be in it. *Debrett's* would be the place to start.'

When she went back into her office, just before five, Penrose Spode was not there; she glanced up at the back of the door and saw that his crash-helmet and fluorescent strap had gone, indicating he had left for the day. Then she saw the note in his neat handwriting as she sat down: '2.35p.m. Phoebe Hawkins telephoned. Very urgent that you call her back ASAP. She is in a meeting but they will put you through.'

She wondered, as she dialled, whether speaking to Phoebe had prompted Spode's unusually early departure. Whatever the reason, she was quite glad that he wasn't there to listen in.

'Frannie?' Phoebe sounded edgy.

'Sorry, I only just got your message.'

'Look, I can't talk at the moment. Can we meet up this evening?'

'I can't,' Frannie said. 'Impossible. What about lunchtime tomorrow?'

'No good, I have a meeting – could we meet tomorrow evening? Come round to my flat and have supper?'

'Yes – I – I suppose so,' Frannie said, reluctant to commit herself to an evening in case she and Oliver wanted to meet up. 'Where do you live?'

'In Clapham. Thetford Avenue.'

'I know it. You're only a few streets away from me.'

Phoebe did not react to that. 'It's really important, Frannie, I mean it.'

'Don't worry. I'll come. What time?'

'About seven?'

'Sure.'

'It's number thirty-eight. Flat Three.'

Frannie jotted it down.

'Does the number *twenty-six* mean anything to you, Frannie?'

As Frannie thought for a moment, she said, 'Why?'
She could hear someone calling Phoebe impatiently.

'Look, I've got to go. Just be careful of that
number.'

'Careful? What do you mean?' She heard the impatient shout again.

'See you tomorrow. Seven o'clock.' Then Phoebe
hung up.

CHAPTER FIFTEEN

The rain had stopped some time during the afternoon, and the streets were slicked and shiny beneath the dusk sky. It was five to seven. Frannie waited outside the Museum in her mackintosh. The rush-hour traffic had thinned down now, but the fumes still hung heavily over Great Russell Street. There was a sharp toot, and Oliver roared up in his Renault.

As she climbed in the car he apologized for being late, saying he had been stuck in a meeting, then greeted her with a long kiss that left her breathless and flushed. 'You look gorgeous,' he said.

'You don't look too bad yourself.' She liked his soft blue shirt and striped tie that was predominantly orange. She kissed his knuckles, then they stared into each other's eyes as the engine ran busily on. He was looking relaxed and some of the anxiety wrinkles that had stressed his face over the weekend had gone, making his features even clearer and stronger.

'I missed you,' he said.

'Missed you too.' She was aware they were in full view of anyone coming out of the Museum but she did not care.

'Edward go off to school OK?'

'Yes, he seemed very happy.' He raised a finger. 'I had to make one solemn promise. That'd you'd be at Meston on Saturday afternoon when he comes home for the weekend.' He angled his head and smiled. 'Would that be a possibility?'

Her sadness about Meredith and her concern about Phoebe's words were forgotten for a moment. She slid her arms around him, intoxicated by the sheer warmth he was exuding towards her and by her own response to it. 'I think it could be arranged,' she said softly.

'How are the stings?'

'Hurting a little but they're a lot better today.'

Oliver eased out into the traffic. Frannie leaned back in her seat and asked, 'Edward's allowed home every weekend?'

'From lunchtime Saturdays.'

'Did you miss him today?'

'As I took Monday and Tuesday off work, I had to knuckle down today; didn't have too much time to think about him.'

'What did you do at work today?'

'I've been analysing and discussing motor-accident statistics.'

From the speed and aggression of his driving, Frannie concluded that the statistics must have left him unmoved. 'What was that for?'

'The bank's involved in reinsurance for some of the motor-car insurers. We have to make decisions based on statistics.' He was quiet for a moment as he changed lanes, aware of the direction of her thoughts. 'So, how was the funeral?'

'Grim. Her husband's being very brave. I think he's going to feel the shock later.'

'You got back last night?'

'Yes. I had some good news at work today. I'm going to work on a new exhibition, which I'm really pleased about.'

'Great! Well done!'

'Just a bit of luck, I think. And I had a rather interesting coincidence involving your family,' she said hesitantly.

'Oh yes?'

She told him about the brass tiger, but did not mention the cut she had got from it.

'The fourteenth Marquess. William Halkin,' he said thoughtfully. 'He was involved with the East India Company, I think. And with Indian politics. He gave quite a lot of works of art to museums.'

'Actually, when I first saw it I found it a bit eerie. I think your own fear of coincidences is starting to get to me.' She was jerked forward against her seat-belt as he braked hard for a red light.

'How do you mean?'

'You know on the drive back to London we saw that accident?'

He nodded, his expression turning more serious.

'Well, as soon as I got home the phone rang with the terrible news about Meredith. And after what you'd said about coincidences always seeming to mean something, I thought that was quite weird.'

The lights changed and Oliver accelerated more slowly. 'I didn't have very good news either on Sunday night. I didn't mention it on the phone. Charles rang to tell me another six cows have gone down with the virus, and the vet has said we have to stop selling our milk until the herd's clear of it.'

'Are you going to lose a lot of money?'

The traffic was snarled up ahead of them in the Charing Cross Road. Oliver halted behind a taxi that was disgorging some passengers. 'Yes; and our insurance doesn't cover it.'

'Maybe the homeopathy you're going to try will help.'

'Maybe,' he said without conviction.

They drove around Trafalgar Square into Pall Mall, then Oliver slowed, found a parking space, and backed into it. Frannie enjoyed walking along the front of the white Georgian terrace on the Mall, her hand linked with Oliver's, watching the last spangles of daylight through the trees.

At the entrance to the gallery Oliver showed his invitation, and beyond was the refined hubbub of the party in progress. A waitress stood at the top of a short staircase with a tray of drinks. Frannie could smell smoke and perfume, and a tinge of alcohol. She went across to the cloakroom, slipped off her mackintosh and laid it on the counter. An elderly, silver-haired attendant pushed a hanger inside and gave her a plastic disc.

Frannie opened her handbag and dropped the disc in. As she did so, something jolted her. Something about the disc. She dug her hand into her bag, rummaged with her fingers and retrieved the disc. It was number twenty-six.

Sudden goose-pimples prickled her neck as she remembered Phoebe's words; and her scared voice, quite out of character. *Just be careful of that number*.

She saw, to her surprise, Oliver reading the number also and frowning, with a distinct look of unease on his face; or perhaps he was frowning at something else, she wondered, dropping it back into her bag and trying to brush the moment off with a smile. She was going to enjoy herself tonight. She very definitely was not about to get spooked by a cloakroom tag.

The party was a crush of wall-to-wall glamorous women, and tall men in City suits with loud ties or unstructured jackets with T-shirts. In her black cotton jacket, tailored shorts and white T-shirt, Frannie felt fine, although she knew she should perhaps have been dressier. But Oliver seemed to approve, introducing her proudly to friends and acquaintances.

She met an art dealer called James Shenstone who

had been at Trinity College, Dublin with Declan O'Hare, and who regaled her with stories of the mischief O'Hare had got up to. He then introduced her to the artist, whose name she had already forgotten and which she failed to grasp when she heard it again. The artist was small and rather embarrassed-looking, and repeated several times to Frannie that it had not been his idea at all to hold an exhibition. When he learned that she was an archaeologist, he launched into a deep conversation about the relationship between archaeology and anthropology, before being wheeled away, shyly and rather reluctantly, for a photograph.

Frannie was then collared by an immensely boring man with a voice like gears meshing, who proceeded to lecture her for ten minutes about a lawsuit in which he was engaged, and which he assumed she had read of in the newspapers, whilst asking her not a single question about herself.

She was finally rescued by Oliver who put his arm protectively around her. 'Shall we slope off?'

She nodded gratefully, gave the bore a sweet smile and followed Oliver to the entrance. He helped her on with her mac and they stepped outside; it was almost dark. 'Sorry you got stuck with him. Did you enjoy yourself otherwise?'

'It was great. I've got some good ammunition on my boss.'

'Oh yes?'

'That art historian I was introduced to?'

'Jimmy Shenstone.'

'Yes. He was at university with my boss at the Museum. Another coincid –' She stopped in mid-sentence and gave him a guilty smile.

He gave her a hug. 'You are allowed to mention the word; I'm not totally paranoid about it. Only slightly.'

Frannie laughed. 'Race you up!'

She broke free and ran up the steps to Pall Mall, leaping them two at a time, Oliver shadowing her. They stopped at the top, breathless. 'You're crazy!' Oliver said, exhilarated.

But when they got back to the car, his face fell. 'Bugger!'

In the glare of the street light the wording of the paper square on the windscreen was clear:

WARNING. THIS VEHICLE HAS BEEN CLAMPED. DO NOT ATTEMPT TO MOVE IT. Beneath was the large star emblem of the Metropolitan Police.

Oliver insisted they leave the Renault and said he would sort it out in the morning; they took a taxi to his flat in Cadogan Square.

In contrast to the grand elegance of the exterior of the building, the flat was small and furnished almost entirely in modern furniture. There were a few ancestral oil paintings, but most of the decor and pictures were modern also. The place felt snug.

Frannie smiled, but was feeling subdued. Phoebe Hawkins' warning, *Just be careful of that number*, was lodged in her mind like an old tune. She followed Oliver into the tiny, high-tech kitchen, and waited as he removed a bottle of wine from the fridge and a couple of glasses from a cupboard.

'Are you hungry? Would you like an omelette or something?' he asked.

'I'll make it if you like.'

'Don't worry; I'll do it in a minute – let's have a drink first.' He pulled a corkscrew out of a drawer and began opening the bottle.

'Do you think there are different types of coincidence?' she said.

'How do you mean?'

'Can you make a distinction between what's just pure chance, and – I don't know – something supernatural, I suppose?'

He carried a tray through into the drawing-room, and put on a jazz cassette she did not recognize, then sat down beside her on a comfortable sofa. Behind her, through the window, she could hear the muffled sound of the traffic.

'Man has an innate need to try to make sense of things he cannot understand. One of the perverse paradoxes of physics is that there is order in chaos. As I said, I was working with road-accident statistics today. In England in 1986, 5,618 people died in road accidents. In 1987, 5,339. In 1988, 5,230. In 1989, 5,554. In 1990, 5,402. You have the same constancy in the United States only the figures are much higher.' He raised his hands in a despairing gesture. 'How the hell can they be so consistent, year after year?'

She looked at him in amazement. 'You can remember those in your head?'

'Uh huh.' He poured some wine into the glasses and handed her one. 'Cheers. Don't you think it's strange? If you think of all the combinations of bad luck and chance that make up a car crash, you would expect to get peaks and troughs – some years more, some less. But it's almost exactly the same number every year. It's constant for road deaths, for dog bites, for air-travel deaths, for cancer, heart attacks. Everything.'

'So why is that?' Frannie asked.

Oliver drank some wine then looked serious. 'There is a mathematical law of large numbers, but I don't believe that's the answer. I think there has to be something behind how the world works that we don't yet begin to understand.'

'Something supernatural?'

'I think coincidences *are* signals that a greater intelligence or consciousness is at work. But I don't have a firm conviction as to whether it is some supernatural force or entity, some God figure, or something that is simply inside us all – part of our programming.'

The music was soothing her, now. 'So was our meeting part of the chaos or part of the cosmic order?'

'Not necessarily either.' He said the words sharply, almost chidingly.

'Isn't there a theory that we read too much into coincidence? That given infinity everything is possible? That if you sat a monkey at a typewriter it would eventually recreate the entire works of Shakespeare?'

'I don't believe in infinity. Life is finite; neither humans nor monkeys live for ever. It would be far more interesting if playwrights in three different parts of the world, who had never met, all sat down and wrote exactly the same play.'

'I've heard of things like that happening.'

'Yes. They do happen. All sorts of strange things happen that are dismissed as chance. People meet on railway stations and dismiss that as chance.'

Frannie smiled.

Oliver took a small sip of his wine and pondered it for some moments. 'When we met at King's Cross, Edward and I should have been on an earlier train; we only missed it because I remembered I had to make a phone call.'

'Hey! I should have caught an earlier train also. I missed it because I had a phone call just as I was leaving the office.' She watched his face, but could read no reaction.

'We meet three years ago in your parents' café. We meet three years later at a railway station. I place an advertisement in a magazine you don't read, and you see it.' He dipped his head and raised his eyes at her.

'Didn't Jung believe in meaningful coincidence? What did he call it – Synchronicity?'

'He never explained it to his satisfaction. I think he accepted that telepathy had something to do with it.' Oliver traced a finger around the rim of his glass. 'Who was it who said that man doubts everything that can be doubted and hopes what is left over is the truth?'

'I don't know,' she said. 'That's rather beautiful.'

'I think it's a sad indictment.'

'Don't mathematicians tend to be sceptical about coincidences because the odds on things such as meeting someone you know – like at a station or an airport, or someone phoning just as you're thinking about them – are much smaller than we realize?'

'I used to think that once.' His eyes widened and he looked sad, suddenly. 'I used to really hope that was the case.' He cupped his glass in both hands beneath his chin and mustered a weak smile.

'I'm sorry, I'm talking about a sensitive subject.'

'It's OK. It's good to talk about it.'

She reached across and squeezed one of his hands. His skin was like ice. She lifted her hand away with a start and studied him. In his eyes was the same look of fear that she had seen in his car the first time he had taken her out. Then it had been fleeting, so fast she might have imagined it. This time she gripped his hand and squeezed again, alarmed. 'What is it?'

He smiled. 'I'm fine.' He squeezed her hand back. 'I'm fine,' he repeated, then stood up abruptly and walked towards the kitchen.

CHAPTER SIXTEEN

Frannie walked down Phoebe Hawkins' street shortly after seven, tired and in a bad mood. Oliver had been given tickets to a royal movie première and had asked her to go with him.

It was a damp night and a light drizzle was falling. She walked with her head bowed, clutching a bottle of Valpolicella in its tissue wrapping from the off-licence.

She itched to see Oliver again, had been missing him all day. He had rung and left a message at the office in the late morning, but she had been tied up almost the whole day with Declan O'Hare and a group of colleagues and had not seen the message until half past six.

Now, instead of being with him, she was plodding through the rain to spend an uncertain evening with someone she did not like, and her doubts were increasing. Phoebe Hawkins was sly; a manipulator who had become unpopular for that reason. At university you'd had to be careful what you told her because it would come back at you weeks later, distorted. An innocent comment about a friend would be turned into an insult and recycled to the person concerned in a quiet, underhand way, as a chance remark. Or a message would be subtly altered. For Phoebe the truth was no more than a raw material waiting to be fashioned. Frannie wondered if that was all Phoebe was up to now. Her old tricks. Making something out of nothing.

If Meredith's death and Jonathan Mountjoy's death and Susie Verbeeten's blindness were nothing.

With every step she took closer to Phoebe's street,

she felt a growing feeling of gloom. A taxi drove past, and she was tempted to hail it, to get it to take her to Leicester Square, to join the crowds outside the cinema and watch for Oliver, see who he was with. The more time she spent with him, the more she enjoyed being with him. After he'd relaxed again last night, they had made love all night through, as tenderly and as forcefully as they had on Saturday.

It had not escaped Penrose Spode's notice that she had arrived for work in the same clothes as the previous day. The shorts were not her usual office togs. He had not commented, of course, not in words; he had conveyed it all with one brief and complex manoeuvre of his facial muscles. Declan O'Hare had also noticed, because he missed nothing, and made a subtle joke connecting the brevity of her attention span to her sartorial consistency, but she had been able to keep him at bay by casually dropping that she had met an old friend of his, James Shenstone, and that he had been reminiscing about their days at Trinity College, Dublin.

She walked slowly past the parked cars that lined both sides of the street. She smelled cooking as she passed an open window, something garlicky, but she was not hungry, did not want to spend the evening drinking Valpolicella and eating nut rissoles, or whatever else Phoebe might cook, in a grotty kitchen.

A strobe flash of blue light skidded down the pavement and she heard the wailing of a siren. Frannie felt something walk over her grave. A gust of wind shook the trees in the street and a solitary leaf shuffled along the pavement.

Two coincidences yesterday: finding the bronze tiger; the number twenty-six. Then Oliver's car getting clamped. Was that a connection? Any more than

Meredith's death had been a connection after the up-turned car? Getting paranoid. She shivered. It seemed bitterly cold suddenly. Winter, not late summer. An old Buddy Holly song blasted from a window across the street. As she turned the corner, she saw ahead of her a jumble of vehicles and the stark white glare of an arc light.

For a second she wondered if there was someone filming, then a solitary blue cube of strobed light hurtled towards her and was gone. A policeman in a luminous yellow waistcoat was standing in the middle of the road, stopping a car. The next cube of blue light turned green on his chest.

In the brilliant white light behind him the first thing she saw was a bicycle wheel. Then the huge shadow of a lorry halted at an angle across the pavement. Its cab had demolished the brick wall of someone's front garden. A small crowd of people stood on the street corner, watching.

'Sorry, sir,' the policeman was saying to the driver of the car. 'Could you use another route?'

The bicycle wheel glinted in the glare of the light mounted on a tripod near it. A gear whined. A man shouted. She saw an ambulance. A fire-engine. A tender. A vast truck with a crane on the back from which a large metal hook was being lowered. Two men were trying to find a purchase beneath the front bumper of the lorry. On the panelled sides of the lorry were emblazoned in large letters: HUNSTONS WHOLE-SALE FRUITERERS. GARDEN-FRESH PRODUCE!

Frannie looked at the bicycle wheel again. It was buckled like the rest of the bike, twisted and broken like some weird modern sculpture in the Tate. *Bicycle on Paving Slab*, she thought, her brain trying to occupy itself, to distract her, to draw her away from the body under the front wheel of the lorry.

Is that lady dead, Daddy?

Edward's words as they had driven up to London on Sunday night came into her mind. Shards of blue light skidded across the wet pavement, across the woman lying in the road. Sparks of orange light followed intermittently from the roof light of the truck with the crane. Puffs of dark diesel smoke drifted across. The woman was in her twenties; Phoebe's build, she thought. About Phoebe's height. She was dressed in a kaftan and Roman sandals.

Frannie's knees collided together. Her stomach was pitching. She did not want to look any more. The woman wasn't moving but she might not be dead, she was not underneath the lorry herself; just had one arm pinned beneath its massive front wheel, as though she were stretching underneath it to reach something.

A shopping bag lay in the gutter beside her. A carton of yoghurt was on its side a short distance from it, its contents spilled on the tarmac; apples, a bunch of bananas; a polythene pack of fresh tagliatelle; a tube of tomato purée. A large shoulder-bag lay in the gutter also, a comb and a notebook beside it.

An ambulanceman walked towards the woman, shining a powerful lamp and taking slow, wary steps on the slick black tarmac as if he were walking on ice. The wheel of the lorry was turned at an angle and in the beam of the light she could see the woman's hand splayed out on the far side, flat, like a dead starfish.

Blood oozed from under the tyre. Her eye caught the word 'Pirelli' embossed close to the rim, and she read it and reread it until it became meaningless. It gave her something to concentrate on, saved her from having to look back at the woman.

Then the beam of the ambulanceman's lamp struck the woman's face. It was turned forwards, eyes closed, trails of blood already congealing.

Frannie's scream got caught in her throat and came out at first as a yammering wail of disbelief as she mouthed Phoebe's name, then ran towards her.

'Stand back, please! Stand well back, please!' a policeman shouted.

Frannie ignored him, knelt and took Phoebe's free hand, her good hand, squeezed it. 'It's OK, Phoebe, it's me,' she said, but the words came out silently, high-pitched, inaudible, like a dog whistle. Something metallic clanged above her. Someone was easing her away. A doom-laden bell clanged deep inside her. She had heard its warning knell before.

'Have to move, please,' a voice said. 'We're lifting now.'

The shadow of the lorry's bumper quivered. Frannie shook helplessly with shock. A voice called out; an engine roared; she heard the rattle of a chain. The wheel lifted a fraction of an inch and then some more, lifted clear, and a shadow swung beneath it.

Frannie could see underneath now; could see that what had once been an arm was now a flattened pulp of flesh indistinguishable from crushed bone, obscenely printed with the zigzag tread pattern of the tyre.

CHAPTER SEVENTEEN

The plastic cup dropped into place: hot black coffee jetted from the nozzle; then frothing milk; there was a sharp clunk and the machine fell silent.

Frannie removed the cup carefully, trying not to slop any over the side, and carried it back to the waiting-room, which had a depressing, lifeless feel, enhanced by the dreary green paint of the walls and the smell of vinyl from the slashed and torn leatherette seat covers.

A trolley clattered past the door. Then silence. After about five minutes a flurry of footsteps came down the corridor and Frannie looked round as the door opened. A nurse whom she recognized from earlier walked in, followed by a tall bear of a man with a tired and rather belligerent expression beneath shaggy eyebrows. He was wearing a grey suit which fitted him sloppily, the top button of his shirt was undone and his tie was loose.

'This is Miss Monsanto,' the nurse said. 'Mr Gower has been operating on your friend.'

When Frannie stood up, the surgeon gestured for her to sit and perched himself on the edge of a chair. 'We haven't been able to contact Phoebe's parents,' he said tersely. 'They'll keep on trying.' He fixed a lengthy stare on Frannie, sizing her up. 'We couldn't save her arm, I'm afraid; the bones were too badly crushed.'

Frannie heard the words one at a time, in slow motion. She felt as if something had been injected into her stomach, numbing it, and the numbness was spreading through her, up her chest, her neck, into her brain. She shook her head in dismay as the words kept on coming, each resonating, made noisier by the buzz of the faulty fluorescent above her.

'We had to amputate above the elbow. But at least she's alive.'

'Yes,' Frannie said, blankly.

'Did you see the accident happen?'

'No – I was –' She suddenly noticed the bottle of Valpolicella on the chair beside her, still wrapped in the off-licence's green tissue. 'Just going round to have supper with her.' She touched the bottle; it felt hard and cold. 'When can I visit her?'

'She'll be conscious enough to talk a bit tomorrow afternoon, but she'll be rather woozy for a day or two from the painkillers.'

Frannie walked out of the front gates of the hospital shortly after half past ten, turning her collar up and bowing her head against the worsening weather.

She was shivering, wanted someone to hold her, to put their arms around her, to tell her that she was going to be all right, that she was silly to be worried, that it was just a series of appalling coincidences, that was all.

She entered the tube station and bought a ticket. Just saying the name of the station seemed oddly comforting.

'Bethnal Green,' the man behind the glass screen repeated, an Indian with a soft voice; he smiled at her, as if the destination was special to him too, a shared secret, the place for everyone in the world who needed help. He pushed her change into the metal dish beneath his glass window and a ticket fluttered from a chute.

A long, empty escalator carried her down to the

platform. Phoebe Hawkins was not ill. But she was never going to get better. Something about that did not make sense; that was the hard part. The arm was never going to grow back. The same way that Meredith was never going to come back. Nor Jonathan Mount-joy. Susie Verbeeten was never going to see again. And young Dominic's right hand would never be the same.

Rain as hard as grit stung Frannie's face as she came out of Bethnal Green Station and hurried along the road. She enjoyed a brief respite under the twin railway bridges, running her hand along the metal railing like she used to as a child, lifting it at each join, her nostrils filled with the familiar unpleasant reek of urine.

She came out into the rain again, passed a used-car lot, a filling-station forecourt, and a grubby parade of take-away cafés and shops. There were few people around. Across the road was the playground of her school. Once, it had seemed so big you could get lost in it, now it was just a small tarmac yard with painted lines and a practice basketball net fixed to a wall; a place where a little girl she could now barely remember had once gone every day except holidays, for twelve years.

A few blocks away, set back from the main road in a backwater of quiet darkness, was the church and priory of Our Lady of Assumption. It was an old, solid church, red brick Gothic, traditional.

Frannie had gone with her parents to mass every Sunday of her childhood. Her faith had begun to dwindle during her mid-teens, but it wasn't until she had left school for university that she had given up going altogether. There was no one thing that had changed her heart, only a gradual build-up of doubts over the years, and a need to search for answers her own way.

An old woman at a bus-stop struggled with a small umbrella. The cinema had 'Kevin Costner' in lights above the porch. The fish-and-chip shop was closed; the Quikburger two doors along was open, with a solitary punter slouched against the counter, reading the menu. The smell of frying onions made Frannie feel queasy. Her thoughts swung around inside her head.

One by one. Chance. Coincidence. Nothing more. Please God, nothing more.

Fear was inside her bones. A bus thundered past; a truck. Her feet were sodden and her right leg ached badly. She removed her right hand from her pocket, slid it inside her mackintosh and up to her neck. Lapsed Catholic Francesca Monsanto pulled on the thin chain around her neck until she could feel the small silver crucifix, and squeezed it lightly. She had put it on this morning for the first time in ages.

It was half past eleven when she rang the bell of the door that was bounded on one side by the dark premises of Sandwich Paradiso and on the other by the dingily lit and smoky office of King Minicabs.

After a few moments a light appeared in the window above the door. She heard the stairs creak and the door juddered, once. A motor cycle caterwauled up the street behind her and a cloud of oily two-stroke fumes drifted over her; her father's voice shouted: 'Yessawhoseit?'

'It's me, Papa. Frannie.'

She heard the rattle of a chain; bolts sliding; then the door opened. Her father stared at her in surprise, his face heavy with stubble as it always was in the evenings. He was wearing a ragged towelling dressing-gown over striped pyjamas; his hair was tousled and she suddenly saw how grey it had become, surprised she had not noticed before.

'Francesca! Hey! Why you here so late?' He put his arms around her and they hugged each other, kissing both cheeks in turn, and she held him tightly, the slight, bony man who was no taller than herself. She smelled the wine and tobacco on his breath, the hair oil he still used and the laundered freshness of his pyjamas. She felt the hard bristles of his stubble against her cheek. She wished he could envelop her in his arms the way he had when she was small, wished he still felt like her father and not a stranger.

He released her gently, standing back a little, shaking his head. 'Where you was on Sunday? Why you no phone? We was worried abou' you.' The bones of his face pressed through the sallow skin and his eyes were sunken, as if he had a wasting disease, but it was just the years of working long hours, the lack of exercise and fresh air that had left him with a weary air of defeat; as if he was aware that life was too big for him and he had abandoned trying to match up to it. Instead he lived vicariously through movies, to which he was addicted, spending almost all his free time in front of the television. He looked down at her leg and his face became tender with concern. 'Was happen? You had an accident?'

She glanced down and was surprised to see a rip in the right leg of her jeans. She touched it with her finger and it hurt. 'I – I hadn't noticed.'

'Where you fell?' He touched her cheek lightly with his finger. 'You look terrible.' There was a sudden flash of suspicion in his eyes. 'You had a fight? Boy kick you? Come in.' He pressed against the wall to let her past and closed the door.

She climbed the steep stairs, still clutching the Valpolicella. She heard the television; there were loud voices, shots, an engine roared and tyres squealed. Her mother's voice called out: '*Chi è, Papa?*'

'Francesca. *Ha avuto un incidente!*' he replied urgently.

Tyres squealed again; there were more shots; the sound of a siren. At the top of the stairs her father opened the door to the sitting-room and switched on the light. 'Get you some stuff; bandage; antiseptic. You like coffee? Glass of wine?' There was a faint aroma of fried garlic.

The walls were bare, but the small room with a dining alcove was cluttered by a huge three-piece suite, too many chairs, and by the china ornaments her mother collected.

'Coffee would be nice.' Frannie held out the wine. 'A present,' she said. 'To say sorry for Sunday.' She sat in an armchair and looked at the artificial brick fireplace. On the mantelpiece there were photographs of herself, her sister and her two brothers, as well as a vase of silk orchids, a Capo di Monte tramp on a park bench and a white plastic Virgin Mary statuette. The window faced the busy street; through the net curtains she saw the lights of a lorry that was grinding up the street, then she saw the top deck of a bus slide past, empty apart from one glum-looking man. The car chase continued on the television in her parents' bedroom, down the landing.

'So who kick you, who wasa it? You gotta boyfriend?'

'No one kicked me, Papa. A friend of mine has just had a horrible accident on her bicycle. I must have got cut when I knelt down.'

'*Mamma mia! Povera Francesca!*' Frannie turned,

alarmed by the hysterical high-pitched yell of her mother who ran towards her in her dressing-gown, her hair inside a bath cap and cream on her face. She knelt beside Frannie, gave her a kiss on each cheek. 'Accident? You have accident?' She ran a finger through Frannie's hair, shaking her head in distress, and talking quickly in Italian, barely giving Frannie a chance to reply or explain. She left the room and came back moments later with a towel, a wet flannel, iodine and sticking-plaster, firing questions in Italian at Frannie as she helped her out of her jeans.

Her father came in with coffee on a tray and sweet biscuits, and she suddenly felt weepy at the simple kindness of her parents, feeling as if she did not deserve their pampering. She had no appetite but remembered she had skipped lunch, had had no supper and needed something to give her energy, so she managed a sandwich forced on her by her father.

'You know what?' her father said. 'Saturday I went into the City to see the new building where the café was. And you know something? They don't built it yet.' There was astonishment in his voice; and despair. 'They don't start it! Poulterers' Alley, the café, not demolished yet!'

'Nothing at all, Papa?'

'They is working on the demolishing – but that should have been two years ago. Is another two years we could have stayed there.' He lit a cigarette and she saw her mother's frown of disapproval. 'Is probably archaeologists digging.'

'I have a new boyfriend,' she said, changing the subject, not wanting to rise to his bait.

Her father's eyes widened with interest and he leaned forward further.

'Boyfrenna?' her mother said, her expression also changing. '*Come si chiama?*'

'Oliver,' Frannie said.

'Olivier!' her mother pronounced, boldly. '*Un bel nome!*'

'Oliver,' her father echoed.

Frannie smiled, feeling faintly embarrassed, wishing she hadn't mentioned it now, afraid that it might be bad luck; they had only been going out for just over a week.

'So what he do, this Oliver?' her father said. 'Archaeologist or he got a real job?'

She shook her head lamely. 'No, he's not an archaeologist; he's a mathematician.'

Her father stared at her sadly. 'Archaeologist; mathematician; what the difference? *Ecco.* You come here in the middle of the night in this state . . .' He drew on his cigarette, pinching it between his finger and thumb, and shook his head despairingly. 'When you gonna grow up, Francesca?' He stroked her hair down over the back of her head. 'When you gonna understand the real world?'

She looked back at him, the distance between them as great as ever.

Her father sighed. There was a long silence, which he finally broke. 'You stay here tonight, OK? I clean your clothes, make them nice and dry for the morning, give you a good breakfast.'

She closed her eyes and nodded, too tired to argue, even to think. A wave of exhaustion overcame her, sapping her. She wanted to sleep.

In the morning, when Frannie woke, her clothes were laid out on the chair in the tiny spare room. It was seven o'clock and the flat was empty. She showered and dressed, then went down to the café beneath. The radio was on, playing schmaltz. Her father was cutting and buttering bread, and her mother was silently mixing tuna and onion.

'Can I do anything?' she said.

Her mother wiped her hands down the front of her apron and kissed her on both cheeks; her mother's skin felt soft and cold.

'You sit, I going to make you nice breakfast,' her father said. 'Get soma food inside you.'

'Thanks,' she smiled and it felt like old times, suddenly. It was a fine morning outside, and the sun shone straight in through the window. A street cleaner drove past and the rush-hour traffic was already building up, heading into London.

She sat on one of the familiar hard chairs at a narrow table, moving the ketchup and bottle of brown sauce out of the way.

'How you sleep?' her father asked, cracking eggs into a bowl. Butter sizzled.

She told him she had slept soundly. Not adding that it was for the first time in several days; deep, dreamless sleep. She felt more refreshed this morning; and hungry.

Her father held up an egg, then looked at her uncertainly. 'But you was a having bad dreams, huh?'

She shook her head. 'No.' She smiled.

'You give your mother and I a big fright.' He tapped the egg gently without breaking it, then looked at her again. 'You talking in your sleep.'

She frowned and a little of the light seemed to fade from the room. 'What did I say?'

He shrugged, broke the egg with one hand and released the contents into the bowl. Then he beat them hard with a fork, before grinding in some black pepper. 'Is mumbo-jumbo. No make sense. Is a foreign language.' Her father looked worried. 'You scared us, your mama and I.'

'What do you mean?'

'Not like you talking. Like someone else is a talking through you.'

She saw the seriousness on both their faces, and felt her skin go clammy.

'Something is no good, Francesca,' he said solemnly. 'Something no good at all.'

CHAPTER EIGHTEEN

'You look very white,' Penrose Spode said across the barren gloss of his desk. 'Are you all right?'

Frannie nodded.

'Late night?' The perfect circle of his mouth stretched into a knowing smile.

'Wasn't like that, Penrose. I'm afraid I didn't get lucky last night.' She still didn't know how well he'd got to know Phoebe, but she wasn't ready to face telling him about the accident.

Her reply caused a rather stranded expression to appear on his face, as if he did not know quite how to take it. He opened his mouth, then closed it again, cancelling whatever further observation he had been contemplating.

As soon as he left his desk to go down the corridor, she looked up the phone number of a florist and ordered some flowers to be sent to Phoebe in hospital, and a note with them, charged to her Access card. Whilst part of her brain did that on autopilot, her active waking consciousness contemplated the coincidence of four people from the same year at university dead or maimed within a short space of time.

She confronted it with clear logic; with rational thought; with the probability theory that had rubbed off from a few conversations with Oliver Halkin. She could also hear her father's worried words echoing through her, but everyone sleep-talked when they were worried; and mostly in gibberish.

Later in the morning Oliver rang to ask how she was, and about her evening. She told him about

Phoebe's accident and he was both horrified and sympathetic. Just as he had been about Meredith's. She asked him how the première had gone. Even when he said it had not been any fun without her, it only lifted her spirits a little.

'Pick you up at half nine tomorrow?'

'Right.' She kept it simple, aware of Spode's ears.

She held the receiver to her ear for several seconds after he had hung up, scared suddenly that it might be the last link between them; that she might never see him again.

Scared of the rest of her life.

Frannie stared at the name of the ward written in grey lettering on a green strip above the double doors: LYTTLETON. She steeled herself.

Hospitals scared her; they always had done: their smells, their sounds. You walked into a hospital and you took a step too close to death for comfort.

She pushed open the door and went over to the nursing station. The ward sister told her that Phoebe was down at the end, around the corner; she said her parents had just left, and asked her not to stay too long as Phoebe was sedated and tired, and should go back to sleep soon.

There was a reek of polish and disinfectant and the bland, lingering smell of mashed potato. A commotion was going on behind the curtains screening one bed. She passed an elderly, almost bald woman whose cheeks were indented, making her mouth look like a belly-button, and a woman in her fifties, knitting busily and holding court to her family.

The ward opened into an L-shape at the end. Phoebe was in the far corner, lying prostrate with a cage over her midriff. There was a window beyond her with blue curtains that had not yet been drawn against the darkness. Frannie felt a lump in her throat. Phoebe was staring at the ceiling, eyes half closed, her face the colour of chewing gum. Headphones hung from a hook above her; the anglepoise lamp was switched off; a bowl of fruit, a vase of flowers and several cards sat on the table.

There was a drip stand beside the bed that was not connected. Phoebe's right hand lay outside the bed-clothes; a cannula was taped to the back of it and a yellow plastic bracelet was strapped around her wrist.

Frannie saw flesh coming out of the other sleeve of the hospital gown and for a brief moment thought that Phoebe was all right, that the surgeon, Mr Gower, had been wrong, had been able to save her arm after all.

Then she saw where it ended, a thin little stump with the bandage over the end like an outsize thumb-stall. A dwarf, handless arm, like a Thalidomide child's. Slender and pathetic.

Her head suddenly felt hot and a swell of giddiness disorientated her. She looked at Phoebe's face, then at her stump again. For a moment the two became discon-nected, belonged to separate people. The stump be-longed to someone else. The Phoebe she knew had two arms.

She stepped closer, then stood still again, struggling to keep her composure. She looked harder, just to make sure Phoebe wasn't playing a joke on her the way Declan O'Hare had played a joke on her yesterday, and that the arm wasn't bent back, the way her father used to bend back his pinkie, hold up his hand, show the rest of his fingers and pretend he had bitten the pinkie off.

On Phoebe's forehead there was a small Band-aid and a larger strip on her cheek. Her eyes registered

Frannie's presence impassively. Frannie tried to keep a bright face, knowing that she must be strong, must not let Phoebe think losing an arm was a disaster, mustn't let her think it was any worse than having her tonsils out; needed her to understand that people lost arms and stuff all the time and it was no big deal. No bigger deal than having a cold or missing a bus. Or leaving the fridge door open.

Who the hell needed two arms?

She breathed in hard, stood by the bed and numbly took Phoebe's right hand. There was a faint hint of a squeeze back.

'Hello, Phoebe,' she said.

There was a delay of several seconds before Phoebe responded, in a weak and slurred voice. 'Frnne.'

Frannie sat down on the chair beside the bed and looked at a large humorous card with nurses whizzing across a ward on skateboards. She squeezed Phoebe's hand again. 'You poor thing.'

Phoebe's eyes moved slowly to Frannie's face. The lids closed, then opened again as she struggled against sleep. Frannie again felt a light pressure reciprocated on her hand. She felt she had better not waste time.

'You were going to tell me something last night, Phoebe, that was very important. Can you remember?'

After a few seconds, the girl in the bed gave a single nod. Then there was confusion in her eyes. 'Made me ride out in front of she lorry. Made me shink I could beat she lorry.'

'*Who* made you?'

There was a long silence. Phoebe's eyes closed and Frannie waited, praying they would open again, that she wasn't going to drift into sleep. She looked around, saw that there were no nurses looking, and shook

Phoebe's good arm gently. 'Who made you ride in front of the lorry, Phoebe?'

Phoebe's eyes opened and she looked at Frannie in confusion and surprise. 'Ouija,' she said.

'Ouija?' Frannie repeated.

Phoebe reached out suddenly, tugging feebly, pulling Frannie towards her, pleading with her eyes. Her lips parted. Her eyes were trying to communicate something; she spoke but it was too faint. Frannie leaned further forward, laying her cheek close to Phoebe's own.

'The Ouija. Warn them, Frannie.'

Frannie was confused. 'Ouija? Can you explain? Please.'

Then suddenly she realized what Phoebe was talking about; and a small bomb of fear exploded inside her.

CHAPTER NINETEEN

March 1988

As the dilapidated Volkswagen, crammed with eight other third-year students from London University, pulled into the kerb, Frannie Monsanto slipped her fingers inside her T-shirt and felt comforted by the touch of her crucifix. She knew that what they were doing was wrong. An hour ago it had seemed a great idea, but now the booze was wearing off, and the courage it had given her was replaced with a deepening disquiet, and the knowledge of what had happened the last time she had been down there.

'Just over on the left, past the garbage bags,' she said.

The camper halted with a lurch and the thump of music died with the engine. They piled out and stood on the pavement, an incongruous gaggle with wild hair and beat-up clothes, blinking in the fine rain and the orange sodium twilight of the street lamps as if they had been deposited in an alien land by a spacecraft. Above them on either side rose the dark, silent windows of banks and insurance companies. In the square mile of the City of London, the streets that teemed with people in the daytime were quiet every night; on Saturday they were dead.

A solitary car drove past, its tyres cutting crisply through the puddles, the reflections of its tail-lights following like a ghost across the varnished tarmac. Seb Holland locked the camper's doors. Flecks of drizzle tickled Frannie's cheeks as she led the way around the corner, past the John Templar Employment Bureau

with its cards in the window: SECRETARY FOR MD. SALES
– COMMISSION ONLY. PART-TIME 2-DAY BOOK KPR. SHIP-
PING CLERK. And into a narrow alley that was much
darker. She walked past a barber, a newsagent, a heel
bar and a tailor, then stopped and rummaged in her
bag for her keys. Water seeped through the cork soles
of her canvas shoes.

'Hey, wow!' Seb said. 'This your dad's place?'

Frannie nodded.

'Great!' said someone else.

Above the small shop-window was a row of twelve-
inch-high dayglo letters, two of which were missing:
SANDW CH S LUIGI CAFE.

Four small suction cups held a white plastic menu
against the inside of the window. EAT IN OR TAKE AWAY
was printed along the bottom. A cracked plastic sign
suspended across the window on a thin chain proclaimed: BREAKFAST SPECIAL! Salamis and sausages
hung from butcher's hooks; an ultraviolet fly-trap
above the counter filled the dark interior of the café
with a purple sheen.

Frannie unlocked the front door and went inside,
into the familiar smells of the spiced meats and olive
oil, coffee beans and cleaning fluid. She pressed one of
the light switches; a fluorescent threw a stark pool of
light over the rear of the sandwich bar, emitting a
steady buzz that joined the hum of the fridges.

The shelves inside the glass counter were bare. A
solitary wicker basket containing packets of crisps sat
on top. There was an electronic cash register, a row of
bar stools in front of a formica-topped shelf along the
far wall, and a cluster of tiny tables with banquette
seats and plastic chairs. A creased poster of Naples
and one of Amalfi adorned the back wall. Both posters
were old, their colours faded, their corners uneven,

with bits missing where they had many times in the past torn away from the crude strips of Sellotape that held them up.

The posters were as much a part of the place as her father's cheery greeting to each customer, whether he knew them or not: 'Hi, how y'doin? What y'gonna 'ave today?' Together with her mother's silent concentration, preparing sandwiches, making hot drinks, pushing earthenware bowls of pasta into the microwave. People mistook this silence for sullenness, but it was only that in the twenty-eight years since they had left the backstreets of Naples to come to England in search of prosperity, her mother had never succeeded in mastering enough of the language even to hold the most basic conversation.

A moth fizzed and crackled on the mesh of the fly-trap. The place was old, unchanged since her parents had taken the lease in 1957, and spotlessly clean, the way they left it every evening, Mondays to Fridays, at around six, when they closed. Frannie had spent more time in here as a child than she had at their flat in Bethnal Green. Almost every day of her school holidays she had worked in here, and she still came in and helped during vacations now she was at university, although less than before.

'I'll have a pastrami and dill on rye,' Max Gabriel said, staring across the blank counter, shaking his tousled blond hair away from his eyes.

'Hey, Luigi, one alligator sandwich – and make it snappy!' Seb Holland boomed, towering over the counter, then looking round and grinning. 'Hey, Luigi! Service, hey!'

There was a sharp crackle as the moth's wing burnt and the creature fell to the floor of the trap where it lay twitching among the carcasses of the flies and wasps. Frannie locked the front door. The sign SORRY CLOSED swung gently against the glass, and she made sure it was still facing outwards; she felt a lump in her throat and was not sure whether it was fear or guilt, or the realization that she had made a mistake in having brought all her friends in, in having suggested the place, in having gone along with the idea at all.

The trapdoor to the cellar was in the tiny passage that separated the front of the café from the kitchenette and toilets. As a child Frannie had been fascinated by the cellar and at the same time terrified by it. Paolo, her eldest brother, said the bogeyman lived down there, and Frannie had believed him; it was big enough, and dark enough. The bogeyman could have lived there for ever, scraping water off the damp walls, nibbling at the stores her father kept. The bogeyman stayed out of sight, lurking somewhere in the shadows (watching her, Paolo said) whenever she went down with her father to open one of the crates of cheeses, meats and olives that were regularly delivered from Palermo when she was a child; the bogeyman was afraid of her father. But not of her.

She had seen the bogeyman once: the last time she had been down there.

At least, she had seen his shadow. It was five years ago, maybe longer. They didn't use the cellar any more, hadn't really used it for a good ten years; a wholesaler started stocking all the items her father needed and he found it easier and more profitable to pick up his requirements on a weekly basis than to have goods shipped in bulk from Italy.

'We need some paper,' Susie Verbeeten was saying bossily. Her black hair was cropped short around the sides then spread vertically above her scalp as if it had sprung from a jack-in-the-box. Her mother was supposed to be a white witch, which was how Susie Verbeeten knew about the occult. 'And a thick marker pen.'

Jonathan Mountjoy stood as he usually did with his hands in his pockets, staring vacantly upwards, his brain focused on a different spectrum. Lynn Frickers, small and bird-like, looked nervously at Frannie. 'I'm just wondering whether I ought to get back. I have a lot of reading to get done by Monday.'

Bob Castle, whose face muscles rose and sagged between the fronds of his flimsy ginger beard, nodded. 'Yes, I –' His eyes darted around the room. 'I have to be up early – I think I – ought . . .'

Frannie went into the tiny alcove behind the fridges, to the cabinet where the stationery was kept. 'How much paper?' she called out, and was startled by how edgy her voice sounded.

'We need to make twenty-eight squares about three inches by three inches,' Susie Verbeeten replied.

Frannie took out several sheets, some scissors and a black marker pen. Lynn Frickers, with Bob Castle standing like a faithful dog behind her, was trying to open the front door. Frannie unlocked it and let them both out, then locked it again behind them, secretly wishing she could follow. The back of her scalp felt tight and her throat was dry.

'Dunno why they bothered coming in the first place,' Meredith Minns said. 'They're no bloody use to any-body!'

Frannie tossed her long brown hair away from her face and grinned, the cheery normality of Meredith's voice allaying her fears for a moment. She handed the paper to Susie, then went into the back of the shop, knelt on the old linoleum beside the trapdoor, slid her fingers under the metal hoops and lifted hard. The heavy door came free with a crackling sound, and a cobweb rose up with it. An angry spider scuttled out of sight. Cold, musty air that smelled of damp stone and rotting wood poured out, enveloping her, seeped through her wet clothes into her skin, and she stared at the wooden steps that descended almost vertically, their bottom rungs swallowed by the blackness, with a sudden sickening feeling of dread.

Five years ago she had scrambled, whimpering, up those steps. Chased by the bogeyman. She had been looking for the entrance to a secret passage that was supposed to lead down to the Thames and that had been bricked in centuries ago. Then a shadow had moved behind her, and with it had come a sharp scrape. As she had turned her torch towards it, the bulb had failed.

It might have been her imagination, she knew. Or a tramp or a wino. The cellars interconnected. You could crawl under the arches, working your way beneath half the City of London. This part of London was riddled with secret passages dating back to the Middle Ages and which were used by prisoners escaping from the Tower, by Royalists during the Civil War, by smugglers.

For five years she had wanted to go back down to that cellar and prove to herself that the shadow had been nothing, just a trick of light. Each time she had plucked up courage she had chickened out because there had been no one else to accompany her. But tonight in the downstairs room of the pizzeria they had been fooling around, joking, a little drunk, telling ghost stories and trying to scare each other. So when Seb Holland had suggested a Ouija board session, or maybe it had been Meredith Minns, and Susie Verbeeten had said it needed total darkness, Frannie told them she knew the ideal place.

'Seb, do you have a torch in your van?' she said, remembering now that there was no light in the cellar.

'Yes, I'll get it.'

Meredith Minns wandered over and stood beside her, staring down. 'Yeeech! God, what's down there?'

'Nothing,' Frannie said. 'Empty boxes and stuff.'

'Perfect,' Susie said, peering over her shoulder.

'Looks horrible,' Max said. 'Why don't we do it up here?'

'Because you need somewhere where there isn't anyone else around, and total darkness,' Susie said.

'Why total darkness?' Meredith asked.

'Because, daaahlink,' Seb said, his voice turning Slavic, and running his fingers up her back, 've are going to summon up ze Prince of Darkness. Yee ha hahhh!'

Meredith shivered and grinned. 'Stopppit!'

Seb unlocked the front door and went to get his torch. Susie cut twenty-eight squares of paper, wrote in capitals a single letter of the alphabet on each one in turn and on the final two the single word *Yes* and the single word *No*.

'We need a glass,' Susie said, 'and a flat surface, and a candle.'

'There's probably a crate down there that's suitable, otherwise we can bring down a table,' Frannie said, resting the trapdoor back against its hinges.

Max stared around the café. 'Should think this place is a gold-mine – right in the middle of the City – perfect.'

'The rent's very high,' Frannie said, and thought for a moment about her parents: up at five every morning making the sandwiches; always struggling to pay the bills, struggling to gain a few more years on the lease the landlords wanted to terminate for redevelopment; always dreaming of returning to Naples laden with riches. But the reality was that they would never return, not now. Their family and friends had died, or moved or changed; the past they had left behind them in Italy was as threadbare as the future that lay before them in England. In a couple of years the lease ran out, this time for good, and the whole building would be coming down. Her parents would have to move on, start again elsewhere; tired, ageing people, their hope beaten flat like old metal.

Frannie found a box of candles in the cupboard beside the kitchen sink, took one out, picked up the matches off the gas ring and waited for Seb. He came back in the front door, locked it behind him and gave her a large rubber torch.

She switched it on, flashed the powerful beam down into the darkness and saw the blob of white light slide across the floor. Then, tucking the candle and matches into the back pockets of her jeans, she climbed slowly down the wooden steps, holding the torch with one hand and each step, in turn, tightly with the other.

As she reached the bottom she felt an uncomfortable sense of isolation. Susie Verbeeten's face seemed a long way above her. The cold air bit through her clothes, blew on her skin. She shone the torch out into the bitumen blackness that surrounded her, tried to dispel her unease. Shadows jumped. A steady, echoing ping . . . ping . . . ping rang out as rainwater leaked through from somewhere above.

Columns stretched out into the distance either side of her and behind her: squat stone columns and ribbed arches that had been built to shore up the cellars after the spreading waters of the Thames had eaten away some of the foundations centuries ago. Far thicker than they probably needed to be, they dated from a time long before engineering stresses and tolerances had been understood. The walls were brick, damp and crumbling, and it was rumoured that victims of the Plague were cemented in behind them.

She played the beam around, but could see nothing she didn't recognize. Several empty cardboard boxes listed badly, their bases eaten by the damp that came up through the floor. Then she swung the beam away with a shudder as she realized it was shining on a decomposing rat.

'OK?' Susie called down, and her voice echoed. *Ok-ayyy?*

'Yup, fine!' she called back. *Yup-ine-ine-ine*, her voice echoed; then she guided each of them down the steps with the torch.

'Spoooooky!' Seb said, shoving his hands into his pockets and looking around.

'Perfect,' Susie said, then looked dubiously upwards. 'I think we ought to shut the trapdoor. We don't want any light at all.'

Seb climbed up and reached for the handle. The trapdoor fell with a heavy thud that gave Frannie a sudden claustrophobic feeling.

She guided him back down, then swept the torch over each of her friends' faces in turn for reassurance. They nearly all looked uncomfortable. Even Seb seemed to have lost some of his bravado. Only Susie seemed unconcerned as she selected a wide plywood packing-case with a flat base, placed the glass upturned in the middle, then laid the letters randomly in a surrounding circle, with the words *Yes* and *No* among them. 'Make a circle round the packing-case with things to sit on,' she said.

'Yeek!' Meredith screamed, clutching Jonathan Mountjoy. 'I saw something move.'

Frannie swung the torch and saw a rat or a large mouse disappear behind the arches at the far end.

'Have you got the candle, Frannie?' Susie asked.

Frannie pulled the candle out of her pocket and struck a match. The acrid smell of the sulphur was comforting against the dank mustiness. Susie took the candle, let a few drops of molten wax fall on the packing-case and stood the candle firmly in it, cursing as a drop of hot wax fell on her finger. A barrel scraped across the floor as Jonathan Mountjoy moved it. Frannie turned her head, startled by the sound, the memory of the shadow and the scrape returning. Then everyone sat down.

'Torch off, please, Frannie,' Susie said.

Frannie switched it off. The darkness seemed to jump in towards them, the weak, oval, yellow glow of candlelight barely keeping it at bay. A small pool of shadow rocked around the base of the candle as the flame guttered. A cold draught blew like a breath across Frannie's neck. She could smell the hot wax and the fainter smell of the spent match. The drip of rainwater out in the darkness still pinged steadily. The flame guttered again, more so, and Frannie felt the downy, invisible hairs on her arms stiffen. Her cotton 'Free Nelson Mandela' T-shirt clung to her like a wet towel.

Three sharp raps rang out, startling her. Then a ghostly voice boomed: 'Is anyone there?'

Meredith giggled.

Three raps again.

'Seb,' Susie said sharply.

'Yeeh-hahh-hahhh!' he replied, his voice low and resonating.

Fingers crawled up Frannie's neck and she jumped. 'Seb – for God's sake!' Then she grinned, momentarily relieved of the oppressive tension she felt. Maybe this was the best thing, just joke, fool around, don't get too serious.

'I can feel the spirits,' Seb said. 'I can feel them all over me.' He wriggled.

'Seb,' Max said quietly, 'I think we should all calm down now and be serious.'

Meredith Minns was smiling uncertainly. In the weak light, the pasty whiteness of her skin against her brilliant red lipstick and her gelled black hair presented a ghostly appearance. Susie Verbeeten stared imperiously around.

'Hey, darlings, I'm just wondering whether I should really stay,' Meredith said, tossing her head theatrically. 'I have to get some reading done – I have another exam on Monday.'

'You can't possibly leave now!' Susie said. 'We need at least six to create enough energy to summon the spirit. And someone to control it.'

Meredith chewed the inside of her cheek.

'Right,' Susie said, 'everyone put one finger on the glass. Very lightly, don't push. It's really important you don't push.'

Frannie could read the name 'Helix' stamped in the base of the glass as she reached out tentatively, touching other hands that were jostling for space, then rested her index finger on the glass. It was vibrating, jerking in different directions.

'Stop pushing it,' Susie said. 'You're all pushing it!'

The glass became still.

'Now close your eyes, everyone.'

Frannie stared out into the darkness beyond the glow of the candle, then down at the fingers on the glass. She closed her eyes.

They sat in silence for some moments. Frannie could feel the pressure on the glass.

'Is there a spirit here?' Susie said, quietly. 'If there is a spirit who has joined us will you answer us by moving the glass.'

There was a low rumbling in the distance. It grew louder. Louder still. Frannie could feel the glass twitching. The rumbling increased, echoing around the cellar, rising to a crescendo din.

'Jesus!' Jonathan said.

'Tube,' Frannie said, her eyes shut. 'Just a tube train – Central Line.'

'Bloody good, Susie,' Seb said. 'You've managed to call up the spirit of a tube train.'

Meredith giggled. The rumble faded.

'Could you get us a cross-Channel ferry next?' Seb said.

Meredith giggled again.

'How about a Boeing 747,' Max said.

'Quiet,' Susie hissed angrily. 'Concentrate!'

The glass jigged.

'There *is* something here. Something is in here with us. I can feel it.' Susie raised her voice. 'Is there a spirit with us? Is there a spirit here who wants to talk to us?'

Frannie swallowed; the silence of the cellar magnified every sound. She could hear the boomf-boomf-boomf of her heart, the blood coursing through her veins like the roar of distant traffic, the gurgling as she swallowed again. The cellar became sharply colder, as if the door to a freezer had been opened. She stiffened. She could sense the change, as if there was something or someone else in here with them now. It was standing behind her, passing a magnet or a sheet of cellophane a few inches over her skin, drawing up the hairs, its icy breath blowing through her bones as if she were transparent. She kept her eyes tightly shut, clenched the lids together, too frightened to see.

'A spirit has joined us,' Susie Verbeeten announced.

Icy claws raked Frannie's skin. She wanted to stop now, she was too afraid to go on any more.

'We have a spirit with us,' Susie said, louder. 'Do you want to talk to us?'

The glass jerked sharply with a loud scrape, several inches to the right, and then stopped.

'*Yes*,' Susie said, her voice rising in pitch with excitement. 'It says *yes*!' Her voice regained its imperiousness. 'Who are you? Please tell us your name.'

Frannie felt the glass move again. It skidded across the surface of the packing-case and stopped abruptly.

'The letter N,' Susie said.

The glass moved again. 'Don't push it, just let it move, let the spirit move it. O,' she said, her voice tight with concentration.

It moved again.

'N.'

'*Non*,' Jonathan Mountjoy said. 'French for *no*.'

The glass moved again. 'O – M – N – I – S,' Susie spelled out.

'*Omnis*,' Max Gabriel said.

'It's Latin,' Seb said. 'You've got hold of a Roman centurion. Hi there, Polonius!'

Meredith giggled.

The glass moved again, startling them all. 'M – O – R – I – A – R,' Susie spelt. '*Non omnis moriar*.'

'*Non omnis moriar*,' Max Gabriel echoed.

'Who can remember their Latin?' Susie said.

'Me – I can,' Frannie croaked. Her throat was now so dry that she was barely able to speak.

'What does it mean?'

'It's a quote from Horace,' she said, her voice barely louder than a whisper.

'*Doris* did you say?' said Seb.

Meredith giggled again, a forced, nervous sound this time.

'Horace,' Frannie repeated quietly. Her arm was trembling. '*Non omnis moriar*. It means: I shall not altogether die.'

CHAPTER TWENTY

September 1991

The tube doors opened and Frannie looked up with a start, snapping out of her thoughts. Clapham South. She scrambled to her feet and just made it out of the doors before they closed again, then stood on the platform, remembering.

Oliver's family motto. *Non omnis moriar.*

Tension coiled through her. Another coincidence. Unless her memory was wrong. The train slid out of the station behind her, accelerating with a fierce whine. A gust of grimy underground wind curled around her, then followed the tail of the train into the tunnel.

Altering the past to make it fit. The mind did that; the mind played tricks constantly. She thought back hard as the escalator carried her upwards. Three years ago – longer – three and a half years ago; it had been near the end of the spring term in her last year at university and they had been out celebrating someone's birthday in the basement of the cheap pizzeria they used to frequent.

It was Susie Verbeeten who had suggested the Ouija session. Susie Verbeeten who had run it. Bossy Susie, far bossier than Phoebe. Susie had claimed her mother was a white witch, and that was how she knew about doing the Ouija properly.

But Susie was now blind.

As Frannie hurried back to her flat she wondered how she could get hold of her. She knew that her mother lived in Sussex, remembered Susie telling her it was the village where Virginia Woolf had once lived. Rodmell! She remembered that, although she wasn't sure why. The number should be easy to get, Verbeeten wasn't a common name.

She picked two days' worth of post from the hall floor: bills, mostly, and a birthday card with Italian stamps and a Naples postmark, from her aunt, who every year sent her a card that unfailingly defeated the Italian postal system and arrived early. Then she went into the living-room and dialled Directory Enquiries, doodling on the back of a telephone bill envelope as she waited.

NON OMNIS MORIAR, she wrote in capitals, then scrawled down the number and dialled it immediately.

The phone was answered by a woman with a small, high-pitched voice that had a hint of a smoker's gravelliness about it: 'I'll just get her for you. Who's calling, please?'

'Frannie Monsanto. We were at university together.'

She heard the sound of the receiver being lifted. Then Susie greeted her with a warm and cheery 'Spags! How are you?!'

Frannie was taken aback. It was as if they hadn't spoken for a couple of days; not for over three years. 'Fine, I'm fine.'

'What are you up to?'

Frannie told her. Susie seemed genuinely interested to know about her work, to know exactly what she had been doing since university, with whom she had kept in touch.

'I wondered if you are going to be down in Sussex over the weekend?' Frannie said.

'Yes, I'm here all the time.'

'Are you anywhere near a village called Meston, outside Lewes?'

'Yes, why?'

'That's where I'll be this weekend.'

'For heaven's sake, Frannie! That's about four miles away! Come over and see us – have a drink or a meal.'

'Love to. When would be best?'

'Any time at all – I've got no plans.'

Frannie hesitated. 'Susie – do you remember that Ouija session we once had underneath my parents' café?'

'Funny you should mention that.'

'Why?'

'Phoebe Hawkins asked me the same thing.'

'Recently?'

'Yes. She rang me on Tuesday evening and told me she had just been to Meredith's funeral. That's when she asked about the Ouija. She asked if I could remember who had been there.'

Frannie was silent. It did not sound as if she had heard about Phoebe's accident. 'Can you?'

'I always used to keep a diary; I would probably have written the names down in it. It's rather difficult looking through things like that in my –' her voice tailed.

'Perhaps I could give you a hand? I think I can remember but I need to make sure.'

'What is it, Frannie? What's up?'

Frannie didn't want to talk about it on the telephone. 'Can you think about it overnight? I know it was some time ago. See what you could find, or remember?'

'Yes,' Susie said uneasily, 'I'll do my best. Do you think there's something –?'

'I don't know. I think it's just coincidence.'

'I've always thought that.'

'Oh?'

'I've always remembered the message the Ouija gave me.'

'What was it?'

'It was just one word, that was all. *Dark*.'

The traffic heading south out of London crawled forwards then stopped again. Oliver braked and put the Range Rover's gear into neutral. It was a blustery day: fat, overripe clouds wallowed in the blue sky; trees bent in the wind; leaves and empty cartons scudded down the pavements.

Oliver was wearing a thin blue jumper over a rugger shirt, and blue jeans; his hair was untidy and he looked tired. Frannie wondered if he was all right, as they sat in silence, each preoccupied with their own worries.

Phoebe Hawkins. Phoebe had gone straight back from the funeral and phoned Susie Verbeeten to ask her who had been at the Ouija session. Then she had rung to warn Frannie of the number twenty-six. Why? She thought about the cloakroom tag at the art gallery on Wednesday night, then Oliver getting clamped. Ridiculous. Then she thought about her birthday next week and felt a prickle of unease. Her twenty-sixth. What did Phoebe know?

Non omnis moriar. The harder she thought back, the more uncertain she became. She could remember being scared, blocking her ears at some point, not wanting to hear the message that came through for her. More than scared; she could remember being terrified.

The Ouija had given each of them a message, but she could not remember what they were. She had never known what her own was, had asked them not to tell her. She knew that sometimes, if you were told something bad, you could end up turning it into a self-fulfilling prophecy.

Dark. Could Susie Verbeeten have willed herself to go blind?

Oliver took her hand suddenly, and kissed it. 'I never apologized to you for getting angry at you on Sunday. I'm sorry.'

She shook her head. 'It was my fault. I was in such pain I wasn't thinking straight. I didn't mean to accuse Edward. I just –'

They joined the motorway; the traffic was lighter and moving more freely now. Oliver accelerated hard, moving over into the fast lane. 'I should have explained to you about him earlier.' He ran his right hand through his hair, then lowered his window a fraction. There was a sharp hiss of air. 'He has a behavioural problem; what the shrinks call a disturbed child. I don't know whether it's his mother's death or whether it's me.'

'You?'

He talked quietly, keeping his eyes on the road ahead and she had to listen hard to hear him.

'I never had much of a relationship with my parents. I was sent to boarding-school from the time I was seven and I was brought up by staff in the holidays. My brother and I had nannies until we were quite old; and Mrs Beakbane. I was never able to relate to my mother or father. So I don't find it easy to be close to Edward. After what happened to his mother, I knew that he was going to need me to be there for him, but I'm not sure I've ever succeeded.'

'You seem to have a really good relationship with each other,' she said, feeling sad for him. Sad for his son. 'I haven't seen that much of you together –' She stopped, as she remembered when she had met them at King's Cross: Edward's tantrum and Oliver's helplessness. And then her mind went back further to the morning the woman was decapitated in Poultry. The father and son coming into the café: the son's tantrum.

'Only since I've met you,' Oliver said. He slowed down, his mind wandering from his driving, and moved back into the nearside lane. The traffic they had just passed began to overtake them. 'You seem to work wonders with him. That time I met you at King's Cross, he had been vile the whole journey; he was good as gold the rest of the day. Last Saturday he was great; and Sunday, except –'

'Except when I accused him of giving me the plum deliberately. God, I'm sorry!'

He took his left hand from the wheel and patted her thigh. 'Listen, he might have done it.'

'No,' she said. 'It was an accident.' She looked at him. 'There's no reason on earth why he should have wanted to hurt me, is there?'

I hope you're not planning to sleep with my daddy.

'No,' he said with a weary smile that contained no conviction, and placed his left hand back on the wheel.

She experienced the familiar feeling that he was holding something back. 'When you say he's "disturbed", what do you mean? The strange silences he lapses into, and the Latin he starts speaking?'

'It's a whole raft of things. He's very disruptive at school – some of the other boys are quite wary of him. I've had a couple of warnings from the headmaster that they might not be able to keep him there.'

'Disruptive?'

'Things like refusing to attend the chapel, which they're meant to do every morning. How do you convince him God loves him when he knows that God took away his mother?' He looked at Frannie and she had no reply. 'Gets into a lot of fights with other children. And the worst thing was last term when he set fire to a wastebin.'

Frannie stifled a grin, guiltily, her heart going out to

Edward. 'Bloody nearly burned the school down,' Oliver said.

'Has he seen anyone?'

'Shrinks?'

'Yes.'

'I've done the rounds. Behavioural psychologists; psychiatrists. Been to the best people. He's sweet as pie with them. Angelic; they end up getting nowhere with him. I've tried a homeopath; dietary changes; drugs.' He shrugged. 'So far you're the only thing that's worked.'

'I'm very flattered.'

He took her hand and squeezed it, then drove on in silence for a while. She saw a police car sitting on a motorway bridge ahead, but Oliver was driving below the limit. A jumbo jet came alarmingly close and flew low across the motorway in front of them, landing at Gatwick, filling the air with the screams of its engines.

She stroked his hand. 'With your fear of coincidence, what do you make of my finding the tiger in the cupboard at the Museum?' She detected a faint tremor in his hand.

'I don't know,' he said.

'It's odd, isn't it? It's almost as if there's something that's drawing us together, bit by bit. One connection after another.'

'Yes,' he said tersely.

The road slid beneath them. The Range Rover's grimy bonnet vibrated a little; a large fly exploded on the windscreen in a smear of blood; its wings continued flapping as if they were trying desperately to fly off without the body.

Oliver drove on for a couple of miles in silence, then indicated left and they turned off the motorway at an earlier junction than last weekend. 'Edward's school,' he said by way of explanation.

A short distance on, he braked and turned into a driveway between brick pillars and over a cattle-grid, past a large sign saying STOWELL PARK PREPARATORY SCHOOL. As they drove up a long avenue of poplars and beech, Oliver's face came slowly back to life, like a creature awakening from hibernation; as if he was filled with yearning at the prospect of seeing Edward again, and Frannie was touched; it was the first time she had really felt the intensity of Oliver's love for his son.

'If there's anything I can do to help with Edward in any way, do tell me. I'll gladly do it.'

'You are helping,' he said. 'Just by being around. It'll be a real surprise for him that you've come with me to collect him.'

There was farmland beyond the trees on both sides; sheep were grazing and the soft hills of the Downs lay beyond. Frannie compared the idyllic setting with her own old school yard in Bethnal Green, and wondered how she would have viewed life if she had been here instead. Yet she felt no resentment; that was life's lottery. She also wondered how she would have viewed life if she had seen her mother decapitated when she was five.

It was warm in the car and she wound her window down a little. 'Rodmell's quite close to you, isn't it?'

'Yes, just down the road.'

'There's an old student friend of mine who lives there. I'd like to pop over and see her some time today or tomorrow. The poor girl's gone blind.'

'Christ. What happened?'

'I'm not exactly sure. I gather it was some virus she picked up in the Far East.'

'You're not having much luck with your friends,' he said grimly.

She did not reply.

'Why don't you go over this morning? I have to go and look at some machinery with Charles in the afternoon and I was hoping you might keep an eye on the boys for a couple of hours. I can run you over and pick you up, or you can take the car, if you like.'

'Sure, if you don't need it; thanks.'

'Mrs Beakbane would normally look after them but she's going to a wedding or something. You don't mind?'

'No, not at all.' And she didn't. She had got over her feeling of being a surrogate nanny and looked forward to spending some time with Edward and gaining his confidence.

'Tristram can be a bit of a monkey sometimes; and Edward rather encourages him.'

A squat Victorian baroque pile came into view. Oliver slowed for a sleeping policeman and the Range Rover bumped down on it. Two boys pedalled down on bicycles towards them.

'A lot of children can be pretty mischievous,' she said. 'Maybe Edward gets blamed for more than his fair share.'

Oliver said nothing.

Her eyes rested on the signet ring on his wedding finger. She could just make out the wyverns on the crest.

Non omnis moriar. She swallowed.

CHAPTER TWENTY-ONE

Frannie steered the Range Rover through the narrow wooden posts of the gates, craning her neck as she tried to gauge the width of the vehicle. She pressed the accelerator and the engine bellowed; the tyres munched the balding gravel drive and her wing mirror slid past the post with a centimetre to spare.

There was a ramshackle farmhouse fifty yards ahead, looking as if it had recently weathered a trip around the world lashed to the deck of a ship. A tired Volvo station-wagon sat in the yard, sagging on its suspension, its sills shot with rust, a faded yellow *Nuclear Power – No Thanks!* sticker visible through the grime on the rear window.

She pulled the handbrake on with difficulty, and switched off the engine. Then she unbuckled her seatbelt slowly, in no hurry to get out now that she had found the house. She felt anxious about meeting Susie, worried about how blindness might have changed her.

As she climbed down, she heard hens clucking and smelled the stench of pigs. A strong gust scattered her hair and she pushed several strands away from her eyes. A combine harvester droned through a large cornfield behind the house. Harvest. Autumn was coming. If she lived that long.

High above her the mid-morning sun glinted like a mirror but gave her no warmth. She walked up to the house, glancing through the double doors of a barn across the yard. Inside she could see a canvas on an easel; a window had been cut into the far wall, opening a view out on to the fields.

Bits of gravel stuck in the tread of her trainers and clicked as she stepped on the porch tiles. She pressed the doorbell but heard nothing ring and wondered if it worked. She waited a moment, then lifted the rusty iron knocker and rapped loudly.

The door was opened by a woman in her late forties wearing a grubby artist's smock and plastic flip-flops. Her hair was a bush of brown and grey wire. She wore no make-up and although ravaged by pock-marks from childhood acne she had a doll-like prettiness about her, spoiled by yellow and black nicotine-stained teeth as she smiled. A lump of rock crystal hung from a leather thong around her neck and there was a heavy charm-bracelet on her wrist. She held a cigarette in one hand and knelt, brushing two cats away from the door with the other. 'Hello, Frannie?' Frannie recognized the voice immediately from the phone last night, like a little girl's, with the faintest hint of a smoker's rasp.

'Yes! Mrs Verbeeten?'

'So sweet of you to come. Susie's thrilled.' She stepped back and waved the cats away again with paint-covered hands. 'Tonga, Biba, my little honeys, shoo, out of the way for Frannie, go on, dears!'

Frannie stepped into a shabby hallway that smelled of cats and joss-sticks. A moth-eaten Aztec rug hung on the wall in front of her, and dusty-looking ethnic rugs were scattered on the floor. A huge tapestry filled the wall on her right and it took a moment for her to notice the five-pointed star motif that was its main design. A pentagram, she thought. Pentacle. A floorboard creaked above them and they both turned. Susie was coming down the stairs, confidently, as if she could see perfectly well.

She was wearing a blouse, cotton skirt and leather

slippers, and clutching a small blue book in her hand. She looked exactly the same as when Frannie had last seen her three years ago. The upright, angular figure, the slender, handsome face harshened by her hairstyle, which was also the same: shorn at the sides and sticking up like a topiaried hedge on top. Only the way she stared past Frannie with a rather vacant expression gave her blindness away. And Frannie noticed that she had made a mistake buttoning her blouse; it was one out in the sequence.

'Spags!' Her greeting was cheery but carried a hint of uncertainty.

'Hi, Susie!' Frannie tried to sound natural, as if nothing was different, but it came out all wrong, sounded as if she was greeting an imbecile. She reached out and took Susie's right hand, then put her free arm around her and hugged her, clumsily. Susie hugged her back warmly and they kissed on each cheek. Frannie smelled the raw, astringent smell of underarm perspiration. Susie was nervous of this meeting also.

She released her hand, and was surprised when Susie suddenly touched her on the arms, patted her ribs, then lifted her hands up and felt her hair.

'Slim as ever,' Susie said. 'And your hair's still long.'

Frannie relaxed for an instant from the tension.

'You're looking great, you know? Really pretty.'

In the silence that followed she wondered if she had said the wrong thing. She watched Susie's eyes uncomfortably; for a brief moment they seemed almost to focus on her, then they moved away.

'Would you like a drink? Some tea, or coffee?' Susie asked.

'Love some coffee.'

'I'm going back to the studio, darling. Call me if you want anything.' Mrs Verbeeten looked at Frannie, giving her a stare she could not read. 'So nice to meet you. Susie's talked so much about you over the years.'

'And you too,' Frannie said, thrown by the stare.

'You're very welcome to stay for lunch, if you like. It'll just be a salad.'

'Thank you, but I have to get back.'

Susie led the way through into the kitchen which was old-fashioned and grimy. A cat slunk out. 'God, I don't know what happens to time, Frannie. I've been meaning to call you. I did try a couple of times but you were away on digs.'

'I would have called you too, but I thought you were out in the Far East.'

'So tell me about you,' Susie said. She put the book down on the wooden table in the middle of the room, and Frannie saw that it was an old diary. She watched Susie open cupboards, remove coffee, mugs, and open the fridge. She did everything slowly, methodically, setting things down carefully. She shook the kettle, switched it on, unscrewed the jar of coffee, then felt below the worktop for the drawer with the spoons.

'Do you have a boyfriend?' Susie asked.

Frannie hesitated. 'Yes.'

'Great!' Susie said with a warmth that surprised her. 'What does he do? You're at the British Museum, you said? Is he an archaeologist?'

'No – he's a –' Frannie wasn't quite sure how to describe Oliver. 'Mathematician. A statistician.'

The kettle started to boil. Susie pulled a gadget from behind it that looked like a radio pager, with one short and one long wire. She clipped it to the side of the mug, the wires dangling in, and poured from the kettle. As the water reached the top of the first mug, a sharp electronic beep rang out. She clipped the gadget to the second mug and filled that.

'That's clever,' Frannie said.

'There's tons of tricks,' Susie said with a trace of bitterness. 'I've got a machine I'm learning on that can read printed books – scans the words and converts them into Braille. In six months' time I'm getting a guide-dog – I have to go on a training course.'

'Is there any chance of getting your sight back?'

'Milk?'

'Just black, thanks.'

'No chance at all,' Susie said with finality, as if she did not even want to discuss it. She poured some milk into her mug, then set the bottle dangerously close to the edge of the worktop, turned away, picked a tray off a shelf behind and put the two mugs on it, her arm passing inches from the bottle. Alarmed, Frannie reached across and moved the bottle.

'Sugar?'

'No, I don't take it, thanks.'

To her horror, she saw Susie reaching towards the back of the worktop, her hand sweeping towards the sugar bowl. She had put the milk bottle right in her path.

She lunged forward, but it was too late. Susie's hand struck the bottle, sending it flying like a skittle. It spun across the surface, spewing out milk, striking one mug, sending it smashing to the floor. Scalding coffee exploded in all directions, lashing Frannie's jeans and burning her legs, splashing over Susie's legs and over her cotton skirt, spraying the units.

Frannie grabbed a tea towel, ran it under the cold tap, and pressed it against Susie's legs, apologizing frantically, explaining that it was her fault.

'Afraid I'm not much good at clearing things up,' Susie said.

Frannie steered her away to the other side of the

kitchen, and Susie told her where to find the squeegee and mop and bucket.

'I'm so sorry,' Frannie said, feeling very small, making herself another cup of coffee after she'd mopped up.

'It's OK. I have to get used to people helping me,' she said ironically.

They went through into the drawing-room. It was dark, with a battered sofa and two armchairs with their backs draped in antimacassars. There were several pictures on the wall, strange, rather disturbing abstracts, which she wondered if Susie's mother had painted. An assortment of stones and crystals were arranged on the mantelpiece, along with some small, rather ugly figurines. A creased pack of tarot cards sat on a lace cloth on a round table.

She waited until Susie had set the tray down and had removed her mug before taking the other, wary of any more mishaps.

'Did you have any thoughts about that Ouija session, Susie?' she asked.

'Mummy found my old diary – damn – I left it in the kitchen.' She jumped up and went out, neatly sidestepping a cat; Frannie watched her agility in amazement. She came back and handed the diary to Frannie. 'Seven of us,' she said. 'You, me, Meredith, Phoebe, Jonathan Mountjoy, Seb Holland and Max Gabriel.'

'That's what I thought,' Frannie said, a band of tension tightening in her. 'And you were given the message *Dark*?'

Susie gave a hollow laugh. 'Yes. We were all given stupid messages.' She hesitated. 'Except Meredith. I'd forgotten until Phoebe rang me.'

'Do you hear much from Phoebe?'

'Not a lot, because I've been out of the country most of the time since university. When her contract ended in Bath she was going to come with me out to China, a few months ago, to join a dig in Szechwan, but then she got the job offer in London. She was lucky. Might have got the same thing as me.'

'It was a *virus*?' Frannie said.

'Yes. I got it on the way, in Malaya. It's from the pollution in the South China Sea. The locals are immune to it, and they like to keep it a secret from tourists. Most people who get it come back with a bad eye infection and are fine after a few days – but if you get it really badly, like I did, it destroys your retinas.'

'I'm sorry I didn't know about it sooner,' Frannie said awkwardly. 'I'd have come to see you.'

'I didn't want to see anybody until recently. I'm not very good company, I'm afraid. I just keep thinking about all the things I'll never be able to do.'

'Medicine and technology are improving all the time.' Frannie said the only thing she could say. 'There might be some real breakthroughs in a year or two's time.'

Susie was silent for a moment. 'Our year from university has done pretty well in the disaster stakes, hasn't it?'

'Is it *us*? Or is it something else?'

'The Ouija?'

'Yes.'

'Is that what you think?'

'It was Phoebe who – I guess – made the connection.'

'Actually, I'm surprised Phoebe hasn't rung me back – she said she might come down this weekend.'

Frannie looked at her. 'You haven't heard?'

Susie stiffened and her voice turned to alarm. 'No?

What?' When Frannie told her about the accident, she seemed dazed by the news. 'I – I ought to go and see her. I'll get Mummy to drive me up. How's she taking it?'

'She was pretty doped up when I saw her last night.'

'She'll go through a lot of emotions. Same as I did. God!' She put her mug down and gripped the edge of the sofa, as if for reassurance.

'Four of the seven who were there have had something happen,' Frannie said. 'That's quite a coincidence.'

Susie thought for some moments before speaking. 'Four?' she echoed, dubiously. 'Have a look in the diary, Frannie. It's around about 24th March.'

Frannie picked up the diary and opened it. The cover was battered and the pages were creased, filled with large, untidy handwriting. There was a page to a day and almost every inch of space was crammed with lists, telephone numbers, reminders heavily underlined. Several pages were missing or partially torn out. She turned to the page with 24th March on it and noticed that the bottom two inches of that, also, were missing. Through the morass of writing she could see, heavily underlined, the word: 'Seance!!!' Packed in beneath it were the names of everyone who had been there. Beneath them, in list form, was written:

Me – DARK
Phoebe – FRUIT MACHINE
Jonathan – CASH AND CARRY
Max – LOSE WEIGHT
Meredith – DEAD BY 25. CAR CRASH

Frannie looked up with a start. '*Dead by twenty-five. Car crash.* Meredith?' she said.

'Yes.'

'You wrote this down at the time?'

'Yes. Well – probably a few days later. How old was Meredith when she died?'

'She'd have been twenty-five in October.'

'Shit,' uttered Susie and then repeated it. 'Shit.'

'That's really freaky,' Frannie said.

She shivered, turned the page, compelled to look for her own message.

Susie was silent. 'Fruit machine,' she said suddenly. 'That was Phoebe's message.'

Frannie could find nothing relevant on the reverse page. It looked as if her own and Seb Holland's messages had been on the strip that was torn off the bottom. She looked back at the list. 'Yes, *fruit machine.*'

'One-armed bandit,' Susie said.

Frannie didn't react at first; she was hunting again in case her own entry was written somewhere else. Then she stopped and stared at Susie, understanding the gruesome connection. 'You were told *dark*, and this has happened to you. Jonathan *cash and carry* and he's shot by a mugger. Phoebe *fruit machine* and she's lost an arm. It's easy to make them fit. But that doesn't make them predictions or prophecies, does it?' She could hear the anxiety in her own voice.

'What does it say for you?' Susie asked.

'Mine and Seb Holland's are missing. Someone's torn off the bottom of the page. Can you remember what they were?'

Susie thought for a moment then shook her head. 'No. Too long ago. It was just a lark, I didn't take it seriously.'

'Some lark,' Frannie said.

Susie grimaced.

'You don't remember if I had a number in mine, Susie? The number twenty-six?'

'No, I really can't remember. Is that what you think it was?'

'Phoebe told me to be careful of that number the day before she had her accident.' She shrugged and looked back down at the diary. 'Max Gabriel – *lose weight*,' she read out.

Susie seemed not to react for a few moments, then she said, 'Well, he's doing that all right.'

'What do you mean?'

'I was going out with him – before – what happened. He was working with some loony environmentalists; tried to sabotage a French nuclear power station and ended up getting heavily irradiated. He's in a hospice dying of leukaemia. It's not four out of the seven who were there, Frannie. It's five.'

Frannie looked down at the knuckles of charred wood and the grey ash in the cold grate, and wondered distractedly if they had been there since last winter. The ceiling was low, a grubby cream that was unevenly stained with nicotine. The room felt so gloomy and dark she had to look through the window at the blue sky to convince herself that it was not raining outside.

Her hands opened and shut. Her body felt leaden, as if she had buoyancy tanks inside her that had been ruptured and she was going to sink. The sofa sagged beneath her weight; there was a stone floor beneath the sofa, and earth beneath that. She felt the vastness of the planet and the smallness of the room, and the strength of the pull of gravity drawing her downwards.

'Why's all this happening to us?' she whispered.

Susie began to pull each finger in turn, cracking her

knuckles. Frannie remembered she used to do that at university and it had got on her nerves. 'I'm scared, Susie,' she said. 'I'm really scared.'

She heard birds singing and the distant drone of the combine harvester. She closed her eyes, trying to staunch a flood of tears. 'I'm sorry. You're the one who's had the awful thing happen and I'm sitting here crying.'

'I've done plenty of crying,' Susie said quietly.

'It needn't have happened,' Frannie said. 'Maybe if we'd thought about the things the Ouija said, we could have stopped all these –'

Susie leaned towards her. 'I don't think there's anything anyone could have done that would have made any difference. They're all so vague, so joky, you could interpret them in dozens of ways.'

Frannie hunched her shoulders, closing them in protectively, cocooning herself. 'Not Meredith's.'

'Do you really think if any of us had worked out what they meant we'd have done anything different? If I'd known I was going to go blind, do you think it would have occurred to me not to go swimming in the South China Sea? That Phoebe would have never gone bicycling? It's easy to understand things after they've happened, isn't it?'

Through the window Frannie watched a blackbird on the lawn and envied the creature's innocence, and freedom. She watched it dip its head then look up, and saw a worm writhing from its beak. She had never in her life felt so completely helpless.

She looked at the books crammed round the fireplace: *Astral Projection*; *Paranormal or Normal?*; *The Presence of the Past*. She had never taken much interest in the occult before; now she read the titles hungrily, wondering if there was one amongst them that might have an answer.

'I ought to warn Seb,' she said. 'If he's still all right.'

'Do you know how to get hold of him?'

'Yes. But what do I tell him?'

Susie did not answer.

'How do I stop this, Susie?'

The blind woman lifted her arms helplessly, and the gesture swung Frannie's mood suddenly, to anger.

'Susie,' she said, her voice rising. 'If it is the Ouija that's brought all this on us, and not some other freak explanation, there must be a way of stopping it. You were the one who knew the rules about it, told us all what to do. You said your mother was a white witch.'

'Mummy a witch?' Susie sounded astonished. 'She's not a witch, she's just a bit – I don't know – fey.'

'Why's she got a pentagram on the wall?'

'She's got hundreds of occulty things all over the place. She dabbles in everything that's going, but she's not a witch. God, she can't even do the tarot without looking it all up!'

Frannie retorted in disbelief. 'But you're the one who knew all about the Ouija. You insisted we had to have darkness, which is why we went down into the cellar.'

'Mummy used to do the Ouija here sometimes, that's how I knew.'

'Great,' Frannie said bitterly. 'Just great!'

Susie's voice stayed calm. 'Frannie, it never occurred to me that it was anything other than a game. Do you think I want to be like this? I wake up in the morning sometimes and wish I were dead.' She lowered her head and sank her face into her hands. Then she stood up unsteadily, and walked towards her friend, putting her arms around her. Frannie felt the wetness of her tears.

'I'm sorry, Frannie.'

Frannie squeezed her back, she was crying too.

'Jonathan Mountjoy,' Susie sobbed. 'Seb. Meredith. Max. Phoebe. All such good people.'

'I'm going to beat it,' Frannie said. 'I'm going to put a stop to it, whatever it is. And get your sight back.'

'Nothing's going to get my sight back, but I want you to be OK. I'll help you and Seb any way I can. But I don't know how. Perhaps you should go to a priest?'

'Your mother's done the Ouija before. Has she ever had any problems?'

'She never told me. You could have a word with her, but I don't think she'll be much help.'

They went across the yard into the studio in the barn. The reek of linseed oil and turps reminded Frannie of the picture-restoration room at the Museum. It was surprisingly tidy and airy; there were modern skylights in the roof as well as the window looking on to the fields, and the walls had recently been whitewashed. Canvases hung on display and dozens more were stacked on the floor.

Mrs Verbeeten was working at her easel with her back to them, and did not appear to notice their arrival. Her palette was gripped firmly in one hand and with a fine camel brush in the other she was adding colour to a detail. A cigarette burned in a tin lid crammed with butts on a milking stool. The picture was of a group of hooded people crowded on a rocky promontory below a castle wall.

Frannie looked closely at the couple of portraits on the wall. One was of Susie in her teens; the other of a bearded man behind an untidy desk. Then she looked at one of the landscapes. It was a disturbing work, with a foreboding sky, eerie buildings and a tormented quality which she did not care for, but she was impressed by the technique.

'Do you paint, Frannie?' Mrs Verbeeten spoke loudly without looking round and her voice startled Frannie.

'No.'

'Susie's blindness has taught me to see things in a different way. She can tell people apart by their footsteps. I've learned to do that. I'm learning to paint what the mind sees, not the eyes.'

Frannie fingered through a stack of canvases leaning against the wall, glancing at each one: all expressing the same troubled theme as the landscape she had just looked at on the wall.

'Images,' Mrs Verbeeten said. 'They come to me all the time. From every thought I get an image.'

'They're very good.'

Mrs Verbeeten turned and tilted her head in a childlike way. 'How very sweet of you, Frannie.' She laid her brush down at the edge of the easel, picked up her cigarette and dragged on it.

'Frannie wants some advice about the Ouija, Mummy.'

Mrs Verbeeten studied the end of her cigarette for a moment, then stared right through Frannie. 'The best advice I can give is not to touch it,' she said.

'It's a bit late for that, Mummy!'

'I haven't touched it for years,' the woman said. She inhaled deeply and jetted the smoke out through her nostrils.

'Why's that?' Frannie said, still flicking compulsively through the pictures.

Mrs Verbeeten glanced at her picture as if she was anxious to get back to it. 'There were too many occasions when –' she hesitated. 'When it was just too accurate, and unpleasant. Tarot cards give you a bit of guidance. The beastly Ouija just gives you a *fait accompli. You will die in three days' time*, you know? That sort of stuff. And people do.' She crushed out her cigarette in the metal tin, picked up her brush and stroked a vermilion splodge on her palette, signalling the interruption was over.

CHAPTER TWENTY-TWO

The needle of the speedometer bounced wildly between 60 and 80 m.p.h., and the Range Rover swayed and lurched along the uneven two-lane road as Frannie wrestled with the steering-wheel. She knew she was going too fast, but she kept the accelerator pressed to the floor up a gentle gradient, the engine bellowing gruffly, the needle bouncing higher on the dial, touching the 90 mark. She felt strangely light-headed, enjoying the recklessness, the sense of freedom; pleased to be away from the claustrophobic gloom of Susie Verbeeten's house, pleased to be away from Susie's strange mother. High on adrenaline, she was experiencing a forgotten feeling of confidence.

The tailgate of a truck she was gaining on vanished over the brow ahead. The clock which was sited to the left of the dash in front of the passenger seat, and was hard to read, said 1.10. She had promised Oliver she would be back by one.

The road curved left more sharply than she expected, and the row of trees on the far side of the bend hurtled towards her. She jabbed her foot off the accelerator as the Range Rover heeled over and her shoulder slammed against the door, the tyres yowling beneath her as if they were shedding their treads. They slewed over on to the wrong side. She jerked the wheel hard, too much; the heavy vehicle yawed, snaked, veered left then right, crossed the white line again. A car was coming in the opposite direction, flashing its lights and blaring its horn angrily. She tramped on the brake pedal, her mouth dry. Going to hit it. Going to hit it!

Her throat expelled a gasp of choked air. The car screamed towards her; she could see the horror on the driver's face, could see him wrenching his wheel. Their wings missed by inches. She heard the shriek of his horn like a train passing through a station. She thought her wing mirror was going to go, but that missed too.

Relief pumped through her. She felt clammy with shock. The truck in front was two hundred yards ahead now and there was a long, straight stretch of road. A fresh shot of adrenaline pumped through her. She could get past. She pressed the accelerator back to the floor, indicated, looked in her rear-view mirror. And froze.

Edward was sitting behind her.

A shockwave kicked through her whole body as if the wheel she was holding were electrified, and she swerved wildly. 'Edward,' she mouthed, turning her head round.

The seat was empty. She blinked. A chill blast of air blew down her neck. Something flashed in the corner of her eye. Red. Danger. Amber. Her mouth opened. Her eyes widened, levered by terror.

The lorry had stopped and was indicating right.

Her foot dived for the brake pedal, and she threw her weight forward on to it. The wheels locked, the tyres howled across the dry tarmac; the bonnet snaked right, left. Now the tailgate of the lorry hurtled towards her as if someone had pulled the lever on a zoom lens. She saw its brake lights go off. Its right indicator still flashed. It was starting to turn, moving slowly, crawling.

Faster. Please move. For God's sake faster.

She was locked too, just like the wheels. A passenger. The Range Rover lurched left, jolted hard, and the howl stopped abruptly as the tyres tobogganed across the grass verge. For a moment the vehicle slid in almost complete silence; not even the sound of the engine. It missed a bus shelter, but was hauled in by the hedgerow. Brambles clattered like hail against the windscreen, ripped and tore. The car then dipped forward, tobogganing still, its shocks creaking as it bounced on to the soft earth of a ploughed field. Several rooks took off and a panicked pheasant lumbered into the air. The car bounced again, then slewed round in an arc to the right, as if caught in a giant rut.

When Frannie opened her eyes a red light was shining on the dash in front of her. She hugged herself. And she looked in the mirror again, then turned. Nothing. No Edward in the car. Just the empty rear seat.

Something ticked busily. The engine had stalled, she realized. She opened the door and leaned out, peering behind her. There was a wide, messy hole in the hedge, and she could see the black tarmac of the road beyond. She heard the distant roar of a lorry changing gear, moving away, fading. Then just the ticking of the fuel pump again.

She looked around, feeling slightly foolish now, and pulled the door shut. Water trickled down her wrist. The palms of her hands were wringing wet. She wiped them on her jeans, then turned the ignition key. The car jumped forward and stopped. She pressed the clutch and put the gear into neutral, then tried again. The engine revolved several times without firing. Come on, please! She twisted the key hard over, then pressed the accelerator slowly forwards as the starter motor clattered. Oily blue smoke rafted past the windows. She put the car into first gear, then slowly let out the clutch.

The wheels spun and mud and stones rattled against

the underside. Then the car slid sideways. She stopped. Think. She knew she ought to be able to get out. On a dig she had once been in a Land Rover that had got bogged to its axles in sand. The driver had pulled something on the transmission tunnel and it had got them going. She scanned the carpeted hump and saw a small plastic knob. Faded white lettering on the top said: 'Diff Lock', and there was a plate screwed to the bulkhead in front with instructions. She pulled the lever up then pushed the gear forwards and let out the clutch again.

The Range Rover slewed sideways; she accelerated harder and suddenly they began to crab forward. Turning in a wide arc towards the gap in the hedge, she drove through it and stopped. There were deep brown furrows where the locked wheels had gouged out the grass. The wing mirror had been knocked flat against the door, but that was the least of her worries.

She looked guiltily at the hole in the hedge, then scanned the road once more. No sign of anyone. Oliver might know the farmer who owned it; she'd phone him and pay for the damage. Then she turned her head once more and stared at the empty rear seat. She unbuckled her belt, climbed on her knees on to the seat and peered over into the tailgate area, just to be sure: some jump leads lay on the carpeted floor; a chewed plimsole from the days of Captain Kirk; a can of de-icing spray and part of a chocolate wrapper. No Edward. She sat back down. She had imagined it.

Cracking up.

She edged forwards and pulled out on to the road. Then she began to shake.

CHAPTER TWENTY-THREE

Frannie turned in beneath the wyverns on the gate pillars, past the sign that said MESTON HALL. OPEN TODAY 10 A.M. – 5 P.M. and down through the arch beneath the stable block. The hands of the clock said 1.25.

She slowed as she emerged into the milling visitors, acknowledged a prim smile from a woman member of staff, and parked on the gravel drive along the front of the house.

Then she climbed out and inspected the front of the Range Rover. The tyres and the wheel arches were coated in mud and there were brambles tangled in the bull bar, which she hurriedly removed and dumped on the bonfire tip beyond the formal garden.

As she walked up to the front door of Oliver's wing, a muffled bang rang out in the distance, followed by a roar, then a steady drone. She had heard the same sound last week, she realized: Oliver's aeroplane. Good. She hoped that meant he wasn't back yet.

She closed the oak door behind her with a heavy clunk, still shaken, wondering whether she should tell Oliver about her accident, and fretting about the damage to the hedge.

She called out 'Hello!' but there was no response. Motes of dust drifted silently, and the eye of a dead pheasant glinted from an oil painting on the far wall. She walked through into the kitchen; there was ham salad on the kitchen table and five places laid, together with a note from Mrs Beakbane saying that baked potatoes were in the bottom oven.

She collapsed on to the decrepit sofa, but the rubber bone that rolled on to the floor only reminded her of what Edward had called 'the bad thing'. Her mind went upstairs to the cutting of Jonathan Mountjoy's death in the nursery. Then to the glass showcase with the book written on human skin. The *Maleficarium*, or whatever it was called. She wondered if there was a curse on the family, and whether the violent death of Oliver's wife could be explained by it. And if so, was she next in line for presuming to love him?

Declan O'Hare had told her there were mentions of the Halkins in quite a few books; she had been planning to go to the British Library all week but had not had the time. She now walked back down the corridor and across the hall, through the grand panelled door into Oliver's library-cum-study.

There was a damp chill, as if the room had never been heated, and a strong smell of stale leather and decaying paper. The sky was darkening; through the window she could see heavy grey clouds. She glanced at the sheets of mathematical calculations on the desk and the charts with their hieroglyphics on the wall, then up at the bookshelves, scanning the titles, uncertain where to begin.

Winston Churchill's *History of the Second World War*. *The Canterbury Tales*. Walter Pater's *History of the Renaissance Studies*. Tomes and tomes of military history, political history, biographies. A whole section on mathematics, and several books on numerology. She hesitated, then went across to the charts on the wall. Numbers; algebraic equations; she noticed the number twenty-six at the core of a ring of concentric circles. But as she leaned forward to look closer, Frannie heard an electronic ting-tack-tang sound, and a shadow fell across the desk. She spun round in alarm and nearly knocked Edward over. He was standing right behind her.

'God, you gave me a fright!'

'I just got four thousand, Frannie.' He showed her the Game Boy's screen. 'Score. On Level Four. Level Four's the hardest. It's my new record,' he said.

'That's very good,' she said, slightly lost.

'What are you doing?'

She blushed. 'I was seeing if I could find any books on your family history.'

He looked at her solemnly. There were dark bags beneath his eyes as if he had not been sleeping well, which she had not noticed before. Or was it just the lighting? 'Can I talk to you for a moment, Frannie?' he said. As he did so, he glanced around, as if checking there was no one else there.

'Of course,' she said, his expression making her feel nervous.

'Can you help me, Frannie?'

'Help you do what?' She smiled at him, because he looked as if he was close to tears. When he said nothing for a while, she wondered if he was lapsing back into one of his silences. Then he spoke again.

'Do you ever have funny thoughts about people, Frannie?'

'How do you mean?'

'Like there's some bad thing inside you that makes you do things you don't want to do?'

She knew this was an important moment and she tried to handle it without fluffing. 'I sometimes think of things I'd like to do which I know I can't.'

'No, I don't mean that. I mean do you have something inside you that makes you want to harm people?' He fixed his warm brown eyes on her, looking scared and vulnerable. 'I have this bad thing, Frannie. I don't want it.'

'What does it do?'

'It makes things happen when I just think about them.'

'What sort of things?'

'Do you remember last Saturday when Dom got his fingers caught in the car door?'

'Yes.'

'I made that happen.'

'But you were with me.'

'I know; but I saw it in my mind first; I wanted it to happen. Except I didn't after it happened.'

Impossible, she thought. It was impossible. Then she remembered the strange, almost suicidal feeling she had had in the Range Rover, as if she were high on a drug, indestructible, could do anything; and how vividly Edward had appeared to her. She squeezed her hands together, then picked at her nails. 'How often has this happened?'

'Sometimes it happens at school. And I got really scared just now, while Daddy was working on his aeroplane engine, because I had this bad thought about you.'

'What was it?' she said, conscious of the chill rippling through her.

Tears began rolling down his cheeks. 'I wanted you to crash the Range Rover,' he said.

She stared at him numbly. 'Why, Edward?'

'I don't know. Sometimes there's a bad part of me that I can't stop.' His eyes widened. 'You can help me, can't you, Frannie?'

'How? Tell me more about it, about this bad thing.'

He said nothing, lapsing into a long silence.

She took a deep breath. 'Did you have it when your mummy was killed?'

His eyes flashed at her, startling her; they had

changed completely, seemed to be burning with venom.

He ran out of the library and the next thing she heard was the slam of a door upstairs.

She was left wondering if she should go up and apologize, calm him; but she felt drained. She sat down and tried to work out what on earth he'd meant. To make some sense. She lowered her face into her hands. All she knew was that Edward had been in the back of the Range Rover; she had seen him clearly.

Willing things to happen? Dom's fingers? The wasps? Captain Kirk? Was it possible? With voodoo it might be, but not with an eight-year-old boy? His mother was decapitated. Why would he will that? Was it the bad thing inside him?

I hope you're not planning to sleep with my daddy.

Was he possessed?

She tried to laugh the idea off but it stuck in her mind. *Possessed*. She barely noticed the sky darkening further as she sat engulfed in her thoughts, looking round unfocusing at the shelves of books and then looking up at the strange mathematical hieroglyphics on the wall, her mind churning, searching for logic.

She tried to tag everything the way she would on a dig, every fragment that might eventually help make an identifiable object, that in turn would build up an image of the site in which it was found, and the people who had put it there. In archaeology tiny fragments were all you needed. They were all she had now. Jonathan Mountjoy. Meredith Minns. Max Gabriel. Phoebe Hawkins. Susie Verbeeten. Edward. Oliver's wife. The boy's fingers. The wasps. Where was the connection? Was Edward possessed? Mad? Or psychic? Telepathic? Reading her mind? That might explain the Range Rover where something had definitely influenced her own behaviour, but not Dom's fingers; or the wasps.

As she had done so many times recently, Frannie thought back to when she had first seen Oliver and Edward. In the café; the boy's tantrum. Then at King's Cross, and the tantrum again. *Can you help me, Frannie?* Something about her that he seemed to trust, to respond to. And at the same time hate?

There were stories about disturbed people having strange powers. Particularly children being psychic; disturbed children caused poltergeists, that was well known. Oliver had said Edward was disturbed. You could hardly see your mother being decapitated and not be.

Especially if you'd made it happen.

Her thoughts were broken by the sound of the front door opening and closing, then Oliver came into the library in grubby overalls, his hands covered in grease and streaks of it on his face. He kissed her lightly on the lips.

'Hi, sorry to be so late.' Then he gave a triumphant smile. 'Got the plane's engine running properly at last!'

She reciprocated the smile. 'Good. I'm looking forward to my first flight.'

'Won't be long.' He looked at his hands. 'Better go and clean myself up. Charles is on his way; he and I are going to skip lunch and shoot straight off – do you mind terribly having lunch with the boys?'

'No, that's fine,' she said, hoping it would be.

'How was your friend in Rodmell?'

'She was OK. Up and down, I guess.'

There was a sharp rap on the front door.

'That's them,' he said and went out. She heard the door open, then Tristram's voice.

'Uncle Oliver!'

'Hello, little brute!' Oliver said.

'Hello, big brute!' the boy replied.

Frannie went out into the hall. Oliver's brother was a little taller than she remembered and more gangly. He was looking very much a farmer in an old shirt, worn-out grey flannel trousers and wellingtons.

'You met Frannie last week,' Oliver said to him.

'Yes,' Charles said. He pushed his fingers shyly through his straw hair, taking a step towards her. 'Hi, nice to see you again.' He gave her hand a rather clumsy shake.

Tristram stared at her silently, his small frame engulfed by a yellow Snoopy T-shirt that was a couple of sizes too big, and pink Bermudas that hung below his knees. She remembered last week his blond hair had been plastered down in an attempt to make him look neat for a party, but no such effort had been made this time; it flopped, unruly, over his forehead and it suited him better. She smiled at him warmly. 'How are you, Tristram?'

He raised his eyebrows quizzically. 'OK.' He shrugged.

She heard the musical ting-tack-tang of the Game Boy again, and saw Edward standing in front of the suit of armour on the half-landing, looking down at them with a distant expression in his eyes, as if he was not registering them. He turned his attention back to his toy and slowly walked down into the hall without taking his eyes off the screen.

'Uncle Charles and I are going in a sec, Edward,' Oliver said. 'You and Tristram are going to have lunch with Frannie.'

Edward continued concentrating on his game and did not acknowledge his father.

'Did you hear, Edward?' Oliver said, irritated.

Edward flapped a hand, equally irritated. 'I'm busy.'

'Aren't you going to say hello to your uncle, or to Tristram?' Edward looked up. 'Hello, Uncle Charles.' Then he looked at his father. 'Can I show Tristram the aeroplane?'

'No, I don't think that's a very good idea.'

His face fell. 'Why not?'

'The engine's been running and it'll still be very hot. We'll go down there when I come back.'

'Promise?'

'As long as we're not too late.'

The ting-tack-tang beat of the Game Boy resumed, and Frannie saw Edward pressing the buttons again, biting his tongue in concentration.

While Oliver went to have a quick wash, Frannie asked his brother how the cattle were. He told her there seemed to be some improvement but it was too early to tell, and explained the homeopathic treatment the vet was giving them.

Oliver came back out, wiping his still grimy hands on his overalls. 'Right,' he said breezily. 'We're off! Think you can handle these monsters, Frannie?'

'OK, you guys, what would you like for pudding?' Frannie said, clearing away the plates.

'Ice-cream and hot choccy sauce!' Edward said. 'Can you make hot choccy sauce, Frannie?'

'If there's some chocolate.'

Tristram whispered in Edward's ear and the two boys burst into giggles.

Frannie found some chocolate and made the sauce. When Edward had finished, leaving a brown-and-white trail around his mouth, he looked up at her and asked if he and Tristram could go out and play.

Frannie tried to engage his eyes, to read behind them, but could see nothing. 'Wait until I've cleared up, and I'll come with you.' She was in charge of him and she felt he needed watching.

He dug his hands into the patch-pockets of his cotton trousers and his forehead furrowed in thought, making him look for an instant like an elder statesman. 'I think we might go and see the horses. If you come with us we could give you a riding lesson.'

'No, not today.'

'It won't be dangerous, Frannie, honestly. We'll just go out in the field. If you ride Sheba she's very gentle.'

'I think your father should be with us if I'm going to have a riding lesson.'

'Daddy's useless with horses; he only knows about aeroplanes. It won't hurt, Frannie. I'll hold her by the reins.'

Tristram was absorbed in scraping his bowl clean. 'I'll hold him too, Frannie,' he said without looking up.

She smiled, not wanting to seem a coward, but equally determined she was not getting on a horse. 'I'll just get ready then we'll go down and have a look at them.'

'Promise?'

'I promise I'll come with you, but I don't promise I'm going to ride.'

'OK.' The boys scrambled off, chattering excitedly.

'Hey! Where are you going?' she called, following them into the hall.

'I want to show Tristram my Game Boy score,' Edward said. 'In my room.'

She returned to the kitchen, glad of a few moments' quiet to try to collect her thoughts. The shakes were coming back in another wave of shock from the accident, and she was deeply disturbed by her visit to Susie Verbeeten. She switched on the kettle to make herself a cup of coffee, stacked the dishwasher and washed the remains of the chocolate from the saucepan.

She blew on her coffee, sipped it, and went out into the hall. The house sounded quiet; the boys were probably engrossed with Edward's game. She went back into the kitchen, wiped the table clean, sat down and glanced through the 'Weekend' section of *The Times*. But she was unable to read more than a short way through any of the articles before her attention wandered.

She finished her coffee, then went up to Edward's room, hoping they might have changed their minds about going down to the horses. As she opened the door she felt the first prick of concern. They were not there. And when she went up to the nursery they were not there either.

Her concern deepening, Frannie ran back downstairs, and out of the front door into the bright sunlight, but there was still no sign of the boys. She glanced at her watch. It was about twenty minutes since they had left the kitchen. There was a muffled bang in the distance. A few moments later she heard another, and she felt a sharp jolt inside her.

Couldn't be.

Then another bang, followed by a blattering roar that died almost instantly.

No.

She was already racing down the gravel path before the noise had faded in her ears.

Faces blurred as she tore along the front of the house. She weaved through a group of visitors moving away from the ticket office and collided with a large man taking a photograph, who was as solid as a sand-bag. Her mouth would not work; she apologized with her eyes, holding him at arm's length as if to get her bearings, slipping past him, and sprinted up the road past the chapel, towards the noise. Again, there was an ear-blistering roar, much louder, an angry sound that rasped through the grounds, shattering the peace of the still afternoon.

She cut across the grass, then on to the asphalt path, the route Edward had taken her last Saturday, just a week ago. A week ago when she was unaware that Meredith was dead and that Max Gabriel was dying. When Phoebe Hawkins still had two arms. She prayed silently as she ran.

Please don't let anything bad happen. Please let them be all right.

Past a huge cornfield that was all cut and baled up, she saw the tall, rusting corrugated iron barn ahead of her. There was a bang, a short, fiendish roar that drummed the walls of the barn, then silence. Rafts of oily smoke drifted towards her. Her speed quickened in panic. Then as she hurtled round to the front she saw Edward and Tristram standing on two oil drums in front of the aeroplane, turning the propeller, that was much higher than either of them, with difficulty, having to stretch up and strain hard. Having a great game. Frannie stopped, horrified.

'OK!' Edward yelled, bracing himself.

'OK!' Tristram yelled back, bracing himself also, holding the propeller steady for a moment.

'Edward!' Frannie screamed. 'Edward! Tristram!'

There was a clattering sound as they swung the propeller sharply downwards. Then it began revolving, slowly, on its own, and with a deafening noise the engine burst into life, picking up speed, the blades of the propeller vanishing into a transparent blur. Thick exhaust fumes billowed out. The biplane shook and the barn drummed with the din.

The boys were swaying, fighting to keep their balance in the vortex of suction from the propeller. Edward windmilled his arms desperately, the drum rocking crazily beneath him, pitching him forward; he was beginning to fall towards the propeller.

Frannie was half demented with horror. 'Edward!' she screamed but she could not even hear if her voice had come out. 'Edwa –'

He struggled to get his balance back, grabbed Tristram by the shoulders and they both fell forwards, then rocked back, swayed forwards again. Then, suddenly, the drums pitched over, throwing them both backwards on to the ground. Tristram lay motionless. Edward covered his head with his hands and rolled clear.

Frannie never forgot what happened next. Tristram climbed to his knees, and remained there, dazed, looking directly at her. The plane began to creep forwards towards him. 'Tristr –' she choked on her own terror. Launched herself towards him. Her foot caught in a crack and the hard concrete slammed into her chest.

Winded, she saw movement to her left, someone running, it was just a blob. The blob became a man in his late fifties, wearing a soiled lumberjack shirt. But Tristram stayed on his knees, looking at her and at the approaching man.

The concrete tearing skin from her hands, Frannie powered herself forward to the little boy who was kneeling less than two yards in front of the propeller. She stumbled back to her feet, felt the air sucking at her, 'TRISTRAAAAMMMM!'

By now her T-shirt was ripped from inside her jeans and icy air flailed her bare back; her hair beat her face like knotted string.

A look of guilty panic sheeted over Tristram's face and he stood up, then backed away. Backed towards the propeller that was looming up on him.

'Tristram! It's OK, Tristram!' Frannie called, but her voice was choked and raw, and it came out as a squeak rather than a shout. She stretched forward with her hands, only a few feet away from grabbing him. The propeller closed on the boy like a shadow.

Out of the corner of her eye she could see the man closing also. Then everything slowed as if suddenly there was all the time in the world. She was aware of strange details: the rubber soles of her trainers compacting on the concrete then expanding, springing her into the air, absorbing her weight as she landed again, compacting, expanding, the wind from the propeller lifting the strands of grey hair from the man's head, exposing the bald area beneath; the wind billowing his shirt like a sail.

There was a strange sound that echoed in her head. A *chinnggg* like a lawnmower blade striking a stone. At first she thought Tristram had been hit by a pillow. Thousands of tiny little shreds hung in the air, like feathers. Then they were gone.

He'd disappeared.

The propeller was inches from her own face now, its draught tearing her mouth open, freezing her eyes. She flung herself sideways and the blade scythed over her; the din of the engine drilling out her eardrums, fumes filling her lungs like cotton wool. A wheel struck her in the back and the shadow of the wing passed across her as she lay flattened. Dust, pebbles and grit peppered her face, stinging it like hail.

Slowly, she climbed to her feet. Through blurred eyes she saw Tristram standing near her. He was fine. He was OK! Relief surged through her. Then she realized it wasn't Tristram, it was Edward, with fluff in his hair and spots of blood all over him. He was staring at a pair of Bermudas that had legs sticking out of them at one end, the feet in tiny trainers. Out of the other end protruded ragged flesh, unwinding coils of intestine and a few inches of sharp, white backbone like the shaft of a broken spear. A small lake of blood was slowly spreading out across the concrete and draining into the weed-filled cracks.

Someone was clambering into the cockpit of the plane: the man in the lumberjack shirt, she dimly registered. The roar of the engine ceased suddenly and there was just the shuttering sound of the propeller. Then silence. The plane was no longer moving. The tiny shreds of hair and bone and flesh that hung from the fuselage and wings also lay scattered across the concrete. Later, when she looked in the mirror, she saw that she was covered in them, too.

CHAPTER TWENTY-FOUR

Fragments of the afternoon played themselves back to Frannie at random. Moments; segments of moments; details. She could not focus on any one part of what had happened for more than a few seconds without her brain switching channels.

She stared blankly around the drawing-room, trying to orientate herself. The drawing-room was real time. She was in the drawing-room. Then she was outside on the concrete hard, hurtling herself towards Tristram. Brambles tore at the windscreen of the Range Rover, rattling and shrieking. The roar of the aeroengine drummed through the barn. The Tiger Moth rolled forwards. The propeller came up behind Tristram like a shadow. The Range Rover was returning with Charles and Oliver inside it: the lusty bellow of its engine; the crunch of its tyres on the gravel; the two men emerging, cheery voiced, innocent of what lay ahead, glancing with only mild curiosity at the police car drawn up behind Charles's battered Toyota Landcruiser and the sign that said PRIVATE. NO VISITORS BEYOND THIS POINT. The policeman approaching Charles and Oliver, Frannie beside him. Edward at that moment coming around the side of the building with his Game Boy, and the ting-tack-tang . . . ting-tack-tang . . . that seemed for a brief instant to be the only sound in the world.

Then the hideous sound Charles had made, a howl of anguish that sounded as if it were drawn from the bowels of the earth.

Now she sat on a sofa, holding a glass in her hand,

in front of an unlit fire. Wind rattled the window-panes. 'My fault, all my fault.' She heard herself speaking as if she were somewhere else, in another room, detached.

There was whisky in the glass: hard, neat Scotch that singed her mouth, burned her stomach. It did not relieve the shock or the pain, but it battened them in another compartment and as long as it did, she would be all right.

The pills helped too, helped to dull everything a little, delay reality by a few more hours. Oliver had given them to her. The doctor had given them to Oliver. The doctor who had made her stings better last weekend, who had come and taken Charles away. Oliver's face seemed to get bigger and smaller. It stretched out sideways then shrank. The doctor had told Oliver she should not drink with the pills.

The channel changed. Tiny scraps clung to the silver fuselage and to the engine cowling. The propeller still spun but the sound had gone mute. Then she was back in the drawing-room again. Bands of tension etched like scratches across her scalp.

'My fault,' she repeated.

Oliver sat beside her. 'No,' he said.

'It is.'

'Kids have to be watched all the time. No one understands that until they have kids of their own. It's not your fault.'

His voice sounded strange as if she were hearing it through glass. She wondered if she had died. Oliver was looking at her oddly. Maybe I was killed by the plane and no one told me. She reached out to touch his hand but closed on air. She tried again, took his wrist, felt the hairs and the firm muscle, pressed her face into his neck, smelled his ears, his shampoo, his skin, held him tightly.

There was a picture of the aeroplane on the mantel-piece, and in the kitchen; there seemed to be pictures of it in every room. Oliver, Edward and Edward's mother standing in front of it, laughing at the camera.

'I should have stayed with them, followed them.'

'I should have padlocked the barn,' he said.

'Where was the ignition key for the plane?'

'It doesn't have a key; just a couple of magneto switches on the dash. It never occurred to me that he – they –' his voice shuttered off, like the propeller, into silence.

Frannie drank some more, held the glass close to her face, inhaling the fumes. Everything was out of kilter, as if new laws of the universe had been written and nobody had told her. The world was now a place where a group of kids could get killed and maimed just by sitting around a table with an upturned glass; where a small boy could kill and maim just by thinking about it. Maybe it was Oliver who had written the new laws? The stuff on the wall in the library. The hieroglyphics. She closed her eyes. Madness was not very far away; just a glass of whisky or a small blue pill separated her from it.

Her own turn was not very far away either. And she did not know what separated her from that.

A crash of breaking glass upstairs startled them both. Oliver jumped up and ran out into the corridor. She followed him into the hall, and up the stairs to the landing where all they could hear was a low moaning sound that Frannie thought at first was the wind.

It was coming from Edward's room. She realized it was not moaning but chanting. Oliver gripped the round brass handle; his knuckles were white. For a moment he remained motionless then he slowly opened the door, pushing hard against the draught of cold air that blasted out at them.

The room was in darkness, the windows were broken. The curtains thrashed, tearing at their rods, the rings sliding and clacking, the fabric hissing. In the midst of it all Edward lay in his bed, asleep on his back, the steady chant coming from his mouth.

'. . . *murotaccep menoissimer ni rutednuffe sitlum orp te sibov orp iuq iedif muiretsym iitnematset inretea te ivon iem siniugnas xilac mine tse cih . . .*'

Frannie felt panicked. A toy car rolled along a shelf and fell at her feet. Oliver ushered her back out of the room and closed the door softly.

'What on earth is it?' she whispered. 'What's going on.'

He raised a hand, motioning her to stay, strode down to his own room and came back moments later with a small ghetto-blaster. He opened Edward's door a few inches and switched on the red recording light, and the tape revolved with a shuffle. Edward's flat monotone sounded along the passageway: '. . . *muem suproc mine tse coh. Senmo coh xe etacudnam te, etipicca: snecid, sius silupicsid euqtided, tigerf, tixid eneb, snega saitarg metnetopinmo muus mertap mued et da muleac ni siluco sitavele te saus sunam selibarenev ca satcnas ni menap tipecca ruteretap mauq eidirp iuq . . .*'

Oliver closed the door and stopped the tape, then walked back along the corridor to his room, switched on the light, waited for her to come in and closed the door. The room looked neat and orderly, but it felt very cold. The candles in the two iron holders either side of the bed had been replaced. In the bright light the room felt strange. Oliver's face was white and lined, had aged twenty years since the morning. He sat on the edge of the four-poster bed and put the recorder down beside him, then looked at her gravely. 'You didn't recognize that?'

She stayed close to the door, feeling unwelcome.

'What is it? One of the Arabic languages?' She observed the cherubs and nudes painted on the walls; the thick rugs, the shirts on their metal hangers hooked on to the wardrobe door. The row of polished shoes with their wooden trees on the floor. Alien. It was all alien.

'I'll play it backwards,' he said. 'You might find that helps.' He opened the wardrobe, rummaged in the back and pulled out an old reel-to-reel tape recorder. He played back the tape, recording it on to the reel-to-reel, then pressed the machine's reverse play button. Edward's voice immediately sounded clearer.

'. . . *Hic est enim Calix Sanguinis mei, novi et aeterni testamenti: mysterium fidei: qui pro vobis et pro multis effundetur in remissionem peccatorum.*'

She prowled near the door like a caged animal. He watched her with haunted eyes. His worn plimsoles were sunk into the shag rug beside the bed and his head was sunk into his shoulders. She translated, her voice trembling, the words that she knew so well, had memorized since earliest childhood. It had been a long time since she had heard them in Latin.

'For this is the Chalice of my Blood of the new and eternal testament,' she said falteringly, unable to take her eyes from Oliver. 'The mystery of the faith; which shall be shed for you and for the multitude of mankind so that sins may be forgiven.'

He stopped the tape.

'Mass,' she said. 'He's reciting the canon of the mass backwards.' She walked across the room and put her hand on the cold ribbed radiator beneath the window. The ghost of her face stared back from the glass. She turned and faced Oliver. 'Mass isn't – isn't held in Latin – in this country –' She faltered. 'Backwards. I –' She stopped and suddenly thought of the plants he had reeled off in Latin. And the animals.

He spoke in Latin to you? Oliver had said when they were in bed in this room last Saturday, sounding surprised, but not commenting further. The way he had not probed deeply when Edward had started reeling off Latin names in the car on Sunday night going back to London.

'Isn't saying mass backwards something to do with black magic?' she said.

'Yes,' he said stiffly. 'I looked it up after the first time he did it.'

'He's done it before?'

'He's been doing it at school for years. Three and a half years, to be precise,' he said, giving her a strange look.

'And the windows? Did that happen?'

'No.' He was silent for a moment. 'That hasn't happened before. He'll calm down. And in the morning he won't remember anything.'

'Where's it coming from?'

Oliver said nothing.

'The doctors and shrinks you've taken him to – did you tell them about this?'

'I've played them tapes.'

'And what did they say?'

'That it's not uncommon. Apparently, disturbed children often speak strange languages or gibberish in their sleep.'

Frannie felt trapped between the light of the room and the darkness outside, the darkness that pressed against the glass, trying to push through it and to crush her up against the light. She shuddered, her skin absorbing the coldness like blotting-paper.

Oliver stopped the machine, then pulled another tape out of the drawer of his bedside table and slotted it into place. 'Last Saturday when we slept together,

273

Frannie, you began talking in your sleep. It woke me up. I thought you'd stop, but you kept going on, talking complete mumbo-jumbo. I couldn't work out what the hell you were saying. I recorded a bit of it because I thought it might amuse you; then I realized it might embarrass you so I didn't say anything about it.' He stared at the floor, then back at her.

She remembered now, being woken by a click in the middle of the night and wondering what it was.

'Then I suddenly realized on Sunday night when Edward started his chanting that it was the same sound. I knew there had to be a connection – it couldn't be coincidence.' He started the tape.

'*Muem suproc mine tse coh senmo coh xe etacudman te etipicca snecid sius silupicsid euqtided tigerf tixid eneb snega saitarg ibit metnetopinmo muus mertap mued et da mulaec ni siluco sitavele te . . .*'

Frannie listened, transfixed, to the chanting sound of her own voice.

Oliver pressed the stop button. 'I don't know what gave me the idea to play it backwards.' She watched Oliver's finger hover, hunting for the reverse play button, then push down on it, and she listened to her words again, mechanically translating the Latin into English as she did:

'. . . and looking up to Heaven to thee, God, his almighty Father, giving thanks to thee, he blessed the bread, broke it, and gave it to his disciples, saying: Take and eat of this, all of you. For this is my Body –'

Oliver stopped the tape abruptly, leaving the house in silence. She was numb.

'You asked me where it's coming from.' Oliver's face was tight. 'The first time it happened was that night after we had seen you at your parents' café – although we didn't know you then.'

The cold air in the room was now burrowing deep into her veins, into her bones. She felt as cold as dead flesh.

'It's you, Frannie,' he said quietly. 'That's where it's coming from.'

CHAPTER TWENTY-FIVE

Frannie sat in silence whilst Oliver's words sank through her, dissolving like chemicals, paralysing her. As long as she did not believe it, she would be all right. She could cope with what he had said as long as she knew he was making it up.

She stared at the chromium-plated grilles of the speakers at each end of the ghetto-blaster, and the shiny red plastic casing. She wondered, irrelevantly, why he owned such an ugly thing. Perhaps it belonged to Edward. Or to Oliver's late wife. Perhaps Sarah Henrietta Louise Halkin had liked music blaring wherever she went. Perhaps she had played it loudly to keep out the silence of the house that was now closing around Frannie herself and entering into her.

She wondered how long she had been talking in her sleep. A few months? A year? Six years? All her life? A memory released itself, rose, like a bubble detaching itself from the floor of the ocean, to the surface of her mind. Her father yesterday morning.

You scared us, your mama and I . . . Not like you talking . . . Like someone else is a talking through you.

Who else had heard her? The bubble of memory expanded. Tom Dufferin, her last boyfriend, had said she mumbled in her sleep. So had Elliot Dumas before him. And on the dig in Iraq after leaving university, when she had shared a tent with three others, they had commented then that she woke them sometimes with her mumbling. The end of her last year at university. She thought back harder; no one had commented before then; no one at home, where she had shared a bedroom with her kid sister. Maria-Angela would have said something. The many previous occasions when she had shared tents on digs; others would have commented. She had shared a room in her second year at university with Meredith; she had not said anything. The end of her third year was when it had started. From worry about her exams?

Or –? She tried to dismiss the thought, but it persisted. The Ouija. They had done the Ouija at the end of that last year. Only days before the end of term. They had all been so happy that night; most of the term's coursework was over and they were winding down for the breather of the Easter holiday before the onslaught of finals. So innocent then. Unaware of what lay ahead; of the spirit they had attracted, angered, the thing that had come after them, pursued them.

Possessed her.

She looked down at her hands, unable to meet Oliver's gaze. She studied her nails; the tips of the fingers went blue after death; she remembered seeing her grandmother's fingernails in an open coffin in Naples; almost black.

Edward in the library came back to her.

I have this bad thing, Frannie. I don't want it . . . It makes things happen when I just think about them.

Edward influencing people. Surely it was coming from him. She spoke to Oliver. 'Edward said –' she stopped.

He raised his eyebrows, waiting for her to continue. But confusion swirled in her brain, because it might begin with herself, not Edward, in which case it was she who was making Edward will bad things on other people. It couldn't be.

'Why do you say it's coming from me?' she said.

'How do you know that Edward's picking it up from me, and not the other way round?'

'It's inconceivable from pure chance that you would both say mass backwards in your sleep, isn't it?'

She said nothing.

'You told me you'd heard about what Jung called Synchronicity; well, that's what I believe. That one of the explanations for what people call chance is unconscious telepathy between them. Channelling of thoughts.'

She watched him blankly.

'I think that one of you is instigating it, the other picking it up.' He uncrossed his legs, folded his arms and leaned forwards. 'Edward had never done this before he met you.'

You're wrong, she wanted to say. *You're wrong!* But she did not have the conviction.

'It's not you, Frannie, not your conscious self, any more than Edward knows what he's doing when he suddenly drifts off into those silences of his in the daytime. There's something else causing it. You're just the channel for it.'

'For what?'

He stood up and walked across to rest his hands on her shoulders. He squeezed them gently. She felt his warm, whisky-laced breath, saw the shadow of stubble that had begun to form, emphasizing his harrowed expression, his drained complexion. She became aware of the tears that were trickling down her own cheeks, and pressed her face into his chest, nestling against the skin of his neck and the soft wool of his pullover.

'Have you ever done the Ouija?' she asked.

'No.'

'I did, once.'

'What happened?'

Frannie told him everything and he listened carefully, leaning on the window-sill. When she had finished, his first reaction was, 'Have you checked on any of your other fellow students? Ones who weren't at the Ouija session?'

'Why?'

'To make sure you have the right causal connection. You're assuming it's the Ouija session, but it could be something else.' He flexed his toes inside his ancient plimsoles, studied them for a moment then went on. 'If odd things have been happening to other students who weren't at that Ouija session, that would put a different light on things.'

'You mean contact every student who was at London University during the three years I was there?'

'Yes. It wouldn't be impossible.'

'It would in the time,' she said quietly. 'And what would I say?' *Hello, just wondering if you're still alive?*

Oliver was silent for a while, deep in thought again. 'Do you have a tame priest?' he said finally.

'No. Not any more.'

He looked at her with heavy eyes. 'I think we need to find one.'

They made love because they each needed solace, but afterwards Frannie lay in Oliver's bed unable to sleep. The booze had worn off and she was troubled by her thoughts. She started to picture her own funeral, wondered which of her old boyfriends would turn up. Perhaps they'd feel guilty for not having loved her enough. Then she wondered whether she should phone Directory Enquiries to see if there was a Ouija helpline. Like Alcoholics Anonymous.

Beside her, Oliver's breathing deepened: strong, deep intakes of air. Physical strength, all the privileges of his birth and yet he still had his fears. Scared of coincidence.

Twenty-six.

She opened her eyes in a cold sweat. The hieroglyphics on the wall. And the number twenty-six inside the concentric circles! The tragedy with Tristram had knocked her out and because of that she still hadn't asked Oliver about what she'd seen in his own library. Now, suddenly, she couldn't wait.

Oliver moved; the bed clanked as he slipped out, and she heard him pulling something on, then treading carefully across the floor. The click of the door then another click as he closed it quietly behind him. She switched on her bedside light and sat up a little. A lavatory flushed, then Oliver returned.

'Hi,' he said.

She gave him a tired, strained smile, then the words poured out. 'In the library you've got charts on the walls with calculations all over them. What are they?'

He sat on the edge of the bed hunched in his paisley dressing-gown. 'Numerology,' he said simply.

'What is that?'

He yawned. 'Part of it is a theory that numbers provide the clues to understanding – I suppose – the underlying mysteries of the universe.'

'What sort of numbers?' She had to understand.

'All numbers have significance.'

'How are they worked out?'

He remained on the edge of the bed. 'It's a combination of metaphysics and religion. There are numbers in the Bible. Aristotle was very into them. Pythagoras. It all stems from a very logical base. Numbers provide a principle of order in a seemingly chaotic universe.'

'And how do you get the numbers?'

'Do you know what a palimpsest is?'

Frannie reached for her glass of water beside the bed. 'Yes – you get them a lot on parchment used by the old monks. When a text is erased and a new one written over it, you can still read the imprint of the old writing if you look hard enough, or in the right light.'

Oliver nodded. 'Numbers are in everything if you look hard enough. In the atomic molecules of everything we see and touch. In the Bible, there are hundreds of codes, messages. In our names and dates of birth.'

'How did you get interested in this?'

He leaned back against the headboard. 'Part of what mathematics is all about is order; patterns; trying to make sense out of chaos.' He reflected for a moment. 'The universe is chaotic, but our solar system is ordered – we have life on this planet because we happen to be exactly the right distance from the sun, the moon. Just a bit further away from the sun and it would be too cold to exist; a bit closer and it would be too hot. Is that chance? Or design?' He gave her a half smile. 'Human life is chaotic, yet we create ordered society, of a sort. We divide our planet into countries, establish governments, laws, education, codes of behaviour. All from random evolution? Natural selection? Or some greater design?'

She watched him, wondering where it was all leading. The despair in his eyes gave him the look of a man who has stared into the pit of Hell and cannot get the image from his mind. He seemed to be talking to himself, rambling almost, as if in doing so he might stumble across the answer. His bewilderment frightened her; she needed him to be strong. In the darkness beyond the undrawn curtains the stable clock was striking two.

'When Sarah died, for a long time I just couldn't

accept it; and when I finally did, I wanted to die too. I loved her so much, and I couldn't believe that I could ever –' He fell silent and Frannie drank some water. 'It was only Edward who kept me going. I had to be there for him; so I buried myself in work during the week, and I made myself a project down here for the weekends, to give me a focus on something. I was handling the theme of connected coincidence in my work at the bank and I thought it would be interesting to look back through my family to see whether coincidence ran through our history in any way.'

'Do you mean genetically?'

'No, not specifically.'

'Did you find anything?'

'Just one very odd coincidence. About a number.'

'What number?'

'Twenty-six,' he said.

Some water slopped over the rim of Frannie's glass and trickled down between her fingers and thumb.

He studied her, registering her lost composure. 'It's a rather interesting number in numerology. *Two* is a number that has a lot of evil significance. And so does *six*. The combination of the two digits, making twenty-six, is twice thirteen. Thirteen is a two-six number. Two times one is two. Two times three is six.'

'I think you're losing me,' she said.

He pushed some hair from his forehead then traced the contours of his face with his fingers, as if to reassure himself that he was still intact. 'I'm lost half the time as well; there are layers and layers. A sort of multiple palimpsest.'

'Why the number twenty-six though?' she persisted. 'Is there a reason for that particular number?'

'That's what I'm trying to find out. I came up with

one connection that's quite curious, although it doesn't mean anything. I mentioned to you that the second Marquess was into numerology?'

'He was the evil one?'

'Yes. I've discovered he was very keen on this number for some reason – it was sort of his signature, his mark. Except it didn't do him much good in the end. He was executed – murdered, whatever – on 26th March, 1652.'

Frannie smiled weakly.

'Does twenty-six mean anything to you?' he said.

'Yes it – might. Phoebe Hawkins warned me off it just before her accident, but I couldn't get much sense out of her when I saw her later in hospital. She was too shattered. I need to see her again.'

He frowned, returning to his previous line of thought. 'My wife, Sarah, also died on 26th March. And it was her twenty-sixth birthday.'

Frannie absorbed the words in silence. Her mouth felt dry. She looked at Oliver for an explanation, for an assurance which he couldn't give. Fear rose up her spine then spread like cold water across the base of her scalp. She bit her lip before she spoke again, tried to affect a normal tone of voice and failed.

'It's my twenty-sixth birthday next week,' she said. 'On the twenty-sixth.'

CHAPTER TWENTY-SIX

In the morning, Frannie left Oliver's room for her own shortly before six. At breakfast, they were all subdued.

The police came back whilst they were clearing up, took a lengthy statement from Frannie and increased her feeling of guilt, and were then closeted in the library with Oliver and Edward for over an hour.

When they finally left, Oliver said that he had to go to the farm and give Charles a hand as his brother was in no fit state to do anything. Frannie and Edward spent the remains of the morning mooching around the estate hunting fossils, and by lunchtime had collected a dozen good samples, which Edward proudly washed and told her he would be taking back to school with him.

She tried more than once to steer him back to the conversation they had had yesterday in the library but, each time, instead of answering her, he plied her with questions about fossils, about archaeology in general. And she had to promise, with a heavy heart, that if she was down next weekend they would do a mini dig in the grounds, just the two of them, somewhere around the site of the old Roman villa.

Then she turned and confronted him directly. 'Edward, in the library yesterday you told me how you could make things happen to people just by thinking about them. Did you have bad thoughts about Tristram before he got hit by the propeller?'

His response startled her. His eyes became hard and fierce, and his face tightened into a similar expression of fury. 'No!' he said in a voice that was almost a shout. Then he burst into tears and ran upstairs.

Frannie waited some minutes then followed him. She found him in his bedroom, sitting in a chair, sobbing. She put her arm around him and talked quietly. 'Tell me more about this bad thing, Edward.'

He reached out a hand and picked a small white sports car off a shelf beside him; he pressed a switch underneath it and the rear wheels began to spin.

'Want to dry your eyes?' she said.

He shook his head.

'Do you have any bad thoughts about anyone else? Do you have any about me?'

He switched his car off then on again without replying, back in one of his silences again.

Frannie tested him. 'What would you like for lunch? Shall I make you something nice?'

He stayed silent. Eventually she left him and went back downstairs. She hesitated in the hall, listening hard for any sign of Oliver, then walked through to the kitchen, and listened carefully again. Then, as quickly as she could, she removed one small shot of Edward from the photographic collage, and slipped it into the pocket inside her handbag.

At six o'clock they dropped Edward back at school and he went off glumly, his fossils carefully wrapped in paper in his small bag, having reminded Frannie of her promise of the dig. Then they drove to London.

'I've been thinking hard all day about a priest I could contact,' Oliver said. 'I have met the Archbishop of Canterbury; we're both in the House of Lords. I could have a word – but –' he shrugged. 'I don't really know if that's such a good idea. If he believed the story he'd probably delegate and it would take time.'

A lorry thundered past, its slipstream rocking them. 'But I could go and see the Bishop of Lewes tomorrow. He's quite a reasonable chap.' He squeezed Frannie's hand. 'It'll be OK.'

'And I ought to go and see your brother,' she said.

'Not for a bit; I don't think he can cope with seeing anyone.' He put his hand on her shoulder and stroked it lightly. 'Come with me tomorrow; we'll go and see the Bishop of Lewes. I'll ask him if he can see us tomorrow evening?'

She nodded bleakly.

'Stay with me tonight?'

She tilted her head and pressed her cheek against his hand. 'Could we make a detour?'

'Where to?'

'I'd like to pop in just for a few minutes to see Phoebe.'

The linoleum floor of the ward was spongy beneath Frannie's shoes. A trolley laden with surgical instruments rattled and she stepped aside to let it pass, the discomfort of being in a hospital adding to the leaden fear inside her.

There was a young woman sleeping deeply in the bed next to Phoebe, her face a sickly grey. Phoebe's table and the tray across her bed were stacked with flowers and cards, and more cards surrounded a massive basket of fruit. She was sitting up in bed, looking a better colour than Thursday, and even greeted Frannie with a smile.

'Thank you for the flowers you sent, Frannie – they're really beautiful.' She pointed to one of the vases on the table.

'You've got some life back in your face.'

'Drugs,' Phoebe said.

Frannie saw her dilated pupils and realized she was right, doped up; reality was at bay. She looked away so Phoebe could not see her grimace. Declan O'Hare had talked about the warriors who wore masks into battle so as to hide their fear. Frannie hoped she was not going into battle but knew that she had looked away to hide her fear from Phoebe just now.

'You went to see Susie,' Phoebe said.

'Yes.'

'I'm glad. I spoke to her today.'

Frannie sat down heavily on the chair beside the bed. 'When you rang me on Tuesday, Phoebe, you asked me if the number twenty-six meant anything to me, and you told me to be careful of it. Why exactly?'

'I always remembered it from the Ouija session. It stuck in my mind.'

'What was my message?'

'I seem to think that was it.'

'What do you mean?'

'*Twenty-six.* Or maybe it was *the twenty-sixth.*'

'Just the number?'

Phoebe nodded. 'I think so.'

'That was the whole message?'

'I don't know if it was a message, Frannie, or a prophecy.'

Frannie closed her eyes, then opened them again, afraid of the thoughts that waited behind her lids. 'Seb Holland,' she said, weakly. 'Do you remember what he was told?'

'No, Susie asked me that. I can only remember mine, yours, Jonathan and Meredith's.'

'Do you think all this is just chance? Coincidence?'

'No.'

'What is it?'

'I don't know.'

Frannie pushed some strands of hair from her face and glanced down evasively, waiting for some moments before speaking. 'How did your accident happen, Phoebe?'

'I'm not sure. I don't understand.'

'Understand?'

'Why I didn't stop.'

The expression in Phoebe's eyes changed as Frannie watched them; her blinking became faster and the lids quivered.

'Was it your brakes? Did they fail?'

'I didn't try to brake. I didn't put my brakes on at all.'

Frannie studied the dilated pupils. 'Why not?'

'That's what I don't understand.'

'Are you sure you're not still a little confused – the anaesthetics can – you know –?'

Phoebe shook her head. 'It's not the happy pills either. They think I don't know they're giving me happy pills.' Her voice was slurring as she raised it in anger. 'But I do know.' Her face contracted and the anger scared Frannie. 'I know. Right? I know.'

Frannie smiled gently, trying to defuse her anger. 'Yes, I'm sure.'

'They won't pull fast ones on me. I know which way's up in here.'

Frannie heard the sharp clack of a curtain being pulled around the bed next door. 'You saw the lorry, but you didn't brake; is that right?'

Phoebe shrugged and the stump rose and fell. 'Maybe I thought that if I stopped I would be late.'

'Late for what?'

'I don't know. I don't remember. Late for the game.'

'Game?'

'Playing fruit machines.' Phoebe's voice was slurring and her mind was drifting. She smiled.

Frannie summoned up a smile in return, but as she did, Phoebe's face changed, began to rumple and crinkle as if she were an inflatable doll from which the air was leaking. Changed from adult to child; to a pink-faced baby bawling in its cot.

Frannie pulled out her handkerchief, dabbed Phoebe's eyes, trying to staunch the flow of tears. She squeezed her hand, cradled her face, trying to stop the sobs.

A nurse came over. 'I think I'd better give her something.'

Phoebe shook her head fiercely. 'Go away. I don't want your fucking pills. I want my fucking arm back.'

She sobbed some more and then the tears subsided and she lay back, spent, against the pillow, her mouth open, gulping air as if she had emerged from swimming several lengths underwater. 'Sorry. Sorry, Frannie,' she whispered hoarsely.

'It's OK,' she whispered back and stroked her hand.

In the distance a floor polisher whined. 'Fruit machine,' Phoebe said. 'One-armed bandit. Obvious, wasn't it?'

Frannie hesitated. 'Phoebe, I want to ask you something. This might sound silly – but – did you see a small boy before the accident?'

Phoebe looked at her, puzzled. 'A small ginger-haired boy?'

Frannie stiffened.

Phoebe's mind seemed to clarify; her eyes brightened. 'Yes, Frannie, I did. He's been on my mind quite a lot.'

'What do you mean?'

'There was a boy standing on the kerb. I passed him

289

just before the accident. I remember thinking it was strange that he was out there on his own – and the way he was standing there – as if he wasn't wanting to cross the road, but was waiting for something.'

'Strange?' Frannie echoed, but her thoughts were elsewhere. Oliver's words last night. *It's you . . . That's where it's coming from.* She was remembering the Latin she learned at school. Remembering the Latin teacher who was a crabby, elderly man with a voice like a saw. Remembering when she was thirteen and asking him why it was necessary to learn a dead language. He had exploded in rage. Then, when he had calmed down, he had made her learn by heart, first the names of dozens of plants, then dozens of animals. Made her recite them out loud to the class. She was remembering Edward giving the plants their Latin names as they had both walked through the grounds of Meston. Edward reciting the names of the animals in the Range Rover driving back to London last Sunday night.

Frannie removed the photograph from her handbag and handed it to Phoebe. 'Is this him?'

Phoebe studied it carefully, then stared back at her suspiciously. 'Is he a witness? Has he said anything?'

Frannie was trembling. 'Is it him? Is it the boy you saw?'

Phoebe looked again. 'Yes,' she said. 'Definitely. Because I can remember him so clearly. When I saw him, it was like one of those freeze-frames on a video – as if time had stopped. He didn't look real. It was almost as if I was imagining him.' She smiled distantly. 'Or as if he was a ghost.'

CHAPTER TWENTY-SEVEN

The boy was curled in a foetal position, face downwards in a scooped-out hollow of rock inside the glass case. Urns and vases lay in there with him, as well as some metal bangles and an earthenware drinking-vessel. His face had long gone and his desiccated skin had hardened so that he looked more like a grotesque wooden sculpture than someone who had once been flesh and blood.

Declan O'Hare patted the top of the case with a paternal air. 'Egyptian Predynastic, this fellow,' he said. 'Gebelein. We date him around 3250 BC. The baubles and jugs are typical of the grave goods that would have been buried with him at the time.'

Frannie stared through the glass; she had done so several times before and she was never comfortable with the sight. There was something she found both morbidly fascinating and at the same time deeply disturbing about a dead human being in a display cabinet.

She watched the reactions of the other two research assistants who had been assigned to the preparation of the exhibition: Hermione Wallis, a friendly but slightly dozy girl with a beaky nose, hair swept back by an elastic band, hands rammed into her dungaree pockets, was glancing uncomfortably round the mummy room; Roger Wencelas, in Doc Marten boots, starched blue jeans and a pristine white T-shirt, was peering fiercely through his wire-framed spectacles at the corpse's tiny buttocks.

Mummies lined the walls of the room: several in

upright showcases, and one in a rotting wooden box. Frannie was tired. The monochromatic overhead lighting in the exhibit rooms became oppressive after a while. You forgot whether you were above ground or below it.

It was half past ten and the room was already teeming with tourists. The living posed in front of the dead, smiling to hide their unease; and smiling because they were on the right side of the glass, Frannie thought, suddenly.

'Attitudes to death,' O'Hare said. 'The way a civilization views its own mortality tells you a great deal.' He looked at each of them in turn, then nodded at Frannie. 'You're a good Catholic girl, perhaps you can enlarge on that for us?'

'Our civilization's afraid of death,' she said.

'Very good. Indeed we are. Afraid of that Great Unknown. Afraid of what we can't take with us.' His gaze scanned all three of them again, his bright blue eyes sparkling with the near-manic passion with which he addressed his work. 'Look at this chap.' He tapped the glass cabinet again. 'What kind of a world did he leave behind? What did he think of in those last moments before death?'

Frannie stared at the cabinet. The remains of Tristram were lying in there. The pink Bermudas with his thin legs and the tiny trainers. The coil of intestines like a dead snake; the splintered shaft of his backbone.

She pressed her hand over her mouth and turned. Jonathan Mountjoy stared out from another cabinet. His mouth was open and there was a bullet hole in his forehead. She spun her head, saw a blackened, shrivelled mummy; but it wasn't a mummy, it was Meredith, her socketless eyes staring back through the glass.

Frannie backed away, perspiration running down her neck, bumped into a cabinet, put a hand out to steady herself. Declan O'Hare was looking at her, so were her two colleagues. 'Sorry,' she whispered. 'I'm sorry.'

The meeting finally ended at twelve. Frannie hurried back to her office, wanting desperately to phone Seb Holland.

Penrose Spode was seated primly behind his desk, looking unusually fashionable in a yellow Lacoste shirt buttoned to the neck beneath a white jacket; he gave her a rather self-conscious smile as she came into the office, as if he were seeking reassurance.

He was normally in before Frannie, but this morning he had been late and it was the first time she had seen him today.

'Hi, nice weekend?' she said.

'Yes, thank you.' He watched her expectantly, like a puppy awaiting praise. 'Did you?'

'I've had better.' She gave a smile that felt like a twitch. 'I like the gear – is it new?'

'It's – ah – a birthday present to myself.' He blushed.

'When's your birthday?'

He blushed even harder. 'Today.'

'Oh, Penrose! I wish I'd known.' She switched on her word processor and sat down, then began rummaging in her bag for Seb Holland's business card. 'Are you celebrating tonight? Having a party?'

Spode wetted the point of his pencil with his tongue and tested it on his pad. 'Having a quiet dinner,' he said.

She thought he sounded rather sad. 'I think small celebrations are the nicest,' she said as cheerily as she could.

Spode opened his mouth as if to say something more then seemed to change his mind and returned to his work.

She found the card. It was embossed with the address of a skyscraper office block in the City which she had always liked immensely. She dialled, praying silently that Seb Holland was going to be all right. She was put on hold by a faintly hostile secretary, then Seb's cheery voice came on the line. 'Great seeing you last week – no – the week before,' he said. 'Real surprise!'

'Congratulations on your engagement.' Her relief that he was all right was tempered by anxiety.

'Have to give me your latest address – you must come to the wedding. Anyhow – we have to get together before that, have a drink or a bite or something.'

'Actually I'd like to – there's something I need to talk to you about.'

'Oh? Business?'

'No –' She saw Spode's ears were busy. 'It's not something I can talk about that easily over the phone.'

'Sounds mysterious!'

'I need to see you as soon as poss.'

'You've just caught me – I'm off to New York on Wednesday, and I won't be back until . . .' he paused and she heard the flick of a page, '5th October. How about that following week sometime? Are you free for lunch?'

'I need to see you before then, Seb. It's really urgent.'

'It can't wait?'

'No.'

There was a pause. 'Christ – I just haven't got any time – how long do we need?'

'Not long. Half an hour?'

'Could you come here at lunchtime tomorrow – we'll shoot off round the corner somewhere?'

'Yes, that would be fine.'

'Know where we are?'

'Yes, I do.'

'Come up to the fortieth floor and ask for me in reception. About one?'

'One. Fine.'

'You'd better give me your number in case something comes up.'

She gave him her home and office numbers, then hesitated. 'Seb, listen – this may sound a bit daft, but will you be really careful until I see you?'

'Careful? Of what?'

She wished Spode would mind his own business and stop listening; he was making her feel even more foolish. 'I – I'll explain tomorrow.'

'Right. OK.' He sounded uneasy; not about her warning, but about her. She tried to think of something to salvage the situation, but Seb terminated the conversation before she had a chance. 'Listen, I have to dash. I didn't want to be rude and not take your call. See you tomorrow, here, OK?'

She turned back to her screen and tried to apply her mind for the next hour, compiling the list Declan O'Hare had asked her to do from the central memory bank of every item of Egyptology in the Museum. She thought, glumly, that only a few days ago she had been relieved to be taken off a monotonous cataloguing job. This one was going to be even worse. If she lived long enough to complete it.

She stared at the screen; the cursor blinked, waiting for her next tap on the keyboard, for her next command, for the next piece of stored information she wanted to access.

Information. She thought about Oliver's research into numerology. When he had dropped her at the Museum this morning he had made a big effort to be bright, positive, to reassure her. But she could see it in his eyes: he was as scared as she was.

She thought hard, her brain tired, blunted by the pills she was taking to help her sleep and damp the shock. They were doing neither. There had to be more she could unravel. She had met Oliver at King's Cross. Before that their paths had crossed in the café. Maybe she had even met him before then, somewhere else. A connection. Something between her and the Halkins. Or her family and the Halkins. All this horror wasn't limited just to the group who were at the Ouija. Tristram hadn't been there. Nor had Dom. Nor had Edward's mother. Oliver was blaming her. But maybe there was something in his past, which he was hiding from her.

Or wasn't aware of.

At one o'clock Frannie hurried outside, weaving through the tourists and the pigeons. She crossed Great Russell Street, went into a newsagent and found a selection of birthday cards that were all either dull, or lewd and suggestive. She opted for one with a picture of the Horse Guards Parade, bought a packet of tiny candles then went into the café next door where she bought a pastrami sandwich, a lemon cupcake and a can of lime-flavoured Perrier. She perched on one of the stools, ate quickly, signed the card and put the cupcake into her handbag. Then she went back into the Museum, glancing at her watch. It was twenty past one.

She showed her pass and went into the hallowed domed silence of the British Library. There was a sharp contrast between the Library and the Museum even though they shared, for a short while longer, the same building. Whilst the interior of the Museum had a modern, progressive feel, the Reading Room of the Library felt as if it had been unchanged for centuries. Ancient volumes lined the grand circular shelves. The room smelt of old bindings, old paper, buffed leather and wood polish. The silence was disturbed only by the squeak of shoes, the rustle of turned pages, the putter of word-processor keys.

Frannie noticed Archie Weir, a genealogist she had met a couple of times. A kindly, worried-looking man, he sat behind piles of tomes that were stacked like a barricade, engrossed in some research. He was wearing an ancient tweed jacket with leather patches on the elbows, and an even more ancient shirt and tie. The tufts of grey hair on either side of his bald dome looked as if they had been glued on as an afterthought, and his wire half-framed glasses were perched halfway down his nose. His lips chattered wordlessly as he scanned a document, reminding Frannie of the rabbit in *Alice in Wonderland*.

Frannie quietly stood in front of him. After some moments, he looked up with a start, a frown of recognition spreading across his forehead as if a name and a face were speeding somewhere through his memory banks but had not yet collided.

'Frannie – Francesca Monsanto,' she said. 'Oriental Antiquities.'

'Ah, yes, yes, yes!' He put down the document. 'With Mr O'Hare.'

'That's right.'

'Ah, yes, yes, yes.' He was blushing and she wondered why. Then through a chink in the barricade she saw a flattened paper bag and a half-eaten sandwich.

Eating was strictly forbidden in here. 'I'm sorry,' she said. 'I don't want to disturb you.'

'Not at all, no, no, not at all.' To emphasize this he placed his hands firmly to either side of him on the desk and sat more upright.

'I was wondering if you could tell me the best books in here on the English aristocracy?'

'English aristocracy, yes,' he said. 'Yes. General history or a specific family?'

'A specific family. The Halkins – Marquess of Sherfield.' She thought as she whispered the name that she detected the faintest hint of distaste in his expression.

'Ah, Sherfield, the Halkins, yes.' A slight brake seemed to have been applied to his enthusiasm. 'Ah, yes, let me see, we're bound to have their family archive here if it's been printed up; most of them have been at some time, fortunately. Might be under the family name or in the name of their principal residence. There'd be something in *Debrett's* of course, and *Burke's Peerage*. Let me see.' His fingers, soft and wrinkled like old carrots, drummed the table. '*Arkwright's History of the British Aristocracy*, might be something in that. How much detail do you need?'

'As much as I can find.'

'You might also find a few mentions in one or two books on witchcraft.'

Before she'd digested this last remark, he'd picked up a stub of a pencil, a piece of notepaper and was writing down some titles in fat, slanting writing. When he'd finished, he gave her a list of a dozen books.

She thanked him and walked across into the vast Reading Room, awed as she always was in here by the sheer quantity of the volumes stacked floor to ceiling. Her watch said it was half past one. In her haste she walked straight past the Genealogy section the first time, and did a complete circuit of the room before finding it and scanning the titles.

She searched first for the name Halkin, then Sherfield. Then she went along the Ms. Marlborough, she read. Montagu. Melbourne Castle. Melksham. Mentmore. Then she saw it. A blue volume an inch and a half thick, with the wording *The Meston Hall Archives* embossed in gold on the spine. Next to it was *Meston and the Halkins – A History* by Keenan Towse.

Frannie pulled it out. Although the book was slim, it felt heavy. There was a ring on the cover where someone had once stood a glass or a mug. She opened it where she stood and smelled the dry, faintly woody smell that rose up from the pages. The frontispiece was an oval vignette of Meston Hall, in much better condition than now, with a horse and carriage outside. On the facing page was the family crest.

She glanced at a few pages further on. There were references to the Halkin family pedigree, the family archives, manorial records, title deeds and leases . . . She turned forwards a few more pages and came to the family tree which was on a triple page, folded over. She read some of the names: Sir Godfrey Halkin; Marie, dau. of Henry Le Sabanne; Agnes de Bournelle; Francis Edward Alwynne, second Marquess; Thomas; Lady Prudence.

There were several pages detailing the contents, followed by a dozen introductory pages in minute type that gave the French origins of the family, the first recorded instance of a Halkynne arriving in England in 1066, and where he'd settled.

She turned back to the contents: The First English Halkins 1066–1300, Halkin Rôles in the Crusades – Home and Abroad, Elizabethan Halkins, Halkins and the English Civil War.

She turned to that chapter and scanned through it. Six pages along, the second Marquess of Sherfield's name jumped out at her. She went back several paragraphs until she found the start of the section, then read through it slowly.

Francis Halkin. Second Marquess of Sherfield. 1600–1652. Unscrupulous and tenacious in asserting the right of the Halkin family, he inherited the title and the family's estates on the death of the first Marquess in 1625, and immediately came into conflict with his overlord, the Archbishop of Canterbury, and even with a group of tenants of his manor of Meston who complained of his 'daryke and bullynge behaviour and hideousness to defie ymaginacion amonges them'.

It is fair to say that Lord Francis Halkin was unique among nine centuries of Halkins for his sheer evil and depravity, a one-off in a family that in general contributed in many ways to the growth of the country and British Empire.

Francis Halkin, a true Jekyll-and-Hyde nature, outwardly a fickle political animal, inwardly a greedy and brutal sadist, deeply involved in the dark arts of Satanism and Numerology which he manipulated both for political and financial gain and for sexual gratification of the most perverse nature. In the Civil War he sided first for his own protection with the Parliamentarians, providing finance and men to Cromwell but subsequently provided help to the Royalists in the City of London, in particular the use of the underground passageway from the Halkin residence to the Thames, in exchange for a supply of children for sexual favours and ritual sacrifice.

In 1652 his younger brother, Thomas Halkin, informed on him to the Parliamentarians (whether from disgust at his perversions or in order to inherit the title is not established). His arrest warrant was signed personally by Oliver Cromwell, but soldiers, sickened by what they found in the premises, carried out their own fitting execution.

She turned forward, flipping through several pages of detailed information on the Halkin family properties – covering, in the thirteenth and fourteenth centuries, several counties. Then several plates of photographs. As she flipped through them, she stopped with a start, turning back to a scene of London that looked familiar.

Frannie felt her skin tightening around her body. The book shook in her hands as she was confronted by a print of Victorian London. The City. Hansom cabs and horse-drawn carts travelled down the street, and the shops were different. But she knew exactly where it was. She had spent most of her childhood there. The junction of Poultry with Cheapside. The front few buildings of Poulterers' Alley were clearly visible in the centre of the print.

Her eyes dived down to the caption at the bottom. Her focus blurred and she had to concentrate her vision: 'Site of original London residence of Halkin family. (Destroyed in Great Fire of 1666.) Now occupied by offices and shops of Poulterers' Alley.'

Where their sandwich bar had been.

CHAPTER TWENTY-EIGHT

Frannie ran out of the gallery and down the stairs, raced down the corridor to the phone booths, wanting to be more private than back in her office. She spilled a handful of coins on to the surface of the box and dialled Oliver's office number.

His secretary informed her, in a very formal voice, that Lord Sherfield had left at midday to go to the country, owing to a family bereavement and was not expected back today.

She rang Meston and Mrs Beakbane answered. She had not seen Oliver and gave Frannie Charles's number. Hesitantly, she tried that, but there was no reply.

She headed back to her office, her heart thumping. Declan O'Hare appeared out of a doorway and walked down towards her, moving in slow motion like a character in a dream.

'Are you all right, Frannie? With us? You don't look as if you've quite made it to Planet Earth today.'

'I'm OK,' she said.

OK OK OK. The word reverberated down the corridor.

'Well that's good. Not happy about working on the exhibition?'

'Very happy.'

'Good.'

GOOD OOD OOD. The echo followed her boss's footsteps. The corridor stretched and shrank, then a double door swallowed him and closed with a bang like a muffled shot.

She opened the clasp of her handbag with fingers

that were not working properly, fumblingly removed the lemon cupcake, pressed in one of the tiny candles she had bought, then tried to strike a book match. It fell from her fingers. She tore another out, lit it and carried the cake into her office. 'Happy birthday!' she said, trying to sound cheerful.

Spode looked up, startled, from a phone conversation. She put the tiny cake on his desk, pulled the card from her handbag, put that beside the cake and went to her own desk.

Spode terminated his conversation hastily. His eyes went from the card to the cake to Frannie and back. He read the card then set it carefully on his desk.

'Thank you,' he said. 'Thank you, Frannie. Thank you very much.' His voice was choked with emotion.

Her phone rang, startling her. It was Oliver.

'How are you, Frannie?' he said.

'I was trying to get hold of you,' she told him. Her throat felt as if it were full of rocks. 'I've found it!'

'Found what?'

'The connection. I've found the connection!' Her voice wasn't working properly, wouldn't let her speak at the speed at which she was thinking. 'You're not going to believe it. It's the café. Poulterers' Alley. Does that address mean anything to you?'

'Not a thing,' he said blankly.

'Your family home in London that got burned down in the Great Fire, in 1666?'

'What about it? I'm not with you.'

'It was on the site that is now Poulterers' Alley. That's where my parents had their café!'

He was silent for some moments. 'Godfathers,' he said. 'That's where you had the Ouija session?'

'Yes. That's the link, isn't it? It must be!'

'You're certain about the site?'

'It's in the library here.'

'*Non omnis moriar*,' he said.

Fear crawled across her skin like a living thing. '*Non omnis moriar*,' she repeated. She no longer cared whether Spode was listening or not. 'I think I'm beginning to understand,' she said.

'I haven't been able to speak to the Bishop yet – he's away until late tonight. His secretary's trying to get hold of him to ask him to call me. Charles is in a terrible state, I had to come down and try and get him a bit organized, make some arrangements. Got to sort out the funeral, got to get the body released by the coroner after the post-mortem. There's more cattle gone sick and I've got the vet coming this evening but he doesn't think he'll be able to get here until nine.'

'Can I do anything to help?'

'No. I just want you to be careful. Best thing is I'll call you later, as soon as I hear from the Bishop – I hope we can see him some time tomorrow.'

After he had hung up, Frannie stared bleakly at the kinked and twisted cord attached to the receiver. At the grubby dial; at the grain of the wood of her desk, noticing holes, scratches, the dull shine from the light bulb above.

The cursor on her word-processor screen blinked at her. She untwisted the plastic cord with her fingers. Spode's fountain pen scratched busily across the lined paper of a notebook. She smelled a faint trace of molten wax from the candle he had extinguished on his cupcake, and it reminded her of the candles in Oliver's bedroom.

She tapped in a fresh file access code on her keyboard, her brain on autopilot, her thoughts on Oliver, on Tristram, on Poulterers' Alley, on a night three and a half years ago.

She shivered. Tentacles stretched back into the past. She closed her eyes. If she could turn the clock back. Could have told Seb Holland that night to keep on driving, not to stop, could have told him she had changed her mind, that the cellar wasn't really a good idea after all . . .

Twenty-five years they had had that café. Her parents had taken it before she was born. All her childhood she had played in there, worked in there. On the site of Oliver's ancestral London home. The site where the second Marquess had murdered small boys. Where he himself had been murdered; by a red-hot poker.

What the hell had they contacted and picked up down there in that cellar? What had been there all along? All the time she had been scared as a child to go down? The bogeyman? The shadow, the scrape that was like a dragging foot – was that who it was?

The wrong file came up on the screen. She read the words, too scared by her thoughts to be irritated. 'Homo habilis. Skhul. Vindja. Upper Palaeolithic. Java Man. Peking Man.' Bones. Dead, long dead, whatever had happened mattered no more, unless you lived in some kind of parallel universe or whatever it was Declan O'Hare had gone on about not long ago.

There were no such things as ghosts.

Penrose Spode was looking at her. 'Are you all right, Frannie?'

'Yes, I'm fine.'

'You're crying.'

She put her hands to her cheeks, startled. They were wet. She sniffed, pulled out her handkerchief and dabbed them. 'Sorry,' she said, sniffed again and forced a smile.

His lips closed in a silent apology for his intrusion, but he continued to stare at her. She thought he was never going to return to his work. Then he laid his elbows on his desk, pressed the fingertips of both hands together and inclined his head, shyly. 'I don't know – if you have any other plans – but – er – if you don't – er – would you have dinner with me?'

'Come to your birthday party?'

'I'm not having a birthday party,' he said quietly. 'I wasn't doing anything tonight.'

She looked back at him, surprised, and feeling sorry for him. Considered the prospect of going back to her empty flat, waiting for Oliver to ring, sitting alone with her thoughts. Did not want to be alone.

'Sure,' she said. 'I'd love to.'

Penrose Spode was getting drunk. Frannie could see it in his co-ordination, in the way he was articulating with his hands; in the way his expression was becoming soppier and his voice slurring. She was getting drunk too; the booze cheered her, made her feel safe, made everything seem all right, just a bad dream, that was all.

Spode tried to pick a peanut out of the goo of dark sauce with his chopsticks. The points of the sticks clacked together a full inch short of the nut. He persevered, focusing with difficulty, and finally held the nut up triumphantly. As he moved it towards his mouth, it slipped free and tumbled down his chest leaving a sticky brown trail through the grains of rice that already adorned his yellow T-shirt.

'Ooopsh!' he said.

Frannie wanted to stay drunk, to get drunker still. She signalled to the waiter for another bottle of Pinot Grigio. Spode registered mock alarm with his eyes and went for a mushroom in another of the array of Thai dishes on the table. He hoisted it up, trapped between the points of his sticks, then it shot out and skidded across the white tablecloth like an ice-hockey puck.

'Have you always been interested in archaeology?' Frannie asked him.

He hovered his chopsticks over the errant mushroom as if he was hoping to catch it unawares. 'Yes.'

'What in particular interests you?'

He inclined his head, leaning forwards a fraction, and drawing her in towards him as if he was letting her into a great secret. 'The past speaks to me.'

'Speaks?'

'Yes.'

She plucked out a hot, spicy prawn, and Spode's eyes followed her chopsticks as if he was watching a conjuring trick. 'You mean you have conversations with the past? What do you say to each other?'

Spode grinned, then hastily covered his mouth with his hand and resumed his inert expression of seriousness.

'Psychometry,' Spode said, keeping his voice low.

'Huh?'

'I have this gift.'

'Psychometry?'

The waitress presented the bottle for inspection, hovered between Frannie and Spode and was rescued by Frannie. Her mouth burned from a hot prawn and she could barely detect any flavour as she tasted it. 'Fine,' she said, then looked back at Spode. 'What's psychometry?'

'I can tell things about the past by touching objects.'

'You mean you're psychic?'

Spode blushed. 'Sort of.'

She ate a mouthful of cod in ginger. 'You're a dark horse, aren't you!'

He cradled his freshly filled glass, and drank by

lowering his mouth to it. Wine trickled down his chin. 'People think you're a bit –' he tapped the side of his head. 'You know – if you talk about these things.'

'So what sort of things can you tell by touching objects?'

'Depends.'

'On what?'

'On the strength of the imprints.' He eyed a prawn, then stared dubiously at his chopsticks. 'On the condition of the object. Where it's been stored.'

'Why does that affect it?'

'Objects pick up everything emotional that happens close to them.'

'How?'

He leaned forwards and she thought for a moment he was going to try to kiss her. 'They absorb things, the same as walls do, in their subatomic particles, or somewhere. I can read them. Usually works best if it's a personal object – or something that's been buried and undisturbed for years.'

'What sort of personal objects?'

'Rings. Watches. Bracelets.'

'Could you read my watch?'

He looked at her scratched and battered Citizen quartz. 'How long have you had it?'

'My father gave it to me for my sixteenth birthday.'

He put down his chopsticks. She unclipped it and gave it to him. He closed his hand around it and stared up at the ceiling with such intensity that his pupils almost disappeared and all she could see were the whites of his eyes. His expression alarmed her, short-circuiting her feelings of pleasant oblivion.

'I'm getting a young man with a red sports car, and a link with fish. I think you had a boyfriend who was a fishmonger. Not really a boyfriend, a boy you went out with but did not like. People wanted you to marry him but you were not interested; almost like an arranged marriage, I am sensing. A source of anger between you and your father. Your father was keen for you to marry him, there was plenty of money in the boy's family. And now I'm getting more anguish between you and your father. Always you and your father, your mother is meek; it's your father you fight and you feel guilty about it but you never give in because you are a very determined girl.'

She stared at him in amazement. He was talking louder, his voice sounding increasingly excited. 'Yes, yes, archaeology; a source of contention! Your father was angry that you wanted to do archaeology because there is no money in it. You have fought with him often over this. You have a younger sister who always wears a black hat. You are deeply in love at this moment with a man you met at a railway station.' He fell silent.

People were turning round and looking at them. Frannie was aware that conversation at other tables in the restaurant had subsided; she was trembling with a strange current that was flowing through her, disturbing the rhythm of her body, and she was blushing hard. It took her some moments before she had collected her thoughts enough to speak.

'That's extraordinary, Penrose.' Her face was in a tight frown, trying to think back, to remember if she had ever told him any of this. They had exchanged pleasantries and talked about work, but never conversed about anything personal before. 'Can you tell me any more about this man I met at a railway station?'

He closed his eyes. 'He has a boy. No wife. She is dead.'

'And the boy? Can you tell me about him?'

She watched him sit in silent concentration. Again the pupils almost completely disappeared; his fist was clenched tightly around the watch, shaking with the tension. He looked as if he was about to say something. Then suddenly, quite unexpectedly, he shot his hand out towards her and uncurled his fingers, presenting the watch to her with an intensely reproachful expression. 'You'd better take it back.'

She felt herself sobering and her nerves shimmying. 'What's the matter?'

'Take it,' he said. 'Please take it.'

'Can't you tell me some more? Please, Penrose.'

'It's just a blur – too many conflicting emotions. Too much to drink. I can only pick up the past not the present.'

'I thought mediums could divine the future through psychometry?' She clipped her watch back on, reluctantly.

Spode ran his eye suspiciously across the dishes, as if he was surveying enemy territory. 'That's a rather presumptuous thing to do,' he said, hovering the chopsticks over a mange-tout that stuck like a green fin out of a dish that she did not remember ordering. 'Objects are not crystal balls; they are like video-recorders; the past is imprinted in them, not the future. And I'm not a medium.' He looked uncomfortable; evasive.

The mange-tout fell on to the tablecloth and he picked it up with his chopsticks with a sudden deftness that surprised Frannie, and clearly surprised him also. She heard the crunch as his teeth bit the crisp vegetable, then saw him lick his lips with the satisfaction of someone who has achieved a small but significant personal landmark of progress. He studied his chopsticks through new, triumphant eyes, as if they had changed from being his enemies into his friends.

'That wasn't just telepathy, what you did? You didn't subconsciously pick those thoughts out of my head?'

'I might have done.' He suddenly looked sullen and she saw a trace of the old Penrose Spode she knew in the office, the supercilious, petulant introvert. 'But when I hold the teabowl that belonged to an Ashokan warrior two thousand years ago and learn about things that happened to him, I don't imagine his decomposed remains are in much of a condition to communicate to me telepathically.'

'I didn't mean to be rude – it's just – I mean – what you told me is incredible – so accurate.'

He looked appeased and drank some more wine. Then he lowered his voice right down and leaned close again, glancing warily around him before he spoke. 'I've helped my brother a couple of times.' He nodded, knowingly.

'I didn't know you had a brother.'

'He's a priest.' He raised his glass to his mouth and noticed to his surprise that it was empty. He lifted the bottle out of the ice bucket and a rivulet of water trickled on to his plate as he filled both Frannie's glass and his own to the brim.

'Are you religious, also?'

He shook his head. 'We don't get on very well.'

'How've you helped him?'

'Hauntings. Place memories. He's a diocesan exorcist. He knows what I can do isn't telepathy.'

'Exorcist?'

'Not his title – but that's what he is.'

'Who does he work for?'

'Church of England.'

'They have an exorcist?'

'Several. He has to investigate – when people in his

parish think they have a ghost in their house or their pub or something. He has to go and see what it is. I've gone along and done my bit.'

'By reading objects?'

'Objects. Or walls.'

'I don't see the connection with exorcism.'

'Some ghosts are place memories that people trigger off. I can read what they are for him.'

'Off the walls?'

'Mostly.'

'Does that scare you?'

He carefully raised his full glass. 'There's nothing scary about the past; it can't harm you.' He looked down as if he did not want to meet her eye.

'Do you know anything about Ouija boards?'

He inspected the top of his glass, lowered it unsteadily and picked up his chopsticks again. 'My brother doesn't like them.' He ran his gaze across each of the dishes and fished out another mushroom. 'He gets a lot of people with problems after the Ouija.'

'What sort of problems?'

The mushroom fell from the chopsticks inches from his mouth but he did not notice; he suddenly stood up, the colour drained from his face, and without saying anything, walked hurriedly and erratically to the back of the restaurant. Ten minutes later he had not reappeared. Frannie went down the narrow stairs at the back of the restaurant to look for him. At the bottom were two doors, one with the silhouette of a man, the other a woman. She knocked on the one with the man but there was no response. Timidly she opened it and there was a strong reek of vomit. Spode was curled up on the floor beneath the wash-basin, asleep.

Frannie cleaned her colleague's face with a damp paper towel and the manager called a taxi. She paid

312

the bill for the two of them and Spode recovered enough to stagger to the taxi, supported by herself and a waiter, and tried to give his address to the driver. 'Spenrose Pode, Number Sheventy-sheven.'

The taxi stopped outside the Victorian mansion block in Wandsworth where Frannie knew he lived, and she helped him along the corridor to his flat and made sure he was safely in. His flat was as neat and bland as his desk. He looked at her with barely focusing eyes, and made a supreme effort to be coherent, 'My brother could help you,' he said, then she had to catch him as he stumbled.

'Yes, please.'

'Call him in morning.'

She climbed back into the waiting taxi, her own head swimming from the wine and the exertion, and fell asleep herself. She woke with a start to find she was outside her flat, paid the driver a sum which would normally have grieved her and heaved herself out, walking unsteadily down the steps, clinging to the rail as she went, and bashed noisily into the dustbins at the bottom.

She let herself in, staring at the post scattered on the floor. As she closed the front door, silence enclosed her.

Too silent.

Suddenly as sober as a judge, she stared down the empty hallway with a feeling of apprehension, backed towards the door, put her hand on the Yale latch, listening. Something was not right. Silence except for the hum of the fridge. Took a step forward. Then another. Her bedroom door was open. So was the kitchen door. Darkness spilled out of them into the hall. The sitting-room door was open also. The faint haze of orange from the street lighting shone through.

Through the silence.

She took another step forward. Waited. Heard the voices above her. A man shouting. Then a woman. The couple rowing as they often did. The baby crying. The sounds of other life in the building gave Frannie courage and she stepped forward again. Then pushed the sitting-room door open, reached in her hand and snapped on the light.

Nothing moved. Nothing there. Empty. The curtains hung open, undisturbed. Her Roman vase sat on the coffee table. She walked in slowly, looking around. Something caught her eye in the hallway; a shadow moving; or maybe it was her imagination. She stared at the doorway, watching the emptiness. Her ears popped as if she were going up in an aeroplane and she swallowed to relieve them. Then the phone rang and the stillness was shattered like exploding glass.

She snatched at the receiver, brought it to her ear. 'Yeshallo?' she said, talking quietly, as if afraid someone in the flat would overhear her.

'Frannie?' It was Oliver's voice.

'Frannie? You all right?'

'Yes.' Just a whisper again.

'I've been calling you all evening. I've been worried out of my wits.'

She watched the hall. The shadow moved again. Stopped. Moved again. 'Where are you?'

'Down at Meston.'

Shadows suddenly jumped all around her. She looked up. The light that hung from the ceiling was swaying wildly in the breeze.

Except there was no breeze.

Alarm coursed through her nerves. The light began to swing faster. The cheap fringed shade the colour of parchment; the brown flex. Faster. The wire frame creaked against the bakelite collar. Faster. The shade hit the ceiling and the flex went slack for a moment; then it swung and hit the ceiling on the opposite side; the shade cracked and a piece of dry, papery material fell to the floor.

'Frannie? Frannie? Are you there?'

The light swung the other way, hit the ceiling even harder, hurled in anger; a huge chunk of the shade fell away. It swung back the opposite way. Hit the ceiling again. Hit it in fury.

She shrieked, putting her hands up as a chunk of the shade and its wire frame fell away, missing her by inches. She jumped to her feet, pulling the phone with her behind the sofa, staring at the lamp in blind terror.

'Frannie?'

This time the lamp swung even harder. The rest of the shade fell away, leaving the bare bulb and a few spikes of wire.

'I'm leaving right now, Frannie. I'll be with you in an hour.'

There was a flash above her head. Then the entire flat was plunged into darkness.

She threw down the phone and ran out into the hall, down to the front door, jerked it open and stumbled up the steps to the pavement, then stood gulping down air, leaning against the railings in a cold sweat.

Without moving and without looking back at the flat, she stayed there for over an hour until the lights of Oliver's Range Rover shone in her face, and he was cradling her in his arms.

'I didn't imagine it, Oliver.'

He had mended the fuses and they were sitting on the sofa in her living-room.

'I didn't.' She noticed for the first time how

exhausted he looked. His face was white, with a patina of grease, and his hair was limp. His dark grey pin-striped suit was crumpled, his top shirt-button was undone and his tie hanging loose. His hands were grimy. He stared at the Roman vase. 'The Bishop rang. He was very helpful. I told him you're a Catholic – or used to be, but he said it made no difference – he's referred me to a rector in London who's the diocesan exorcist for the area. Protocol, I suppose.' He shoved his hands into his trouser pockets. 'I tried ringing him, but he must have been out. I left a message on his answering machine. Are you free any time tomorrow?'

'I'm having lunch with Seb Holland.'

'Perhaps he ought to come too if we go to this clergy-man?'

'If I can persuade him.'

'Are you going to work in the morning?'

'Yes.'

'The message I left the rector – I asked him to call you if he couldn't get hold of me – I gave him both your numbers.'

'What's his name?'

'It's – ah –' He clicked his finger and thumb a couple of times. 'Rather odd name.' He pulled out his diary, opened it and turned several pages; then he seemed to have difficulty deciphering his writing. 'Canon Benedict Spode,' he read out finally.

'Spode?'

He nodded. 'I think so.'

'S-P-O-D-E?' she spelled out.

'Yes.' He looked at her with surprise. 'Why? Do you know him?'

She stared back at him. 'Where do they stop, these coincidences?'

He frowned. 'I'm not with you.'

She shook her head in disbelief. 'I share an office with his brother. We had dinner together tonight.'

The page of Frannie's diary said 'Tue 25th Sept'.

She sat at her desk trying to work, waiting for the phone to ring, running through in her mind what she was going to say to Seb Holland. She was trying hard to hold her sanity together, trying to think of everything that had happened and not think about it at the same time. Not thinking about Tristram. Phoebe's stump. Max Gabriel being eaten away.

Her head ached fiercely. It was a damp, overcast morning and a strong wind was blowing outside; a chill fear soaked through the whole of her body, mildewing her insides and making her feel sick. She wished she had dressed in warmer clothes than her navy linen two-piece and the cerise blouse which she had put on to look smart for Seb, as well as for seeing the priest.

Penrose Spode did not appear until after eleven o'clock, and when he did he slipped in wordlessly, hung his cycling kit on the hook and walked across the office in a curious, upright manner as if he had just come from a lesson in deportment.

He eased himself into his chair and carefully placed his hands on his desk. His face was a similar shade of white to when Frannie had found him on the washroom floor. He smiled apologetically then winced, as if the act of stretching his lips had hurt his face.

'Morning,' she said.

Spode mouthed a silent reply.

'How are you feeling?'

'Rather fragile.' He stared around the office as if trying to remember where he was. 'I think the food

must have been a little rich for me. Thank you for –'
He raised his hands and dropped them, blushing. He
sat down, closed his eyes and pinched his forehead
tightly between his hands. 'I'm not very good at
drinking.'

'We had quite a lot.'

He looked as if he was about to stand up again.
'I think I might get a coffee – would you like
one?'

'You were talking about your brother last night.'

He cradled his forehead in his hand for some moments, then he nodded slowly. 'I spoke to him already.'

'You have?'

'That's why I'm late in. I went round to him.'

'Oh?'

'I wanted to make sure he understood.'

'Thank you,' she said, surprised.

'I've arranged for you to see him at half past six this
evening. All right?'

'Yes – yes, thank you.'

'Good. I –' He fell silent and his mind seemed to
wander. Then he stood up. 'Black, no sugar?'

'Yes, thanks. Want me to get them?'

'No, it's OK.' He shuffled across the room like an
old man. As he reached the door, he stopped and
looked at her for some moments. 'You will go, won't
you?'

'Of course.'

'It's very important.'

'Yes, I know.'

'It's just sometimes I'm never quite sure when you
are being serious.'

'I am serious. Penrose. Really serious. There's someone else I'd like to take with me if it would be all

right.' She looked at him, but was unable to read his reaction. 'His name's Seb Holland.'

He said nothing else, and shuffled out of the door down the corridor.

CHAPTER TWENTY-NINE

Frannie came out of Bank tube station at a quarter to one, blinking in the sunlight which had broken through the cloud. The autumnal wind was freshening, blowing right through her thin clothes. Her hair thrashed irritatingly around her face, her jacket and skirt flapped and billowed.

She waited for the lights to change before she crossed over. A sightseeing coach chuntered past. A taxi followed, then a BMW, its driver talking on his telephone. A motor-cycle courier weaved by, its engine blasting. A road drill pounded and her own nerves pounded with it.

On the far side, a pretty girl came tripping out of an office and greeted a young man in a suit with a hug and a long kiss. Frannie enviously watched the carefree way they linked arms and walked away. Normal life was going on and she felt excluded from it.

The pavements were crammed with people moving quickly, urgently. Men jostled past her in funereal suits and peacock ties, women in two-pieces, their necks trussed importantly in Hermès and Cornelia James scarves. The traffic stopped and she crossed over.

People were queueing in the sandwich bars, and she heard the usual lunchtime hubbub as she passed a pub, then silence as she walked through the shadow laid across the pavement by the Gothic façade of a church. She glanced up at the windowless wall. Fear pressed to her skin like brass against tracing-paper, rubbing dark lines across her face. A siren wailed. She slowed her pace, her feet weighted with uncertainty. An ambulance flashed across, ahead, its siren a swirling banshee that beat her stomach like an egg whisk.

She passed sights so familiar from childhood that she scarcely noticed them. In the City, things rarely changed; when they did it was brutal: radical surgery; a familiar comfortable sight cut away like a mastectomy; cranes, skeletal girders rising like prosthetic limbs. She passed the Record Album shop, Boots the Chemist, Austin Reed, reassuringly unchanged, then orange lights winked ahead of her. Temporary bollards in the middle of the road. A triangle of barriers; the reflectors of unlit red lanterns. She felt the first prickle of apprehension as she saw the hoarding sticking out into the road, encasing an entire block of empty buildings; as she saw the huge sign on it: MACFAZEDEAN BROTHERS PLC. CITY FIELDS DEVELOPMENT.

MacFazedean Brothers. The name lodged in her gullet. Bastards. The slick young men in their grey striped suits who served the eviction notices, took her father's ranting with barely a twitch of their facial muscles and had the gall to tell him it was the best thing for everyone.

It was a large development. Seven acres. Two giant cranes rose from its midst, one with a demolition ball suspended from its jib and swinging menacingly in the wind. There was a cacophony to jar the ears and a pall of dust hung in the air above the entire site.

On some of the buildings visible above the tall hoarding the façades had been torn off, leaving rooms that were open to the elements, like a scene from a war movie of the Blitz, and Frannie felt for an instant as if something had been torn from herself, leaving her raw and exposed. Number 14 Poulterers' Alley was behind that hoarding; somewhere. She crossed over and ran along a boarded walkway where the pavement had once been, past the words GARBUTT MCMILLAN ARCHITECTS on a smart red sign.

Taking her bearings from the shops opposite, she reached what should have been the start of Poulterers' Alley, but the hoarding went across it, sealing it off. There were small viewing slits cut into the hoarding and she pressed her face to one and found herself looking straight down the alley. It was gloomy and forlorn; the windows were boarded up and all that remained were the names of the shops and offices, and closed doors. She could see the café, and the sadness she felt was tempered by a rising fear.

The whole central core of the site had been disembowelled. She could see right into the cellars. One was filled with water; another was now bare mud, shored up with iron pilings. A hook was sinking down from the jib of the massive crane and she saw the demolition ball swing out of sight. There followed a crash of rubble, the gears of a bulldozer meshing, metal clanging, and then a steady hiss of compressed air.

Dust dried the back of her throat as Frannie walked on and reached the site entrance. She went in through the wide-open gates, on to rubble-strewn mud that was rutted with tyre treads, and was confronted by a hive of activity: bulldozers; dumper trucks; tippers unloading; men in hard hats measuring, digging, drilling. Two men were attaching an iron piling to the hook of the crane. Three others on a rooftop were hauling up tools on a rope. Someone was shouting instructions. Over to her right the demolition ball swung against an unsupported wall belonging to one of the buildings immediately behind Poulterers' Alley. The wall buckled. The ball swung again. In its wake a bulldozer was clawing at the rubble like a crab scavenging a carcass on the seabed. In one of the deep rectangular pits a yellow JCB digger was pounding a stone floor, tearing great chunks of it out, lifting them up and dumping them in a skip. It looked as though it were ripping out the entrails of the earth itself. She stepped over some cables, then had to move out of the way of another truck. She checked her watch. Five to one.

She turned and left the site, then crossed the road, quickening her pace. As she reached the end of the next street, she could see Seb Holland's office building ahead. The Winston Churchill Tower, its bronze walls rising sixty storeys high out of the open square in which it sat. Her favourite modern building, which she had watched go up as a child, but which she had never been inside.

She remembered how it had always seemed to absorb the different moods of the weather and now it darkened suddenly as a cloud slid across the narrow corridor of sky like a roof hatch closing. A ferocious gust ripped across the open square, whistling eerily like a mountain wind, bending the conifers in their marble tubs and blowing the spray of the fountains sideways; the spots of water striking Frannie's cheek gave the illusion for a moment that it was raining. Her jacket thrashed like a loose sail and she had to hold it tight around her chest. One of the local criticisms was that the building created a wind tunnel around it.

Frannie pushed through the revolving door into a vast marble lobby that was strangely quiet. She heard the ping of an elevator, then another. The names of the companies housed in the building were engraved on a tall brass plate like a roll of honour on a cathedral wall. She scanned down it.

The fortieth floor, she remembered Seb Holland had told her.

The centre of the lobby was dominated by a Henry Moore sculpture, and presided over by an elderly commissionaire in black serge, his jacket breast covered in rows of decorations and his shoulders looped with bright white rope. Beyond him the lobby narrowed to an alcove containing two banks of four elevators each. One of them disgorged a group of men who walked across the lobby in silence. Two office girls came out of another and walked past Frannie, snippets of their chatter trailing behind them.

A man and a woman emerged from another, the woman talking emphatically. Frannie stepped into the elevator. It had a deep bronze carpet, black lacquered walls with bronze-tinted mirrors and reeked of a perfume she did not recognize.

She touched the button marked *40* on the panel and it lit up, but for a moment nothing happened. She tidied her hair in the mirror, then pulled a tissue out of her handbag and quickly wiped the mud from the building site off her dark blue shoes. The doors closed, decisively and smoothly. For an instant, again, nothing happened. Then an unseen hand lifted her by the insides of her stomach. The carpet pressed up hard against her feet. She felt a great weight on her knees. There was a rush of air and a faint drumming. Numbers spun on the digital dial above the doors. Her stomach rose up through her body. 15 20 25 30 35.

The pressure eased. The floor shrank away from her

feet. Her stomach was lowered gently. The display slowed, 38, 39, then halted. 40. Ping. The doors opened. She walked out, slightly dazed, into a hallway. The four elevator doors opposite faced her, and there were double oak doors to her right and left. The one to her left had a large brass plate which said: HOLLAND DELARUE PLC. RECEPTION.

Frannie went through into a sumptuous oak-panelled room, with deep leather armchairs and sofas on either side of the reception console. Large gold letters on the wall behind her proclaimed the dozen countries around the world in which Holland Delarue plc had offices, and the centre-piece was a large blue and gold 'Queen's Award for Export' emblem.

The receptionist was a woman in her late forties with silver highlights in her coiffed black hair, chatting busily on the telephone in a nasal voice and filing her nails at the same time. 'Melanie didn't come in today, another of her migraines, so I'm stuck over lunch hour. I thought I might try the new Asda superstore this evening. I'll just put you on hold a moment, don't go away.' She pressed a switch then looked inquisitively at Frannie.

'Could you tell Sebastian Holland that Frannie Monsanto is here, please.'

'He's expecting you, is he?'

'Yes.'

She pressed two buttons on her telephone, lifting the receiver to her ear. 'Oh, would you tell Mr Sebastian that Frannie Monsanto is in reception. Yes, no, I'm still here. Melanie didn't come in today, so I'm covering lunch hour.' She held the receiver to her ear in silence for a moment. 'Righty-ho. Thank you very much.' She looked at Frannie again. 'He'll be out in a couple of minutes. Take a seat.' She flicked a switch and resumed her conversation.

Frannie sat in a deep leather armchair and glanced at the magazines and papers on the table beside it. The *Financial Times. Fortune. Business Week. Lloyd's Log.* The walls were hung with framed colour photographs of modern office blocks. The telephone warbled again. It was a different world in here; a long way from the one in which Seb Holland, the archaeology student, had gone down into a cellar beneath a sandwich bar for a lark.

The doors behind her opened. 'Frannie! Hi! Sorry to keep you!'

She stood up and turned round. Seb was looking tired but cheery, the same slightly larger-than-life Seb: tall and hefty with his generous grinning face, big white teeth, black hair fashionably long and with a hint of gel, and his rich green eyes. His well-cut clothes and the executive trappings suited him. He looked good on them.

He gripped her shoulders and kissed her on each cheek, smelling heavily of aftershave as she remembered he always did. 'God, you look great! Hope you're still available in case Lucy dumps me at the last minute!'

She smiled. 'You look good too. Being engaged suits you.'

'Yah. It's great! Right, let's dash. I've booked at a little place around the corner. We'll have to be quick if you don't mind – bit of a crisis has come up and I've got to be back here by two o'clock.'

'You're off to New York tomorrow?'

'A hassle. We've got some real problems over there at the moment. So where are you working? British Museum, did you tell me?' He held the door for her,

326

then stepped across and pressed the elevator button. 'Are you doing something with archaeology? You don't look like an archaeologist.'

'How are we supposed to look?' she said with mock indignation.

'Thought you'd be in an anorak and wellies.'

'Like I was wearing at dinner?'

He grinned. 'So, smart dates, eh? You're going out with Ollie Halkin?'

'Yes.' It sounded strange hearing Oliver's name abbreviated.

'Good stuff. How long?'

There was a ping behind her and they turned. A strip of green lights was flashing on an art deco display above an elevator. The same one she had come up in, she noticed.

The door slid open and Seb stepped forward quickly, holding his arm out to catch the door. 'Hello, young fellow!' he called out. Frannie felt a blast of cold air. 'Have to get in these things quickly,' he said; 'the doors are really vicious bru –'

His voice stopped in mid sentence. She saw his eyes widen in wonder. Another blast of wind curled around her, sucked her, as if it was trying to draw her in towards him. There was blackness all around him. The wrong blackness. Not the black lacquer of the elevator walls and the bronze tint of the mirror.

No bronze-carpeted floor.

A dark, matt blackness. Air poured out. Cold air that smelled dank like a cellar. The blackness of the bare shaft. Cables ran down the back wall. Grooves were cut into it; ridges and guides.

There was no fear in his eyes; just a look of surprise; like a child opening a parcel and finding nothing inside it. His hand grabbed once at the steel door-frame; his fingers slid for a few inches down its shiny surface, without any hope of purchase.

Then he dropped from her sight in complete silence.

CHAPTER THIRTY

For a moment, for just a fleeting instant, Frannie thought it was one of his pranks. She stepped two inches forwards, moving slowly as if she were wading through water. Her hand touched the cold steel frame of the door and she stared into the darkness, breathed in its dank, oily smell.

A bunch of bright yellow wires, held together by thick black tape, ran down the far wall into a junction box with a warning bolt-of-lightning label on the outside. Ducting pipes ran down beside them; she dropped to her knees and inched forward on her hands, still protected by a layer of disbelief.

'Seb?' she called out in a feeble croak, her throat clamped shut like a sprung trap.

Her hands touched the metal rim and her eyes strained into the square black tunnel that dropped sheer away for forty storeys. The dust in the draught made them smart. 'Seb?' it was a whimper now. She looked up. The ribbed black ceiling was only ten feet above her; wires looped down from it. It was a moment before she realized it wasn't the ceiling, but the floor of the elevator that had stopped inches above the top of the door. 'Seb?' the darkness sucked up her voice. She looked up at the elevator and down into the shaft again.

Then the reality hit her and tore the scream from her throat.

She backed away from the edge, scrambled to her feet and burst, stammering, through the double doors into the reception area, her eyes transmitting her terror like semaphore flags to the woman she'd seen earlier and who was still chatting merrily.

'Get help! Oh God, get help!' Frannie screamed. 'He's fallen. He's fallen down the lift. Call an ambulance. For God's sake call an ambulance! Keep people away from the lift. Don't use the lift, the door's open.'

She ran back out through the doors, stared at the open elevator shaft, then looked around wildly. There was a fire extinguisher against the wall and a flat hose on a reel. She grabbed the extinguisher and stood it in front of the open door, then hefted the hose reel down and laid that beside it, blocking the way.

The double doors opened behind her. It was the receptionist. She looked at Frannie then at the open shaft. Horror shrivelled her face as if it had been punctured. 'Mr Sebastian? Did you say Mr Sebastian?'

'Where are the stairs down?' Frannie yelled at her, too afraid to risk another elevator.

'Just inside the other doors, on the right,' the woman's voice had become a whisper. 'Mr Sebastian?'

Frannie nodded.

The woman covered her mouth with her hand.

'Call an ambulance! Please call an ambulance!' Frannie said. She ran through the double doors and came into a large open-plan office, most of the desks abandoned for lunch. She saw immediately on her right a door marked FIRE EXIT, pushed it open and found herself on a stone staircase. She ran down, clutching the metal guide rail, turned, turned, turned again, saw the number 39 crudely painted in black on the raw concrete wall.

She raced on down, the echo of her tapping feet chasing her. 36 . . . 35 . . . 34. She was getting giddy, her hand was burning from the rail. 33 . . . 32 . . . 31 . . .

She passed fire buckets, a discarded cigarette pack, a grubby J-cloth. The light was weak and for a couple of floors the bulbs had gone and she ran in almost total darkness. 25 ... 24 ... She was conscious of the sound of her own breathing, her own sobbing. 20 ... 19 ... The walls swirled past her. 14 ... 13 ... 12 ... She could feel the ground getting nearer. 7 ... 6 ... 5 ... She stumbled, lost her balance, grabbed the rail tightly and swung against the wall. One of her shoes came off and tumbled down several steps, rolling to a rest on the landing.

She hobbled down, gasping, tears streaming down her face, pulled the shoe back on and began to run again. 3 ... 2 ... 1 ... Then she reached the bottom, a poorly lit basement corridor with thickly cladded pipes along the ceiling. There was a steady roar of a machine and a hiss of air, the whine of pumps. She saw a bucket and a mop just beyond the banks of the elevator doors; a squeegee was propped against the wall beside them and a plastic drum of cleaning fluid. Further along was an open doorway and she heard a tapping sound, like a hammer on metal, and called out.

Her voice was swallowed by the roaring. She ran down the corridor, saw an open door and went in. She heard the rumble of a furnace. There were racks of stores on metal shelving: lavatory paper and towelling paper, plastic containers of soaps and detergents. The ceiling was low and gridded with pipes. It was as hot as an airing cupboard and the air was thick with flecks of lint. At the far end a light shone through an open doorway. 'Help!' she called out.

A shadow moved across the light. She heard the tapping again and ran across. A black man in a blue boiler suit was hammering a bracket in a vice inside a small workshop, his face glazed in concentration.

She dashed up to him. 'Please, are you in charge of the elevators?' She was so short of breath she could barely speak.

He looked up at her in surprise. 'I'm the caretaker, yes, ma'am.'

'Please come! Someone's fallen down the lift shaft . . .'

His face was streaked with grease and his hair was a grizzled grey. He wiped his hands on his overalls, studying her for a moment, absorbing her expression with tired brown eyes, one of which had a burst blood vessel. 'That can't happen, that's impossible.'

'Please, I was with him on the fortieth floor. The doors opened. The elevator wasn't there. Please come.' She shook her head in desperation. 'Please!'

He looked at her as if about to argue, then his expression softened. 'They've only just been checked. It can't happen,' he said, slightly defensively.

'It has. Oh God, it has.'

The tone of her voice seemed to get through to him.

'On the fortieth floor?'

'Yes. The door opened – he said he had to grab it quickly and stepped in and there was nothing there. Please,' she said. 'Please.'

He ran his hand along a row of shelves, hitched a long ribbed instrument and a bunch of keys off a hook, picked up a rubber torch, then walked with a limping gait out into the corridor and down to the elevators. 'Which one?'

Frannie had to think for a moment, trying to regain her bearings. She turned around and pointed to the third one along on the right.

He gave her a chance to reconsider. 'You sure?'

'Yes.'

He hesitated. 'Fortieth floor?'

'Yes.'

'A man, you say?'

'Yes.'

'I don't think anyone could have fallen, ma'am.'

'Please,' she whispered, the salty taste of her tears in her mouth. Perspiration torrented down her chest and back. 'Please check.'

She noticed the framed maintenance certificate that was fixed beside the elevator door.

> MAINTENANCE RECORD.
> DATE OF LAST SAFETY CHECK.
> DATE OF ANNUAL INSPECTION.
> SAFETY OFFICER. D. PAPWORTH.

The records were neatly typed. She could see the last date clearly. 27th August. Less than a month ago.

The caretaker tapped it with his forefinger; his nail was dark blue as if it had recently been hit by a hammer. 'Been checked, you see.'

She nodded.

'It's impossible. The doors can't open. Not without the elevator car there.' He pushed a key into a box on the wall, turned it and pulled open a small metal door. There was a battery of switches and winking lights inside. One orange light was static and he stared at it for a moment, pressed a switch a couple of times and looked dubious. He then pressed two more switches and a bell sounded. He pressed another and the bell stopped ringing. 'Have to stop the whole system,' he said. 'Won't be too popular.' He pulled a lever and there was a loud clunk. All the lights stopped winking and remained on.

He knelt down and inserted the long ribbed tool into a tiny hole in the bottom of one of the elevator's doors and turned it sharply. He repeated the procedure in a hole at the top, and then again in the other door. Then he slowly levered his fingers into the gap and began to prise the doors open. They slid back until there was enough gap for him to get his head through.

He gave Frannie a cautioning signal with his hand for her to stay back, picked up his torch, leaned in and pointed the torch downwards.

'Oh God . . .' he stepped back, gagging. His eyes looked at Frannie without focusing, then swung away unco-ordinated. His mouth quivered. The torch fell from his fingers. He lurched towards the bucket, knelt and threw up.

Frannie picked up the lighted torch and stepped, terrified of what she would see, towards the gap in the door. She slowly lowered the white blob of torch beam down the back wall of the shaft.

Where it met the bottom she saw dust spun into a fine moss, cigarette butts, keys, a milk carton, a child's rattle. There was a vile stench of excrement. Her chest tightened as the beam slid across a crumpled shape in pinstriped cloth. A shiny loafer shoe with a green and red band across it, and a gold buckle. Her heart jigged. Something pale white gleamed out at her. It was Seb's face, his eyes wide open as if something was trying to push them out of their sockets, and for a brief moment she thought he was all right, thought he was fine, just in shock.

Until she realized his body was chest and stomach down, and his head had been wrenched round 180 degrees, saw a gleam of white bone sticking out of the side of his neck. And then she saw, also, the mess of red and orange pulp that was spreading through his hair and which lay like a cushion behind his ears. She whimpered. Something was sticking several inches out of his back like a bent spar impaling him; sharp and pointed, it had pierced cleanly through the centre of his jacket, between his shoulder-blades. A bone, she realized; one of his ribs.

She gulped, and her insides rattled as she staggered back, the image of his face imprinted like a developing photograph in her brain. She backed into the wall. Bells were ringing one after the other: desperate, panicky drilling sounds. She breathed in hard rasps, horror guttering through her, staring at the dark slit between the doors as if expecting Seb to climb out of it at any moment.

She turned her head. The caretaker was dialling a phone on the wall. The smell of his vomit churned her own stomach; she turned and ran, up the stairs, out into the lobby. Bells were ringing there, also, and she saw the commissionaire in his smart braided outfit walking anxiously past her towards the basement door.

She ran across the marble floor on legs that would barely hold her weight, pushed through a revolving door into the howling wind and slumped down on a teak bench, still holding the rubber torch in her hands. She switched it off, then on. Off then on again, the rubber button bending then clicking under the pressure of her finger.

She watched the spray from the fountains being bent by the relentless wind. Where a pigeon landed with a crack of its wings and eyed her expectantly, she saw only a grey blur on the ground. People were still at lunch. She could hear the distant clatter of their knives and forks, of laughter and chatter. She and Sebastian should have been in the restaurant now, talking about how to stay alive. She buried her face in her arms, plugged her ears with her fingers against the whoosh of the approaching siren and shook silently in grief. And in terror.

*

The tea was sweet and she sipped it gratefully, then placed her mug back down on the cork coaster on the mahogany boardroom table that shone like an ice-rink. A man who bore a family resemblance to Seb looked down from a portrait on the wall opposite her, a hard-looking man with Seb's large features, but not his warmth, wearing ermine and with a shrieval chain around his neck.

She turned to the policeman, Constable Boyle, who sat opposite her, his notebook in front of him on the table. He held himself well, sat upright with broad shoulders. In his mid thirties, his face had babyish, underdeveloped features, with half-moon eyes and thick, rubbery lips, but his manner was firm, adult, toughened with street wisdom. He exuded a faint aura of sadness as if there were things about human life that were beyond his comprehension, beyond his ability to change.

He smiled at her periodically, and each time the small act of kindness made her feel weepy again, and she sniffed, blinked away some tears and continued with her story, inching it forward, then being taken back, retracing each step a dozen times, adding fresh detail.

'You're sure it was ten past one, Francesca?' His voice was flat and pedantic and she had to fight the urge to snap at him with irritation.

'Yes.'

Then she managed, 'I can remember looking at my watch as we went out to the lifts.' But she was thinking, *He's dead. Nothing's going to bring him back. What the hell does it matter what time it was?*

'I was meeting him for lunch at one, and I was late. I didn't get here until ten past and when he came out he told me we'd have to be quick because he had to be back by two. He had some problems in the office he had to deal with.'

'What made you late?'

She drew her breath in sharply, fighting irritation again. The clock on the wall said 2.45. Her stomach ached. She sipped more tea. Someone on the construction site would remember her she thought, knowing it was irrational. 'I didn't leave enough time, I suppose. And whilst I was in the area I wanted to take a look at my family's old sandwich bar – it's on the City Fields development – so I took a detour over there.' She shrugged.

'And no one else came out to the lifts with you?'

'No one.'

Hello, young fellow!

'Did you have lunch with – er – Mr Holland regularly?'

Hello, young fellow! Seb's voice like an echo.

'No. We were at university together.'

'What was the reason for your lunch today?'

I wanted to warn him about the Ouija.

'We – hadn't seen each other since we were students – and we bumped into each other in a restaurant a couple of weeks ago. He told me he was engaged and said we ought to have lunch some time.'

His eyebrows rose. 'Excuse me being personal, Francesca, but was there anything – you know – between you and Mr Holland?'

'No.'

'Not at university?'

She hesitated. Almost. Once. They had snogged on a sofa at a party. But she had been dating someone else at the time and it had gone no further. It was one of those things that might have been. 'No.' She looked at him. 'You think I pushed him or something? In a fit of

337

jealousy? Or so that I could get to marry him?' Her face flushed with anger and she saw he had at least the grace to blush a little.

'I'm afraid it is my job to look at all the angles.'

Hello, young fellow! The expression on Seb's face as he had stepped into the lift. As if he was greeting someone in there. A small boy.

Edward.

He had seen Edward.

'So I'm a murder suspect, is that it?'

He raised his hands. 'Please! Nothing like that. But I do have to make a full report.' He smiled. 'You have to understand that I've come into this cold. A man is dead; the circumstances are very odd. At the inquest we will have to show we have looked at every possibility, for everyone's sake – and particularly for the deceased and his relatives.'

Wet, heavy sand heaved in her guts. The image of Seb's face brightened in her brain. She saw him again, lying there, amongst the dirt. The policeman's face dissolved into Seb's and drifted up away from the table. The table slid sideways; she gripped it, tried to prevent it from crashing to the ground. Her cheek pressed against it and she saw her blurred reflection in its mirrored shine, and tears flooded from her eyes.

A hand touched her arm, gently. 'I'll get someone to run you home. Do you have the number of your doctor? We'll ask him to pop in and see you.'

She lifted her head slowly, feeling giddy. The table was fine, solid, had not moved and she looked at it in confusion. 'I have to go to the office. I have a meeting this afternoon at three. My boss is going to be really angry.'

'Would you like to phone him?'

'How much longer do I have to stay here?'

'We're almost finished.' He smiled. 'Don't worry; no one's accusing you of anything.'

I'm guilty, she wanted to say. *I'm guilty. You're quite right to accuse me. It was my idea to have the Ouija session in the cellar. I made it happen. Seb would be alive now if –*

She sipped some more of her tea, as tears welled in her eyes again. 'I'm sorry,' she said to the policeman.

'I think you should go home and go to bed, have your doctor give you something that'll make you have a good night's sleep.'

She shook her head. 'I can't. There isn't time.'

He smiled again, but did not ask her what she meant.

CHAPTER THIRTY-ONE

Frannie got back to the Museum shortly after half past three. She stopped in the middle of the hall, feeling giddy and sick, and looked numbly at the crowds, at the queues for the bookshop tills, the souvenir shop, the information desk. Feet clacked all around her on the hard floor. Voices. She fumbled in her bag for a handkerchief and dabbed her eyes, tried to still the image of Seb's last look of amazement, which spun like a fairground centrifuge in her brain, pressing her back against the walls of her skull. If she had been quicker she could have dived forward and –

Hello, young fellow!

Constable Boyle had told her she could not have done anything, that she'd never have held his weight, that she would have been dragged down also. She felt the floor swaying beneath her. She could have seen the elevator was not there, could have screamed out.

Could have realized when he had said *Hello, young fellow!*

She collected her key, nodded at the security guard without noticing him, walking in a trance, then stopped outside her office, forgetting where she was for a moment, shock and fear clogging her mind. Eventually she opened the door and went in. Penrose Spode was not there, and had left a note on her desk: 'Not feeling well. Have gone home. Benedict is expecting you at 6.30, address and directions on reverse. If I can help, call me at home.'

There was another note also in his handwriting: 'Kate Hemingway phoned, *Evening Standard*. 2.50. Will call back.'

She looked with a feeling of hopelessness at the message from the newspaper. Calling about Seb, no doubt. She sat down, closed her eyes and began to pray. The phone rang and she answered it warily, afraid it might be the *Evening Standard* reporter. But it was Oliver, and he sounded distraught.

'Edward's disappeared,' he said.

'From school?'

'He had breakfast, then he didn't turn up for any classes. No one's seen him.'

Spode's neat handwriting blurred. 'What does the – the headmaster – say?'

'He doesn't know what to do.'

'Are the police –?'

'They're looking for him.'

'God, I'm sorry.' She bit her lip. 'What's happening?' she said quietly. 'What are we caught up in, Oliver?'

'I don't know.'

Her knees were knocking together; she felt the pressure of her knuckles against her cheek as she held the phone to her ear. She had to tell him. 'It's even worse than you think. Seb's dead.'

'Seb? Holland?'

She started telling him what had happened, but her voice became too choked with tears to go on.

'Christ, you poor thing,' he said, and was quiet for a moment. Then he grasped at the only shred of hope they had left. 'Did the priest – rector – get in touch?'

She stared into the tiny holes in the mouthpiece. 'I'm seeing him this evening.'

'If Edward turns up, I'll come straight to London.'

'I'm sure he's all right. He's very resourceful.'

'Yes,' Oliver said grimly. 'What time are you seeing the priest?'

'Half past six.'

'Will you call me afterwards?'

She promised she would in a choked whisper.

The Reverend Benedict Spode's address turned out to be a grimy, detached Georgian house on a busy main road south of the Thames, behind London Bridge Station.

Dark clouds with pink underbellies from the setting sun slid like burning boats across the sky. The wind was freshening, and occasional fat splodges of rain burst on the pavement around her as Frannie approached the front door and rang the bell.

She was surprised by the appearance of the man who answered it, quite different from the image she had in her mind. He was ten years older than his brother, short and bald, with a small round head as solid as a cannon ball and thyroid eyes. The only feature he shared in common with Penrose was the same bung-shaped mouth. His body was parcelled inside a billowing black cassock and what neck he had was squashed, fleshily, inside a tight dog-collar.

'Frannie Monsanto?' he said fiercely.

'Yes.' She held out an uncertain hand. The clergyman discarded it almost before he had shaken it, as if it were a package he had been handed for an Oxfam sale and should have been passed on to someone else. 'I was expecting you at six o'clock.'

'I'm sorry. Penrose told me half past.'

He looked at his watch. 'I really don't have any time

left – perhaps you could come and see me at the beginning of next week? Say Monday evening?'

She looked at him aghast. 'But I need help now. It can't wait that long. Please could we have a talk tonight? I can wait if it's not convenient; I must see you tonight.'

He looked exasperated. 'Bloody brother of mine. I told him six quite clearly.'

'*Please*,' she said again.

He hesitated, assessing her, then stepped back and gestured for her to come in.

The hallway had a shabbiness that reminded Frannie of a student rooming-house, and stank of wet dog. The hall carpet was worn down in places to the underlay, and strewn with moulted hairs; the paint was yellowed and chipped, and the walls virtually bare. The clergyman took her mackintosh and hung it on a Victorian coat stand, which stood out rather proudly, and then led her into a small, austere study.

There was a marble fireplace with an unlit gas fire in the grate, and a crucifix dutifully resting on the mantelpiece – a postcard of a pyramid beside it. A plain oak desk cluttered with papers, amid which sat a weary-looking manual typewriter and a small fax machine, fronted a typist's chair that looked as if it had been salvaged from a skip. The room also boasted a beat-up armchair and a sofa with shot springs that appeared as lumps in its blue covering. The window beyond the desk looked out on to the street, and rattled from the passing traffic.

Frannie heard a pattering sound, and an elderly Old English sheepdog limped inquisitively into the room.

'Basket, Shula!' Benedict Spode said in an equally

dictatorial but kinder tone than the one in which he had greeted her. 'Back to your basket!'

The dog turned and padded slowly back out. Benedict Spode gestured Frannie to the sofa, then perched on the swivel typing chair and gave her a more thorough inspection. With his air of disdain and conceit, he reminded her of a portrait she had seen of one of the Borgias.

He raised his head a fraction when he spoke, as if in order to throw his voice to an entire congregation, and his aggressive tone was belittling. 'Penrose tells me you've been mucking around with the Ouija?'

'Once. When I was a student,' Frannie said.

'Once!' He tapped his foot on the carpet; he was wearing polished black loafers that seemed too small and dainty for him. 'What is it about this word *once* that seems to make everything all right? There are circumstances where once is more than enough, young woman. Went bankrupt *once*. Mugged an old lady *once*.'

He shook his head in frustration, as if there were some inner demon trapped within him. 'I'm fed up with intelligent young people who should know better, who dabble with the Ouija then come running to me for help, expecting me to wave some magic wand and make everything all right.'

Frannie's spirits dropped to an even lower ebb. This was all wrong. She should not have trusted Penrose, not listened to him. She balled her fists in anger and despair. And yet, last night: Penrose at the table. The things he had said were not lucky guesses. And she tried to remind herself that the Bishop of Lewes had recommended this clergyman. The diocesan exorcist. He must know what he was doing. *Must*.

'I don't imagine you even go to church, do you?

Except for Christmas carols?' he added with a faint sneer.

'I used to.'

'How long ago is *used to*?'

'Seven or eight years.'

He squeezed his hands together. 'I'm fed up with non-attenders! They either come to me because they want a church wedding – so they can have pretty pictures to stick on the mantelpiece, or else because they've been dabbling with the occult.' Then his tone mellowed, just a fraction. 'OK. Lecture over; time is short.' There was even a hint of sympathy in his face. 'Would you like to tell me the full story?'

'How much has Penrose filled you in?'

'Let's make no assumptions, then we won't make any mistakes.' He leaned back, waiting.

Frannie began. The clergyman nodded impatiently several times as she told him all about the Ouija session and the messages that had turned into predictions. He sat motionless as she related Edward's plea to her in the library, the Latin he had been reciting in his sleep, and which she had too. And he listened without comment as she told him about Oliver's research into his family background, his studies in numerology, and her discovery of the common ground shared by her parents' sandwich bar and the Halkin residence.

'Twenty-six,' Benedict Spode said when she had finished, sucking in his cheeks as though he had a boiled sweet in his mouth. '*Twenty-six*. This man who died today, this friend, Seb Holland, you don't know what he was told by the Ouija?'

'No.'

'Do you really think it would have made any difference if you had known?'

345

She stared back bleakly. 'I don't know.'

He gathered a fold of his cassock, lifting the hem a few inches and inspecting his shoes. Then he looked at Frannie with a new intensity. 'Birds never sing at Auschwitz. Did you know that?'

'No,' she said, surprised by the apparent *non sequitur*.

'There's a reason. All the suffering that went on there is imprinted in the land. Animals sense it and they avoid it; those that do pass over it are silent.' He lapsed into silence himself for a moment. 'People leave imprints behind them when they die. Imprints of their energy, emotions. Some, like my brother, can read these imprints. There are other people who simply act, without knowing it, as channels, like radio receivers and transmitters, passing those imprints on to others who can either visualize them in the form of ghosts, or be subconsciously influenced by them.'

Channel. The word Oliver had used.

'It sounds,' Benedict Spode continued, 'as if you might be channelling the spirit of this second Marquess to Lord Sherfield's son, Edward.'

Her voice faltered. 'Do you really think that's possible?'

'What do you think?' he retorted sharply.

She regressed, pushed herself back through her mind, back into the darkness of the cellar. Something in there imprinted in the walls? The spirit of a man dead for 350 years who was still thinking, scheming, planning; still able to make others do his bidding? Able to make her do it? Edward do it? To kill Meredith, Jonathan Mountjoy, Seb Holland. And to strike Max Gabriel, maim Phoebe, blind Susie Verbeeten? To kill Oliver's wife? Tristram?

'I don't understand what it is – exactly – that lives on – how it works.'

The clergyman spoke more civilly. 'I believe there are forces of evil that exist in their own right and which we all have the choice to accept or reject. Every time we accept evil, allow it to enter, we feed it and it becomes stronger; and sometimes when we die it remains behind. The second Marquess accepted and embraced evil. It perhaps did not die with him but remained dormant; a strong enough force to survive for 350 years.'

'To survive in bricks and mortar? In stone?'

'Bricks and stone are inert, but they contain many elements – including electricity and carbon – that are capable of storing energy. When people play with the Ouija they are inviting intense energy into one focal point. Creating a fusion of energies. The energies of six or seven people all focused into one glass. That concentrated mass can disturb whatever is in the room around them, and sometimes reactivate the place memories – or a dormant evil force. I would think that cellar, with all the evil that has taken place around it, was a highly dangerous place to play the Ouija. I can't imagine anywhere that could be worse: sexual perversion; mass murder; a hideous end.' He shook his head. 'What do you expect?'

Frannie was silent.

'Evil is immensely cunning, but it can only work through adult humans who will accept it, or through young children who are not yet aware of the distinction.' He smiled ironically. 'The second Marquess was murdered on the premises, more than likely down in the cellar, by *seven* soldiers. Numerology was his big thing.' He looked hard at Frannie. '*Seven* students held the Ouija session.' He shrugged. 'Maybe significant, maybe not. What *is* significant is that Lord Sherfield, with his five-year-old son, came into the café after you had re-energized the force. You were the natural link.'

'Why?'

'A young child's consciousness is not fully formed until at least the age of seven. Here the evil force or the spirit, or whatever you care to call it, saw a child not only young, but also with direct ancestral and therefore genetic lineage back to the second Marquess. By using you as a channel, it could slowly become part of that child's consciousness; test the boy out without him realizing, until he became used to it, accepted it as part of himself. And then –' he looked away for a moment.

'And then what?'

'Then it – or he – doesn't need either of you any more.' His ironic smile returned.

'Why?' said Frannie. 'Why would it want to carry on? Surely there – there's no reason –' her train of thought stumbled.

'Evil is the corruption of good. That is its sole purpose: to corrupt, destroy, nullify. It requires no reason, only energy. The energy of a seance; the energy of a host body.'

'Why would it harm everyone who was at the Ouija session?'

'You know the expression "Let sleeping dogs lie"?'

'Of course.'

'A sleeping dog has no gratitude for being woken.' He rested his hands on his lap and surveyed the room imperiously. 'If the second Marquess was into numerology, the spirit probably finds it amusing to continue. Seven soldiers put him to death. Seven people bring him back into existence. Repeat the pattern.' He parted his hands. 'Evil does not have to account to anyone for its actions.'

'But how does that explain the friend of mine who went blind? She picked up a virus swimming – how could a spirit have made her do that?'

He flicked some tiny fleck off his cassock. 'We understand very little about the body's abilities to look after itself. The immune system is still largely a mystery. I should think most people don't go blind from the virus your friend caught. Probably only a tiny percentage do. Was she unlucky? Or did something get channelled into her subconscious, blocking her immune system for her? To make her prophecy come true?'

Frannie felt as though a nerve had snapped inside her. 'Is there nothing I can do?'

'There's only one thing we can do. We go to that cellar and we hold a requiem mass. And we go now.'

'Who?'

'Just you and me.'

She bit the back of her hand. 'I don't know if we can get in.'

'We'll worry about that when we get there.'

'What – what happens in a requiem mass?'

'We hold a simple communion service to lay the spirit to rest.'

'And if that doesn't work?'

He looked at her as if she was mad. The skin around his mouth tightened in determination, 'We are going armed with the authority of the Church. The authority of God. That is stronger than anything belonging to Satan. You do understand that, don't you?'

She could feel the hairs rising on her body and the goose-pimples creeping across her flesh. She had hoped that in coming to the clergyman she would somehow find comfort. Instead she had found even greater fear.

CHAPTER THIRTY-TWO

Frannie walked with Benedict Spode across London Bridge, her mackintosh pocket weighted with the torch he had lent her. The clergyman carried a small vinyl holdall which he swung at his side in a deliberately carefree manner that did not reflect the anxiety in his face.

They waited for a stream of traffic to pass, then crossed into King William Street and walked down towards Bank. Over to their right, brightly lit against the night sky when Frannie looked down one of the side streets, was the Winston Churchill Tower. But she had to look away again.

'Do you think,' she said, 'this could be the reason why Oliver and I met? That it was all manipulated, contrived – by – the – this –?' She stopped, uncertain of the word she was searching for. *Spirit? Force?*

'I believe that there is order in disorder,' Benedict Spode said tersely.

She remembered Oliver had said the same thing. 'How do you mean?'

He did not reply until they had stopped to wait for the traffic lights at the end of the street. 'I mean that there are patterns even in apparent chaos. Sometimes one is too close to them to see them.'

'I'm not sure I understand; I –'

The lights changed and they crossed into Poultry. The air in her lungs felt heavier by the second. Ahead, up to the left, she could see the lights of the hoarding. She slowed her pace and the clergyman slowed his also.

'I just want to say something before we –' she said, and she saw the soft, baby-like skin of the clergyman's cheek in the glare of a street light as he half turned towards her. 'I'm sorry for everything. For all the grief I've brought to everyone. For being so bloody stupid.'

Benedict Spode turned further to face her full on. The anxiety had not left his face but his voice was calm. 'Seven of you made the decision to play the Ouija, Frannie,' he said quietly. 'It's not for you to take the blame alone. God will be the judge of that.'

A sharp blast of wind seized her hair and her clothes. The clergyman's cassock billowed beneath his raincoat and his holdall swayed in his hand. The hoarding rocked; even from a hundred yards away Frannie could hear the loose boards banging and tarpaulins cracking like sails, metal chinking.

She looked back at Benedict Spode. 'Can I ask you something really naïve? If people can do this – attract evil spirits – on their own, why does it need a priest to stop it? Couldn't anyone stop it with prayers?'

'Priests have no magic,' he said. 'Good is stronger than evil; but when evil becomes out of control, those who have the authority of the Church are stronger in dealing with it than anyone else. The Church acts on God's behalf, with His authority. And God is stronger than Satan. God defeated Satan.'

A bus rumbled past. The door of a pub across the road opened and two men came out. Behind them the interior looked cheery, and Frannie felt a pang of envy.

'I still find it hard to believe – with all that's gone on – that just saying a few prayers will end it.'

Her companion stopped, 'Why?'

'It seems too simple.'

He rounded on her with logic. 'Is it any less simple than the way it started? Just a bunch of drunken friends with an upturned wine glass and some scraps of paper?'

She smiled weakly, but Benedict Spode did not smile back. She looked at her watch. A quarter past eight. It was much brighter lit here than she had expected. The pavement, the hoarding, the site; they were all bathed in a milky-orange haze. Conspicuous. But towards the tops of the buildings that towered around them, the artificial light faded. And far above, only hard white stars pricked the oily blackness of the sky.

The landscape was as Frannie had seen it earlier that day: the jib of a crane towering over the alley; the silhouette of a massive lead demolition ball suspended beneath it like something hanging from the beak of a giant bird of prey. But the building that had been there at lunchtime was no longer standing. Shock ripped through her guts. She raced across the road towards the hoarding and peered through a viewing slit but could see nothing. She ran on to the next slit, which looked straight on to the remains of the corner building at the start of Poulterers' Alley. It had been almost completely demolished, its façade torn off, its innards opened to the elements. But, on either side of the alley behind it, the rest of the buildings were still standing.

Part of her wished they weren't; wanted to pretend that it was too late. The clergyman wouldn't know. Then Seb Holland's face came into her mind. Then Tristram's. Meredith's coffin on the catafalque. Frannie shuddered. She imagined never seeing Oliver again. Nor her family. Being crippled, or dead or disfigured. She nodded at Benedict Spode and pointed.

He looked up at the hoarding. 'Let's see if we can find a gap,' he said decisively.

They stopped outside the main gates, which were chained shut. She tested them, but there was no play in them. A taxi drove by, the knocking rattle of its engine echoing in the quietness, the fumes of its exhaust staying in their nostrils after it had gone. She walked on, leading the way down to the end of the block, then turned left and the pavement became a covered boardwalk as they followed the hoarding along a street that was quiet and less well lit. Benedict Spode pressed a section of hoarding on the join with the scaffolding and it gave, reluctantly, then sprung sharply back. He glanced around, rather shiftily, pushed hard and held it for Frannie, then followed her through, releasing it behind him with a fierce bang.

They stood on an unstable mound of rubble; the sounds of flapping and loose metal were much louder now. Frannie switched the torch on, and the beam jumped hungrily into the shadows beyond the haze of light from the street lamps. It struck the caterpillar tracks of a bulldozer. Then the cabin of a crane. She played it along the partially demolished terrace that housed the site office. The air was full of the oddly sweet smell of rotten wood and damp, and the harder, drier smell of old plaster. The beam slid over a stepladder, a skip, then flared off the windows of a Portakabin. She stepped forward nervously, picking her way past a broken supermarket trolley, then walked across rotten plasterboard which broke beneath her feet and on to a track of churned mud.

Benedict Spode walked on tiptoe, his cassock hitched up like a skirt. As they passed a Portakabin with 'Supplies' stencilled on the door, a van drove fast down the road and halted outside the gates, its engine still running. Frannie snapped off the torch as footsteps and the crackle of a two-way radio were heard. Then a man's voice.

'City Fields. One nine five five. Site secure. Moving on to Docklands. Roger and out.'

A chain rattled and the vehicle sped away. Frannie switched on the torch, revealing the clergyman's raised eyebrows. 'Could have been a bit embarrassing,' he said.

Frannie couldn't raise a smile, and walked on until Poulterers' Alley stretched out in front of them like a ghost town on a movie studio lot.

Fear had returned to the clergyman's face and she felt it infecting her, flowing into her. Had to keep going now; to somehow be brave. Had to keep going. Had to. She imagined two eyes watching them from behind the boarded windows. A small boy's eyes. She felt her heart bang like a shuttle inside her chest, weaving a tapestry from the raw yarn of her nerves.

She almost walked right past it. What had once seemed such a very big place now looked so small. She swung the torch up above the door as if she needed to make sure: SANDW CH S LUIGI CAFE.

The windows were boarded like all the others, but the door still had its glass panels. She took her key-ring from her bag, separated the old Banham and pushed it into the lock. It slid in almost too easily, and allowed herself and Canon Spode to gain entry to the premises she'd known for most of her life.

Inside, the floor was a mess. Part of the ceiling had come down, leaving exposed beams. Frannie trod slowly, waited for Benedict Spode, and played the torchlight around, scooping the darkness out. A flesh-white rectangle indicated where the counter had stood. The old poster of Naples had fallen and lay on the floor. The other, of Amalfi, was still on the back wall. And it was this one on which the clergyman had fixed his gaze, eyes widening. Frannie followed his stare.

The poster was moving, the top left-hand corner tearing as if an invisible hand were pulling it. The other corner was already free. She felt her own flesh tearing in sympathy, parting. The whole place felt as if it was charged with electricity as the poster carried on moving from the top downwards until it dropped to the floor, curled over on itself and lay still.

The effect was petrifying. Just the draught from opening the door, Frannie tried to convince herself, pushing her way through the darkness to the hoop of the trapdoor which she could see glinting dully. She laid the torch down, knelt and signalled to Spode to do the same.

The cold metal bit into her fingers like ice as she pulled. The bogeyman was down there beneath the hatch, waiting for her in his dark, silent lair. He lived in the cellar. The bogeyman who pricked every bone in her body now with sharp needles of terror. The second Marquess – Francis Edward Alwynne Halkin.

The hatch lifted a few inches and dropped back down. She had forgotten how heavy it was. She resisted the clergyman's attempts to help and, bracing herself, lifted harder; it came away, pulling a stringy cobweb with it. A draught of air poured out, as cold as if she had opened the door of a freezer.

She pulled the hatch right back until it was resting against its hinges then shone the torch down the wooden steps into the darkness. Dark as a lift shaft. Frannie was shaking uncontrollably by now, as if she had convulsions. She rocked on her knees, staring down as darkness coiled like smoke around her.

The clergyman offered, 'Shall I go first?'

'I'll go,' she heard herself say, 'and you can pass your bag down.'

Slowly she eased herself over, and grabbed the torch with one hand. She felt as if she were descending into a bottomless pit. But eventually her feet touched the hard flagstones. They felt unsteady, then she realized that it was herself, swaying in her fear.

'OK,' she called out, shining the torch back up. The word echoed back at her. *OK . . . OK . . . OK.*

Benedict Spode's foot clumsily struck the top step. 'Careful!' she shouted out into the blackness. *CAREFUL . . . FUUULLLL.*

The cold of the flagstones seeped through her shoes. Her skin prickled and she felt the downy hairs on her arms, her legs, on the small of her back rising and her skin erupting into goose-pimples. She could hear the steady metallic drip . . . ping . . . ping . . . ping and remembered it from the last time she had been down here.

She raked the steps with the torch, too afraid to look around her, stretching for the bag which Spode was holding down to her.

The clergyman reached the bottom but stayed holding on to the rails with both hands, collecting his breath. 'My bag,' he said anxiously, as if he was frightened to be separated from it.

She handed it back to him to the accompaniment of a low, rumbling echo that came out of the darkness, growing deeper and louder, like a hundred boulders rolling towards them. She had heard the sound thousands of times but it always scared her. It began to fade as rapidly as it had started, becoming a distant hum, and then died completely. 'Tube train,' she said. 'Central Line.'

Spode released his grip on the rail and walked a few

steps away from her as if drawn across the room. She watched him open his bag; he removed a small torch of his own then went over to one of several upright barrels, and using it as a table began to unpack. In the extra light of the second torch, she saw a packing-case with a candle stuck on the top, a pool of wax around the base. Scraps of paper lay on it. It was the packing-crate they had used as a table for the Ouija.

Memories washed over her. She walked over, afraid to go too close. The letters of the alphabet lay in random order, the words *Yes* and *No* in their midst, mottled now with black spots of mildew.

The clergyman had pulled a phial of holy water and a silver salt cellar from his bag and set them on the barrel. Then two silver candlesticks, into which he pushed candles, which he lit. A chalice, a silver tray and a silver stoup were also produced. Mouthing a silent prayer, he poured some water into the stoup and added some salt. Working in the flickering candlelight, he was slow, tidy, methodical, as if he had all the time in the world.

He raised the stoup, 'Protect us, O Lord, we beseech you.' He said the words firmly, but without raising his voice. Then he pulled what looked like a silver ball and chain from his bag. The ball had tiny holes, like a sugar shaker. An aspergillum, Frannie realized.

He carefully immersed the head in holy water, before raising the aspergillum by its chain so that it swung gently. Then he raised it higher as if making sure that whoever or whatever was present could see it. He began to swing it on its chain, slowly at first, then faster, until flecks of water sprinkled the wall. At the same time the clergyman began to move around the cellar, repeating the words and procedure over and over.

'Protect us, O Lord, we beseech you.'

★

Outside the lead demolition ball that hung from the jib of the crane, twenty feet above the rod, moved a fraction in a gust of wind. As the gust died away it continued to move, in a faint, barely discernible, rocking motion; the ball gradually began to swing faster, making wide, sweeping arcs until it was swinging too hard for the jib to contain it and the whole crane began to sway with it. The lead ball swung like the aspergillum in the clergyman's hand. Like the lampshade in Frannie's sitting-room. Harder and harder. Until it rose too high and the chain went slack. Then it fell with a dead-weight of five tons. Plummeted unchecked through the air as the slack of the chain paid out. Then tightened. Sharply. Too sharply.

The top of the jib's superstructure sheared away and was yanked sharply downwards by the demolition ball as it plunged straight down through roof tiles and rotting timbers.

Below in the cellar, Benedict Spode made another swing with the aspergillum. Holy water spattered on the brickwork.

'Protect us, O Lord, we beseech you.'

He took a step to the left and began the same performance. As he did so, Frannie heard a faint splitting sound like sticks of firewood being snapped. Then a deep rumble. A train, she thought at first, but it was different: deeper, more threatening. She saw jagged spidery cracks rip across the walls and ceiling. Dust and small stones showered down on them, striking her head, her hands.

'Get out!' she shouted. 'Get out!'

The whole cellar was shaking and dust was avalanching down through the open hatch. Frannie shouted again, then something slammed into her shoulder, sending her crashing to the floor. The noise had become deafening. She heard someone scream, but dust and plaster filled her own mouth and she choked, blinded by dust.

Then there was silence.

She felt wind on her face and tried to move. But she was pinioned, trapped. She spat out a mouthful of dust. 'Mr Spode?'

A faint haze of light made its way through the mist that was stinging her eyes. Then the mist itself started to clear. Dust, settling. Above her was a strange orange glow and familiar pinpricks of white in an oily blackness beyond. Shadowy walls rising up. Then Frannie realized, confused, that she was looking straight up at the night outside.

There was a face. Someone staring down at her. A small man standing looking down through the crater in the floor above. He was smiling and she thought that was incongruous. Smiling, and there was a gleam in his eye. Then she saw with blind terror that it was not a man at all.

It was Edward.

CHAPTER THIRTY-THREE

As Frannie watched, Edward disappeared.

She struggled to free herself from the dead-weight crushing her legs and her left shoulder, but panic snaked up and down inside her.

'Mr Spode?' she called out.

Silence. She felt like an insect trapped in a match-box. *Beetles are vermin, Daddy.*

'Mr Spode?'

She choked on dust and coughed again. She strained her eyes but could see nothing. Something sharp was digging into her wrist; she pulled, twisted, but it dug in further. She looked up again but could see nothing except the faint orange haze.

A shadow moved. She heard a scrape, like a dragging foot, and her muscles went into spasm. But still she couldn't shift her legs; they felt set in cement.

She heard another scrape. Louder. Then again. Behind her. She could still move her head and now she spun it round frantically.

A silhouette standing; someone small. A torch came on and the beam blinded her. It moved away from her eyes and in the spill of light she could see that it was Edward.

He was motionless, concentrating on her.

'Edward!' she called out. Try to talk to him, get through to him, she thought desperately.

His lips moved but she could not hear what they said. The beam of his torch raked the cellar. It had caved in and she was in an enclosed pocket. Then the beam struck a face to her left.

It was Benedict Spode; his back and his legs crushed flat by the demolition ball. His tongue was sticking out and a trail of yellow bile dribbled from it, down into the pool of blood that was spreading slowly out across the floor and towards Frannie.

Bursts of a throttled scream gouted from her throat. Edward took a step towards her. Then another, his lips moving, talking, saying something she could not hear.

Her right arm was the only limb she could move and she slid it across the rubble without taking her eyes off him, then closed her fingers around a chunk of masonry, gripped it tightly and swung it back, demented enough to use it.

Edward walked solemnly towards her, eyes glazed, lips still chanting inaudibly; he was wearing his school uniform of grey jacket and shorts, and striped tie. She lifted the stone chunk higher, bracing herself. He continued chanting, and as he came closer she realized with rising terror that it was not his own voice coming from his mouth, but that of someone much older.

He walked on past her, knelt and picked up the aspergillum that lay just beyond the outstretched fingers of the dead clergyman, stood and swung it from the chain. Droplets of holy water struck Frannie in the face.

'Protect us, O Lord, we beseech you. Protect us, O Lord, we beseech you,' he repeated much louder and clearer in a no-nonsense voice that she recognized.

He knelt again and began pulling away the rubble beside Canon Spode, chanting to himself. Now he was saying the Lord's Prayer. Frannie watched as he unearthed the silver tray and the chalice, as if he knew exactly what he was looking for, and what to do next. From the buried holdall he removed a bottle of communion wine and some wafers.

'Listen to our prayers, Lord,' he said. 'As we humbly beg Your mercy.'

Frannie could not comprehend it, but the voice coming from Edward was that of the clergyman who was lying dead on the floor. The clergyman was speaking through the boy.

Edward continued with calm assurance. With authority. 'Listen to our prayers, Lord, as we humbly beg Your mercy, that the soul of Your servant Francis Edward Alwynne Halkin, whom You have called from this life, may be brought by You to a place of peace and light, and so be enabled to share the life of all Your saints. Through Christ our Lord, Amen.'

'Amen,' Frannie echoed involuntarily, releasing her grip on the masonry.

'We pray You, Lord our God, to receive the soul of this Your servant Francis, for whom Your blood was shed. Remember, Lord, that we are but dust and that man is like grass and the flower of the field. Lord grant him everlasting rest, and let perpetual light shine upon him. O God it is Your nature to have mercy and to spare. Grant to Your servant Francis, Lord, a place of rest and pardon.'

The boy with the presence of an adult was quiet for a moment. A siren faded into the distance, and Frannie had the strange impression that someone else was standing beside them. But she did not dare look away from the miracle taking place in front of her. Edward had begun saying the Lord's Prayer again, and she joined him.

When they had finished, he picked up the Host and broke a piece into the chalice. 'Lamb of God,' he said, 'You take away the sins of the world; have mercy on us. May this mingling of the Body and Blood of our Lord Jesus Christ bring eternal life to us who receive it.' He carried the host to Frannie and placed it in her hand.

'Take, eat,' he said.

She raised it to her mouth and put it on her tongue. The sweet, papery wafer dissolved.

Then he brought her the chalice, and placed the rim to her lips. She tasted silver polish; then heavy, sweet wine, swallowing gratefully.

'This is the Blood of Christ.' Edward's words were spoken confidently and he put the chalice down. 'Lord God, Your Son gave us the sacrament of His Body to support us in our last journey. Grant that our brother Francis may take his seat with Christ at His eternal banquet: Who lives and reigns for ever and ever.'

'Amen,' whispered Frannie.

The air felt warmer and she was no longer afraid. Edward knelt beside her. The darkness had lifted and she could see that his eyes looked bright, and he was smiling. His voice was normal again.

'Are you OK, Frannie?'

She nodded.

'It's all right now, isn't it, Frannie?' He knelt and began to pull the rubble off her. As he worked, she stared at the small boy's face and remembered his question: *Do the dead stay dead?*

Benedict Spode had been armed with the authority of the Church and he had died. But not quite. By killing Spode, the second Marquess had not diminished the clergyman's authority, but had given him a new weapon: Edward.

Non omnis moriar.

In his death Canon Spode had channelled his spirit through Edward.

Frannie put her arm up and gently took Edward's hand, the clergyman's words echoing in her head.

When evil becomes out of control, those who have the authority of the Church are stronger in dealing with it than anyone else.

Something else that he had said echoed also. *I believe that there is order in disorder.*

Frannie pulled Edward tightly to her; he did not seem to mind that tears were streaming down her face. It was as if they both knew that here in the rubble of the past, and in the presence of death, somehow they were now free.

Epilogue

July, 1999

When Charles Richard William Halkin was seven he discovered his half-brother's secret place, where Edward would go and smoke. He discovered it by following him through the attics beyond the nursery. He had watched Edward crawl out of a window, and had crawled after him, along the parapet and into a hollow beside one of the massive chimneys.

Edward had been annoyed the first time, but now he let Charles join him whenever he wanted. On a fine day you could see across the hills and far out into the English Channel. Edward said that the line on the horizon was France, although Charles didn't really believe him. There were a lot of things Edward told him that he didn't really believe and he preferred to try to find the truth out for himself. Discovering things gave him a great thrill. He liked to work everything out and had inherited a logical, analytical mind from his mother; he was always piecing things together from little fragments.

Once when he was bored and rummaging through some old suitcases in one of the attics, he found a battered case with a faded Alitalia luggage label. Inside it was full of photographs of his mother and some of his uncles and aunts, as well as old magazines and bundles of letters. As he was closing the case, he noticed an envelope that looked more recent than the rest and he glanced at it. It was addressed: 'Francesca, Lady Sherfield, Meston Hall, Meston, East Sussex.'

Inside was a brief letter with a strip of paper attached. The letter was in rather scrawly handwriting.

Dear Frannie,
Mama found this the other day when she was helping
me clear out some old stuff when I was down for the
weekend. I thought you might like to see it in case
you've always wondered. Horribly appropriate for
poor old Seb, but I don't know about yours. It seems
Phoebe was wrong in her recollection, it wasn't just
the number 26, after all. Not that any of it matters
now.

I will try and call you next time I'm down. Second
baby's due in August. Lots of love.
    Susie.

Charles unclipped the strip of paper. It was about two inches wide, and lined, and looked as if it had been torn from a diary. On one side there was an address. On the other were two names, in list form:

Seb Holland – HUMPTY DUMPTY
Frannie – YOU'LL BEAR THE 26th

When he was younger, Edward had told Charles that he wasn't like a proper brother because they did not have the same mummy. Charles understood that; he knew Edward's mummy had died a long time ago.

He understood also that it was Edward who would inherit his father's title one day. His father was the twenty-fourth Marquess of Sherfield, and Edward would become the twenty-fifth Marquess. When Edward died, his eldest son would become the twenty-sixth Marquess. Unless Edward died without having a son, in which case the title would pass to Charles.

On the whole, Charles liked Edward, and in spite of their age difference they got on well, although sometimes he had a weird thought about him. He would imagine that he was watching Edward falling to his death from the parapet.

THE TRUTH

Peter James

What if you were about to lose everything . . . What if a bizarre offer from a stranger was your only option . . . What's your price?

When the bank pulls the plug John and Susan Carter have thirty days to find one-and-a-half million pounds or they will lose everything they've worked for. Then out of the blue the mysterious Mr Sarotzini offers them a deal. Their financial problems solved on one condition: Susan must be the surrogate mother of his child. But who is Sarotzini, and how come he knows so much about the Carters. And why is it that Susan's pregnancy hurts so much . . . ?

Price: £5.99
ISBN: 0 75281 666 7

ALCHEMIST

Peter James

At first, Monty Bannerman did not believe the newspaper reporter who came to her house with his story. She thought he was just trying to trash the pharmaceutical giant that had recently taken over her geneticist father's laboratory. But within weeks, the seemingly fantastic story he had told her seemed to be increasingly and horrifyingly plausible. Behind the respectable public face of 'The World's Most Caring Company' an outrage was taking place . . . against the entire human race.

Price: £5.99
ISBN: 0 75281 729 9

All Orion/Phoenix titles are available at your local bookshop or from the following address:

> Littlehampton Book Services
> Cash Sales Department L
> 14 Eldon Way, Lineside Industrial Estate
> Littlehampton
> West Sussex BN17 7HE
> *telephone* 01903 721596, *facsimile* 01903 730914

Payment can either be made by credit card (Visa and Mastercard accepted) or by sending a cheque or postal order made payable to *Littlehampton Book Services*.
DO NOT SEND CASH OR CURRENCY.

Please add the following to cover postage and packing

UK and BFPO:
£1.50 for the first book, and 50P for each additional book to a maximum of £3.50

Overseas and Eire:
£2.50 for the first book plus £1.00 for the second book and 50p for each additional book ordered

----

BLOCK CAPITALS PLEASE

name of cardholder ....

address of cardholder ....

....

....

postcode ....

delivery address
(if different from cardholder)

....

....

....

postcode ....

☐ I enclose my remittance for £............................

☐ please debit my Mastercard/Visa (delete as appropriate)

card number ☐☐☐☐☐☐☐☐☐☐☐☐☐☐☐☐☐☐

expiry date ☐☐☐☐

signature ....

prices and availability are subject to change without notice